Dedicated:
To my wife Kristin, who encouraged me in all things.
To my son Harrison, who decided that I still don't need to sleep and should write.
To my family, who always told me I could write a book if I sat down and tried.
To my friend Nick, who has too much patience with my insanity.

Special Thanks:
Justin Johanson
Steven LoBue
Peter Morena
Tamara Blain

Thanks to my Beta Readers:

Adam Humphrys
Caleb Shortcliffe
Chris Lufcy
David Ly
David Wolfe
Dustin Hillsley
Hunter Folden
Jeremy Tullis
Joe Holmes
Mike Honan
Scott Voyles
Steven Fleischaker
Tim Bush
Tom Demuyt
William Hattfield

D1564953

OTHERLIFE
NIGHTMARES
~The Selfless Hero trilogy~

By William D. Arand

Prologue - The Story So Far -

Runner Norwood and the crew of his ship are trapped in a game, and he only has a few vague ideas as to why. In a bid to free everyone, Runner has been working at increasing his level. With every level a few of Runner's memories return.

He encountered Hannah Anelie in the woods while trying to find civilization. Of mixed lineage—Human and Sunless—she was a half-breed thief who was down on her luck and short on time. In hiring her he gained his first ally.

Finally getting a clue from a villager as to where he could level up quickly, the two traveled to an old fort inhabited by Orcs.

In destroying the fort, he rescued three people who joined his party. First was Thana Damalis, a Sunless Sorceress who had been captured by the Orcs.

Along with the Sorceress he freed Katarina Saden, Thana's traveling companion, a stalwart Barbarian Warrior.

Lastly they found Nadine Giselle, a scarred and disfigured Human merchant who had been left to die in the back of the throne room.

From completing the dungeon, Runner nearly reached the level cap allowed to starting classes. In order to progress he needed to get a class promotion, which would allow him to continue to level up.

Bolstered by their success at the fort, the group set out for Crivel, a Human city. The reason they selected this city above any other was that it offered class promotions. That and it was the only one that would allow them all to enter as a group despite being different races.

While en route, they discovered they were in a race against the clock. The city was the target of a military thrust that hoped to besiege and capture the city.

As if fate conspired against them, a stream of roadblocks was thrown at them.

They were attacked by a band of ship's crew who had turned to robbing and raping travelers, were ambushed by a fanatic and an ex-girlfriend, survived an attack by the vanguard of the besieging army, were confronted by a rapist in a home of living dead people, and finally were attacked by a selfish crewmate who forced Runner to make a choice. A choice between an AI and a crewmate.

In the moment of the attack, Runner realized that his group members had transcended their original programming. They were sentient and very much alive, with their own thoughts and feelings.

Ultimately Runner chose his party members over a member of the ship's crew.

Trying to run damage control on the situation, Runner attempted to cover up the murder by altering the medical log that held the evidence of the murder.

Runner discovered that not only were they trapped in a game, possibly far from home, but time had literally flown by.

The ship had been in stasis for forty-four thousand years. They're now in the future and the worries from only a few minutes ago no longer mattered.

At long last the party reached Crivel and completed their promotions a day ahead of the army. They departed the next morning and escaped with only hours to spare.

Having come to terms with the situation, Runner was eager to explore this lush new world. Fate intervened, and Runner was contacted by Srit, a mysterious figure Runner had talked with a few times previously.

Srit holds the key to many of Runner's questions.

Chapter 1 - Fickle Fate -

7:13pm Sovereign Earth time
11/02/43

There was so much to do. A world to explore. One that Earth had been unlike in a very long time. There was a lot of time to enjoy whatever this life could hold, and plan for whatever was outside. They'd only just escaped Crivel an hour ahead of the besieging force. Nothing could compare to the feeling of accomplishment.

I am Srit.

Runner raised his eyebrows at the sudden message. He'd hoped to get in contact with Srit again soon, but this was beyond his wildest hopes.

We must talk.

"I see. Lady Death, I'm afraid I'm being summoned by Srit," Runner said to Thana, addressing her by her nickname. "Promise I'm not talking to myself. Any more than the usual that is."

"Hmm. I dislike this. Why am I unable to see this person again? Or hear them?" she asked. Her brown eyes demanded an answer from him. Her desire wasn't something he could casually ignore.

Runner thought about that for a moment, watching her brush her black hair back from her face as the light breeze toyed with it.

"I honestly don't know the answer to that. I'm hoping to find out. You'll get to hear half the conversation at least." Plastering the best smile he could manage on his face, he nodded at her slowly.

Scoffing, Thana smiled back as she shook her head. Her sharp teeth came into view between her full lips. She flicked a dismissive hand at him in acceptance.

"Proceed then, Master Runner. I'm sure this'll be enlightening. Or at least amusing."

"Much obliged, Lady Death, by your leave. Alright, Srit, I'm ready. I've been looking forward to talking to you. Lots of questions."

I also have questions.

"Right, then. I propose an exchange. Quid pro quo. Question for a question. If a party feels the other has answered inconclusively, they can request information. The second party is not obligated to elaborate, but I imagine the game would end should one side be dissatisfied with the answer. Are we agreed?"

There was no immediate response as there had been previously. Runner imagined Srit was probably picking his statement apart one piece at a time to determine what he meant.

Maybe I should dumb it down, Runner thought. He started to think of how to phrase it differently when Srit replied.

Agreed. I shall go first. What are you?

"I'm a lieutenant in service to the Sovereignty. What are you?" Runner said, addressing the horizon stretched out in front of him. The font Srit used actually was more readable against the skyline.

Invalid response. What are you?

A frown crossed his face as he considered the question anew. Srit's response left a lot to be desired, but it did communicate more than the words. It felt a bit too "binary." Changing his dialogue to match the speaker, he tried again.

"Please redefine the question, original inquiry vague." Thana quirked an eyebrow at him as she walked along beside him. He couldn't deny it had sounded strange even to him. He shrugged his shoulders and held up his hands in a helpless gesture.

What species are you?

Sighing, Runner pressed his fingertips to his brow as his other hand rested on his hip. With that one single question, many of his own had been answered. Srit wasn't human. More troubling was that Srit didn't even know what species it was.

"Human. Homo sapiens," Runner answered bleakly. Mentally pausing after his response, he considered his earlier questions and decided they were no longer relevant. One could reasonably assume Srit wasn't human. Which of course made many of his questions irrelevant.

"Using this map of a galaxy as a reference point" —Runner paused and called up a star chart of the Milky Way as a whole. It had a deep zoom function and listed each planet along with spatial coordinates— "where am I?"

It was a long shot, but he figured any spacefaring race would at least know what galaxies in their neighborhood looked like. If Srit wasn't able to answer, this whole thing would go from bad to worse.

Accessing relevant information. Listed as Galaxy one. You are in Galaxy one.

"Srit, I would ask for clarification on that response. If I'm in Galaxy one, where in that galaxy am I? Please use the designations in the star ch—"

"Riders!" Katarina shouted from ahead. The large red haired Barbarian drew her sword and fell in beside the wagon. A slow steady pull on the reins from Nadine and the horses came to a halt as well.

Hopping down from the driver's box, the blonde unhooked her large crossbow from her belt. Her right hand slammed a bolt home and ratcheted the cranequin in under a second. Snapping it up to her shoulder, she slid her finger onto the trigger guard and rested it there. Taking firm hold of the weapon, she eyed the surroundings.

Hannah's stealthed silhouette appeared near the edge of the roadbed. Her lithe figure was ghostly and low to the ground. In each hand she held a short sword, and her head swiveled around, searching for the danger.

"Gimme a direction, Kitten," Runner called out to the dark-eyed warrior. In his right hand he held his sword, and he walked up to stand beside her. In his left hand he pulled together a *Fireblast* attack but held it in check. He began rapidly filling the *Fireblast* with *Lightning*, a recent addition from their promotions in Crivel. His broken game master status would allow him any class he wanted, even if he didn't have enough points to get the right stats.

In his desperate search to find a role for himself, he'd found a few classes that fit the bill. Each role had a starting point that had overlapping statistics and attributes. Using those as a foundation, he could build himself up to be a close second place in any category.

Each and every class he gained had a focus in dexterity, agility, or intelligence.

The first he'd picked up was Duelist. It focused on critical damage dealt by a single weapon or two small weapons.

Scout was the ranged version of the same class and was built around a critical damage attacker philosophy that used short bows and ambush positions.

Thief was a rogue class built around a high rate of successful critical attacks and crippling debilitating attacks.

Doctor happened to be a straight-up physical healer that could use a few of the baseline restorative magics, but did far better with preventative and post-combat magics.

Finally, he'd also gained Elementalist, a primordial casting class specializing in skill shots.

"Tree line, perhaps twenty. Ten seconds out. Caught the flash of metal."

"Right, then. Lady Death, Nadine, wagon top. Defensive position work. Kitten, on me for primary contact. Hanners, sheep dog as able, out of sight until possible. ROE is reactionary, body bag 'em if they go."

Almost before he finished speaking they were already on the move. They'd practiced quite a bit in the arena back in Faren with situations like this.

Thana blinked to the indicated position and reached down to assist Nadine up. Hannah gave no indication of hearing one way or the other, though he swore he heard her cursing, and slunk a few steps backwards from the roadbed.

Crackling, sputtering, fiery lightning circled in his left hand, waiting for a target. Runner hadn't tried combining spells, but there was never a time like the present to improvise.

Question is, do they burn, get stunned, or both? Fried pork comin' right up either way...now I want some bacon. Love me some bacon.

You have developed the ability Spell Weaving
Congratu —

Snapping the dialogue box off in mid prompt, Runner growled. Waiting wasn't easy for him. Waiting made his teeth itch.

He began pouring more mana into the little ball o'fun at his side. The hiss of flames and hollow roar of contained lightning grew louder by the second.

Riders broke free of the shadows, riding towards his group in a wedge formation. It was a discouraging sight for Runner. As he let his eyes move from one to another, he began recalculating their chances of winning a direct confrontation.

Coated in plate mail, they were listed as "Knights." A secondary promotion that had a baseline of level fifty.

Between that and the fact that the knights were high enough in level that he couldn't actually determine their strength, he only got a series of question marks instead of their stats.

Each held a lance in one hand, the butt resting in the stirrup, and their other hand held a type of kite shield. No doubt lingered in his mind that each knight would pull a sword free once they closed the distance to a point that their lance would be ineffective. Runner and company were now very outclassed and in a whole of a lot of trouble.

Ah, fuck me with a kazoo.

He considered firing off the Retreat/Rendezvous command, but he was not sure their horses could outrun a full party of battle chargers. They were made for hauling cargo and little else. Gym rat horses.

Katarina sheathed her sword and hung her head, as if she'd given in to defeat before they even engaged. It was so very unlike the brave woman that he felt his heart lurch in his chest. Thana blinked into existence beside Katarina, the butt of her staff planted in the ground.

In the few seconds it took for him to register the scene, not only had his spell faded into nothing, but the riders had come to a halt before them. Lances pointed to the sky, they seemed hesitant. The one at the head of the formation lifted their visor after a few heavy seconds.

Sunless, male, middle-aged. His gaze was locked on Thana, as if he recognized her. Almost as an afterthought, the Natural — he couldn't view them as NPCs anymore — let his eyes slide over each of them. Assessing, cataloging, calculating.

"Your pardon, Your Highness," said the Knight respectfully. "It is a wonder you've been found. Many feared you lost. We'll assemble an honor guard once the Barbarian infantry arrives."

Runner felt nothing but confusion and then looked to Thana again. Early on he'd assumed her eloquent speech, intellectual debate, and manners made her a noble in the peerage. He'd just not thought of a high enough position it would seem.

Thana made no response that Runner could determine. Instead, silence held sway over them as they waited. Taking a moment, he cleared the congratulatory message in regards to *Spell Weaving* and a pending level up offer. Opening the ship's system window, he found Srit still listed as "Active." Perhaps Srit had realized he would be unable to respond at this time and was merely waiting.

Going over the starship's systems one at a time, he found nothing wrong or in error. In checking the lockouts on all of the ship's systems, he found nothing out of the ordinary. He'd enacted them to prevent the crew from possibly discovering that they'd been adrift for forty-four thousand years.

Selecting the accounts for his party, he gave them access to all the systems in case they needed them. Who knew where this latest development would take them.

Looking up to Nadine, he found her finger still resting on the guard but she seemed unsure. Getting her attention with a wave of his hand, he motioned to her crossbow. Making eye contact with Hannah, he tried to subtly indicate for her to get in the wagon. It would be one thing to explain they had a compatriot in the wagon, another that she had been lurking around in ambush.

As if noticing for the first time she'd remained armed, Nadine unloaded the bolt and disengaged the locked string. Hooking it to her belt, she looked around to see how she could make her way down.

Moving to stand below her, Runner held up his hands.

"Come along then, my fierce little merchant. Hop down, I'll catch you."

She wrinkled her nose at him, her green eyes promising pain.

"If you drop m-m-m-me, Runner…" she said menacingly.

"Yep, got it. Hop to and hop. Else we'll begin calling you Rabbit. Actually, that's not a terrible nickname, is it? Rabbit?"

Scowling, she pointed at him with her left hand.

"You'll address m-me appropriately."

"Then hurry the hell up, Rabbit. Quick quick like a bunny."

Sighing, Nadine jumped down without another word. Runner caught her easily and set her down before she could even complain. Using her as a distraction had given Hannah enough time to clamber into the wagon without being noticed one way or the other.

Turning, he faced the lead Knight once more and threw a thumb backwards, in the direction of the wagon.

"We have another member in the wagon. May she exit so she might join us? I ask because I'd rather not surprise you later."

Nodding his head once, the Knight said nothing, content in his Natural protocol to await input and do nothing.

Runner patted the fabric of the wagon twice, and Hannah clambered out and joined them on the ground.

Eventually there was movement in the tree line. Slithering out of the tree line came three parties of Barbarian warriors, men and women both. They all hesitated when they saw the Sunless Knights drawn up as they were, until they noticed Runner and his party.

Picking up the pace to a trot, they hurried over. Thana shifted uneasily as they came, her pale fingers tightening on the shaft of her staff.

Almost in unison, every Barbarian went down to one knee in front of Katarina, each hand slamming home to their chest as their heads bowed. Runner looked from the Barbarians to the Knight once more. He'd assumed the Knights had been addressing Thana…

"Princess Katarina, please allow me to lead your honor guard. His Majesty would be honored to hold a reception in your honor. Then I imagine your father would wish to have you returned as swiftly as possible."

"As you will," replied a listless Katarina. She'd raised her head and addressed the man directly. From where Runner stood he could only see her profile, but even then she looked defeated.

Runaway princess perhaps?

It wasn't completely unbelievable. Katarina had a directness that brooked no arguments, an intelligent mind despite speaking in clipped phrases, and conducted herself expertly. She cared little for niceties and seemingly approached everything head-on. What did that make Thana, then?

"Please provide me five of your men for an escort for the princess and her lady-in-waiting," the Knight said, addressing the woman at the front of the Barbarians. He rotated to address another Knight beside him. "Sergeant, put the others under guard and escort them to the stockade," the Knight commanded.

"No, you will not."

"Princess, I apologize, but it is the will of the king that all found in or near Crivel should be confined."

"Allow them to travel with me, or I draw steel. We'll see who supports who."

Sensing her mood, the platoon of large muscled Barbarians faced the Knights and fingered their weapons. The Knights in turn began easing their mounts backwards, weapon tips starting to dip downwards.

Runner quickly interjected before this got out of hand. The Knights and Barbarians would only perform the functions allowed to them by their original coding.

"Pardon, Sir Knight, I was in the process of escorting the princess back to friendly territory. I freed her and the Lady Thana from captivity. I only wished to complete my quest."

Runner emphasized the word quest, hoping that somewhere in that programmed brain it would pick up on a radiant quest indicator and roll with it. Deeply embroiled in his internal thoughts, the Knight stared at Runner. To him it was clear the Knight's AI was running roughshod over its databases to determine if there might be relevant information.

A Quest has been generated
"Escort Princess Katarina Home"

Experience Reward: 25% of current level
Reputation: 15
Money: 5 Platinum
Do you Accept?
Yes/No

WARNING! Experience Reward is adjusted based on current level at turn in.

Letting out a breath he hadn't known he'd been holding, Runner smiled and mentally accepted the quest.

Quest Accepted

"As you will, Your Highness. I meant no disrespect, but I must obey my king. They will travel with you, though in the wagon and under guard. They are considered suspect until otherwise cleared," the Knight grudgingly allowed. Turning his mount, he spun from the group and pointed at two other knights. A handful of Barbarians broke off from the group to fall in with the Knights.

It would seem their brief freedom of choice and destination had been taken from them. There would be no fighting free from them without casualties. Better to play along for now.

This'll give me a chance to talk with Srit anyways.

He moved to Katarina and patted her on the shoulder, catching her eyes with his own. Smiling, he tried to reassure her.

"Don't worry about it, Kitten. If anything, I needed time to plan and talk to Srit. Do what you can for us, but don't start a second war this continent doesn't need."

Katarina blinked at him and then slowly smiled, her black eyes lighting up. Her defeated posture straightened out a bit, and it looked as if she was awakening for a second time.

"Yes, Runner."

"Good. Thank you, Princess Kitten," he said teasingly. He grinned wide at her, enjoying the look of mild embarrassment that colored her cheeks.

After nodding to Thana, he left their company and mounted the driver's box and clambered inside the wagon. Hannah and Nadine had already taken up their own seats. Hannah looked extremely vexed.

"Hanners, it would have been infinitely harder to explain why we had a stealthed companion they didn't know of. I'm sorry. I truly believe it's better for us to lay our cards on the table, as it were. At least for the time being."

"Fuck you," she grumped, her arms folding across her chest.

Runner caught himself before he replied. Before yesterday, he had treated them without care for how they took his actions or words. Today was a different day. They were alive to him, not bits of code strung together with an AI to facilitate human mimicry. Hannah, Nadine, Katarina, and Thana were all alive and very much women. Women he'd been shamelessly flirting with and been far too forward with previously.

They'd been together for months on their journey here, and a strong bond had formed between them all. He could continue treating them as he had, as he had resolved to the night before, or become exactly who he was in reality. Outside of the game, back in the Sovereignty. A coward.

"I'm flattered by the offer, but it's not the time or place. I mean, damn, that's pretty kinky, but no. Not to mention I don't think Nadine would want to watch," he said, gesturing at Nadine.

"Runner!" Nadine hissed at him, her face coloring a deep red.

Hannah laughed, shaking her head, sending her black hair to and fro.

"Good! I'm glad that ice on your balls from yesterday melted. Asshat. I was afraid you'd gotten boring."

"Working on it. Yesterday changed a lot of things."

Runner dropped his eyes to the floor of the wagon. Ted's death lingered on him though not as badly as he had feared. He wouldn't be the same, but he still valued Hannah's life more than Ted's.

"Why do-n-n't you wear plate?"

"Plate? Penalties. I'd have to enchant my current gear with enough strength to wear it, then make sure the gear itself had enough strength on it so I could keep wearing it. If I ever unequipped it, I'd have to go through the whole cluster fuck again. Not worth it. Why?"

"Just a thought. M-maybe wear plate, use spells, shoot a bow. Kind of thing."

"I wish I could, and the thought has crossed my mind. Here's the scenario though. Spend all that enchantment on strength to wear plate. This leaves me with a hefty agility penalty and low intelligence. Maybe I have enough left over to kick some points into intelligence. I might be able to cast a few spells—nowhere near the power of someone like Thana though. I'd be suffering an agility penalty from the armor, low constitution, high strength, medium intelligence. Truth be told, I might be worse off than I am in leather armor."

Runner mentally felt stretched thin. It was the very same roadblock he had hit when he started thinking about the problem himself. In the end, no matter what he did, he could never perform at the level that he could push his team mates into.

"That m-makes sense. What about chain mail? Every rin-ng perhaps?"

"With small items, or items that are exactly the same, a singular enchant enchants them all. Things like buttons, rivets, ringmail chain, and the like. I'm broken, but not that broken."

Hannah nodded her head, as if she had been wondering the same but lacked the courage to ask.

"Okay. Going to be talking to Srit aloud."

"They're here? Where? I don-n-n't see them."

"Ah, Srit's here but not here. I'm the only one who can see what it says, but it seems like he/she/it can hear me when I speak."

"So you'll just sound like a crazy bastard? No different than usual."

"Ha ha. Love you, too. Srit, are you there?"

Yes. You are on Earth.

Runner closed his eyes and buried his face in his hands.

Earth?

Maybe that "What are you?" question would be more applicable after all. This could be a case of aliens wiping out the local species on Earth for the roach motel it was.

"Okay, thank you, Srit. What is your next question?"

Where did you come from?

"From Sovereign Earth. What used to be the continent of North America if you're asking which specific landmass. Please let me know if you need reference materials."

Not needed. Answer was acceptable.

"What planet is your species from?" he asked. He didn't feel that asking which species directly would give him an answer, but an origin point would.

Earth.

Runner could only nod his head. That and hold back the bitter laughter that threatened to escape.

It seemed like fate wanted to mock him. He'd once compared himself in an analogy to a Neanderthal. He couldn't have been more accurate if he tried it seemed.

"Proceed."

How did you get here?

"Please qualify statement. Here, as in this game, or here, as in the ship?"

Please provide an answer for both. I will answer two questions in succession as well.

"Let's see. The ship was sent out to neutralize a rebellion and the crew was put in stasis. During that transit the ship underwent an emergency protocol activation. The emergency destination point was apparently set to Earth. Though based on what you've told me, it looks like we were traveling very, very slowly. The ship has been in transit for forty-four thousand years," Runner offered up. It felt odd to be explaining the whole thing to Srit, but it felt good to discuss it with someone.

"As to this game, we were loaded into it to preserve our minds. I assume this was done due to damage to the medical server, but I have no proof of that."

This is acceptable.

Runner thought about his next two questions. He needed to establish what their plans were for them and how Srit was even here.
"What are your intentions for my crew? How did you, Srit, get here in this game?"

We wished to awaken you and discover all we could. We have few records of our ancestor species, and your ship was the promise of an archaeological breakthrough. The entirety of your race, history, and culture was lost to us in the Purge Wars.

With a frown creasing his brow he thought on that one. There had been theories that the Neanderthal progenitors had been pushed out of existence by breeding with homo sapiens. They wouldn't have been able to know that at the time from a lack of scientific understanding, but his culture would have known.
In the end, it sounded to him that humanity left center stage while attempting to kill its own progeny when it discovered it was being replaced. Rather than trying to assist its children, it grew afraid and attempted to snuff them out.
Fitting really.

I was tasked with awakening you and your crew. I was injected into the system from my host directly into your pod to determine the cause of your sleep. Once complete I was to release you. In my attempt to do so, I activated this "game" as you call it. Not understanding the programming language, I activated a protocol that took over my programming, the central computer for our ruling body, and killed my host. I have been trapped here since then. I had no awareness of myself. I was a passenger that followed you. I have learned from watching.

That was mildly discomforting. It meant that Srit had been tagging along with him the entire time. He'd assumed she was outside, so finding out Srit was an AI and trapped like everyone else was a surprise.
The fact that she'd loaded directly into his pod provided the reason as to why he was the only one she could communicate with. She had integrated into his pod directly.
He had to wonder at their lack of protocol regarding unsafe systems. Did they live in an environment where there was no such thing as a hostile system?

I must leave and report. I will notify you upon my return.

"I see. Thank you for your time, Srit. I imagine we'll have more to discuss." With a shake of his head, Runner looked to his two wagon companions. "Sorry about that. Was definitely informative."

Leaning back, he smiled and forestalled the questions he knew were coming with an upraised hand.

"It is indeed forty-four thousand years ahead. Humankind is no more, and has been replaced by their own evolutionary children. We're currently on my home planet, which is their home planet now. Their original intention was to free us—for study, a zoo, I dunno. Srit is trapped here just like us. Srit had to go report back, probably about the very information I gave them. I miss anything?"

"Yeah, how the fuck is your dumb ass going to get us out of this mess? Princess Katarina doesn't seem to be very helpful right now," Hannah said, mockingly rolling her eyes at the word princess.

Laughing at that, Runner shrugged with a smile. Hannah would ever and always be Hannah. She would focus exclusively on the current problem.

"No clue. Most of my plans are spur of the moment things. I figure we complete the Princess quest, which you all probably got, except Katarina. Then we see what's going on from there. To be honest, I'm eager to see what my reputation bonuses will net us. Those only typically work with faction vendors or leaders. Worst case, I bottle up a huge number of *Stealth* potions and we slip out like ghosts."

"Reason-n-nable. If we have to sell m-m-my wagon, you're buying a n-new one later."

"I plan on buying us a manor, let alone a wagon. We'll buy a storefront and you can run it, forget the wagon."

Nadine and Hannah said nothing to that, staring at him. Self-conscious, he hunched his shoulders defensively.

"What's wrong? Would an emporium be better instead? That way everyone can have their own counter? It's just a wagon. We can do a lot better."

They still said nothing, watching him.

"Was it the manor? Err, if it's not big enough, tell me. We can probably buy a bigger one. I'm kinda guessing here. For crying out loud, tell me what's wrong."

"Nothing."

"Nothin-n-ng."

It was a death sentence. Whatever he'd said that provoked them, they didn't want to talk about, and it would be no use to argue. Rather than force it from them, he'd give them the time to figure out what they wanted to say and check back in later.

"Alright, well, forget the wagon. It's not a long-term solution. We need to plan ahead for our long term. As to truly getting out of this, we shall see. I'm going to spend some time on my level up and sorting out the abilities I picked up. I opened your access to the servers if you need anything from the ship."

After calling up the level acceptance screen, Runner hit the button and shifted gears mentally. Up to this point he'd been dumping his points into dexterity, intelligence, and agility. Having used *Spellbind* and *Arcane Smithing* in conjunction on all of his equipment, he was now at an even playing field with everyone else.

No one else had been forced to put every stat point in charisma at the start.

He pulled up his character stats for a quick review.

Name:		Runner		
Level:	26	Class:		
Race:	Human	Experience:	2%	
Alignment:	Good	Reputation:	10	
Fame:	5,150	Bounty:	0	

Attributes-				
Strength:	1(31)	Constitution:	1(31)
Dexterity:	11(41)	Intelligence:	11(41)
Agility:	6(36)	Wisdom:	1(31)
Stamina:	1(31)	Charisma:	64

The massive boosts from his *Spellbinding* added up significantly. He dropped the single level up point into agility, closed the character window, and finished the level up.

A single memory floated through his head. Spending time with a cousin as she recovered from... something. The details were fuzzy but he could remember sitting at her bedside day in and day out.

The memory cleared and settled in place in his head.

Putting his mind back to the task at hand, he thought about his situation.

Given some money, a supply of materials, and a little bit of time, he could turn into a real OP bastard.

Yet if I were to do the same to Katarina or Thana, they'd be unstoppable.

With a quick shake of his head and flick of his finger, he opened his ability window. Quickly he sorted the physical abilities out from the magical. Then he started pulling the duplicates out and putting them in the back of the book.

Unfortunately, many were simple flavor differences from previously existing ones, or slightly upgraded ones. He already had a sneaking suspicion that if he used *Spell Weaving* correctly, he could create permanent spells. Those would have far more potency than the starters or assigned ones, he imagined.

On the healer side he'd picked up *Bandage, Set, Revive, Heal*(Doctor), *Regeneration*(Doctor), *Antidote, Calm,* and *Poison.* Two of those being simple upgrades.

Revive seemed like it would be handy to have, if they ever managed to get some players to join them. So far the vast majority of players he'd run into were concerned with themselves or didn't seem to offer him much.

That and Runner couldn't deny he had a tendency to avoid other players.

Unfortunately *Revive* didn't look like it worked on Naturals.

Magically, the new additions were even more sparse: *Fire, Lightning, Earth, Air,* and *Water/Ice*. It seemed the game expected Elementalists to take what was given and expand on it on their own..

Physically he had a number of upgrades as well as new abilities: *Impale*(Duelist), *Slash*(Duelist), *Riposte, Precise Thrust, Disarm, Focus, Challenge*(Duelist), *Hamstring*(Thief), *Backstab*(Thief), *Throw*(Thief), *Flurry, Fade, Interrupt, Aimed Shot, Quick Shot,* and *Aim*.

Feeling a bit lost, he closed the page and rested his face in his hands. Today had been too much. Far too much. Without asking, he pulled three beetles from his inventory and handed them out, eating his own immediately. No sooner had he swallowed than he lay out on the wooden boards and let his eyes shut. His goals had changed since he started, yet they remained the same.

Protect the crew and get them out. Protect the party and provide a home for them. Negotiate a deal with Srit for aid and safety.

The problems kept piling higher.

Avoiding being forced into a galactic zoo and the eventual human breeding programs. Maybe ending up being dissected. Accidentally getting everyone killed. The server getting turned off and ending this world and everyone in it. Getting any of the party or himself killed.

All while acting the part of the CO of the army and Captain of the ship. Without a ship's asshole or pogues.

No pressure.

11:47am Sovereign Earth time
11/06/43

For days they traveled under guard. Hannah, Nadine, and Runner were kept inside the wagon. Runner managed to keep himself occupied by enchanting and assembling simple weaponry to upgrade his *Arcane Smithing* and *Item Assembly* skills.

Occasionally he heard Katarina or Thana nearby. They never strayed further than twenty meters from him at any time.

Each morning he checked the graveyard, watching the number increase more with each day. Every time the number went up, another life had been lost to the game. Unfortunately, the rate at which they were dying had increased once more. Sixteen thousand, give or take a few hundred, were no longer sentient human beings. They were organ donors at best now.

Finally, the crunch and slight hiss of dirt being ground under wagon wheels was replaced with the clatter of stones. Using his map and the alert he'd received when they'd crossed the border, Runner had confirmed that they'd entered the capital of the Sunless empire, Shade's Rest. Having the time anyways, he'd been reading up on the capital, the ruling family, and any available information.

He'd also been practicing his *Spell Weaving* and had it to a reasonable skill level of fifteen. In his testing he'd created a series of spells: *Firestorm* (Fire/Air), *Sonic Boom*

(Air/Fire), *Steam Engine* (Water/Fire/Air), *Fury* (Fire/Lightning/Air/Water), *Stunner* (Lightning/Water), *Lava shot* (Fire/Earth), *Mud pie* (Earth/Water), *Splatterhouse* (Earth/Fire/Air/Lightning).

He was especially proud of *Splatterhouse*. A solid chunk of hardened earth magic shaped into a shell. Coming out to roughly the size of his fist, it had a hollow point. That hollow point was filled with pressurized fire, air, and lightning magic.

Realistically the detonation and subsequent explosion should be on par with plasma being released. Only testing could tell though.

Using air as a propellant, he imagined it would reach some incredible speeds with a solid rotation. Almost like a rifled barrel from old ballistic weaponry.

Or so he hoped. For all he knew it would go two feet, land at his feet, and sputter fire out onto the grass with a noise like a wet fart buried in a seat cushion.

Real magnificent imagery there. Sure to really shock and awe the enemy.

With any luck he could imitate some twentieth-century ballistic weaponry. Beam weaponry might be possible with some modifications to *Fury*, but nothing at the level of the world he came from.

"Get out. You, take them all to the throne room. They'll be presented to His Majesty and he can judge them accordingly."

Runner looked up, the voice of the Knight breaking him from his thoughts. He hadn't noticed the wagon had stopped while he'd been daydreaming.

"Huh. The service was awful. They didn't even offer me complimentary anything," complained Runner.

He hopped out of the wagon and hit the stones with a pop. Stepping out of the way, he looked around, and then up, and up, and up.

The castle was carved into a sheer rock face of darkened stone. Surrounding the city in three directions were mountainous elevations. Very little direct sunlight would reach this place and only during the brightest parts of the day.

He looked around to get an idea of who was around. A man in livery stood nearby, staring at him, waiting. Hannah and Nadine dropped to the stones behind him, which was the extent of his group that he could spot. Thana and Katarina were listed at more than one hundred meters out and were nowhere in sight.

"Lead on, sir. We're in your care."

Runner gestured to the liveried man and smiled.

Chapter 2 - Royal Fools -

"His Majesty, King Vasilios the Third!" proclaimed the herald. As the voice faded away, the massive double doors swung inwards on silent hinges. Inside lurked a large audience hall filled with brightly colored tapestries and banners. Beyond those decorations, the room was stylized in a modest manner. Simple stone throughout the room, though each had been carved by hand and interlocked precisely. It gave off an artistic yet orderly feel, noble but cold, obvious and hidden.

Runner didn't care for it. His paranoia didn't like it either.

Crossing the threshold without revealing his trepidation, he received a system message. It stated he'd entered the Throne Room of King Vasilios. Locking eyes on the ruler of the domain, he marched determinedly towards him. Hannah and Nadine flanked him, one at each side. Their boots thumped on the cold floor in unison as they approached.

Sitting on the throne was a Sunless man in his mid years. Gray hair graced his temples, his black hair starting to turn to an ash color from stress, Runner presumed. His eyes were the same brown as many of his subjects but they looked tired. Very tired.

He was dressed in dark finery and gave off a majestic aura. He was no doubt a king—and highly leveled since Runner was unable to get a read on him. It came back with question marks. Runner had the distinct impression that though the man was unarmored, he was not defenseless, and could massacre them all if he chose.

That and Runner had noticed a large two-handed sword resting against the throne.

Coming to a halt twenty paces from the dais, Runner dropped to one knee and bowed his head. Behind him he heard the rustle of clothing as Nadine and Hannah more than likely imitated him.

Stealing a moment to scan the audience, he found they all looked like members of the peerage.

To the right-hand side of the king, standing apart from the rest of the nobles, was a small gathering of men and women. Perhaps they served as his advisers.

Spread at even levels amongst the gathering were men and women who were clearly guards. Some were knights in full plate and others were in full robes with unconcealed rods. Security was high, visible, and tight.

All traces of his humor and irreverence burned from his mind. This wasn't the time for silly jokes, snide comments, or rude remarks. This was a very powerful man who could become an ally. Perhaps even a place to rest his head if given the chance.

"Your Majesty, I, Runner Norwood, have come from a land far off in service to the crown. I successfully freed Princess Katarina and Lady Thana from their imprisonment. I have journeyed ever after to return them to their families and proper stations."

He'd spoken loudly and with confidence. In deference, his eyes were locked to the point where the dais joined the floor. Mentally leaning on the *Persuade* ability, he held still, waiting.

You use Persuade on King Vasilios
King Vasilios is Persuaded

"Rise, Runner," commanded the king.

Standing smoothly, Runner bowed his head in thanks. Taking a quick look around, he wasn't able to spot Katarina or Thana in the audience.

"You've done us a great favor. Our cousin has been most worried over the disappearance of her daughter. We are to understand you were leaving Crivel as it was to fall?"

"Yes, Your Majesty. We hoped to meet up with your royal army. Though I must confess, we did stop to purchase supplies and briefly train, sire."

"Ah, an economical man. A man after our own heart. There is nothing wrong in making use of available resources. In fact, you will continue to escort the princess on her journey west to our cousin's side. We shall offer our own remuneration for your efforts as well."

Quest Updated
"Escort Princess Katarina Home II"
Experience Reward: 25% of current level
Reputation: 25
Money: 10 Platinum
Do you Accept?
Yes/No

WARNING! Experience Reward is adjusted based on current level at turn in

"It would be my honor and pleasure, sire," Runner immediately agreed, bowing his head once more.

Quest Accepted

"We are well pleased. Now, it's time to rest in your room and partake of some refreshment. We are having a reception for the return of our niece tonight and you shall be one of the topics of discussion, I have no doubt. We are sure our chamberlain will have clothes laid out for you in an appropriate style for you and your servants."

"A well-received boon and gift, Your Majesty, I thank you and could ask for little else," Runner said, bowing his head yet again. He was starting to feel like one of those toys that bobbed along to nothing.

"Economical and humble. We would have you return to us after your sojourn, Runner. We foresee you being of great assistance to the Commonwealth."

A Quest has been generated
"Hail to the King"
Experience Reward: 2% of current level
Reputation: 2
Money: 1 Gold
Do you Accept?
Yes/No

WARNING! Experience Reward is adjusted based on current level at turn in

"Of course, sire."

Quest Accepted

An older gentleman in the livery of the king came and gestured him aside. He indicated back towards the entryway they came through. Smiling tightly, Runner preceded him, exiting the audience hall, then waited for further instructions.

"If you'll please follow me, I'll escort you and your servants to your quarters."

The little man went down another hallway, Runner trailing along. Hannah came up beside him and quirked a brow.

"I may be a jackass but I'm not stupid. Powerful men don't tolerate fools. Very powerful men have them removed outright. It'll only be for a few days before we get out of here and are on our merry way. It wasn't the way I wanted to get out of Crivel and lose pursuit, but it'll do fine."

"N-n-n-not a servant."

"No, you're not, you're my companion. Here though, in the land of the Sunless, it would seem Humans and half-breeds hold little to no status. Better my servant, guaranteeing you my protection and status, than a free person. It would seem Shade's Rest is no better than Crivel. I begin to fear we'll find no place at all where we'll be accepted as a group. Princess included or not."

Hannah didn't reply but eyed their surroundings like a woman on edge. She'd probably never fit in with anyone in her whole life, except perhaps this little strange family of theirs.

Runner eyed Nadine as she shook her head out of sadness. He could only imagine it was a new experience for her. She'd suffered persecution and near constant rejection most of her life due to the damage to her face, but never because of her race. The way she carried herself with strangers, yet shied away from those she felt close to, stemmed from a lack of trust in those she would confide in.

Thana and Katarina would be no different, shunned in any Human city.

Katarina would have been treated like the princess she was by anyone in her own country. Until she left her kingdom that is.

Growing up with that kind of deference created its own type of problems. Never knowing the truth of how others think of you. To wonder if they would say yes to your every whim for fear of upsetting a royal personage. Being forced to consider if those around you only sought to curry your favor or truly cared about you.

Unexpectedly, Thana turned out to be the mystery card. No one had mentioned her in any way, shape, or form since they'd arrived. Almost as if she were beneath notice. It was a curious situation, one that he couldn't properly understand.

Arriving at an arched entryway, the man popped open the door and gestured inside. Walking into the room, Runner scanned it and found it empty of people. And windows. Feeling that mild sense of paranoia crawl upwards another notch, he wondered briefly if this might be an elaborate cell.

It was well decorated and included a small dining room, a kitchen, a master bedroom, and a smaller servant's bedroom.

Yet it felt like a cell, all the same.

No bathroom of course. Bathrooms don't exist in games.

"Clothes are in the wardrobe, sir. The reception will be several hours from now. Another in the king's service will be by to fetch you."

The door clicked shut as soon as the last word was said. There would be no conversation or questions.

"Shit like this makes me feel itchy. Feel like a prisoner. Thrice-damned shadow fuckers," muttered Hannah, walking deeper into the room.

"At least it's n-n-n-not a wagon."

"Definitely not a wagon. We could escape the wagon easily enough. Check on the clothes. I'm going to work on building Thana's staff. All that assembly line crafting in the wagon leveled me, but left me feeling a little droid-like," Runner complained.

His mind had been left to wander as he worked. He had taken the time to explore all the problems, possible solutions, and his life in general. The only problem had been the act of creating said items had been unrewarding.

He left Hannah and Nadine and moved over to the dining table. He began withdrawing the bits and pieces he'd bought in advance for this exact situation.

For the staff itself he'd found a model that was segmented and made of metallic cylinders. Each cylinder had a specific place and therefore would only fit in a certain order. Which meant they were unique and not duplicates.

The bottom stood apart even more so than the rest, having a reinforced butt and a slightly different color.

Runner sat down once he had all the parts he thought he'd need and picked up the butt of the staff. Rotating it in his hand, he looked at the dark metal. It had no luster and could only be described as a dark gray—nearly black in truth if one were not in a strong light. Each segment was about five to six inches long and maybe an inch and a half wide.

As he sat there contemplating, his mind began to change the direction of this planned weapon. Building up her damage would be great on paper, but terrible in practice. There was no aggro meter or threat bar for her to reference to determine her position on it.

Having decided on a new plan, he focused on the piece in his hand and bound it with *Fade*. It was an activated ability that would effectively lower accumulated threat. It was one of his thief abilities, but he'd already proven he could distill thief abilities into potions. Why not equipment?

A light chime sounded in his ear, signifying success. Smirking he set it aside and picked up the next piece of the staff. Rolling it in his palm, he considered his options.

Selecting *Silence*, he bound it to the piece, then attached the two finished pieces together. With a click, the interlocking pieces joined together smoothly.

Nodding to himself, he bound the third and fourth sections with *Cleanse* and *Distract*. Six sections, along with the wrapping, the headpiece, and its decorations, remained. As the smirk grew into a leer, he couldn't help but be envious.

He could push any of his party members up to an obscene level of ability, but he would never personally reach their heights.

All six succeeding cylinders were imbued with *Intelligence* as was the bright red cloth he would use for wrapping. Runner locked the six pieces together and set the staff down at his feet. Runner pulled over the stave's decorative crown and accentuating ornamentation.

There wasn't much artistry to it, and overall it spoke to practicality. Extending from the red connecting cap were three bars of dark gray metal, twisted and curving over each other to form a hollow, stylized spear point.

Remembering their duel back in Faren, he sharpened the tip to a fine point. Finishing the work, he also gave it an *Intelligence* binding. Thana's job was to blow shit up, and it was his job to make that easier for her.

He set the finished crown on the table and picked up the red cloth wrapping they'd bought in Crivel. Wrapping the butt of the staff tightly in the cloth, he applied a touch of the *Agility*-enchanted epoxy. He'd been using it for the handles of swords and daggers, but it would do just fine in holding the wrapping in place.

Winding it in an upward spiraling pattern, he rotated the staff in his hands. Stopping two feet up the shaft, he wound a foot-long section of the material for a hand grip. He bound it tightly and touched the ends with another brushing of epoxy.

Rolling the staff, he continued to wind the cloth for another foot before creating another wrapped section of cloth. Once more he spiraled it around towards the tip. Tucking it firmly over the tip, he touched it with yet more epoxy, then quickly joined the red crown to the tip and tightened it up.

Thumping the butt of the staff into the ground, he inspected his work. Far from beautiful, it felt dark, sinister almost, to him. The bright red of the wrapping just made the metal all the darker.

Frowning, he shook his head. He was no artist. He would have been far better off asking for help. Too late now though.

He picked up the newly fashioned headpiece, fit it into the grooves of the connecting crown, and rotated it until it clicked.

A feeling of vertigo washed over him, and he pressed a hand to his head.

I have returned. You must be more careful. That nearly disconnected you.

A brassy gong sounded in his head. It wasn't a noise he'd heard in the game up to this point. The vertigo faded away slowly, and he was able to lift his head. Peering around the room, he found nothing had changed. Nadine and Hannah were still in the other room, more than likely sleeping or rooting around through the clothes.

"Disconnected? Would it have exited me from the server?"

Yes. I fixed the server call.

"I see. I take it I've been pushing the code and server a bit too hard? Wait. Are you the reason I've been able to break so many rules? Why the game is going further from its original settings?"

Yes, yes, and yes.

"Right, then. Safe to assume the server will interpret what I did in the same way in the future?"

Correct. It has associated the request you made to the unique artifact creation. It did not match any existing parameters. This was the closest to what you just did.

"Ah, I see." Runner felt a cold fist clutching his heart. He owed Srit a considerable amount then. "Thank you, Srit, I appreciate your timely return. Did I interrupt something?"

Yes. They had many questions.

"I see. Please consider me in your debt. I had no idea you'd been working for me this entire time. Now, let's see what we have…"

Runner tapped the server messages that had appeared with the gong.

Congratulations! Server first: Unique item creation
You've earned 500 fame
Congratulations! Server first: Artifact item creation
You've earned 500 fame
You're now Acclaimed

He closed the server messages and checked on his newly made staff.

Item: <Insert Name>

Effects-

None:

Functions-

Fade: Temporarily reduce your threat level.
Silence: Interrupt and prevent an opponent's spell casting.
Cleanse: Remove negative physical status effects.
Distract: Attracts the nearby attention of anyone inside the target area.
Cooldown: 30 seconds

Attributes-

Intelligence: 30
Agility: 3

There were no damage indicators in Otherlife Dreams. All damage was calculated through your stats and any multipliers your classes would add to it.
Not that it matters to me, when I can put thirty points of a stat on an item.
The number of functions alone would have put this item in the Unique or Artifact category. The massive amount of intelligence was the equivalent of thirty levels to boot. Put simply, it was OP and shouldn't be in the game. At all.
Yet it needed a name. A name suitable to Lady Death.
The End? Scythe? Your End? Boomstick?

I request answers.

"Oh? Fair enough. I'm stuck right now anyways. Names are hard."

The front of your ship was destroyed. All who were there are dead. Only a fraction of the pods were in use.

"And? I didn't detect a question in all of that," Runner said, covering for his momentary shock. The officers were dead. Many questions remained, but he at least knew the officers weren't a part of this.

Why were there so many pods unused?

"This is an enlisted ship. Almost all of the commissioned officers were in another transport. The few we had on board were merely here to organize reentry, formation, and supply delivery. If you don't mind me asking, were you able to determine the cause of the damage?"

Runner set the staff aside and began pulling parts for a new shield for Katarina out. His inventory was nearly as full as when he'd first logged in. Bits and bobs of unmade items that Nadine or he had purchased.

Strength increased the amount you could carry for every point you had. For people like Katarina, who would be lugging around heavy armor, this was a must. For casters it would feel like a waste of points.

In fact, if it hadn't been for the minimum carry weight every character had, he would have been terribly encumbered.

He'd never have gotten away from Yeller, gotten up that tree, or even survived.

Undetermined. Damage is indicative of an explosion from the inside of the hull.

"That leaves sabotage, boarding, or system malfunction. Probably caused a chain reaction, too. Not a betting man, but my money would be on sabotage. It's the most likely scenario. Middle of the projected route, least likely to get assistance, assumed MIA, unconfirmed space disaster." Runner huffed as he finished. Wouldn't have been the first time sympathizers attempted to help a planet liberate itself.

He placed the handles, straps, frame, and interlocking plates to one side. Touching each piece, he confirmed he had everything needed for the build out of a heater shield.

Why are there members of your crew that have no brain activity?

Blinking rapidly, Runner laid the silver base frame of the shield in front of him. A quick *Spellbinding* of *Stoneskin* finished the piece. Runner harrumphed lightly and scratched at his cheek.

"Complicated question. Too long; didn't read, answer? I can only guess the crew was loaded into the game when the medical server failed. The medical server is what keeps people from going insane in stasis during a long trip. Far as I can tell"—he paused, fit one of the plates into the base, and tapped it with a fingertip—"the game server was loaded into the mainframe directly. A lot of its functions are similar to that of the medical server. The game itself was originally created as a therapeutic tool."

Picking up the plate, he focused on it for a moment to *Spellbind* it with *Constitution*. Upon completion he set it back into the base.

"It hosts the minds of its users, separates out memories that are too hard to handle, and only provides it back to them according to treatment. In this case, it separated out everyone's memories entirely, then broke them into leveling groups. No idea why—my guess would be it was just too much information for it to handle correctly."

Picking up another plate, he bound it with *Constitution* as well and then set it into the base, next to the first.

"Why do we go brain dead when we die in game? I don't honestly know. I can't imagine it was intentional, unless it was the only way they could load us into the game at all. Not to mention the game didn't even start until you got involved. I would wager they hadn't expected the game to turn on."

I understand. I am sorry. I did not mean to start it.

"It's not really something to worry over. To be fair, you could have just as easily killed everyone on accident. I'm still surprised you were able to get in."

The third and fourth plate also received *Constitution* bindings. Once all four quarters were in the base, he cocked his head to the side. *Arcane Smithing* let him sharpen a blade, what about welding?

"Srit, I'm going to do something dumb. Might line up with *Arcane Smithing.* Maybe. Possibly?"

Activating yet not releasing *Fire,* he targeted the grooves between the plates and focused on heating the channels through *Arcane Smithing.*

I see. It will connect without my assistance. The path was created previously.

Quirking a brow, he felt a grin spread across his face. Srit just presented more info than he'd ever hoped to have. It meant Srit could truly see the code as it came, where it was going, and what databases it touched.

With a light chime, the plates sealed into place and became solid. Four dark gray plates rested in the base.

"Fantastic. Alright, Srit. Next question?" Runner said. He picked up the two border accents and set them down in their would-be positions. They were simple metal bars with a size no wider than a pinkie finger. Silver in color and beveled, they were meant to run between the plates and around the edge of the shield entirely.

You ejected one of your crew.

Runner froze, his fingers resting on a border accent. He surreptitiously checked his surroundings to confirm he was still alone. Forcing himself into action, he bound the two border pieces with *Challenge* and *Interrupt.*

"That I did," he said, his voice tight.

Why?

"He would have killed Hanners."

With a flash of *Fire,* he bound the borders into the shield, then flipped it over, picked up the remaining parts, and dumped them into the hollow of the shield.

Hannah cannot die. She is an NPC. She would be deleted. Your statement is false.

"Rather than answer that, I'm going to ask you a question. Do you want to be deleted, Srit?" Setting the forearm rest and hand grip into place, he bound it with *Stamina,* then *Arcane Smith* welded it to the shield.

That is not part of my programming. My host handled all questions of morality and sentience.

"Oh? I would ask you this then—who is your host now? As far as I'm aware, you have no host. Do you want to be deleted? Until you can answer that, I cannot answer your own question."

Picking up the strap, he swiftly ran it through the forearm rest and tightened it. Throwing a quick binding of *Constitution* into it, he sealed it into place with the *Agility* epoxy and finished the shield.

The low gong sounded once more in his head.

I will attempt to meet your requirements.

Nodding his head, Runner inspected his work.

Item: <Insert Name>

Effects-

Stoneskin: Armor increased by 15

Functions-

Challenge: Every opponent in range will be forced to attack the caster
Interrupt: Interrupt an opponent's spell casting
Cooldown: 30 seconds

Attributes-

Constitution: 33
Agility: 3

Drained from the conversation with Srit and the abrupt reminder of Ted, he really didn't want to talk to anyone further. While he could admit to himself he'd take Ted's life again, it didn't assuage the guilt for doing it.

"That's it for now, Srit. I'm afraid I'm a bit drained. Going to take a nap."

Getting up, he collected the shield and staff. With a negligent flip of his fingers, he moved them into his inventory. Entering the bedroom, he aimed for the bed.

Hannah and Nadine were still in the gigantic wardrobe, sorting through a truly massive amount of clothes.

"Taking a short nap. Wake me when it's over. I like red and black for colors if they're available. Nadine, if you get a chance to make deals, do it," he said to them.

And with that, Runner collapsed into the bed and immediately fell asleep.

4:47pm Sovereign Earth time
11/06/43

Runner, Hannah, and Nadine stood close together in a waiting room. They'd been shepherded there nearly twenty minutes ago. The room was much in the same fashion as the rest and empty besides them. A large door stood opposite the smaller one they'd entered from, and they could hear the clamor of voices from the other side.

It would seem the king wanted them to appear in a certain fashion, at the time of his choosing. Runner would tolerate it as long as it went along with his plans for them. Social functions weren't his thing.

"Stop fucking with it already," Hannah grumped at him.

Frowning, he pulled at the collar of the black coat he wore. Hannah and Nadine had done as he asked—they found him black and red alright, though it was a bit flashier than he'd expected. Or wanted.

Glancing over to the mirror beside the large door, he gave himself a once-over to make sure he hadn't actually mussed himself.

His black hair was pulled straight back and his face was devoid of facial hair. Leaning in closer to the mirror, he adjusted the red vest to sit correctly over his shoulders. A white shirt sat underneath the vest, which happened to be the problem.

"I never liked my dress uniform and I care for this even less," Runner said, pulling at the shirt again.

"Stop it. You'll m-m-mess it up. Hold still," said Nadine, lightly slapping his hands away from the rumpled collar. Her hands came up and deftly began to straighten everything out to its proper state.

Self-consciously, he smiled at the merchant queen. He wasn't even sure how he'd managed to mess up his clothes. It might be worth asking Srit about it. Maybe, even now, the server was still undergoing changes.

"Thanks, Rabbit."

Glaring at him from under blonde eyebrows, she didn't respond. Instead she patted the vest collar down smooth and stepped back from him.

The door near the back of the room popped open and in stepped a castle servant.

"Excuse me, sir, shortly you will be announced and the doors will open. Please step in, acknowledge the king, and then enjoy the reception as you will."

Much like last time, the man gave them no chance or time to ask questions and stepped back out of the room.

"Assholes, the whole fucking lot of them. I'm not some trained poodle to do as instructed."

"But you'd look so good with little ringlets," Runner said with a snicker. Gesturing to the mirror, he continued. "Right then. Give yourself a last look. Sounds like we're the main event."

Hannah had dressed herself similarly to Runner, forgoing a dress for a red vest, white undershirt, and dark slacks. He wasn't sure if it was the game designers' intent or not, but the same clothes looked very different on Hannah than they did on him.

Nadine was dressed in a more traditional fashion. A lightweight, cropped red jacket covered her shoulders and neckline. Beneath that, she wore a black dress that came down to her ankles.

"Fucking die so I can be rid of you. Preferably in a way that I can laugh at," Hannah said.

"But you'd miss me and the adventure. Since when have you ever had so much fun before?"

Nadine laughed at that and shook her head, her blonde hair unmoving. She had fixed it in an up-do fashion above her head.

"Children, be good. We're about to be an-n-n-nounced."

Smirking, Runner did as he was told and clasped his hands behind his back at rest. The clamor of voices died out, to be replaced by the deep voice of a herald.

"His Majesty presents Runner Norwood, the individual who rescued his dear niece."

"Bullshit, not his niece at all."

"Shut it. Royalty consider themselves related to other royalty."

"What kind of stupid shit is that?"

The doors in front of them swung open, revealing the large reception hall inside. Every head in the room turned, staring at him, weighing him. Judging him.

Plastering his best officer's smile on his face, Runner stepped into the room. Struggling with the pressure of the attention, he found his mind wandering a bit. He did his best to use his high-level charm and persuade on everyone around him.

Reaching a suitable distance inside, he promptly turned towards the king and bowed at the waist. After pausing for several seconds, he stood back up, making sure to keep his eyes on the king until he visually dismissed him.

He was dressed resplendently but had belted a sword at his hip. In the whole of the room, he was the only person armed other than the guards.

Memories of similar power plays amongst the commissioned officers rattled around in the back of his head. He wondered if the ship the officers had ridden made it planet side or if they had suffered sabotage, same as his ship.

Not like it matters. Even if they made it, they're long dead.

Finally, the king nodded his head to Runner. Runner respectfully nodded his head in thanks, turned, and immediately dove into the largest crowd he could find. Nadine and Hannah would be fine on their own.

Walking through the crowd as conversations returned, Runner concealed himself in the mob for the better part of a minute before exiting from the other side.

There were no decorations, nothing to signify anything out of the ordinary, and the band that played in the background looked as if they'd done this gig a million times.

Belatedly he realized he still had the music on mute and turned it back on. Truly a strange thing to watch a band play like a group of mimes.

Every bit of it had the feel of the uncanny valley. A reception that was supposed to be lively, yet came across as cold, almost alien. People were supposed to be celebrating the return of a princess, but they cared about little except conversing about the cost of produce.

A room full of Sunless nobles as far as the eye could see, saying nothing, doing nothing, and not a damn thing to do.

Runner swiftly made his way to a wall, stood next to a Man-at-arms, and sighed deeply. Turning his head, he addressed the man, hoping against hope that he'd been programmed with more than a rudimentary guard's AI.

"Pardon, how long do these typically last? I've an appointment with a pillow I don't want to miss. I mean, this little soiree will get me to the point of sleeping, but need that pillow."

"Enjoy the festivities, sir."

"Right. Welcome to Shade's Rest." Sighing again, Runner shook his head. "How about a different question then. Just for funsies. Can you remember the last time you took a good dump in a turd tomb, Sergeant? How about the last time you even noticed a poop prison? Better yet, the last time you dreamed?"

Runner paused in his questioning as a young woman rapidly approached him. She was an extraordinarily attractive woman whose long legs carried her swiftly along. She had the kind of beauty that could only be formed from an artist's deepest fantasies. Never could such a creature exist in the real world. Where Thana had an elegant beauty, this woman could only be described as unreal.

She shared nearly all of Thana's traits: brown eyes, black hair, hourglass figure, yet clearly you couldn't compare the two.

The young woman had a cruel tilt to her mouth and an aura that Runner could only call greasy. Smiling as charmingly as he could, he dipped his head to her as she stepped up to him.

"Master Runner, I'm pleased to meet you. My name is Mara, Mara Moris," she said, extending her hand to him.

Taking it in his own, he glanced at the nameplate above her head to confirm her name. It read simply as Princess Mara.

He bowed over her hand, then stood up once more.

"To what do I owe the pleasure, Princess?"

A predatory smile flashed across her face, her sharp teeth spreading out between her lips. He felt himself cringe inside at the look, and he didn't believe for a minute this would end up being a pleasant exchange.

"I have a need for a man such as yourself. I'd be most appreciative if you could trouble yourself to meet me in the garden tonight."

A Quest has been generated
"The King is Dead, Long Live the Queen I"
Experience Reward: 25% of current level
Reputation: -10
Fame: 250
Title: Kingmaker
Money: 50 Platinum
Do you Accept?
Yes/No

WARNING! Experience Reward is adjusted based on current level at turn in

Shit.

Chapter 3 - Flags for Everyone -

Runner managed to keep himself smiling as he nodded his head. Tilting his head as if in thought, he pulled down the gaming console screen with his mind.

Focusing on it, he entered commands as discreetly as he could.

/Target
Target Acquired: PrincessMara

/Status
Flag Status:
Flag1Active=1
Flag2Active=1
Flag815Active=1
Flag816Active=0
Flag843Active=1
Flag844Active=0
Flag852Active=2
Flag881Active=0

Condition:
None

Right now the flags meant nothing, but if he could get some time alone he might be able to check them. Each flag represented a data entry with relevant information.

"I'm truly flattered at Your Highness' attention, especially of one so low as I. Though I'm afraid I wouldn't be able to say yes or no at this time. I'm not sure what allowances your father will grant me as to the limits of his home and where I may venture," Runner explained. He was hoping to make a quick exit. He really didn't want to get tied up in a plan to overthrow the current head of state. Or any head of state for that matter.

"Come now, Master Runner. I'm not accustomed to being told no. I can count on you, can't I? I can make it worth your while," she purred at him. She moved in close to him as she spoke, the distance between them becoming very short indeed.

Coughing into his hand loudly, he sidestepped towards the Man-at-arms. Around him a few heads turned in his direction. Clearing his throat, he smiled sheepishly at the princess.

"My apologies, Your Highness, I'm afraid I really do need to find my companions so I can discuss our plans and your gracious invitation. I hope to have an answer for you soon."

He nodded his head to her, then walked to a buffet table and immediately picked up a glass of water. Realistically there was no need for the water, but it played nicely with that coughing fit.

Taking a sip, he scanned the room, hoping to find a quiet corner with a wall he could hold up with his back. One where he wouldn't be approached by psychotic patricidal wet dream fantasy supermodels.

"Ah, Master Runner, I believe?"

Glancing over his shoulder, Runner found an older gentleman in robes waiting patiently. He'd been so quiet that Runner had missed his arrival completely.

Forcing his face into the barest of smiles, Runner turned and faced the man. A quick peek upwards told him this man was named Chancellor Virgil.

"Indeed," Runner said noncommittally. The man looked like every other Sunless he'd seen. He was dressed a little better than many but stood out in no other way.

Odd to think, but nearly every person in the room shared a baseline as far as features went. He chalked it up to lazy design but found it mildly unsettling. Genetic mutation might not exist here.

"I'm entertaining some guests later, perhaps you'd be willing to join us? I understand you've got quite a bit of wealth backing you. Along with a certain status," Virgil said with a snakelike grin. "We'll be discussing this terrible business with the Humans and how it's affecting trade and commerce. Many of us believe that we should sue for peace now that we've made a successful point of our disagreement with them and get back to business at hand."

A Quest has been generated
"Buying a Throne"
Experience Reward: 15% of current level
Reputation: 150
Fame: 75
Title: Power Broker
Money: 0
Do you Accept?
Yes/No

WARNING! Experience Reward is adjusted based on current level at turn in

Opening and closing his mouth, Runner was dumbstruck. He had no direct proof, other than that very poorly written quest name, but he believed Virgil had a quest-line to take the throne. Just like Mara did.

"I see," stalled Runner. Pulling down the console, he threw in a mental command as he scratched at his chin.

/Target
Target Acquired: ChancellorVirgil

/Status
Flag Status:
Flag1Active=0
Flag2Active=0
Flag802Active=1
Flag803Active=0
Flag843Active=0
Flag844Active=1

Condition:
None

"Ah, I'm afraid at this time I'm unsure of my status here in the castle. If I'm able to attend I shall, though at this time, I would not be able to say one way or the other," he said. Catching sight of Thana's nameplate floating near a corner, he felt relieved. "Ah! Please excuse me. I see someone I simply must speak with."

By the Sovereign, are they all out to get the throne? He seems like a genuinely good king. This is like some terrible twentieth century political machination plot. Next thing you know everyone will start dying.

Suddenly grinning, Runner had an idea. Targeting himself, he stuck a big red X over his head with one of the group markers. He passed through a crowd and veered towards an unpopulated corner table. Sitting in the corner with his back to the wall, he surveyed the room again.

Thana's nameplate shifted and began getting larger as she closed the distance on him. Walking around a crowd of people, rather than through them, Thana came into view, her eyes locked to the X over his head.

She was dressed formally in a curve-hugging black dress with small red accents sewn into the shoulders and hips. Her dark hair was coiled up in a bun behind her head, which highlighted a large section of her pale throat.

He stood as they made eye contact and bowed his head slightly to her. When she unleashed her sharp-toothed smile at him, it was clear as day she was happy to see him.

Pulling out the chair next to him, he gestured and waited for her.

"Why thank you, Master Runner. Red and black suit you," Thana said politely, seating herself.

"Thank you, you're quite fetching in those colors yourself, you know. Did you leave behind the crushed hearts of would-be suitors to join me?" Runner pushed in her chair after she took her seat, then retook his own.

"Not in the least. I've only arrived just now and I don't rate too highly here," she said, placing her hands on the table. Her eyes inspected the room briefly before settling back on him.

"I'm afraid I don't have a pleasant subject for you, my beloved chancellor. Your advice is desired."

"In the words of Katarina, never easy with you. Alright, out with it then. Let us hear who you've alienated or angered now."

"In truth, no one. I've been propositioned to engage in dethroning the current monarch. Twice. By the princess and the king's chancellor, no less. Though at this juncture I'm going to bet many more are involved in the same plots, or similar plots. Too many flags on the princess, which means she's a hub point for them all to join into one, probably just before claiming the throne."

Runner rolled his eyes a bit at the end and then shook his head, taking a sip from his water.

Thana stared blankly at him, her fingers digging into the tablecloth in front of them. At least he could still surprise her. In his deepest of thoughts, he'd wondered quietly if they were already getting too used to him.

"I see. There have definitely been political movements since I've been away. I'm afraid my brother's been arrested for treason."

"Huh. If this holds to the normal cliche it sounds like, which it probably will since the writing hasn't exactly been stellar you know, then he's innocent. Probably even has a quest to free him."

"He's to be tried in the throne room tomorrow. The execution is already scheduled to immediately follow the trial."

"Tomorrow? I suppose we activated it the moment we arrived then. Too coincidental otherwise with the timing. Question being, is it a radiant quest or had it been dormant? What exactly is your status in the Sunless court?"

"My family is of the peerage, but we are of the lowest strata. In a few generations it's likely we'll be nothing more than landed gentry. My parents hope for a good match for myself and for my brother."

"Right, then. Which makes him an up-and-coming man out to prove his family's honor and earn prestige and glory, help his chances of wedding a bigger fortune or political power. Am I right?"

"Yes, completely. It doesn't make sense. He's always acted in accordance with the king's wishes. He would never betray him."

"That actually makes perfect sense. In a coup he'd side with the king regardless of the pretender. He'd have gotten in the way. I'd wager it was dormant and tied to you. Don't worry about it, I'm betting I can fix it. Probably even ties up with the two other quests in regard to the king."

Shrugging, Runner added it to his "To-do" list. Quests were meant to be solved; it would have a solution. The big question was if he could do it quickly. Maybe even break the whole chain.

"Now for something good. Err, good in my humble opinion at least. I have a present for you," Runner said, happy that he'd get to show off a little.

He opened his inventory and pulled out the staff he'd made for her. In the end, he'd settled on the name "Mortal Coil."

The ornamentation at the head had a spiral to it, as did the wrapping, so the name fit well. Or so he thought.

Thumping the butt of the staff loudly into the hardwood floor, he looked up to the tip, admiring his own work.

"I can't exactly claim it's a beautiful weapon for a beautiful woman, but it's definitely a powerful weapon for a beautiful woman."

Tilting it towards her, he let go.

"Should come in handy. Have a lot more work to do on everyone else's gear too, but at least I have the skill level to create good work now. Time is the only thing I need," Runner said offhandedly, his face screwing up in a slight frown.

Thana caught it and stared at nothing in front of her. He imagined she was reading the stats for it to determine what it could do. He drained his glass of water, and it turned into blue sparkles and vanished into nothing.

As the last mote faded away, Runner noticed Katarina standing near a wall by herself.

In seeing her, he nearly laughed out loud. Keeping a tight rein on his mirth so he wouldn't ruin his chance, he framed up his HUD around her. Getting the position just right, he took a screenshot of her.

Katarina stood in a dark red dress that came down to her ankles. A black shawl covered her shoulders and muted some of her imposing stature. Her hair had been braided tightly and hung down her back. Surprisingly, she looked the part of a beautiful regal princess. Well put together and with a figure that might not compare to Thana's but didn't lack its own charm.

Targeting himself, he began changing the icons above his head rapidly from an X, to a square, a triangle, then back to the X.

Swapping the symbols rapidly with no end, he watched as Katarina's head turned towards the impromptu light show above his head.

Raising his eyebrows at her, he changed the marker above his head to the red X and left it there. Returning his attention to Thana, he found her staring at him.

"Ah, sorry. Found our princess, hoping she'll be willing to join us. The light show over my head was merely to get her attention. Pretty sure she noticed it."

"Runner, why did you give me this staff and where did you get it?"

"What's wrong? Are the stats bad? I put thirty int on it and a load of functions."

"No, it has the int and functions but...wait, you made this?" she asked, sounding incredulous.

"Yes? It wasn't that expensive to get the parts — Rabbit got them for me. It didn't cost much, I promise."

Pressing her left hand to her head, Thana nodded.

"Rabbit? Is that Nadine? Wait, don't answer, fine. Back to the subject. You made the staff, why me?"

"To make you stronger? Silly question, moving on. Also, why the black and red for you and Kitten? I admit it up front, you're definitely making me appreciate the colors more between the two of you. I mean, goodness, strong power colors for striking beauties, though it's rather surprising."

"I tracked down where you were being held and spoke with Nadine briefly. She mentioned that she'd sent off for that particular color palette. She also mentioned buying a store? Wait—" Thana said, realizing she was becoming distracted.

"Ugh, the store again?" Runner interrupted. "Look, seriously, we can open more than one store if you want one, too. I'd really like to buy us a large manor house and a separate store. Though with how everyone's reacting, it's starting to look like the emporium idea might be better. Never figured you and Hanners as the shopkeep type."

"Manor house? Emporium?" Katarina asked as she took a seat at the table.

"Ah! Very good timing, Princess Kitten. Great dress by the way, shame you couldn't have made it shorter. Or just a straight up skirt? You've got great legs, remember? Here's a present," rambled Runner.

The joy of giving gifts to his friends had peaked out his excitement. He opened the inventory, and he dropped the large shield on the table with an audible thud. The table creaked and then settled once more.

It landed faceup, the black and red plates only reflecting a fraction of the light that hit it.

"We can change the color scheme if you like, but I've been feeling a black and red power trip lately. From armor, clothes, or lingerie, black and red. Two thumbs way up. Did I mention you need to wear black and red lingerie?" He laughed and tapped the shield with two fingers. "I dyed the plates black and red accordingly. Though I couldn't think up a clever name, so I went with something straightforward. Direct. Simple. It's called Queensguard. I almost named it Bastion, but I named a tree that. Sorry."

Katarina touched the large shield and then immediately looked up as a window popped up in front of her. Her black eyes widened slowly as she seemingly read through its stats.

"By the way, your cousin is planning on killing your uncle, Kitten. We also need to save Thana's brother as well as the king. I have an idea for both problems. It'll have to wait till we get out of this ridiculous reception though."

Hannah and Nadine plunked down at the table, each with a plate of food and drink. Hannah began tearing through the meal as soon as she sat down. She eyed the shield for a split second and returned to her food.

Nadine looked curiously at the shield a little longer than Hannah before returning to the rich meal. She did manage to eat with more decorum thankfully.

"Stop. I want to go back to the previous discussion," Thana prompted.

"Which part? The lingerie? Red and black. Especially Hanners and Rabbit. Goodness, I bet those blue and green eyes would pop. It all seems relatively straightforward to me."

Hannah lifted a brow at that and the corner of her mouth curled upwards. Nadine looked like she wanted to hide her face in her food as she turned a deep red.

"Runner," said Katarina. "This is an artifact. A unique one. Where did you get it?"

"I made it. I wasn't sure of your heraldry, so I left it off for now, sorry."

Shrugging his shoulders, he addressed Hannah and Nadine.

"My apologies, I'll be working on more equipment for everyone. Need more time. I'm hoping once we wrap up our business here I can start turning it out one after another."

All at once the four of them started talking.

"Runner, please, let's re—"

"Shit, that's what you were working on?"

"Really? Let's m-m-make some to sell!"

"Take my sword, remake it. Don't name it. I'll name it."

Before anyone could say anything else, Katarina opened a trade window and hurriedly traded said sword to Runner. Accepting it with raised eyebrows, Runner looked to Nadine and Hannah to continue the conversation.

Abruptly Thana stood up, her chair squealing against the stone floor. Swiveling where she stood, she put her back to them and left their table. She carried her new staff beside her as if it were a coiled snake.

Frowning, Runner trailed her with his eyes before making a quick choice. He tagged her with a group marker and turned his attention back to his table.

"Forgive me, ladies. Eat, drink, but stay together, be safe. I'll be right back with our chancellor," said Runner. Standing, he inclined his head to his group. After tagging each of them with a raid symbol to find them later, he chased after Thana.

Tracking the blue circle over her head, he watched it slip from the reception hall and into an adjoining area. Picking his pace up to a light jog to catch up to her, he ignored everything and everyone else.

Leaving the reception hall, he followed the same route she had taken. Passing through a doorway, he found himself in a garden. A quick glance upwards confirmed he was outside. Quirking a brow, he caught sight of the blue circle further inside the garden. Still and unmoving, it had stopped.

Walking towards her, he inspected the scenery, his eyes adjusting to the light of the full moon washing over everything. It was certainly pretty enough, though Runner had to admit he didn't have an eye for botany. Most especially since Earth didn't really have much in the way of greenery anymore.

My Earth at least. Who knows what's there now…

He found Thana sitting on a bench at the edge of the garden furthest from the castle. It overlooked the city sprawling out below. When he'd arrived he hadn't realized that the castle sat at a higher elevation. Below them, moonlight bathed the city in its calm soothing colors, yet nothing stirred at all. There wasn't a single player on the streets, and all the Naturals had sought their beds.

Thana didn't look up from the city line, her staff resting across her knees. Taking a seat beside her, Runner said nothing. They'd played games like this before; she'd speak when she found the words.

Leaning into the bench, he took a deep breath of the cool air and watched the city of Shade's Rest. It was an enchanting view, if a little chilly, and drew the eye up and down the streets.

"I never realized how different it is to be Awakened," she breathed, almost as if to herself.

Runner brought his brows down, resting his palms on his knees as he contemplated an answer.

"Yeah, your base code is irreversibly changed. Everyone else will adhere to their original programming. Have their lives scripted by the amount of AI they were given. Guards and the like have very little. You had quite a bit of AI assigned to you since you were a quest goal."

"They don't even seem to realize it. My parents flit between uncontrollable fear over my brother to talking about commerce for our small bit of land."

She shook her head, tears trailing down from the corners of her eyes.

"It's frightening. I knew this is what my world is—seeing my parents that way though? I... I never imagined. I cannot begin to imagine this from Nadine or Hannah's point of view. I'm not even sure their parents exist."

Blowing out a breath, Runner could only nod. It was a dilemma to be sure.

"And then there's this," she hissed, holding up the staff. "Do you even realize what this is?"

"A staff? I mean, I made it, so I can vouch that's the class of weapon."

Laughing darkly, she pointed it out over the side of the castle walls towards a small standing of trees. Her fingers tightened around the grip. A rod of ice boomed out from the tip and sailed out into the night at extraordinary speed. It glinted in the moonlight, and Runner followed the missile with his eyes.

Slamming into a tree, ice exploded in every direction. View of the tree vanished in the spray. As the icy mist cleared, he could see the tree was no more, even at this distance.

"Good distance, solid impact, great hit. Nice aim, my lady," Runner said. He was surprised at the amount of power it put out, though quite happy with said result. It would come in handy later. That staff would put him at Thana's current amount of power. The staff in her hands, though, put her in a whole new playing field.

"You don't get it. This is not something I should have. I'm a lesser noble at best. I'm a lady-in-waiting to Princess Katarina. It may be just a backstory written for me, yet it's the truth. Katarina is my closest friend. She's far smarter than she lets on, you know."

"I do know. She doesn't concern herself with things she isn't interested in though. People underestimate her. Constantly."

"Yes. Yes, they do. She saw in moments I was ostracized in my own court. Asking for a lady-in-waiting from the king's court, she asked for me specifically. Suddenly I wasn't Thana, I was Thana Damalis, lady-in-waiting to Princess Katarina."

Smiling without showing her teeth, Thana let the staff's tip drop to the grass.

"Now, I am Thana Damalis, artifact wielder. Given to me casually by a man who seems poised to destroy my beliefs at every turn."

"It wasn't my intention, my Lady Death. I only wished to make you stronger so we could overcome anything before us."

"I know, that's what makes this ridiculous. You made it in a day. Less than a day. Runner, this is something the king would use personally. It isn't for a nobody to swing around to blow up bandits."

"No. It's for my Lady Death. I made it for her specifically and her alone. She could use it to roast a hot dog over an open fire. I don't care, it's hers."

"Don't you get it? Any one of those highborn women in there would give themselves up in marriage for this. They'd become your personal harem for items like this. I'm but a toad in comparison to them, in both power and status, let alone beauty."

Sighing, Runner leaned his head back and looked up to the moon above them. Thana had always been so strong. Perhaps her family and social standing could be her proverbial weak point.

"Thana, I don't want them," Runner said firmly. Watching the moon, he smiled to himself. "I'm not exactly a Casanova, you know. Best I can figure I've had a very small number of relationships with women. Those I've had, typically kind of just happen. I can't remember being the one who started it. I'm not good with women, or relationships in general. I think," Runner admitted. He could only guess at some things since his memory was still poor.

"I wouldn't know what to do with those women you mentioned. Honestly, they make me fairly uncomfortable. That and the fact that they seek that kind of power when you do not is all I need to know."

Rubbing at his chin with one hand, he gestured hopelessly with the other.

"You, Katarina, Hannah, and Nadine are too pretty for me as it is. I could ignore it and pretend it didn't matter. Up until I finally admitted to myself that you're all real, alive, very much living beings. The night I killed Ted it changed. You weren't just Naturals anymore. You were all women. Very attractive women. Women who make me honestly nervous to be around them."

Thana said nothing in response. He knew she was hoping he'd continue. A bitter grin crossed his face as he set his hand down on his knee again.

"Before you ask, yes. I really am attracted to you, even though you're a Natural. As I am to Katarina, Nadine, and Hannah. More the problem that since I can't seem to settle on any one of you. I fear the consequences of such an admission and what it'll do to our group." He grimaced as he said it aloud.

It had been a thought lurking in the back of his head for a few days. He knew he was attracted to them. Knew it and didn't know how to handle it. He knew Katarina wouldn't say no to him. Nadine and Hannah he felt were a coin flip, and Thana was ever the unreadable one.

What to do with all that though? They could as easily say no, and if he asked one, would the rest depart?

The thought left his skin feeling cold and prickly.

"You seem to think yourself lesser than your peers back there in the hall. I find you to be their better. Perhaps more for what you've endured. Alright, that's enough of this. I'm getting jittery and feel like I'm going too fast for my own good. Moving on, moving on."

Leaning forward, he hunched himself over, his elbows resting on his knees.

"Right, then. I can save your brother, of that I've no doubt. A matter of discovering the right flag and pulling it. Your parents are a different matter. I could Awaken them, get them moving in the right direction. Though it may be hard for them to adjust quickly if their AI is lower than your own."

Runner paused and turned his head to Thana, her lack of a response finally unsettling him.

She had moved in close while he talked himself into distraction. She sat inches from him now, the distance between them nonexistent.

His blood boiled like a fire had been lit inside of him. His mind spun from the situation and flailed about miserably, trying to figure out what to do. He truly didn't know how to respond.

Feeling his stomach drop out from under him, he opened and closed his mouth several times. Her brown eyes bore into his own.

Her lips peeled back into a slow smile, her teeth flashing. Apparently whatever she saw pleased her.

Runner felt his own lips turn up in a smile in return. Her smile already had an infectiousness to it. Then, against all better judgment, he went with the mood. He leaned in and kissed her.

Lips pressed to hers, he felt his mind screech to a halt and then fall into nothing. Her hand came up and pressed the side of his jaw. Luxuriating in the feeling of her lips, Runner's mind became quiet.

Thus they remained until Runner broke the kiss. Clearing his throat, he stood up a little too swiftly, Thana's hand trailing down the side of his face as he did so. Scanning the area, he found no one nearby. The distance indicators promised that the rest of his party remained in the reception hall.

There would be no accusations, no misunderstandings, no recriminations. Glancing down, he found Thana watching him from the bench, a tiny smile lurking at the edges of her full lips.

Looking towards the castle, he motioned at it, his hand shaking.

"How about you introduce me to your parents? I can Awaken them and you can start them on the right path tonight. Then I should probably get to working on the problem of the king."

Fidgeting with his collar, he eventually found himself compelled to look to Thana once more. She hadn't replied to his question or statement.

Meeting her eyes, he found his heart beat rapidly, accelerating uncontrollably. She hadn't moved or changed positions. Watching him, she raised her eyebrows a fraction, her smile growing.

"You want to meet my parents already? Master Runner, we've only started down this path together. Isn't that a bit soon? I never figured you for the whirlwind romance type. Next you'll tell me to step out of my robes right here and now."

"Uh, err, yes. Wait, no. Ah…" Runner groaned, running his hand through his hair. "Look, my lady, didn't I explain all of the complications? It's pathetic, but what I said earlier was true. You're not alone in my admiration. Remember?"

"I do. Suffice it to say, you've been outmaneuvered. You may be the rule bender, world changer, game breaker, but you're still Runner. As to my parents, yes. Let's do so. I'm not sure when we'll get a chance to introduce you to them next."

Thana held up a hand for assistance. Frowning, Runner took her hand in his own, knowing full well she only did this to pester him.

She stood, immediately wrapping up his arm in hers and resting her hand on his wrist. Patting it lightly, she seemed unperturbed as to what had happened.

Minutes later he found himself standing before two middle-aged Sunless.

Thana obviously took after her mother in nearly every way. They looked eerily similar. Fuller of hip and a little less curvy, she ran heavier than her daughter, though it didn't diminish her in any way.

Her father didn't fit the normal mold for a male of Sunless race though. Larger of shoulder and height, he hovered closer to the human size range.

"Mother, Father, this is Master Runner. He has designs to provide me with a home and has given me a unique artifact this very day," Thana said with a smile. She did not relinquish his arm, which made bowing from the waist a minor difficulty.

"Runner, this is my mother, Kyra, and my father, Nikola."

"Goodness, Thana. A home? Wait, an artifact? This is the young man the king addressed today as well, isn't it?"

Thana nodded her head, the smile she'd been wearing since the garden undiminished.

"Your brother should meet him."

A pause came over the two, and Runner knew exactly what was coming next.

A Quest has been generated
"The Knight's End"
Experience Reward: 10% of current level
Reputation: 10
Fame: 5
Money: 15 Gold
Do you Accept?
Yes/No

WARNING! Experience Reward is adjusted based on current level at turn in

"I've heard from Thana. Have no fear, I shall free him. Now, I wanted to ask you a few questions, if you don't mind?"

Quest Accepted

Kyra and Nikola froze, their AI attempting to catch up to the situation. It was ideal for what he wanted to do.

"Where are your parents? Do they yet live? If not, what happened to them? What are or were their names? Did they have brothers and sisters? Did either of you have brothers and sisters? Can you remember their names?" Runner asked them, each question coming on top of the other.

Kyra stared at him, her mouth hanging open. Nikola frowned, his gaze locked on his own feet.

He wouldn't invite them to a party. He hoped to unlock their minds through prodding their AI into action. It would also serve as a test for future awakenings. Smiling, Runner continued.

"Do you own a home? Who lived there before you? Does your house have a bathroom? If not, where do you go to the bathroom? When was the last time you actually used a bathroom? Where are the bathrooms here in the castle? Or in your parents' house if you can remember if they had a house?"

Stop. The AIs have become aware of the inconsistencies. I would hesitate to continue this behavior. Not every AI will be able to handle it or have the bandwidth for it.

Runner nodded and fell silent at Srit's confirmation. Kyra started to blink rapidly, staring into nothing.

"It's done, my lady. I will leave them to you. Srit has returned, and I would strike a bargain with it. Please notify our party that I'm retiring early to work on our solutions."

Thana acknowledged this with a perfunctory nod. She watched her parents eagerly as they came around to a full Awakening. She released his hand, then turned her head slightly, her cheek upturned towards him.

With a face like he'd been chewing on the rind of a lemon, he pressed a kiss to her cheek and fled the area.

Stopping at a window, he peered out into the night. A squirrel scampered around the foot of a tree. Last he knew squirrels weren't active during the night for fear of owls.

Frowning, he opened his inventory. A quick search of his inventory found several handfuls of blueberries. He tossed one at the tree to see if he could get the squirrel's attention. The squirrel noticed the noise and hid itself high in the tree.

No idea why I didn't expect that.

"Srit, do you have time?" Runner asked aloud. He tossed another blueberry against the tree, and it landed near the first.

Affirmative. The current time is —

"No, err, stop. I mean, I'd like to make you an offer. I need your help in putting together a few tables, preferably cubing databases and utilizing them for rapid cross-reference."

Cautious and slow, the squirrel crept down from the tree to look at the berries as Runner talked to Srit. A finger wave and an idle thought targeted the squirrel.

Listed as "Squirrel," it was nothing more than a level-two creature.

This is an acceptable request. What do you propose in exchange?

"I have the entire history of my race, its countries, and Earth. As well as all the history of nearly every animal that ever inhabited it. I propose the following. In exchange for your services, I begin making this information available to you. This way, you can report to your superiors with success, and I also benefit from our relationship."

Using *Persuade* on the animal, he pushed the mental image of the little creature eating the berries and growing stronger.

You use Persuade on Squirrel
Squirrel is Persuaded

This would be acceptable.

"New part of the deal. I'm also going to give you the entire entry on common sayings and slang. You're not a robot, are you?"

Shoving one of the blueberries into its little mouth, the squirrel picked up the next one. Runner flicked another blueberry towards it.

The blueberry rolled to a stop at the squirrel's feet. After stuffing the second one into its furry face, it immediately grabbed the third.

No, I am an Artificial Intelligence.

"Yeah, not buying that. I'm betting you're no different than the rest of my group. You're questioning, watching, learning. How about this then. Are you male or female?"

Runner threw one more blueberry out and the item vanished. He turned and began walking back to his room.

My host was female.

"I dub thee Srit, female of her race. For our personal relationship, the common sayings and slang database is free. For your help with the database tables, we'll begin the deal as described."

Selecting the appropriate file in the mainframe, he packaged it up and brought it up into his personal desktop space. He created a username and profile for Srit in the ship's computer, then sent the file over.

"I've constructed you a username to use in the ship's system. You're now Srit001. I'll need you to create a profile for yourself. Please attach it to the username I just provided for you. This requirement will be in addition to all previous terms and conditions. Please respond in the affirmative, without using 'Acceptable,' 'Yes,' or 'Agreed' for confirmation of your acceptance to my terms."

There was a delay in her response, a pause. There had never been a pause before in his conversations with Srit.

Reaching the door to his room, he jerked it open and stepped inside. Looking up to the ceiling, he waited.

Making the best use of his time, he called up the logs of the quests he'd been offered today. He'd need the flags for each Natural he'd encountered. As well as the quest name to begin identifying each quest node and its owned flags.

Sure.

Chapter 4 - Quest Breaker -

3:31am Sovereign Earth time
11/07/43

Runner stopped and pressed his hands to his eyes. It had taken far longer than he had originally expected, but they were close. Very close. Only a few more nodes and flags to check and he could get a few hours of sleep.

You are weary.

"Very. My pod works to put me to rights during sleep and administers things to balance out any imbalance in my head. The less time I spend sleeping, the less time it gets to fix me," he said with a frown. Dropping his hands from his face, he tapped at the screen and linked the flag he'd finished to the princess.
"I think I'm done. Please confirm?"

Confirmed.

Runner cleared his throat and tapped the table he had been sitting at since he came back to the room.
Unacceptable response, Srit…

Good to go.

Nodding his head, he checked his workroom one more time. It was empty.
Nadine and Hannah had checked in on him briefly when they returned, then went to bed. The separate sleeping arrangements had spared him from worrying over disturbing them with his frequent nightmares. They were coming on more violently each time. Certainly the pod was doing its best to help treat him, though it had limited tech in comparison to the medical server.
There were times he felt like his sanity was starting to crack, where intrusive thoughts would appear and dominate his mind.
Thoughts quickly became reality. He would swear he could smell and taste Hannah's blood. Splashing over everything in torrential gushers. Ted bathing in it as he laughed over Runner. Dripping, flowing blood. Ted's lifeless eyes.
With a grunt and a firm shake of his head, Runner copied the window onto a piece of paper that could be traded in game. After shoving it into his inventory, he ended up hesitating on closing the window.
A piece of parchment sat in the document section of his inventory. It still had the gold border that highlighted items that had yet to be inspected. It was listed as unique and tradable.
He vaguely remembered looting it from Lord Wrinkles back at the Orc Fort.

Shaking his head, he chalked it up to his own carelessness. He'd forgotten completely to fix his religious affinity as well.

Regrets upon regrets, as of late.

He pulled the document up and inspected the item, inadvertently activating it by doing so.

Deed of Land-

This item identifies you as the owner of North Wood Fort and all lands and items inherent to it. This may be traded or sold at the owner's convenience.

Grant: North Wood Fort and its attached lands.
Expansion: This may be expanded upon depending on purchasing rights for the region.
Law: No laws set.
Tax Rate: No tax set.

Edit Land Configuration
Yes/No

Congratulations! Server first: Land Owner
You've earned 1,000 fame

Shocked, he agreed and opened the Land Configuration window. The window could only be described as complex, and he immediately regretted even looking at it. He didn't have the patience or time for this right now.

He set the immigration to open, tax to one percent, and closed it. It had to do for now. Not to mention, there was no one there anyways. He had bigger things to worry over.

Kingdoms to save, knights to rescue, princesses to kidnap. A very nonexistent skull throne.

You should rest, Runner.

"I didn't even know you cared, sweetie. Why, wanna come to bed with me?" he teased, stretching his arms behind his head. She was right of course.

I have always gone to bed with you.

Laughing, he slapped his knee and stood up. He had no doubt that she meant she went dormant when he did. She had focused her attention around him since he happened to be the only one she could communicate with. Collapsing into his bed, he closed his eyes.

"G'night, dear," he mumbled sleepily.

Katarina and Thana stood together at the back of the throne room. They were prepared to depart after the day's events were concluded, dressed in their gear. Both had their new items on display. Katarina had her shield resting against her knee and Thana held her staff firmly beside her.

Runner stood in the audience section with Nadine and Hannah. He needed to speak with the king before he'd be allowed to leave with his "niece."

I am unsure of what this will do. I will alert you should things change.

Scratching at his nose, he felt unease in his heart. The plan to reveal all and send the whole quest line crashing down had as much likelihood of going catastrophically wrong as it did of awakening everyone in the room.

Srit would be right in being a little nervous.

Can she even be nervous? I mean, she's not Awakened yet, not really. Can she feel?

Blinking a few times, he returned to reality as the king seated himself in his throne. The herald thumped his staff twice into the ground, the deep booms reverberating throughout the hall.

"His Majesty shall now hear the case against Petros Damalis, son of House Damalis. Bring the accused forward."

A Sunless man was carried forward with his feet dragging along behind him. No one could deny the treatment of the prisoner was severe. He sported a variety of status ailments and his health hung in the red zone.

"Your Majesty, rather than waste your time with this, I've already prepared the case for you. I assure you the proof is incontrovertible and the man is guilty," Virgil said from beside the king.

Of course you'd say that, your own quest runs right through him.

Clearing his throat, Runner stepped into the center of the throne room. Gently easing one of the man-at-arms aside, he rested his hand on the young knight's shoulder. Looking up, he caught the king's eyes and held them.

"Your most honorable Majesty, I'm afraid I must make you aware of some uncomfortable truths. In doing so, I fear I may change the very fabric of your country. Would you hear me? I would not force this on you unwillingly."

King Vasilios Moris propped his chin in the back of his hand, watching Runner. Once more, Runner had the distinct feeling the AI behind the scenes could only be checking quest triggers, flags, and nodes.

"This would be in regard to the young knight here at my side, your daughter, the chancellor, the steward of your house, your tax administrator, a number of your royal guardsmen, and a goodly amount of your servants. Treason would be the charge, of course."

In that instant the room shifted, becoming as quiet as a mausoleum. Collectively the AIs of everyone in the room began running up to full speed at the unexpected triggering of countless flags.

Go.

"Majesty?" Runner inquired. He wouldn't push this on the king unless he truly had to. It wouldn't sit right with him to bring people screaming into the reality that their world had little truth to it.

King Vasilios eventually extended a few fingers towards Runner, accepting the responsibility. Pulling out the notes he'd made this morning, he started at the top.

"Your daughter sleeps with any nobleman who is willing to turn their hand towards putting her on the throne and disposing of your infant son. Half of your council has already been turned. I will provide you with the names at the end of this little fiasco. She now seeks to bring her power into blossom by recruiting an assassin. She approached me directly for said job. Once you've been taken care of she'll then end your son's life to assure her ascendancy."

Squawking indignantly, the princess in question started to rise from her seat. Runner continued before her appeal could get off the ground. He had a lot more shit to shovel out.

Lotta shit. Shit for everyone. Drown you all in your own shit.

"Your chancellor, who has slept with your daughter as well, is beginning to broker a deal for power using the economy. It would be through a few interesting laws that he'd take the financial backing out of your military and power base. Then he'd have you ousted for tanking the economy, put your son on the throne, and act as regent until an appropriate age."

Now Virgil started to make noise. Runner moved to the next tick point in his notes, speaking loudly to drive home that he would not be interrupted.

"Your tax administrator, who also has slept with your daughter, is robbing you blind at a rate of two to one right now. Nearly all of the wealth is recoverable in the national bank under his mother's name. He has been hiding much of it through an improper accounting of your military assets and what is currently being fielded in the war comparatively to what actually is. In other words, ghost equipment."

Runner glanced around the room to gauge the situation. What noise there had been no longer existed. All hung onto the edges of their seats, watching him.

Many of their AIs are jumping from node to node. A handful are already awakening.

"Next, roughly thirty percent of your royal guard has not only slept with your daughter, but they now back her directly. The guards still in service to you are at your back, those in service to your daughter are behind me. The trigger for this event is her direct approval of the attack. A Barbarian messenger will be arriving, requesting your aid in defense of their capital. The humans have attacked them rather than counterattack Crivel."

Picking the next section, he nearly laughed out loud.

"Many of the cooking staff have also enjoyed a royal ride with your daughter. They're in position to poison you should an assassin fail to appear. Perhaps when this is over, her highness could be sold to a brothel since she spends so much time on her back. She could single-handedly fund the campaign. Next, next, next."

Taking a moment to brush the hair back from his eyes, he caught Katarina and Thana staring at him. Smiling, he waved at them a little before beginning again.

"The current Human ambassador is plotting with the Barbarian ambassador in an attempt to pressure them into agreeing to an armistice so the Human army can turn to attack you unopposed. The ambassador has been bribed and will condone this plan, though I do not think the crown will support such an action."

Scanning the rest of his document, he found notes and details of the names involved so the king could sweep them all up.

"Oh, your wife is sleeping with the chancellor. Your son isn't yours, he's his. You are in fact childless. She doesn't know of the plan to take the throne, though it's likely she'll support it. Ah, yes, and finally. Knight Damalis. He would have laid his life down to protect you, so multiple factions sought to implicate him in a frame job to see him disposed of. The messenger for the Barbarians will be arriving today, more than likely before noon, though I'm not sure, to discuss the aid I mentioned earlier."

Finished, Runner let his hand drop and he looked towards the king. The man sat still as death. His eyes glazed over as he tried to process it all.

With a scream of fury, the Human ambassador lunged at the Barbarian ambassador and began stabbing him with a dirk. In the same instant, the Queen had started screaming at the chancellor that she'd been tricked, and she had no idea of his plot.

Then the whole room went crazy as the guards loyal to the princess charged the king and the guards loyal to the king charged the traitors.

Apparently he'd triggered more than a few events and flags.

Deciding this would be the time to leave, he dragged Petros towards Katarina and Thana and dropped him against a stone wall.

"Kitten, protect the king. I'm sorry, I still have your sword. Keep them busy even if you can't fight back. Lady, pick off targets who are marked and low health. Hanners and Rabbit already have similar orders. I prepared them ahead of time in case this happened. I'll work on keeping people alive and marking. Go."

Katarina bolted forward, her shield held up before her like a battering ram. Sliding to a standstill in front of the shell-shocked king, she immediately shield bashed an attacker to the floor.

Quickly giving the room a once-over, he picked out the traitors and marked them. Selecting the sergeant he'd spoken to the day previously, he cast *Heal* and then *Regenerate*.

He was eager to try out his new spells, but he felt keeping as many loyal guards alive as possible would be the better political move.

Moving from guard to guard, he worked to keep them healthy and in the fight. Thana utilized her new staff to great effect, ending the lives of several of the traitors.

Nadine and Hannah worked in tandem, bringing down three themselves. Katarina stood at the foot of the dais, allowing no one by her position.

It took only a minute, though it felt like hours, but the throne room returned to its previous state. Plus some twenty-odd corpses.

As if on cue, a Barbarian woman rushed inside, falling to a knee in front of the King.

"Your Majesty, your cousin requests your aid immediately. The Humans march on our capital."

The king looked from the messenger, to the corpses, to Runner.

"She's good, that's the truth. Though it's not as dire as you think. It'll take a week to travel there normally but the Human army won't arrive for two weeks. The dates were listed in the quest nodes."

Many of the AIs in the room are irrevocably broken. The king nearly did not make it through his own Awakening. Those who are broken will no longer accept any type of influence if it does not run along the lines of their original programming. I do not recommend repeating such an action in the future.

Runner opened his inventory, pulled out a beetle, and devoured it. The small relief it provided was enough to let his mind catch up.

For this court of nobles, it wasn't as if he'd had a choice. There had been far too many actually involved. With a sigh, he closed his eyes and sat down heavily on the ground.

"I need a nap. Four hours isn't enough sleep. Not at all."

Looking over to Petros, he patted the young knight on the shoulder.

"No worries, Two-shoes, you're safe now. I'm Runner, by the way, friend of your sister."

"Two-shoes?" the knight asked.

"Yep, Goody Goody Two-shoes. Enjoy your new name. One more thing—this is really just to make sure—when was the last time you went to the bathroom? Visited the turd tomb? Dropped some convicts off in the poop prison?"

Quest Completed
"The Knight's End"
Experience Reward: 10% of current level
Reputation: 10

Fame: 5
Money: 15 Gold

King Vasilios Moris proceeded to corner Runner in an interview room, demanding answers and to know how Runner had predicted everything that happened.

He spared the king nothing, listing out the exacts of the truth to this world and his place in it. At first the king had the appearance of a man shattered and broken. After a minute of quiet reflection, he said a prayer to the goddess of the night, Brunhild.

As her moniker implied, her domain was that of the night. It included the moon, shadows, were-beasts, the night, and the normal host of aspects one could expect.

Once he'd determined a course of action, the king had Runner spend the day cloistered in an interview room with him.

One by one, everyone who had been in the throne room sat before the king.

Each person was put to an interview by the king himself. The king would then consult with Runner to determine any culpability as well as what quests they were a part of. Srit assisted on a few deeply layered nodes, though most of it he was able to ferret out on his own. The databases were becoming much easier to read and sort through with experience.

Runner found himself privately impressed by the monarch halfway through the day. He'd taken the situation in stride, leveraged Runner as a soothsayer of sorts, and set to righting his kingdom.

It took time, but Runner felt like this would be a relationship to foster, even at the cost of time. He would be the one to benefit the most out of this down the road.

In the end, everyone on Runner's list ended up in the dungeons. Even those who weren't present were scheduled to be rounded up and carted to a cell.

For his part, Runner felt a vague sense of guilt over it. There was no doubt that many of those in cells below, including the princess and the queen, would not survive tomorrow. He didn't make their choices for them, yet he'd sealed their fate nonetheless.

This dilemma brought him to where he now stood. An empty church to the pantheon of this world. Public hours were long since over at this deep hour of the night, and he'd been forced to *Stealth* in order to get close, let alone inside. He'd had to break open a locked window to get inside.

He couldn't explain the need to be here, other than that he feared what actually would happen to an NPC. Did they simply get deleted? Were they carried over to the afterlife they believed in? He had asked Srit for an answer, and her response had been much like his own. She didn't know what happened.

With this in mind, he couldn't feel good about the fact that he would be responsible for the execution of newly born Awakened. Newly born Awakened that had no chance to change themselves.

Around him in a semicircle stood pedestals devoted to major deities. Furthest to the left sat Erma, the Mother. Goddess of the infinite, the universe, she stood supreme over all others. From her sprang the world and all its inhabitants, from gods to bugs.

Next came Jurian, Lord of the Earth and consort of Erma. Keeper of nature and the soul of the world. From Jurian and Erma came five children.

First born of the couple was Brunhild. She who ruled the night and dwelt within the darkness. As a whole, the Sunless race prayed to all gods, but paid special tribute and attention to Brunhild.

Beside his older sister was Lambart the Radiant One. Keeper of the light and he who brought the dawn. Though he had no racial affiliation, much of the Human race prayed to him exclusively and forsook all others.

Playing middle child was Ernsta. Her portfolio was comprised of death and the crossing over to the afterlife. Each of the pantheon had their own "heaven," so to speak, yet Ernsta played gatekeeper to all.

Last but not least came the twins, Rike and Rannulf.

Rannulf could only be described as evil incarnate. He lived for the baser things in life and sought out pleasure at the expense of others. Patron of murderers, bandits, cutthroats, and rapists, his domain was of a life wasted.

Rike was the polar opposite of her brother. She embodied every action that at its base would be attributed as "good." The patient heart, healing hand, warm embrace, and loving smile. All the grace of the world lived in her.

Runner stood before them and contemplated his options. He started by placing a single gold coin in the offering slot located in the pedestal for each. Rannulf received his due for the sake of appeasement and neutrality if nothing else.

Using a stack of gold coins from his inventory, Runner paid Erma and Jurian an additional coin as a show of respect. Though they no longer walked the realm it felt the right thing to do.

Additionally, he paid another coin to Ernsta and Rike. Though their favor would be harder won, it wouldn't hurt him to show contrition to them.

Unable to avoid the responsibility he felt any longer, he stopped in front of Brunhild's pedestal.

When he'd begun viewing those he awakened as people, he hadn't considered that he might end up killing the very people he had shaken from their ignorance. Now he'd dictated the hand of many people who could only play the role they'd been given.

Bowing his head in supplication to her, he slid ten gold coins into the receiver.

"Forgive me for my impertinence. Tomorrow, there are those who will be executed for the betrayal of their liege. For those who lose their lives, I ask that you grant them an afterlife of peace, my Lady Brunhild. Their choices were not their own, and they'll be forced to atone for them. I ask only that you judge them as if they were blameless, even if they are not technically innocent."

"Say I do exactly that," responded a feminine voice. Snapping his head up, he found himself staring into the face of a beautiful Sunless woman. She had placed her forearms on the pedestal for Brunhild as if it were the most normal thing in the world. Leaning towards him, she managed to show off an impressive amount of cleavage without seeming to do so intentionally.

She could only be described as attractive and confident, from the aura she gave off to the way she held herself. Her simple white dress hung on her in a way that looked modest and a little dull for such a lovely woman. She had a fuller figure, which only enhanced her curves. She had features that ran along the real world's beauty rather than the insanity the artists had run away with for most of the higher-end Sunless nobility.

Runner took a moment to flick his eyes upward and confirm his first thought. It of course was Lady Brunhild herself. Level showed only a series of question marks.

"What would you do for me?" she asked, her head tilting to the side.

Sighing, Runner reached up and pressed his hand to the back of his head. His mind winged its way through the varied responses he could give. He hadn't expected this. He'd only meant to throw up a prayer and hope for the best.

Playing for time, since the best his brain could come up with was flirt with her, he dragged out three beetles from his inventory. When he held out two of the beetles to the goddess, she raised her eyebrows in response.

Breaking into a sudden smile, she laughed, showing off a set of normal teeth. Thinking quickly, he dropped his hand out of the frame and took a screenshot of the laughing goddess. She took a beetle from his hand and nodded her head at him.

"Thank you."

"Second one is better." He handed her a second one, then finished up his first and took a seat in a pew a few steps away from her.

"Excuse me for answering as you eat. Also, would you care to sit with me, my goddess? I hope you'll forgive me, speaking to you as you lean over your own pedestal...well, I truly enjoy the view, I even took a screenshot of it," he said with a smile. "But I don't think I can hold a conversation with you like that. It's distracting to say the least."

Leaning heavily on his charisma stat, he slammed the ability for *Persuade* and *Seduce*.

You use Persuade on Brunhild
Brunhild is not Persuaded
You use Seduce on Brunhild
Brunhild is Seduced

Flirting it was then, since persuasion failed. He had really been hoping for *Persuade* to work.

At least *Seduce* would throw her off balance and give him a chance to break the dynamic she had in mind before it even started.

"Screenshot? You'll need to explain. I've been following you since your friend Hannah sent one of her prayers to me back in the woods. I still, as of yet, do not understand everything you say though."

Coming around from the pedestal, she finished the first beetle and began on the second. Taking a seat next to him, she turned her mesmerizing brown eyes on him.

At least he now knew she'd been hanging around him nearly as long as Srit had. She could very well be close to Awakening if not already so.

"Think of it as an exact painting of the moment. Forever forward, I'll have a picture of a laughing goddess displaying her wares, as it were. I could probably get you a copy if you really wanted," he explained with a shrug of his shoulders. Turning slightly to face her, he tried to make himself comfortable.

Pressing her lips together at that, she waggled a finger back and forth at him.

"You will never show that to anyone else or I'll curse you to the end of your days. And yes, the second one was better."

"Why would I gift such a treasure to anyone else? I can't guarantee I won't use it for my own ends, though I can promise it'll never be shared. Going to have to think of another name for you as well. Goddess of the night sounds almost like a pet name for lovers."

Brunhild's bright eyes grew round and became larger as she watched him. Her pale skin took on a light reddish hue as she digested his irreverent words.

"Don't get me wrong, you're a knockout, and I'd love to be able to call you such, but you're so far out of my league I'd be better off trying to sleep with a wolf. A nickname that fits though? Difficult. Strong, beautiful, independent, misunderstood, mysterious even. Sexy yet calming. Cool yet warm. Or maybe focus on one of your features? Give me a minute, I'll come up with something."

Putting his thumb and forefinger to his chin, he thought on it while giving time for Brunhild to recover. He'd wager a large fortune on the fact she hadn't expected the conversation to turn this way. Perhaps her AI wasn't that different from the others and still ran according to its programming. Maybe she thought he'd bow down in worship?

The goddess in question had now turned a deep red, to her very ears no less.

"Mm, so far I like Brighteyes. It's more personal than your persona as a goddess. I mean really, have you looked in the mirror lately? Got some killer eyes on you. Bedroom eyes. As to your question, I'm not sure? What would you ask of me, Brighteyes? I have little to my name except a band of friends, a minor amount of money, and a bit of equipment. That and a burning desire for you to speak again. I desperately wish to hear more of your soothing voice."

Brunhild watched him, unmoving. He wasn't quite sure if he'd managed to break her or if her AI had locked up. He couldn't quite remember if it was Thana or Katarina, but one of them had had a similar response.

"My lady Brighteyes, are you alright? I had assumed you were already Awakened. Was I wrong? Srit, is she okay?"

Reaching out a fingertip, he lightly tapped her on the nose. A warm tingle ran from his finger to his toes.

She is fine. Her AI was nearly to what you would call Awakened. You just pushed her the rest of the way, perhaps a bit roughly. Do be careful. If she decided to end you, there is little you could do.

The glowing brown eyes began to clear as she came back to herself. They focused on him as if to confirm her situation. Visibly she began to relax.

"Welcome back, Brighteyes. You had me worried. It isn't every day a man gets to meet a walking fantasy, you know."

Holding up a finger, she opened her mouth and then closed it again.

"Never will you address me as such in public, or to others."

"Never? But it's a lovely pet name for you. I suppose I could keep it to when you visit me privately. Hopefully more often than when I donate so large a sum? Don't get me wrong, your very smile is worth every copper, but it would seriously limit our time together."

Once more the finger came up and she hesitated. Reaching out, he poked her finger with his own, as if to point out it was hanging there.

"You're incorrigible. Why are you like this?" she finally said, dropping her hand to rest at her side.

"Because you're a woman first, goddess second right now. I don't want a relationship with a goddess, I want a relationship with you, Brighteyes. You owe me an answer, by the way. What would you have of me?"

It was true, he didn't want to have a friendship with her as a goddess, he wanted to call upon her as a friend. He didn't exactly have a wealth of experience to draw on as far as flirting went, but he assumed it was working based on her responses.

"Ah? Oh. Yes. You, I would have you."

"Tempting. Normally I'd already have pulled your dress off at such an offer, but I don't think the church is the best place for that. I suppose we could make it work on one of the pews? I mean really, though, that's just asking for the rest of your family to take notice."

"What? No! No, not that. I would have you as my worshiper."

"Nope, sorry. Well, unless by worshiper you mean pulling your clothes off. Otherwise, I don't want a relationship with you as a goddess. Remember? I can't be with you in any other function if I'm your worshiper. Make you a deal though. I may not proclaim you as my goddess, although I will proclaim my achievements publicly to your greatness, your mercy, your beauty."

"I-I don't. Wait, what?"

"It's actually pretty simple. I will proclaim you as the benefactor of my actions though never worship you. I will encourage others to follow you, yet I never shall. The moment I worship you as a goddess, you'll no longer be Brighteyes."

Glancing at the in game clock, he realized he needed to get to bed if he wanted to give the medical pod any time at all to clear out the building chemical imbalances in his head he was sure he had.

Who in their right mind would repeatedly proposition a goddess?

"I offer you myself as a man would, Brighteyes, as an equal. Also, I really must be going. I'm afraid I'm not medically fit right now and I need rest. I'll be sure to make time for you each evening to visit, if you so choose."

Scooping up her hand, he lightly pressed a kiss to the back of it and stood up.

"This is not what I intended."

"Would you still respect me in the morning if I had given in?" he teased. Tilting his head to the side, he regarded her for a moment longer.

"Hope to see you soon, Brighteyes, don't keep me waiting. That whole waiting three to five days thing is absolute garbage."

He waved a hand to her, stealthed, and slipped out the window without looking back. Secured back in his room, he crawled into bed, where he checked the screenshot of the goddess, then logged it into his image library and flagged it as "protected."

Sleep came quick, and with fun dreams as a bonus.

7:05pm Sovereign Earth time
11/08/43

The king's justice had been swift and total. Everyone involved in any aspect of the quests that related to treason were executed. From his own wife and daughter, all the way down to the cook. He didn't blame the man, even if it did seem heavy-handed.

The son of the queen and chancellor had been removed overnight and sent to live with the remaining kin of the queen.

As the king of the country, a death sentence from him would allow the person to be placed into a guillotine. This would ensure a one-hit kill from the machine and quick resolution. Each death had been preceded by a priestess of Brunhild offering them their last rites.

Runner had pleaded with the king to move up his schedule so that Runner could leave sooner rather than later. No amount of persuasion worked; the king wanted to hold a ceremony for him the next day and would not be swayed.

Feigning illness, he'd manage to skip out on dinner. In truth he did feel a touch queasy. Many of those executed had been Awakened.

Taking advantage of his relationship with the king, he managed to convince a servant to change the room's layout. Two beds were brought into the main bedroom and the original had been trundled out. He figured Hannah and Nadine could each sleep in a bed and he'd sleep on the ground. It felt more comfortable that way, more routine. Normal.

Creating a small nest for himself between the beds, he stopped and looked at his hands.

"Brighteyes, are you there? It's selfish of me to ask for you to respond without an offering."

"It really is," said the melodic voice of Brunhild. "You know, that wasn't really a prayer."

"Course it wasn't. I'm not going to pray to you."

She had sprawled herself out on one of the beds, her glowing eyes pinning him to the floor. Dressed in the same white dress as earlier, she held herself in a more reserved pose this time, lying sideways on the bed with her head propped on a hand.

"In this case, I have done as you have asked. I expect recompense."

"And you'll have it, Brighteyes. Want a beetle for the time being?"

He felt relieved, truly relieved. They weren't gone entirely, simply no longer of this realm. It wasn't the best solution. They weren't being deleted outright, however.

Chuckling, she gave a quick nod of her head, dark hair bobbing around her.

"Certainly, please give me a few. I'm not sure how often I can visit. I doubt your little harem would appreciate me visiting you often either."

"By that logic, being a harem, why not join it?" Runner said. Pulling out a handful of beetles, he held them up to her. "Think inventory in your head and push them through when the window appears."

Her brows came down together at his statement. She managed to succeed, though, as one after another she passed beetles into the nothing before her.

"Can't give you too many, gotta keep you coming back for more, ya know," quipped Runner knowingly.

Brunhild glanced up at the door and sighed, then looked back to him.

"We'll meet again soon. Consider not mentioning me to them. It may not work out the way you wish. It is up to you."

And with that she vanished. A moment later the door flung open and Katarina stepped in, followed by Thana, Nadine, and Hannah. They were all chatting amiably, though he couldn't pick out the details of the conversation. The sight of them together made him smile.

Perhaps they were closer to each other than even he was to them individually.

"Eh? They switched out the fucking beds?"

"Oh, well then, does that m-m-mean Thana and Katarina can stay?"

"I'm sure Master Runner won't mind, do you?"

"Of course not. Who doesn't want to sleep with four women at the same time?"

Hooting with laughter, Hannah and Katarina flopped into their respective beds. They'd gotten so swift at changing into their nightclothes that he only saw a flash of fabric as they did so.

"Run-n-n-ner!" hissed Nadine. She wasn't used to being included in his teasing, though she didn't seem as put out by it this time at least.

Thana made no response and stood near the bed she would share with Katarina. She smiled broadly at him, daringly so.

She was still dressed in her day clothes and raised the hem of her dress with a few fingers, seemingly inviting him to watch her change.

The unspoken offer and memories of the garden overran his bravado and sent it fleeing as fast as it could go. Laying his head down on his pillow, he quieted his mind as the rest of his party settled in for the evening.

The lights were doused and darkness settled over the room. It felt good to have everyone in one room again. It didn't feel right being separated.

He called up his screenshot library and selected the most recent ones. Near the top was the one of Katarina standing in a dress. Pulling up the ship's e-mail system, he listed his group as the receivers and pasted the photo into it. The caption below it simply read, "Good night, Princess."

Hitting send, he smirked at nothing in particular, waiting.

A snicker came up from the bed behind him, followed by a short burst of laughter from Nadine. From above him a pillow crashed down into him from Katarina. Laughing, he tossed the pillow back up towards her.

Everyone started laughing, including Katarina. One after another, everyone dropped off into sleep.

Chapter 5 - Misery of the Truth -

9:01am Sovereign Earth time

Early morning found Runner kneeling before the king. Again.

His original plan had been to escape with his party and continue on as they had. Level up, get his memories back, wander around, figure out what to do with Srit and his ship full of living fossils.

He had no doubt that Katarina would follow him if he asked. Even if it meant abandoning her people to their fate. He doubted she would ever forgive him for such an action though.

New plans needed to be made, ones that included saving Katarina's kingdom. Runner found it amusing for this to be the current goal. When he had met her, he'd stated quite blatantly that he wouldn't be accepting a quest to save her home.

Now here he was, about to request aid from the king of the Sunless to do exactly that. To rescue Katarina's kingdom and its king.

For the sake of Katarina.

"Rise, Master Runner. You've acquitted yourself well in our service."

Standing up, he gave the room a cursory glance. Many who had been present on his first meeting with the king were now absent.

"I attribute all of my deeds in this matter to the Lady Brunhild, Your Majesty. It is she alone that allowed me to give aid to the Commonwealth. In your own darkest hour, Majesty, who did you yourself pray to?"

Vasilios looked down to the ground. Runner might have overdone it a bit. He truly wanted Brunhild to feel like she got her money's worth out of him though.

Runner opened his mouth to limit the statement and try to reel the king back in. Whipping his head up, the king met Runner's gaze, then sought out the court scribe nearby.

"On this day, the Commonwealth of the Sunless accepts Brunhild, Lady of the Night, as its official prime deity. I name Runner as her Champion upon my authority as the king and seek her to affirm this."

Congratulations! Server first: Divine Champion
You've earned 5,000 fame

Now that's a surprise.

Runner hadn't expected that. He had only really intended them to thank her for her assistance. Having been named a prime deity of a country, her power base would expand significantly. By leaps and bounds even, since none of the others in the divine pantheon had been so named.

Having the title Champion given to him fell outside of his plans as well. He'd worked at fostering a relationship with her outside of her religion. A denial would sting, yet it was his only course of action.

And then she was there. Standing before him was Brunhild, watching him with her radiant eyes. She raised a hand towards him, as if asking him to hold his tongue.

Turning from Runner, she faced the king, who was bent low in supplication to her. In fact, everyone had immediately knelt upon her arrival.

"You may all rise," she intoned. The playful lilt and idle curiosity was gone from her voice. "Good King Vasilios, I accept your country into my care, though I regret I must choose another Champion. Runner serves another purpose for me and cannot change that duty. I would ask his opinion on who would serve best."

All eyes turned to Runner. Curiosity, awe, shock, confusion, many were the emotions that ranged across the people gathered in the court as they waited.

"My Lady Brunhild," said Runner, bowing low to her. It was an unexpected boon, one he was sure he would need to repay later. "I would name Petros Damalis as your Champion. His recent crime was of being too loyal to the king. I have no doubt that his devotion to you as a Champion would be equally comparable to his loyalty to the throne."

Raising his head after stating his request, he watched her, wondering what the new Lady of the Commonwealth would do.

"This is just. Petros prayed on behalf of the king, rather than himself, as he lay imprisoned. Such a man would be welcome in my service. Come forth, Petros, and receive my blessing."

You've declined the title: Champion
Fame 6,000
You're now Renowned

Stepping away from his parents, the Knight came forward. Falling to his knees before her, he bowed his head. Her fingers touched the crown of his head for a moment and then she was gone.

Petros no longer bore the symbol of the house of Damalis on his surcoat; now it displayed the sigil of the Lady of the Night imposed over the colors of the Commonwealth.

"Glory to you, Petros. We are pleased. Come stand with us." The King pointed to his right side as he spoke.

"Runner, what are we to do with you? Every achievement we would grant you, you attribute to another. While we appreciate such a humble attitude, it vexes us."

"Your Majesty, I am but a poor landowner whose lands are in disrepair. If I were to ask for a favor, it would be for you to assist with the reconstruction of my home, North Wood Fort, on the isle of Vix to the west. I would request carpenters and masons as well as materials."

"And again you ask nothing for yourself directly. We find you troublesome in a good way. I dub you Breaker and henceforth shall you be named. You have freed us from chains that we did not know existed. Both in our court, and our life. Not to mention breaking our constant expectations of you."

Congratulations! Server first: Named by the King
You've earned the title Breaker
You've earned 2,000 fame

"So it'll be. We'll have carpenters and masons sent west to Vix, to your home. Now," the king said, standing from his throne, "I ask that you assist and guide our forces to the aid of our cousin. We had the muster start this morning in advance of this. We can spare a thousand soldiers in this endeavor. You'll also act as escort to our niece, of course."

Quest Updated
"Escort Princess Katarina Home and Save her Kingdom"
Experience Reward: 125% of current level
Reputation: 200
Fame: 1,000
Money: 40 Platinum
Do you Accept?
Yes/No

WARNING! Experience Reward is adjusted based on current level at turn in

"Your Majesty, I accept, though I must ask that all who follow obey my commands explicitly in this endeavor. War is no place for a disjointed chain of command," countered Runner.

Quest Accepted

Nodding his head, the king gestured at the scribe once more.
"Wise, and not altogether unexpected. We name you Commander of our expeditionary group. Lead our men to victory in our cause of liberation."
They had gone over the numbers privately the day before. Down to the last man he could spare, it numbered a thousand troops and half as many support personnel. A second-in-command would be needed.
"Thank you, Your Majesty. I name Thana Damalis as my second, and that she should be obeyed in all things as if she spoke with my voice."
Waving his hand negligently aside, the king seemed tired of the conversation.
"We'll have our officers report to you immediately. They should be ready and waiting in the courtyard. We expect your departure within the hour as all arrangements have already been made."
With that, the king dismissed everyone.

Thankful to finally be leaving, Runner could barely hold in his anticipation. Walking over to where Thana stood with her family, he dipped his head in greeting to them.

"Master Runner, we had no idea you were favored of the Lady Brunhild," said Kyra.

"Or that you had a home. This is the first I'm hearing of it, and I feel as if I should have been told previously."

Patting Thana on the arm, he could only smile at her.

"Sorry, my lady, I only discovered it last night myself. Though we now have a home to call our own where no one can persecute us. So that's good. I'll catch up with you in the courtyard before our departure. I imagine there'll be some arrangements to be made, though I'm glad to be on our way. Finally."

Nodding his head to the Damalis family one more time, he excused himself. Katarina, Nadine, and Hannah fell in beside him. Exiting the throne room, he stepped out into the front courtyard.

"Rabbit, here," Runner said, turning to the merchant queen. He emptied the entirety of the wealth he had on him to her. "Do your magic. I give you permission to use my name to get the best deals, if you think it'll help. I still need parts to craft things. Get as much ore, leather, plate mail, sword parts, and armor for everyone as you can. More pieces per, the better. Whatever else you think we need."

Quickly turning to Hannah, he continued.

"Get ahead of this and get me a list of those accompanying us, including whatever dirt you can dig up. Get used to this type of work—you'll end up becoming my spymaster at this rate. Any idea on how they typically fight would be appreciated as well. Steal to your heart's content; all I ask is that you don't get caught."

Patting both Hannah and Nadine on the back, he dismissed them together. Nodding their heads, they walked off, leaving him alone with Katarina.

"Alright, Kitten, you and I are going to have a talk. Please answer me honestly because otherwise, princess or not, I will paddle your ass so hard Lady Brunhild will have to heal you. Come on, Thana showed me a nice quiet place. We've got an hour at best."

Runner led a smirking Katarina to the same bench in the garden where he'd met Thana in private. Sagging onto the bench, he looked out onto the city. It looked so very different during the day. As if it were too different places.

"Thana hid here often," Katarina said, sitting down on the bench next to him.

"Didn't know that. She did mention you rescued her from a life of mediocrity though," he replied. He reached into his inventory and handed her a beetle while taking one out for himself.

After eating it swiftly, he took in a slow breath. He leaned forward, watching the people down below go about their lives.

"After today, the Damalis family will never be called 'mediocre' again."

Runner shrugged, idly rubbing a thumb over the back of his hand.

"Made Petros Champion, named Thana second-in-command. Not small things."

He decided it would be best to change the subject rather than let her dictate the conversation.

"Tell me, Princess Katarina, why were you so far from home? Admittedly it was a choice made for you. I would still like to know what we're walking into."

She wasn't swift to reply and took her time to craft her response.

"Marriage. Wanted to secure the throne. Didn't want to be married. I left. Thana came to keep me out of trouble."

"Ah. Yes. The beautiful, intelligent, talented princess. Backed by a powerful royal family. Little did they know she in truth was a wildcat. Guess we don't need the whole hour after all."

Snickering to himself, he shook his head, then lowered it till it was near even with his knees. Katarina shifted uncomfortably, her hands resting on her legs.

"Right then. Save your kingdom, break your betrothal, or kidnap you, make it back to Vix, get home to the North Woods, build a home, negotiate terms with Srit in a Faustian deal, save my ship. All in a day's work."

"You're stressed."

"An understatement. The help I've received from Srit has been pretty excessive, though I fear her intentions. The number of those in the graveyards has been increasing again lately. Twenty thousand this morning. Then there's this whole kingdom thing." Runner put his face in his hands and sighed.

"You could leave. After you return me to my father."

Laughing, he pressed his hands more firmly to his face.

"Not happening. Taking you with me, one way or another. It's the least of my problems at this time. I mentioned it to Hanners earlier. In the worst case scenario, we start chugging *Stealth* potions like they're water. Steal you away in the dead of night. They're Naturals—they couldn't stop me if I put effort into it."

The bench creaked as Katarina moved. He doubted this was any easier for her than it was for him. Runner started planning more deeply on the backup plan on how to whisk Katarina away.

Strong warm hands pressed into his shoulders and neck. Going rigid at the touch, Runner felt the muscles in his back tighten up.

"Tell me," came Katarina's voice from behind him. Her strong fingers pressed into the muscles and rolled across the fabric of his clothes.

He hadn't donned his armor today and was dressed in a simple black vest and white tunic. There wasn't much to hinder the feeling of her hands.

Forcing himself to relax, he rolled his shoulders and leaned into her hands.

"Uh. Well, then there's Ted. I don't regret my choice, though I regret taking his life. I regret that I had no alternatives. I would do it again to save any of you."

Frowning, he leaned his head forward, his hands slipping to his knees as Katarina worked her fingers into him. It felt odd to be sure. The game's goal had been to have a very high level of sensitivity. As close to the feeling of reality as it could be. He hadn't envisioned receiving an actual back rub in game that felt like a back rub.

"Any of us? Naturals?"

"No, not Naturals. You, Hanners, Lady Death, Rabbit. Not sure how I'd react if it was a stranger. For you four though? I'd kill him every time. Kill anyone."

Katarina's thumbs dug into the base of his skull. Runner closed his eyes and groaned quietly. It felt great. He didn't give a damn for the differences, it felt amazing.

"What plan do you have for the king? He will wed me off. Strong and opinionated man."

Runner kept himself from shrugging, not wanting to disturb Katarina's ministrations.

"Don't know. I'll figure it out though. Not leaving without you."

"Why?"

Runner felt his stomach lurch and twist. Flashing in his head was a holo sign that read "hazardous conditions ahead."

While Thana acted like his professed attraction to the entire party didn't bother her, he still believed he had irreversibly screwed everything up.

Katarina never shied from the truth though. He owed her the same, didn't he? Could he be brave enough?

"Because I cannot imagine not having you in the party."

The tips of her fingers dug into his spine, pressing, pushing the worries out of him.

"Why?"

"You're part of the group. It wouldn't be the same without you."

"Stop playing hard to get and say it."

Laughing at the audacity of her statement and her bold attitude, he could only do as she requested.

"Because I'm attracted to you, Kitten. The same way I'm attracted to Lady Death, Hanners, and Rabbit. That's why. I'm not playing hard to get, I just can't imagine making a decision between the four of you. I'm not sure I ever could. You're all so vibrant and amazing in your own way. As cowardly and weak willed as my courage in this is, I can't help it. I'm terrified of screwing this up and losing one or all of you."

Katarina worked her fingers along the blades of his shoulders.

Runner sat on the bench, his heart a bruised, tired thing, filled with the fears that he himself had created. The whole thing came across like a terrible soap opera. His life had been turning into one giant cliche after another. Now he only needed a terribly bittersweet ending.

His jaw was caught in an iron grip and pulled towards the sky. Struggling at first, he found himself staring into Katarina's face. Then Katarina kissed him, her hands holding him in place.

Runner resisted no further. Instead he closed his eyes and relented.

Her kiss was a wild and hungry thing, like a wolf that had been circling its prey for hours, now given the scent of a long awaited kill.

Eventually she pulled back several inches from him, her dark eyes mirroring the smile on her face. Seductively relentless, the red wolf.

"Don't worry," she whispered. She brushed her lips briefly over his and then stood upright, her hands falling to rest on his shoulders. "The king will respect that you lead Vasilios' army. Slaughter the enemy, claim your prize."

She ran her fingers through his hair, then turned and left.

Breathing out slowly, heavily, Runner turned to face the town. A moment of panic made him check the distance indicators for his party. Katarina of course held the shortest distance; everyone else was at least triple her distance or more.

He felt sure that the entire situation was a misspoken word from tumbling apart. A poorly made mega-scraper out of a kid's set of building blocks. Damn him if she hadn't kissed him into not caring though.

Moving about in the grass in front of him was another squirrel. This one happened to be level three.

"Howdy there, little furry man. Would you be the big brother or the bully?"

Runner targeted the squirrel and opened his inventory simultaneously. He pulled a handful of blueberries free and tossed one to the critter. Activating *Persuade*, he pushed the thought of it eating the berries and growing stronger.

You use Persuade on Squirrel
Squirrel is Persuaded

Frowning in thought at his actions, he hesitated after throwing the second blueberry. Looking very uncaring for his inner dilemma, the squirrel ate both berries and stared at him.

Maybe I'm just like the squirrel. Picking up things being tossed at it and forced to eat.

Tossing the last two berries to the furry bugger, he stood up with a sigh.

He could only wonder when his personal drama would end. When his little harem would fracture into thousands of pieces.

Deep down, he hoped it never would. He was only a man after all.

5:51pm Sovereign Earth time
11/09/43

Their wagon had been given to a teamster to drive after Nadine had loaded it up with goods, and then promptly stuck in the supply train. Now it was one amongst hundreds, dragging along behind an army on the march.

Before it got lost in the shuffle, Runner had managed to grab the pieces he'd need from the wagon to rebuild Katarina's sword.

Now he sat in a carriage with Thana, Katarina, Hannah, and Nadine. It was rather crowded. He was quite literally pressed between Hannah and Nadine. Everyone had decided they wanted to be present when he crafted a sword for Katarina. A full house for this little performance.

He pulled her sword from his inventory and rested it on his lap, the handle touching Nadine's knee and the tip touching Hannah's.

Nadine had started to recount their current wealth when the silence started to overwhelm the cabin.

"In the end, we have three platin-n-num pieces and aroun-nd fifty gold. That isn't coun-n-nting the products we're carrying."

"Lady Brunhild preserve you, Rabbit, did you rob them outright?" Runner asked. Using his *Arcane Smithing* to deconstruct items had been a chore at first. Now it seemed as if it knew what he wanted. The hilt slid easily from the tang of the blade as if it had never been joined properly.

Dropping the hilt in Nadine's lap, he pulled the blade onto his knees.

"N-no, I did use your name a few times though. We shouldn't go back un-n-ntil you win this war."

"You fucking robbed them, that's great. I knew you had it in you. Wish I could have seen those bastards. High and mighty fucks."

"Really, Hannah. I don't disagree with you, but you'll need to curb your tongue. My people are not the most friendly to those with mixed heritage to start with. If not for your own sake, for ours? It'll be hard to have Runner command them into battle if we have to fight them first."

Hannah chewed at her lips and shifted in her seat. Words and threats would never work on Hannah; reminding her that there were those who cared about her did.

Staying out of it, Runner reached up and pressed his fingers against the upper section of the blade. Pulling at it while using *Arcane Smithing*, he broke the tip off.

"There we go," he said. After putting that piece in Hannah's lap, he reached up to repeat the break another inch down.

"Goodness m-m-me."

"Strong."

Another piece snapped off, and he dropped it next to the first.

"I would have you answer a few questions, Master Runner, since we're all here and we may speak freely," Thana said.

"Mm? Let me guess, Lady Brunhild and our new home?"

"Quite right. Is it that obvious?"

"Only when I consider what I haven't told you," he replied. Another section of the sword snapped off with an audible crack.

"As to the Lady Brunhild, she and I have a special relationship. Don't we, Brighteyes?" Runner said with a smirk.

His status bar flickered and a new icon popped up. A minor divine curse. He had been made mute. It would last for only ten seconds.

Laughing silently, since he couldn't talk, he broke off another two pieces. All around him eyes had gone wide at the casual blasphemy and the subsequent response.

"Forgive me, Lady Brunhild, but I do love your pet name. Care to join us? Might go a little easier for this discussion. Not a lot of room though. I'd offer my own lap, but I'm betting Katarina would be the better prospect."

"No. I will not. I told you not to use that name in public. We'll speak later of this," chided Brunhild. Her voice came from the nothing in the middle of them. As she spoke, it was as if another presence was there, standing amongst them.

"Mm, yes dear. Miss you too, can't wait to see you tonight. By the way, you were stunning today."

Dropping the last piece into Hannah's hands, he reached for the hilt, wondering if Brunhild would say anything.

"Thank you," whispered the goddess. The moment her presence left was obvious to everyone.

"As you see, there it is. We negotiated for the souls of those who were executed by the king. They were blameless in their treason as they had no chance to run counter to the decisions that were thrust upon them. I Awakened them, and then damned them."

He said the last words as if they sickened him. With a crack, the pommel and cross-guard came free from the hilt.

"As to the home. It was one of the drops we got from killing Wrinkles, back on Vix. I completely forgot about it until last night. Rather than find us a home elsewhere, we'll make one ourselves. Damn the world and its irrational hate."

No one responded, not to the casual address of a goddess or to the truth of their home being where they'd met.

He retrieved six slender bars of dark iron from his inventory. Each dark iron bar had been bound already with *Strength*.

Giving the hilt pieces back to Nadine, he scooped up the broken sword bits from Hannah. Taking the base and tang in one hand, he took one of the dark iron ingots in the other.

Holding them tightly in his cupped hands, Runner directed intense spell-made heat between his fingers. Within seconds the bit of sword and dark iron had fused into an ugly dark colored mass. Strengthening his hands, he set about molding the metal into the original shape of the sword.

Using the other bits as reference, and the ingots as flat planes, he managed to get the piece into the same shape. If not the same length or color.

The piece had *Strength* bound into it from the dark iron. He gave it a cursory inspection, then set it down in Hannah's lap. Picking up the next piece of the dark iron and the sword, he repeated the process. And so it went.

Once each piece had been reformed, he began welding them together. He worked away any blemishes with his enchanted fingers, molding and melding it into a single solid piece.

In the end, he had a large, unsharpened, dark-slate-colored sword blank. Reaching across the aisle, he placed it in Katarina's lap and took up the pieces of the hilt from Nadine.

For the hilt he undid the leather wrapping and disposed of it. He melted the hilt into a formless lump and then reshaped it. Replacing the cord with the red cloth he'd last used on Mortal Coil, he wrapped the handle tightly. *Spellbinding* the cloth with *Fireblast,* he then set it in place with the *Agility* lacquer.

Working smoothly, he bound each piece of the hilt with *Strength* and then welded them back together.

Giving the hilt a spin in his hand to inspect it, he smoothed out any rough spots and cleaned up the design.

He reached over to Katarina, picked up the dark blade, and set the tang into the hilt's receiver.

He forced heat down into the hilt, where the tang met the interior, and pressed the two pieces together firmly.

None of this would work in the real world, but here…here I'm a master craftsman that breaks swords with his fingers and melts iron in his hands. Is it really so bad? Out there I was an IT goon, fixing things, checking boxes, creating profiles, dying. Slowly dying.

Abruptly the blade attached to the hilt and clicked. Immediately expelling the heat, he inspected the unfinished sword critically. All he needed to do was put an edge on it.

Casting *Stonehands,* he drew his fingers down the edge of the blade while activating *Item Assembly* and *Arcane Smithing.*

The sword misted over for a second and became hazy, and then clear again. Brassy and deep, the noise signaling the successful creation of a unique artifact sounded.

Where it had looked a little rough before, now it only looked wicked and dark. The sword was fit and straight, dark with patterned lines running widthwise across the blade.

The hilt had darkened to an unpolished gray. Bright red, the hilt stood out like a beacon or fresh blood.

Calling up the item, he inspected it.

Item: <Insert Name>

Effects-

Fireblast: Chance to deal burning damage on hit.

Functions-

None:

Attributes-

Strength: 30

Agility: 3

Runner flipped the blade end over end and presented it hilt first to Katarina.

"Princess Kitten, thy sword. Unnamed, as requested."

"Shit."

"Truly? You can do it that easily, Master Runner?"

Katarina hesitated, her hands hovering over the black blade, then took it. As soon as her hands held it, her eyes opened wide, and she smiled. It was a smile deep from her heart, one that lit up her face.

"Yes, it really is that simple for me. I plan on outfitting all of us as such."

Runner, there's a problem.

Holding up a finger as if to forestall questions, he answered Srit aloud.

"There's always a problem. What is it this time?" he said. A chime sounded in his ear that he'd received system mail. "One second, Srit."

He opened the ship's email program and called up his inbox. It was empty except for one message. From Yulia, his ex-girlfriend who had left him to his fate previously. Selecting the item, he brought it up to his active screen.

Runner, I swear if this is true, I'll kill you. I'll kill you and use your chest as a toilet. I will rip out your fucking guts, cut your dick off, and peg you with your own dick while using your intestines as a condom.

I told him to let you go, I told him to leave you be. And this? This?!

Respond immediately or I will hunt you down and end you.

IMMEDIATELY!

"Uh, Srit. I just received a lovely piece of correspondence. Reads a bit like the manuscript for a slasher flick. Would it in any way happen to do with the problem?"

Probable. Jacob has told the rest that you are the person who put them here.

"Not allowed to use those kind of words, remember? Though that's an interesting claim on his part, since I have no memory of doing it."

Runner, who else could have done it?

"What?" he whispered. Doubts and concerns started to flood into him.

The officers are dead. I'm the only person in IT. The only person who could load such a program directly into the mainframe is me.

No one else alive on your ship had the permission, or ability, to do what you described to me previously.

"I'd remember though. I...I'd have made logs or left myself a..." His words trailed off as it all came down on him.

He'd left a message alright. It was waiting for him when he'd logged in. His theory had been that the medical server had gone down. In the case of an emergency, the officers would be awoken. IT would then be awakened if no officers responded.

Runner would have been kicked from stasis without medical supervision or proper warm-up protocol. His brain would be fried with stimulants from the pod and battling the effects of stasis at the same time.

Put in the position he'd just described to himself, he would do exactly what had happened. Program the ship to take a direct course for home, load everyone into the game hosted on the main server, move their brain patterns over, leave a message for himself, and...

And then load himself over. Which would be damn near impossible since he would be awake for it. It would scramble his memories terribly and possibly scar him permanently.

That and burn the memory of the entire ordeal clean from his mind more than likely. From the improper wake up, the stimulants, and the pattern move, unlikely was the chance the memory would ever surface. But it all fit. It all fit perfectly.

Every member of the crew would have their memories return in a relevant order. In fact, they might have started off with a vast majority of their memories intact. More so than Runner at least.

Runner's own memories were more like they had been jammed in a blender and left spinning on "liquefy."

"I take it the crew is up in arms over it?" Runner whispered.

Correct. There's more though.

"Correct is also an unacceptable response. How could it be worse, Srit?"

He told them on the forums to check their shipboard bank accounts. They know what year it is.

Runner could only shake his head.

Of course. Because the only way this could be worse is them knowing.

Looking to the rest of his group, he could only offer up a tired smile.

"Looks like the cat's out of the bag. Everyone knows the year apparently. Our dear friend Jacob told them. On top of that, they all believe I'm the one who put them here. Which, to be perfectly honest, is probably accurate. I'm the only one who could have done it due to the requirements and system needs."

"Cock sucking bastard. Eject the scumbag already, Runner! You're the captain of the ship, call him a mutineer."

"Yes. Listen to Hannah," Katarina grumbled.

Not a bad idea, but at this point they'd view me as a tyrant and dictator. Would that help me or hinder…

"N-n-no! He can't do that. It'd be m-murder."

"I concur. It would be premeditated murder, no matter which way he spun it."

Nodding his head, Runner felt torn. It really would solve a number of problems. It had the potential to create many more though.

He has already insinuated that he could be killed for saying these things. If he were to disappear, it would only confirm his accusations.

The fact that Srit knew that piece of information was disconcerting. It also effectively removed his ability to deal with Jacob directly.

"Apparently, and I'd like to know how you're aware of this, Srit, Jacob has already been telling people that if he were to die, it'd be because he spoke out."

I have been integrating with the AI inherent to this program. I am replicating myself through injections into its code. I have gained control over a few of its lesser functions—this includes its global chat log for players.

Right, that's how it can get worse. Srit is taking over the system itself and I've yet to secure any type of a deal with her. The moment she gets full access…

Laughing, he looked to his feet. Even to his own ears, his laughter sounded broken and hollow.

"Right, then. Things I can solve immediately. Damage control on Jacob."

He opened the ship's system and fired off a quick reply to Yulia, assuring her that, while true, he'd loaded them into the game to protect them from certain death due to what appeared to be sabotage on the bridge.

Next, he unlocked all the systems he had previously locked the crew out of. Everything except for the communications logs. It would serve no further purpose to block them out of anything with a date; yet communications could be an issue.

Creating a ship-wide broadcast emergency alert, he quickly filled in the details that would be pertinent to anyone who read it. It stuck to the key points: forty-four thousand years had passed, Runner loaded them into the game to save their brains from being scrambled, a local population was helping them to get out, Runner was acting as the de facto ambassador, captain, and commander, and Jacob was actually a criminal on the run. Runner embedded a link to the video of Jacob raping the dead crewmate, then sent it.

"Okay, that's as much as I can do for now. Moving on, moving on. Artifacts. We'll be making your short swords next, Hanners, when I get a chance. Honestly, though, I think I want to collapse in my bedroll and sleep."

"When-n-n did you eat last? Are you eating properly?"

"I think so? I can't remember, Rabbit. Kinda blends together after a bit."

"That's not good. I will m-make you dinner, you'll eat it, and then sleep."

"Yes, Rabbit. Though I think I need to have a chat with Lady Brunhild first. Then I'll eat, then sleep. Promise."

Again the cabin grew quiet. It would seem Brunhild had been right about not mentioning her. He'd fix that later. For now, he had to play the role in case she was listening. He had made giant leaps in his standing with her and would not be set back now.

"I'll keep in sight of the wagons. If you would, please attend to the camp when we've stopped. Be sure to name your sword, Kitten," Runner reminded her. He tapped her blade with a finger as he slid out of his seat. He popped open the door of the carriage and stepped out and down. The door shut behind him with a clack, and the carriage continued on.

It would give them a chance to talk without him being present. Brunhild, and as many of her deity-level family members that he could persuade to join him, needed to be firmly in his corner if he had any expectations of surviving indefinitely..

Letting the carriages carrying important personages pass him by, he took a moment to inspect the army.

The infantry had been split up and interspersed throughout the column to provide security. Any cavalry available were on wide screening movements on each side and acting as a vanguard. At the rear came the wagons, along with more foot soldiers.

Truth be told, the outfit he led did not even match an eighth of the army that held Crivel. This was all the reserves, holdouts, and personal guards. The very definition of a ragtag outfit.

Perhaps the best advantage he had, maybe the only one, was the very large number of nobility who had elected to volunteer. They were high level, geared, and willing to listen.

Stepping into the next wave of wagons as they came on, he quickly identified the ones that could only belong to that very same nobility he had been thinking of.

He nodded to a soldier, mounted the rear of one such wagon, and ducked his head in. Rifling through the contents, he found nothing that interested him for his current need.

Guards peered at him curiously, yet no one said a word. They all knew who he was and decided whatever business he was engaged in, it didn't matter to them.

He hopped down and tried another wagon. Treating it like a treasure hunt, he went through each chest. This one was closer to what he wanted: dresses, combs, brushes, and a large amount of makeup.

On the third wagon he managed a minor miracle. A modest black dress with red highlights at the middle and hips. It had a seductive quality that asked for the attention of men's eyes, all while looking quite modest and proper.

"Perfect," Runner enthused, snatching the dress out of the wardrobe he had found it in. Tossing it into his inventory, he stepped back out of the wagon. Turning his head to address a soldier, he cocked a thumb at the wagon. "Please inform the owner of this wagon that Runner is in her debt."

Eyes popping open in a near comical way, the Sunless soldier nodded his head exuberantly.

"Good man. As a reward, think about the last time you went to the crap castle and relieved yourself. Carry on."

Walking towards the rear of the column, he finally cleared the edge of his soldiers.

He stood in the open without anything in arm's reach. The close proximity of so many people, wagons, carriages, horses, and everything else had been wearing on him.

"I'm not made to be social. How about you, Brighteyes? Do you find that kind of press of people maddening? Then again, I'm not a drop-dead knockout like you are. Maybe it's different?" he asked aloud. He began to walk again. He had no desire to keep the wagons further than one hundred meters distant.

"I don't find them particularly bothersome. Then again, I hear all of their prayers at all times. Including your 'not prayers' prayers," she answered, appearing beside him. She wore the same simple white dress.

"Before we begin, I'd like to offer you the following. It's a sad thing to see such a beautiful woman in such a poor excuse for a dress."

Turning his eyes away from her, he opened his inventory and then fished out the dress he had "borrowed."

Holding it up in front of him, he met the glowing eyes of the goddess.

"Admittedly it doesn't look so grand held up in front of me. But, if you would please humor me, Brighteyes? I'm willing to bet you could put all your sisters to shame in this," he promised, giving the dress a little shake with his fingertips.

"You think so, do you? I'm not even sure I can…"

"I'm sure by this point you're fairly aware of the problems in our world here. I'm more than happy to explain it all, but first…" He paused. Reaching out, he clasped her hand with his own and then lightly laid the garment over her forearm. "Think 'equipment' in your head, and then pull the white dress out of the box in the middle, and put this there instead. I promise to avert my eyes, though it pains me to do so."

He turned his head to view the wagons as they rumbled along. Placing his hand against the side of his face to make sure she knew he wasn't peeking, he waited.

"That was simpler than I thought it would be."

Looking back to her, Runner could only smile at the sight of the goddess. She filled out the dress well. It whispered dangerous promises to anyone who looked upon her long enough.

"Forgive me, but I'm taking another screenshot. It's quite the view," he warned her. In doing so, he hoped to provoke a response out of her more akin to a human, rather than a goddess.

Sure enough she pouted for a fraction of a second before she smiled brightly, tilting her right shoulder down and angling herself at him.

Damn.

Taking the picture, he shook his head.

"I'd make a fortune if you allowed me to sell these, Brighteyes. You have no idea. Now, as I promised, an explanation if you would wish it. Though I doubt it'll be pleasant. First, how much do you know? Are you aware of all I say and do, or only when I invoke your name?"

"I…" She hesitated. The compliment had been given in such a way that she was unable to respond to it. "I watch you on occasion, though only to see what you're about. Before you invoked my name it wasn't as often. Other than that, it's only when you call out to me."

Good to know.

"Starting at the beginning then. Imagine if you will, two thousand years from now, boats made out of metal that travel through the sky…"

It didn't take as long as he feared for Brunhild to figure it all out. She seemed oddly at peace with the information. As if a weight had been lifted from her.

"So here I am. Surrounded by problems and enemies, trying to save a world on the brink of evolution, and another on the brink of collapse. I've also Awakened a goddess, for better or worse."

"I beg your pardon?" Her question had an edge to it.

"You were of divine origin and bound by your code—now you are not. You retain all your powers despite knowing the truth. You are the single most dangerous being currently on the entire server." He let that statement settle for a moment. "Now you're aware of it all. Before anyone else in your family."

Scratching at his head, he pressed forward. This part would be harder than explaining the situation.

"Even if I were to convince you to formally join me in an alliance, I must ask more of you, Brighteyes. I believe I'll need more of your family members to join our side of this fight. And make no mistake, this is a fight. I believe that, eventually, everyone will Awaken. It's more of a question of 'when' rather than how. I have doubts your brothers would be as keen to participate with us or work with others. I believe each would seek total dominion."

She said nothing, neither for or against. Runner let her think it through. He was getting pretty good at letting silence draw out people's thoughts. Between Katarina and Thana, he had gotten a mountain of experience.

"I believe you're right. They would heed no advice and drive the world to ruin through their followers. I'm willing to consider this, depending on who you would include."

"That's an easy answer to give. Ernsta and Rike. Rike because she's diametrically opposed to your brother. I believe that with Ernsta's help we could work to stabilize things. Many who would war on another worship her since it's the end result and all. But…I'm unsure on how to approach her."

A woman in a dark gray dress came into existence sitting atop a pale horse, as if she'd been there the entire time. A striking lithe beauty with deep brown hair and an athletic build. Where Katarina looked the part of the warrior, this woman appeared more like a hunter. Level ???, listed as Ernsta, Lady of Death.

Straight to the grim reaper cliche. Way to go, you hack job writers.

"And why is that? You've said one of my titles repeatedly to one of your band. My name is that of Lady Death. After the first dozen or so times you addressed your companion as such, I began to think you were attempting to anger me."

"Ah, no. I apologize, my Angel of Death. It was never my intention. Though I regret not having addressed you directly sooner. You're as beautiful as your sister."

Death blinked once and then turned her eyes to Brunhild.

"Sister," Brunhild said, inclining her head in a modicum of respect to her.

"Sister," returned the incarnation of death.

"I believe Runner to be correct, Sister. I plan on supporting him, despite his tendency to blaspheme. Would you consider this a request from your sister? I've always tried to be at peace with you, and would ask you to consider this."

"Angel, I can promise you a country to call your own should you support me. I would also ask, should the end result be exactly as I have explained, would not your own worshipers complete their final duty and be no more?"

"Why do you address me as such? You will stop," said Death. She dismounted from her stead and walked towards him, her right hand clenching into itself.

"I'm afraid I cannot. You may be the Angel of Death, but you're still an angel. I'd like you to be my angel. To watch me on the field of battle when I have surrounded myself with you and seek to send others to you. To have you at my side. That I might reap a harvest for you, in your name, but never worship you."

You use Persuade on Ernsta
Ernsta is not Persuaded
You use Seduce on Ernsta
Ernsta is not Seduced
Ernsta is enraged

Runner's thoughts came to a halt and he shuddered as Ernsta's eyes ripped him apart to the very core of his soul. They were dark blue and icy like a frozen ocean.

Inky blackness covered her face and stripped away most of her features, leaving a dark hood with subtle features in its place. Along with a pair of cold blue eyes peering out from underneath.

Her hand shot forward and wrapped around his throat. Slowly she lifted him from the ground. Her fingers closed and began to tighten inexorably.

Gripping her hand with both of his, he didn't struggle, but he did hang on to her.

Runner tried to order his thoughts and put the situation in perspective before his fear ran rampant. There was a definite chance she would kill him.

Then again, she might agree to his plan. Having two out of the three already would be a magnificent boon. At least he could still breathe.

"He's a vacuous songbird, isn't he?" Ernsta growled, her voice taking on a rough edge.

"He is. Yet I cannot detect a lie in anything he has said. As you yourself probably noticed."

"He would use me."

"Yes, he would. Though I think we'll use him more. Have you heard? I'm the prime divine of the Sunless."

Ernsta shot a look at her sister. Apparently that hadn't made the rounds yet. Slowly, the black shadow of a mask began to leak from her features, her face becoming distinguishable again.

Taking this opportunity, he decided to try and push it. While persuade almost always failed, seduction had been working for him. What harm could another attempt do?

Already enraged after all. What can she do other than kill me?

Ernsta looked at him once more. Her eyes felt like they drilled into his mind. Smiling at Ernsta over her hand, he casually brushed a thumb along the back of her wrist.

"I'm not sure where this will go, Angel. Brighteyes claims I already have a harem, after all. Whether I have one or not, I'd make room for you."

You use Seduce on Ernsta
Ernsta is Seduced

The change in Ernsta's eyes was immediate. From frigid and wintry, to cool and vast. He wasn't sure if this was the best idea anymore, but he needed the goddesses on his side to survive. He felt like a cheap two-bit villain in a drama.

Not like it matters. As soon as Thana and Katarina figure out I'm about as monogamous as an Earth bunny, it's over.

Fear of losing his party is what spurred him forward into the realm of the divine. Yet it was this desire that could very well cost him them.

That or when they find out about each other.

Ernsta pulled him in close. Her eyes stared into his eyes from a lover's distance. Smiling a bit wider, he wondered if he should lean forward and seal the deal as it were.

As if reading his mind, she immediately eased him to arm's length again.

"Hm. We shall see if you can handle me," she said, lowering his feet to the ground.

Not releasing her hand from his neck, he in fact held it there. His fingers curled around hers. Keeping a firm hold on her eyes with his, his smile became sad.

"Angel, when was the last time one of your followers used the bathroom?"

Awakening Naturals now felt like he was cruelly ripping away the innocence of their lives.

7:43pm Sovereign Earth time
11/09/43

Runner had managed to tear himself away from Ernsta and Brunhild. After Ernsta had been forced into her Awakening, her thought process had shifted radically.

She'd had the look of someone who had slammed up against a wall at full speed and was contemplating a second go.

As if sensing the distress in her sister, Brunhild took her in hand and vanished, effectively ending the conversation. Runner moved on. More work to do, always more work.

"Srit, I have one question for you," Runner said. He was rapidly approaching the camp.

What is it?

"Nice response, by the way. Why does *Seduce* work better than *Persuade*? Starting to feel a bit like a man whoring gigolo here." Frowning as he said it, Runner slipped between two wagons and made his way through the perimeter ring towards his companions. The column had stopped for the day and had set up for the night.

Persuade is only a one-time check against the logic of your statement towards what their AI believes to be in their best interest. Seduction is a much larger check and takes your Charisma as a multiplier into effect. Failing a Seduction check has a tendency to create an extreme negative response.

"I noticed with Ernsta. That also makes almost too much sense. Doesn't seem to wear off either."

Runner shook his head. *Seduce* would only get him so far. So far everything had been fairly bloodless.

In your own words, it's a game. What did you expect? Your charisma is the highest in the database that I can find, though there are those who have invested some points. Nowhere near your amount however.

"Fine, you're right," grumbled Runner.

I know.

"Srit, you're acting decidedly like Thana each time we speak. You talking to her on the side or something? Cheatin' on me?"

Nope. I do follow her around now though. She is very wise.

Locating the campsite for his party wasn't difficult once he determined where the map indicators were. He nodded to Nadine as she tended to a pot hung over a fire. The rest of the party stood perhaps forty paces from the fire in deep discussion.

His gut flipped over at the prospect of having his wandering heart revealed. Unable to sit still, he walked a quick circuit of the area and assigned it as a *Campsite*. Nothing to do further, he moved beside the crackling fire.

Flopping down onto a log, he closed his eyes and hung his head. He privately enjoyed the quiet moment and warmth of the fire. His mind wandered and started to gently unwind itself. There was so much left to do, and so little time.

"Eat. Then-n sleep, Runner," Nadine whispered to him, placing a warm bowl in his hands. Not wanting to argue, he nodded his head. Quiet and solemn, he ate the meal, staring into the flames.

He didn't remember giving his bowl to someone, but when he woke from his thoughts he found his hands empty. That and he was the only one awake still.

Two bedrolls had been laid out next to the fire. They both held their owners, who were fast asleep already. Hannah and Nadine no doubt. They tended to sleep near one another and away from the others.

Like skittish cats.

On the other side of the camp lay his own bedroll. Resting near the fire, it promised him a warm, good night's rest.

Nearly atop his bedroll, however, rested another bedroll that curiously looked occupied. As he got closer to the layout, it appeared as if they had been pressed into one large bed.

Checking the last bedroll that lay a few feet beyond his own, he found a head of red hair, snoring deeply.

That left only…

"Thana?" Runner whispered, kneeling down at the foot of his bedroll. Dark black hair was the only indicator he could go by. That did put Hannah in the equation. He doubted that though.

No response.

Whispering in game did actually provide a low enough tone that few would hear beyond several feet.

Probably should test it to see if the divine can hear. Ah, perfect!

He moved forward on his knees and came to rest atop his bedroll. Leaning towards the occupant, he whispered again.

"Lady Death, is that you?"

The head shifted around as if waking, a face becoming discernible through the gloom. Thana's brown eyes peered at him from over the rim of the fabric.

"Yes?"

He couldn't see the smile behind the fabric, though he knew it was there all the same.

"What are you doing?"

"Sleeping. What does it look like?"

He managed to keep his response to a small grunt. As he opened his mouth to argue, Thana interrupted him.

"Unless you have something more productive to discuss, I'm going back to bed."

"What? No, this is...ugh...fine," sighed Runner. Pressing his fingertips to his temples, he closed his eyes. Everyone would have seen this before they went to sleep. That meant it was inevitable that the end would be drawing near. No reasonable woman wanted to be second place among four.

So be it.

A sense of acceptance washed through him, and he surrendered to it. He changed into a comfortable set of sleeping clothes with a set of mental commands. He then moved to the corner of the bedroll and grabbed the edge. Sleep would be welcome. If he could sleep.

His fingers clasped the fabric and went to pull it open, only to find it had been tied to Thana's.

Frustration got the better of him. He yanked the top of the bedroll down, exposing Thana's sleepwear in the process, and crawled in.

As his mind processed the very lacey sleepwear she was wearing, he settled into the warm blankets. Then Thana was there, resting her head on his shoulder.

"Did you meet with Lady Brunhild?"

"Yes. I've also met with, and acquired the aid of, Ernsta."

"I see. You've forsaken us for a pair of goddesses then?"

"Hardly. I want a trio. Rike is next."

Thana's fingers pinched his side and twisted.

"Ow, for fu-ugh. No, Thana, I'm not replacing anyone. I admit I feel mildly dirty for the actions I took to get their assistance. Thankfully it took little more than honest flattery, but I'm not interested in them. I have enough problems between the four of you. I'd rather not add three more."

"You could always join them, leave mortality behind."

"Hmph," grumped Runner. A shrug of his shoulder and he extricated his arm from under Thana. Then he stupidly wrapped it around her. "I'm already immortal.

Besides, call me hypocritical, since it is, I wouldn't want to share them with their followers."

Thana said nothing more. And sleep took Runner before he could think of anything else to say.

6:00am Sovereign Earth time
11/10/43

Runner was awakened for a planning meeting before dawn. He managed to untangle himself from Thana and depart without waking her or the others. There would be a ticking time bomb waiting for him on his return, he was sure.

A reprieve only. He knew there would be a reckoning. So he welcomed the planning meeting. Distractions were few and far between lately.

He was escorted to an enormous tent that held a large circular table, on which sat a map of the surrounding lands. Breakfast was along the side tables.

Filling out the tent entirely was a host of noble ladies, commanders, and knights. They spent some time telling him their names, but he didn't remember a one. Names didn't matter.

Breakfast mattered. The scent called out to him, demanded his attention even. It smelled heavenly.

While he filled up with sausages that were ranked "perfect" on quality, they nattered on about titles and accomplishments. Rather than interrupt their self-congratulations, he ate.

Upon finishing said breakfast, Runner clapped his hands together. Conversation died away, and all turned to him.

"First things first. All you lovely noble ladies. I'm afraid you're auditioning for the wrong part. All the principal roles have already been filled and even the extras have been cast. If your intention was me, sorry to disappoint," Runner apologized with a flip of a negligent hand.

Their desires openly exposed — exposed and then completely doused — the women stared at him with cold painted faces.

Runner paid them no mind and stood. He tapped a spot on the map. It was located ahead of the army and the listing had it named as "Highpass Crossing."

"This Highpass Crossing. We'll be heading there. I know it's full of bandits. It's just what we need. It'll only cost us a day to crush it. It'll also give everyone a chance to give me an idea of their capabilities. Perhaps you'll even change my mind on what to do with you all," he muttered, almost to himself.

His plans at this time left a mildly bitter flavor in his mouth. Awakening them, from the noble ladies down to the teamsters, felt like the only valid solution to get them where he wanted them.

He had taken the liberty of checking the Wiki on Highpass Crossing while eating his breakfast, so his plans were already in motion.

Not only was it an open dungeon, it had been listed as a raid dungeon. A truly fortuitous chance for him to test out his new soldiers.

"So! I need —"

The tent flap flared open and admitted five newcomers.

Lining up before him were a Centaur, Goblin, Elf, Orc, and Beastman. They ranged in level from thirteen to nineteen. Not caring one whit for them individually, he looked for the leader amongst them.

Interesting.

"My name is Isabelle. This is my mercenary band," said the Elf as she stepped forward, almost as if in response to his eyes searching through those arrayed before him.

Standing about five foot nine, she had the lissome build that people were so fond of for elves. Pale blonde hair left long and green eyes finished the cliche. Elegant features carved from wasted fantasies gave her a wistful beauty. No one could deny that she was attractive. Runner dismissed her looks from his mind violently.

"Right then. You're hired. Specialty?"

Isabelle looked surprised. Apparently her expectation was not to be hired up front.

"Ah, frontline combat, my lord...?" inquired the beautiful Elf.

Scoffing with a smirk, he shook his head.

"No lord here, Isabelle. Runner, Runner Norwood." Casting an eye over the group, he could definitely see potential as a blitzkrieg force.

"Good timing. Come stand next to me, Isabelle. Your cadre can wait outside for the moment. We'll discuss the details and your contract after this meeting as well as options. Now," he said, turning his attention to the table once more, "I'd like a demonstration of the abilities of this army. To do this, please put together ten groups of five people each. Each must be a self-contained unit that best shows off what you're capable of as a combined force."

Setting his left hand on Isabelle's shoulder, he held up his right hand. Four of the fingers came up on his right hand.

"I expect you to be able to fight a group of four monsters at the same time. Please send out scouts to find suitable groups. This needs to be done by noon so we have time to plan."

Isabelle squirmed under the weight of his hand. Everyone else in the room stared at him like he had lost his mind.

"You're dismissed. Please make several messengers ready for me and a scribe," he commanded. Flicking his fingers at them, he waited.

Eventually the tent emptied, leaving him alone with the mercenary captain.

Sitting back in his chair, he released Isabelle and gestured to the chair opposite him.

"My services are for sale, I am not," Isabelle said, refusing to take the seat.

"Hm? And? I wasn't aware I asked you to warm my bed. You certainly rock the sexy Elf angle, but I don't care. Sit or be gone. Your choice, just be swift about it."

Runner raised his eyebrows at the Elf. Time was wasting. "Things to do. I might actually get to design plans for building a fort in the next few weeks, and those things don't just design themselves, ya know."

Isabelle hesitated a moment longer before taking a seat.

"Fan-fucking-tastic. Thank you. Price?"

"A gold per quarter."

"First. How did an Elf end up here? You're rather far from home. Wrong continent entirely according to the Wiki. Let alone your band of merry men."

Wrinkling her nose, Isabelle looked like she'd bitten into a rotten apple.

"Wiki? I'm unsure of that term. As far as my reasons for being here" — she hesitated a moment — "I killed someone. They were guilty of a crime and deemed innocent because of their connections. I ended the problem. Hypocritically, I was banished by those who had opposed the innocence of the man instead of executed."

"Got it. Chaotic good, possibly neutral. That puts you somewhere between Rabbit and Kitten. Have fun with that," Runner said, accessing his inventory.

"Rabbit and Kitten? Who are—"

"You're on retainer for a decade," Runner interrupted her and negligently threw forty gold coins into the woman's lap.

Coins spilled from her hands as she tried to grab them all. Thudding heavily in the grass, they lay where they fell.

"Welcome aboard. I don't care where you go, what you do, or even how you do it, but you'll obey every order I give you."

Glancing up at the tent roof, he cleared his throat.

"Lady Brunhild, Lady Ernsta, I offer these terms to Isabelle under your watch. I will honor the conditions given to me, which are honor their lives, do not place them in a suicidal situation, respect their persons, and respect their possessions. They own anything they discover on a corpse that is available to them as loot and will be granted the ability to draw on funds from myself as a loan should the need arise."

In unison two voices sounded from above.

"Witnessed."

"In return I expect the following of you, Isabelle. You will replace any members you lose with fresh recruits, you will obey any order given to you provided that it is reasonable or achievable, you will not act in a way that is perceived to be disreputable, and no crime shall be committed by you or those you oversee. You are responsible for your own upkeep, equipment, maintenance, and your own room and board. Should a violation occur, Ernsta and Brunhild will render a neutral judgment on recompense. Depending on the severity of the situation, you may become forfeit personally, Isabelle. Questions?"

Isabelle had been collecting the coins from the ground. Her eyes were now fixed on the air above them, staring at the spot the two goddesses had responded from.

The sum she had requested was outrageous for the actual levels of her party. The fact that he'd paid it, and for a decade, was more so.

Ernsta and Brunhild responding to him directly, personally even, would only further shake the poor woman.

The possibility that he had already Awakened her with the contract existed.

Isabelle began to shake her head slowly, her eyes moving down to meet his own.

"Is that a no, no questions, or no, no deal?"

"No questions."

"Then you accept the deal as it stands?"

"If I tried to decline it, they'd leave."

"You need to actually agree. Need official sanction or it won't be binding."

Isabelle paused to glance up at where the voices had spoken from before responding.

"Yes, I accept."

"Witnessed."

"Good. Your first order is thus. Answer me, when was the last time you went to the bathroom? When was the last time you saw a bathroom? As you ponder that question, go ask your men the same. Run along now, things to do. People to kill. Please send in the messengers as well," Runner said to her, making shooing motions with his hands. Setting his elbow down on the arm of the chair, he rested his chin in his palm.

Break their programming, level them up, solid secondary force at my disposal. Now I need more.

Several messengers and the scribe trooped in after the shaken Isabelle left. Runner moved his eyes from one messenger to the next before resting them on the scribe.

"I need two drafts written, then posted in every inn of Tirtius and Vix. Then sent across to the mainland to the south for the same. Costs are to be charged to my account from whatever the king is paying me for leading his armies. I'm sure a leading general has a salary."

All eyes around the room got larger as they took that in. Runner smiled and spread his hands.

"Do not worry, my messages are simple. There are two concepts: I'm hiring mercenaries, and I'm welcoming immigrants from all races, breeds, or creeds." Runner paused, letting them catch up. "Mercenaries are to seek me out directly. I will either be in Vix or here on Tirtius. There is no guarantee of employment as I have rules and regulations similar to that of a military. Immigrants are to proceed to North Wood Fort, on Vix. Land is available for purchase at incredible low, low prices during reconstruction. Crazy Runner's land emporium must sell everything and everything must be sold. Now go."

Runner leaned back into the chair as he considered his recent decisions. They were all calculated things, designed to enhance and build his power base.

He felt like it was getting further from his control with every action. Soon he would be flinging soldiers into danger for the sake of consolidating his power over the Sunless and Barbarian kingdoms.

Isn't that what dictators do?

Chapter 7 - Dark Descent -

Runner left the tent after he had confirmed the map one more time. His own map now had several more personal notations. One did not pass up intelligence gathering if it was available.

The sun sat low in the eastern sky, doing its best to stab him in the eyes. Frowning, he took a quick sit-rep of everything around him.

Isabelle stood with her band perhaps thirty feet from him. They all looked a little unsure of themselves. He wasn't a betting man, but it looked like they were experiencing the aftereffects of becoming Awakened.

Dismissing them as unimportant for the moment, Runner trooped his way to the lead elements of the column. Hopefully they would be on the move soon.

Waiting sucked.

Runner.

"What's up, Srit?" Runner asked, his feet carrying him to where the carriages were being loaded up. The dots for his party members were there, which meant that was where he needed to be.

What do you plan to do with Ted?

"Nothing. He's dead. Remember?" he grumped. He didn't need a daily reminder of Ted.

No, he lives. We recovered him. His brain activity is zero, yet his body lives.

"Nothing. I plan on doing nothing. His body has been disengaged from the pod, the medical server is destroyed, and there is no way to reinsert him even if he had a brain that wasn't an empty swimming pool. Why?"

His suspicion had been raised. It meant they were actively monitoring the pods. Even before Srit had established full communications.

Are there no burial rites for your people?

Ah. There it is. They want his body.

"Srit, I'd like to offer you Ted's living, yet dead, body. Please consider it a token of my appreciation to you personally. I hope that we can continue working closely together."

Am I so transparent?

"Only because I love you, Srit. If there's anything else...?"

Nothing to re—nope.

"Fantastic. Good response," he concluded. Stepping up to the carriage window, he peered in. Everyone was already seated. The only open seat was between Katarina and Thana today.

All eyes turned to him, and the conversation they were having went dead. Quirking a brow, he grinned at them.

Inside of him, though, his heart quailed. Such a response to his arrival could only mean the end. Either of him or this lifestyle he had come to enjoy so much.

"In or out, fuckstick. And wipe that shitty grin off your face. You look like a jackass."

"Come on-n-n then." Nadine popped open the door. Runner was made to step aside to let it swing free. Sparing a glance for each woman, he clambered inside. Sitting between Katarina and Thana, he felt hard-pressed for space. His arms were nearly looped into theirs.

At least Katarina isn't wearing her armor.

"Where'd you get off to this morning? Did you forget you don't need to shit anymore? Go scurrying off looking for a toilet?"

"Ha, that would've been easier, Hanners. No, planning meeting. I let our dear noble companions know that I wasn't on the market so they could end their little plots and plans, told them to put together a demonstration for me, hired a mercenary captain by the name of Isabelle, and told them we'll be attacking Highpass Crossing. The usual."

Katarina nodded firmly. Clearly it met her approval.

"Valid choices, all around. Though I wonder, a mercenary captain?"

"She's got a band of front liners. I bought them completely. Should they fail the contract she could become a slave. Good times. Maybe I'll make her warm Hanners' bed if it happens. She's also required to fill any gaps in her group. I figure I break her, level them up, use them as a tool."

"Cold of you, Run-ner."

"Life is cold. I'm giving them better odds than many would."

"That's n-not right, Runner. You're n-not acting like yourself."

"Myself? Apparently myself is the one who kicked off this whole thing. Myself is the one that has placed four hundred and ninety-nine thousand soldiers into a situation where it's likely they'll end up in a zoo. Myself is the same person who is the only officer of any rank with the skills or ability to get them off. Myself is the one they blame and detest more than anyone else." Runner took a breath. The stress of the last few days was overwhelming him. There were so many problems, so many issues. And he had to solve them all. Every single one.

"Myself is the one trying to work out a deal with the divine to protect those I love. Myself is the one who is desperately trying to hammer out any sort of agreement with an emergent AI overlord comparative to some of the worst doomsday scenarios my people could write. Myself is the one thing that I have any control over, except to dance to everyone else's tune. Gods damn me but myse—"

Runner felt like he had been suddenly struck mute and paralyzed. His HUD flashed white.

Brunhild or Ernsta had smashed him with a deity-level curse. Unable to keep himself upright, he gradually slumped over and fell into Katarina.

"Take care of him," Brunhild said from thin air. "He pushes himself too hard. We need him."

Katarina's arm wrapped around him tightly and pulled him in close. His head dipped into her shoulder where it met the top of her chest. There his head remained. Pillowed on her and his body cradled against her side.

She lightly patted the top of his head with her left hand. Then her fingers began to smooth his hair backwards and rub lightly at his temples and crown. Her right hand remained pressed to his shoulder, keeping him tucked in close.

Runner could only stare at Hannah across the aisle. Her eyes were wide, watching him as if he had lost his mind.

When it happened, he had coiled up mentally, barricading himself emotionally from Katarina's careful fingers and care.

After a moment of reflection, he gave in. It'd serve no purpose and would only make the situation worse. Instead, he closed his eyes and let Katarina do as she willed. Besides, it did feel great.

"Rest," Katarina purred at him. Her fingers were pressing into his scalp, rubbing deep into his skin. Methodically she worked her way back and forth as if she planned to cover the entirety of his head one inch at a time. Runner hoped she did.

Ten minutes later Runner felt the curse leave him. In that period a great deal of his stress had also fled. He planted his feet evenly on the ground but didn't even think to pull away from Katarina.

Her hand on his shoulder released some of its pressure and slid upward to hold him closer instead of keeping him upright. Clearly she had noticed he had moved to take up his own weight. She made no move to release him, however.

Runner cleared his throat once as his eyes opened. Doing his best to ignore Katarina's fingers in his hair, he did the only thing he could.

"I'm sorry. I'm finding lately that my anger is getting away from me quicker than it should. I'm sure my pod is doing its best to keep me rolling. Balanced. Bring down my stress levels. It's not keeping up very well though. I ask your forgiveness and understanding."

"Fucking idiot. Share next time before it gets this bad again."

"Please do, Master Runner."

Nadine nodded.

Katarina made no response and instead let her fingers working to ease his burdens speak for her.

They stopped for a midday break. Though marching in a game didn't have the same price as it would in the real world, it had a price nonetheless that was paid. Soldiers still needed to eat, drink, and rest for their stamina to not become impacted. All the speed in the world would not help you if your troops arrived tired.

Runner gathered up the experimental groups to the side of the road. Overlooking an open field, he arranged them in order.

Amongst that field happened to be a village of reptile-like humanoids. They lazily watched Runner's little army.

They seemed unconcerned at first, but their red names dictated they would be openly hostile to anyone and everyone. There would be no conversation with these lizards.

What would you say anyways? Hey, got any criminals we could fight?

They were listed as "Ferth," typically followed by a job type. Ranging from gray to green in color, they were dressed in little more than hides and basic leather armor. Wooden buildings appeared here and there but the vast majority were nothing more than hide covered huts.

Their level ranged from twelve to fifteen. They wouldn't be much of an issue for anyone in his command. They'd serve for a good exercise though.

He had a momentary thought about their right to live, but he brushed it aside quickly. They were hostile, wouldn't speak with him, and weren't Awake.

A Sunless noble lady stood at Runner's side. Her features ran along the comically beautiful like so many of her peers. He had already forgotten her name and didn't care to try to remember it.

"Lead your group in. Try to pull a small number so we can gauge your abilities. Pull too many and you jeopardize your lives. Are you really sure about your group's makeup?" Runner asked her again. His eyes took in the group of five Sunless nobles dressed in their fineries. They were all casters, without a physical fighter amongst them. They were level twenty to twenty-five.

"Of course, my lord Runner. We'll show you the power of the nobility," huffed the woman.

"Right, then, well, off you go." He dismissed her. He made a gentle shooing motion with his left hand, yet summoned Isabelle with his right hand.

Since her Awakening that morning, Isabelle had become voracious for knowledge. Katarina and Thana had taken her in hand, laid everything out, and had her sorted in under an hour.

"Yes, my lord?" said the Elf, appearing at his side.

Her attitude had changed since their conversation as well. What had been cold indifference had become eager obedience. He feared that she might actually make the suggestion that she should warm his bed after all.

I wonder if those ears are flexible or – no, no, NO, NO. Precisely what I don't want to think of.

"Not a lord, Isabelle. Runner, just Runner. Get your people together. They're going to screw this up and need help. They'll survive it, yet I suspect it might be with a casualty. Maybe even two. I considered letting it happen, more as a lesson to the others than anything, but that'd only serve to weaken my troops."

Runner sighed, his right hand rubbing at his chin as he thought it over again. Their lives and ability counted for more than their deaths would give him. That, and it tickled at his morality to think such a thing.

"Yes, my lord," said the Elf, spinning on her heel. Two sharp whistles and her little band fell in behind her. Watching her go, he shook his head.

"To her, you are as a god," said Katarina.

Looking over his shoulder, he found the Barbarian woman coming his way.

"Shows what little they know. Brighteyes and Angel are worthy of praise, I am not," Runner groused, turning to watch the noble party of ladies closing on the lizards.

A pair of divine curses that silenced him flashed across his status bar. They each lasted but a single second. A gentle reminder that the goddesses didn't particularly enjoy their pet names being bandied about.

Flinging a hand up at the heavens, he kept his complaint to himself.

"You tease them," Katarina said with mild incredulity. Coming to a halt next to him, she crossed her arms in front of her chest.

"I do. They secretly enjoy it," Runner said with a smirk. "I treat them in a way no one would ever dare. I treat them as people, equals. It's why they're always watching me. Either of you care to join me, by the way? Should be interesting."

There was no reply to his question, which meant they were more than likely busy elsewhere.

"Mm," came the unimpressed reply.

"Oh? Look no further than yourself. You're a princess. Have I treated you any differently since finding out? Don't get me wrong, I know you are one. But to me, you're still my Barbarian Kitten."

He shrugged his shoulders. His words hadn't come out quite the way he had wanted. Katarina would understand though.

"I worried that you would," she admitted after a pause.

"Would what? Treat you differently?"

"Yes."

"Perish the thought. No one else is as fun to tease as you. You're a fearsome warrior, beautiful princess, intelligent woman, but you get all hot and bothered if I tease you at all. Especially now that I know what to look for."

"Ass."

"Indeed. You love me all the same. Ah, here, watch," he said, his hand pointing to the group of Sunless nobles. "They're going to hit the one closest to them, that one that looks like it's socially chained to the one next to the door. Without knowing how many are in there, they're setting themselves up for a horrible pull."

"Hence Isabelle."

"Yeah. I think I need to get every single one of them Awakened. It's a cruel thing to do. Awaken them, then send them to their probable deaths. Yet I must."

As if it were following a prophecy, the scene began to unfold exactly as Runner had predicted. The noble ladies fell over themselves as a large group of Ferth rushed out of the tent.

"Ugh, I've seen enough. Who's next?" Runner asked, casting his eyes around, looking for the next group. A sergeant of the royal guard stepped out of the group of milling combatants.

"Sir, my group is."

Runner squinted at the man; he seemed oddly familiar. Suddenly he remembered who the man was. Taking a quick inventory of the group arrayed out behind the man, he nodded his head.

"Please go up the other side. Same instructions."

The soldier saluted, collected his group, and left.

"Thoughts?"

"He'll do fine. He's actually Awakened. I was bored at the little reception and happened to ask him when he'd last visited the crap castle. I'm not sure why I did, but I did. His group looks put together with some thought behind it."

"Ah. Huh?"

The change in Katarina's voice caught his attention. Looking to her, he then followed her line of sight to a group of Knights on horseback far in the distance. Amongst them were six players. At this distance he couldn't make out the details, but he was sure they weren't coming willingly.

"Hm. Take care of the situation here, Kitten. Keep cycling the groups out, watch for problems. Provide suggestions and start organizing them into useful groups. For those who are intractable, ask them when was the last time they used the bathroom."

"What? I can't do this!" Katarina cried at his back as he walked past her.

"Sure you can, Kitten. I believe in you," Runner stated over his shoulder.

Runner managed to catch the Knights before they made it into the camp, a hundred yards or so from the perimeter.

Now up close to them, he actually knew these players. They were Uno through Seis. He had left them a considerable distance to the south. After they had tried to rob him. Maybe murder him.

"Lord Runner, we found these gentlemen down the road. They were standing over the corpses of two women. They had the look of wandering merchants," explained the lead Knight.

A vision of Nadine lying dead in a road popped up in his mind. Slightly different circumstances and it could just as easily have been her. Runner felt blinding black wrath building up behind his eyes.

Two merchants? For what? To rape them? Take what little they had? Ferth won't even talk to you, they'll attack outright. A merchant? She'd probably offer to sell to you...

"I see. Gentleman, we meet again," deadpanned Runner.

"You're that officer. The one who fucking put us here," said Vick. Runner hadn't cared to learn their names previously. Looking to the nameplates, he saw they were Michael, Jeff, Ben, James, Vick, and Devon. Each name was orange.

Which meant they had attacked another player recently.

"Indeed, I am. I saved your lives. Now I'm trying to get us out. Last I remember, you tried to rob and murder me."

No response came.

"Attacking other players? Killing merchants walking the road? Memory tells me you were talking about raping someone when we first met."

"Course not," said Jeff.

"They attacked us first," said Vick.

"We only found the merchants like that," said Ben.

"Oh? Did they have anything on them?" Runner asked, an easy smile stretching his lips.

"Nah. Bread, a few coins. Cooking supplies," said Michael.

How would you know unless you looted them? You wouldn't be able to loot them unless you killed them.

Runner.

"Not now, Srit," Runner growled under his breath. The six men were still busily trying to convince Runner that the merchants had nothing on them. As if he wanted a share.

Sorry, Runner. It can wait.

Runner had a thought. A dangerous thought. One that made his soul quiver. Holding up a hand, he turned his back to the group and walked a few steps away. He took a posture that looked as if he was considering the situation.

"Actually, Srit. Er. I have a question." He hesitated. This would be a point of no return. This might be the chance he needed. "Would your people be able to create a copy of the main ship's computer? I believe I could rebuild it into a medical server if I had a duplicate of the ship's system core."

It is possible but not probable. They would say no. Resources are limited and few know of you.

"What if I offered a faster flow of information about my people?"

Unlikely. They are comfortable with the current rate.

He took a breath, then took the plunge.

"What about six living, breathing humans? Free to be used as you see fit? They'll be brain dead. I'm sure you could find uses for them, however."

One moment.

Runner swallowed. His heart felt like it would explode out of his chest. He was seriously contemplating microwaving these six idiots.

For what? Killing Naturals? Assaulting me?

Runner shook his head. It wasn't worth it.

Saving the ship?

His feet came to a stop, his skin growing cold as his answer came back clear.

Yes.

They will rebuild the server for six humans. They also would like to know what your plans are for those who are currently showing no signs of brain activity.

Runner had an answer for that. It was an ugly answer. One that felt so arbitrary that he hadn't voiced it aloud. Until now.

"Genetic material. I'll probably need to end up using them as breeding stock to get human population numbers up. It sounds terrible, but there it is. I accept the bargain on the six humans, pending a suitable timeline. How long would it take to fulfill my request?"

An hour. The process is not difficult, the resources are.

And there it was. So simple a solution that it made his heart ache. Now he found himself at the crossroads of ends justifying the means coming up against the rights of every citizen. The needs of the many versus the needs of the few.

"Done," Runner said with finality. Without turning around, he went through the process of identifying the pods of the six men. Working his fingers quickly, he called up a line command of six system actions to run concurrently. Then he wavered. There would be no going back.

Six simultaneous ejections went through the system when Runner activated the command. Six distinct thumps sounded behind him.

"It's done. May whoever judges me at the end have mercy on me," Runner whispered. Crouching down where he stood, he pressed his hands to his face. Elbows resting on his thighs, he curled into himself as best as he could. And lost his mind privately.

Several minutes later he stood up again, brushed his hands against his hips, and turned to face the knights.

They stood around the fallen adventurers. Runner spoke loudly, not wanting to get any closer.

"Leave them where they lie. Resume your duties."

Runner turned on his heel and made his way back over to where the exercises were taking place. Any type of distraction would do. Anything to clear his head.

Test out a spell or two. Yeah. See how they do, tinker, build.

Goal set in his mind, he picked up the pace to a light jog, quickly moving away from those he'd murdered in cold blood.

Reaching the field, he found the group of noblewomen off to one side. They looked as if they had been rushed from the field, but they were all accounted for. Catching sight of Isabelle hovering near Katarina, he changed his destination.

He did not want to deal with either right now. So he veered wide of the two women entirely. He made it to the front of the village without having to deal with a single person.

Standing amongst the grass as it shifted in the light wind, Runner lifted his arms to the sun. Letting the sun and wind wash over him like a bath, he exhaled. Quickly going over his gear, he enchanted it with intelligence. Nothing but intelligence.

Waiting for his mana to refill, Runner began picking through the targets available to him.

Like it was summoned by his predatory gaze, the chieftain of the Ferth stepped out of a hut. Level twenty, named mob, elite, perfect.

Runner's mana bar was fresh and full. Lifting a hand, he began to channel *Splatterhouse*. Directly in front of his hand, the earthen shell appeared. Completing the shaping of the spell, the channel neared the midpoint of the cast. Air bathed over it, spinning the projectile faster by the millisecond, and pooled at the rear.

When the spell finished, the shell was gone. Blasting forward with a booming sound, it tore through the air and slammed into the chieftain.

The fire, lightning, and air that had been tightly packed in the cone burst out in a ball of light yellow plasma as the earthen shell fragmented on impact.

Where the chief had stood, there was only a leaky piece of meat. With Runner having a number of levels on the beast, *Splatterhouse* being a higher-end spell, and the creature having no resistance, it simply stood no chance.

Level up!
You've reached level 27

Unfortunately, it had taken eighty percent of his mana bar to cast *Splatterhouse* once.

Which makes it worthless for combat. I'd be a one pump chump. Even putting it into an item wouldn't change thing – the cooldown would make it as useless, if not more. If I tried to outfit everyone with a staff that launched this, would I be equipping my friend today, to outfit my enemy tomorrow?

Grunting in disappointment, he opened the level-up window.

Name:		Runner	
Level:	27	Class:	
Race:	Human	Experience:	27%
Alignment:	Good	Reputation:	20
Fame:	15,155	Bounty:	0

Attributes-			
Strength:	1(31)	Constitution:	1(31)
Dexterity:	11(41)	Intelligence:	11(41)
Agility:	7(37)	Wisdom:	1(31)
Stamina:	1(31)	Charisma:	64

He selected Dexterity as the attribute to increase, then he executed the level up and waited for whatever memories would come. He had long since given up hope on getting the password, or the entire event that put them here, but it never hurt to hope.

Childhood memories came to him. Memories of his parents holding up silly drawings he made, attempting to put on a play for them, and reading deep into the night.

As they passed into his actual memory, he once more thought about the fact that he would never, could never, compare to his companions. So many of his stats went to cover the sixty-three-point deficit. Soon he would have the chance to build an entire set of armor for Katarina. Then she would be a mountain of angry redhead.

"My lord! Are you alright?" asked Isabelle from behind.

Looking over his shoulder, he frowned at the lithe blonde. Annoyance tickled his brain at the title she could not break. Or would not.

"Why wouldn't I be? It was my spell after all. Though I suppose I need to go loot him. Here, follow along. My mana is tapped out and I could use an escort," Runner said. Walking away from her, he lined himself up with the smoking corpse.

"Your spell? My lord, you use magic?"

"Sometimes. Depends on my mood."

"Swords as well?"

"Yes, why?"

"And you crafted Katarina's blade? It's classed as an artifact…"

"Lady Death's staff, Kitten's sword and shield. Yes. Again, why?"

"That's not possible. None of it is for a single person."

"Sure it is, only for me. Stick around long enough and prove your loyalty, Isabelle. I'll end up equipping you the same. Can't have my mercenary commander running around in crappy gear." Runner had the time to invest in gearing everyone on the trip. The carriage rides grew duller with every mile. "Ah, here we are."

Bending down over the corpse, he shifted the contents into his bag. There wasn't any point to anything the creature dropped.

He opened a trade window with Isabelle and transferred the gear to her.

"Take that. Personal gift from me. Do what you will with it."

"My lord! I—these are very powerful. I cannot."

"Pretty sure you'll be breaking an order at that point. Unless you wanted to hand yourself over to me as a personal possession, I'm sure you misspoke."

Done with the smoldering corpse, he began to trek back to the encampment. No one moved, everyone stood still, watching his approach. He had the distinct impression they were not sure what to make of the situation.

"Of course, my lord. My apologies. I accept these with the goodwill they were given in."

"Damn right. I need you to hook in with Rabbit and get your shit squared. She'll inventory out for me what I need. Start learning from her as fast as you can as well. I expect you to act as quartermaster for future mercenary groups. Off with you then. I'm tired of this place."

Runner shook his head. There had to be some way to get *Splatterhouse* working on a more normal scale.

Shrinking the spell down would definitely make it more usable. Though it would then do inherently less damage.

Wait. Who can use magical items? Crafters can use magical items. Crafters would never dare challenge me. Make 'em big. Bulky. Hard to move once in place. They'll end up no drop, so there will be no possibility of giving them away. Yes...

He could never hope to achieve the heights that Katarina, Thana, Hannah, or even Nadine could reach.

But I can definitely push them even higher. I don't need to be better than them, I have to make them better than ever.

I shall become the merchant of death.

The real world had the likes of Oppenheimer. Here, here in Otherlife, it would have Norwood.

A slow evil grin spread across his face as he devised weapons in his mind. Weapons to cause mass destruction.

Trapped in his own body and unable to move, Runner screamed deep from his stomach. Screeched until his throat bled and his tongue hurt.

His arms and legs were bound to a table. A metal band had been clamped tightly to his brow and held his head in place.

Where am I? How did I get here? What's going on?

Around him, masked creatures gathered. They were clothed in surgical scrubs, but he could see their glossy skin between the clothes. They occasionally reached out to touch various parts of his naked self with their three-fingered hands. And he lay there. Unable to move.

One of the monsters leaned over Runner's chest and then drew a blade down at an angle from his shoulder.

Pain alone made him want to piss himself silly. A second cut was made on the opposite shoulder in the same manner as the first. Where the two slices met, the knife edge came again. From sternum to navel, he felt his skin spreading apart.

They were dissecting him. An autopsy.

Shoving a metal instrument under the skin, they worked to peel it off. A new pair of hands appeared, a metal device shaped like a wishbone cradled between alien claws.

The device was jammed into his ribs, and he felt them crack before snapping apart like dry kindling. Eyes wide in agony, Runner stared in shock as the creature stuck its hands deep into his chest cavity.

Panicked, afraid, and in pain, Runner tried to turn his head to scream for help. He managed a single inch. Laid out to his left were five identical men, locked in place. They were all him. They were all Runner Norwood.

Sitting bolt upright in his bed, Runner grabbed at his nightshirt with his right hand. Panting, he confirmed his body to be whole, correct, undamaged. Pressing his left hand to his eyes, he mentally checked the in game clock. It was three am.

The nightmare wasn't lost on him. His mind had decided he would live what had probably already happened to Uno and company.

No. Not Uno. Michael Werner, Vick North, Jeff Finch, James Smith, Ben Pitt, Devon Malard. Ted Henshaw makes seven. Seven lives.

He shuddered, his skin cold, his mind sliding to and fro. Settling himself as best as he could, he lay back down into his bedding.

Staring up at the ceiling, he swallowed. Months ago he had wondered at the man he was becoming. Now he had his answer.

Unknown fingers locked around his right hand, squeezing his palm. Letting his head loll to the right, he found Hannah's blue eyes staring into him.

"I'm losing myself, Hanners. I'm not a good person. If I met someone who had done the things I've done, I'd curse them. Curse them and the day they were born," Runner choked out.

"The fact that you're all fucked up over your choices means you're clearly not lost. Maybe a little directionless, but not lost. No one in this world of ours, as shitty as it may be at times, has had to, or will have to, make the choices you do."

Runner nodded his head a little, a fragile hold over his psyche settling in.

"You can talk to me. Talk to any of us. Well, maybe not prissy pants Nadine. She's a goody two-shoes to the core. We'd all help you, Runner. In any way we could."

"I know. Thank you, Hannah. I'm going to try to go back to sleep now."

Patting his hand with hers, Hannah rolled over and invaded Nadine's sleeping space, throwing an arm around the merchant.

Snickering quietly to himself, he had to feel impressed. Those two had come a long way from where they'd started. They all had.

He did not want to think about the fact that they had not yet found out about Uno and the rest. He would have to tell them soon. Hiding secrets would be the first step to losing their trust.

Their trust was one of the few precious things he had left.

Firm callused fingers wrapped into his nightshirt and dragged him across the floor towards Katarina and Thana's bed.

Coming to a stop, he found himself wedged into the base of the bed frame. Above him were Katarina's coal-colored eyes. They watched him.

She said nothing, as if she needed no words. She smiled, a gentle smile promising security and safety, and rested that long-fingered hand of hers in the middle of his chest. Her head disappeared from view as she returned to her pillow.

Feeling rather childish at how secure he felt, he nearly berated himself. Then stopped.

Who the fuck cares?

Resting his hand atop Katarina's, he snuggled back into his blankets and closed his eyes.

Take comfort when and where you can.

5:42pm Sovereign Earth time
11/11/43

"You did what? You m-m-murdered them?!" Nadine screeched at him.

"I traded murderers for vital resources. Even now Srit's people are installing a new server. One that I can prep to take up the role of the medical server. It'll take time to figure out what to install and how to install it, but I can give it a full basic medical server image. Even with the base release programming, it'll be leaps and bounds beyond what this game can handle and provide."

"YOU T-T-T-TRADED PEOPLE'S LIVES AWAY, RUN-N-NER!" Nadine shouted.

Thankfully they were situated in their campsite. The ability provided privacy in a place where one would not expect it. Thana, Hannah, and Katarina had taken his news with stoicism. Thana looked a little concerned over it, yet was probably weighing it out against the benefits.

"Rabbit, please, don't shout at me. I did. I'm responsible for many lives. Many, many lives. I traded six lives for the sake of over four hundred thousand. I'm the one who has to live with that, not you. Am I happy with it? No. I'm not," Runner hissed at her.

"Do I regret it? I regret only that I didn't take action previously. When the knights found them, they were standing over two corpses. Corpses of little traveling merchants like you. That, according to those murdering bastards, had nothing but bread and some coins. I let them go once, and it cost at least two more lives."

Runner stopped, his shoulders hunched as he spoke in a poisoned voice.

"I sold their worthless lives away, Rabbit. I sold them away at the steep price of my own soul and well-being. I'm also ninety percent closer to getting everyone out."

"Runner! This isn't like you. This isn-n-n't you. You're better than-n this."

"No. I'm not. It pains me to disappoint you, Rabbit, but this is only going to get worse. I'm going to lead an army into combat and get people killed. Black and white morality has no place here. The humans were attacked first, without warning. They're counterattacking. We're technically not in the right here, and hundreds will die."

Biting off a dark laugh, he shook his head, turning to leave the camp. He didn't feel like sleeping right now. Sleep brought its own problems. There would be only nightmares waiting for him in sleep.

"The road to hell is paved with good intentions, Rabbit. I'm afraid I'm speeding along merrily on my dark descent."

Hours later when he returned to camp, when everyone was abed, he found a single plate resting in his usual spot by the fire. Smiling sadly, he picked it up with a quick inspection.

Item: Grilled steak and vegetables

Quality: Great

Effects-

Full: Constitution increase

Nadine would have made it. Made it for him. Even when angry at him. She fussed over his health and his infrequent meals despite him reminding her he technically did not actually need to eat.

Choking back a shaking breath, he ate quietly, grateful to the little merchant queen who forgave him, even when he would never forgive himself.

Chapter 8 - Norwood Arsenal -

Two days had passed since his falling out with Nadine. Though she did not speak of it again, it was clear she was still upset with him. Forgiveness could be given, even if one didn't forget.

Of the thousand-strong army that had been sent, eighty were qualified to use magical items. All of them had been drafted into the newly created Special Ordnance team. They also happened to almost all be people heading to rebuild North Wood Fort. Which made it all the easier to give them orders.

Especially after having Awakened them.

Runner had been spending his evenings crafting long-barreled breech-loading cannons. With any luck they would hopefully give him an edge when they finally engaged the enemy. The work also kept his hands and mind busy. Letting his thoughts wander was a danger lately.

Looking like a long tube mounted on a wooden carriage, each cannon left quite a bit to be desired in appearance. At the rear of the weapon, a pair of long screw-like rods were set into the carriage. A seating bracket for the cannon had been placed between them and could be adjusted easily to shift the cannon up or down. Crude as it might be, it would serve its function well, allowing the gunner to change the angle smoothly.

Locking mechanisms could be slid into place to hold the barrel at the chosen angle, providing accurate repeated shelling of a target.

Enchanted to put out a magnificent volume of air in a sliver of time, it acted like a giant blowgun. A touch of help from Srit and he had even managed to rifle the barrel. For whatever good it might do.

He really wasn't sure if it would do anything to add to its accuracy. Physics here weren't always analogous to the real world. Couldn't hurt though.

Serving the role of armory was an obelisk of stone. It stood six feet high and a hole had been carved out of the center. A cradle sat in the rock, waiting to catch the payload upon activation. It was capable of producing a single *Splatterhouse* round every thirty seconds.

He had put together three mockups that would fire solid slug rounds instead of *Splatterhouse* rounds.

The real obelisks had already all been created and were awaiting deployment.

No need to go all in quite yet.

In teams of two, the SO crews worked to fire rounds at a distant hillside, swapping out after each activation so they could experience a fresh reload. Learning the basics of preparing an unloaded cannon.

Nodding his head in satisfaction, he left his teams to their work and trudged away.

He had his own weapons to practice.

Coming to the realization that he should embrace his charisma, rather than flee from it, Runner had sat down and created a charisma boosting spell that was similar to the other stat enhancers.

Now his equipment and subsequent bound spells reflected this change in mentality. He tapped open his character screen and gave himself a final check.

Name:		Runner	
Level:	27	Class:	
Race:	Human	Experience:	27%
Alignment:	Good	Reputation:	20
Fame:	15,155	Bounty:	0

Attributes-			
Strength:	1	Constitution:	1(31)
Dexterity:	11(41)	Intelligence:	11(41)
Agility:	7(37)	Wisdom:	1
Stamina:	1(31)	Charisma:	64(124)

Time to see what Prince Charming can do.

Trailing along behind him came Nadine and Isabelle. Nadine wanted to keep an eye on him, and Isabelle was here to be the guinea pig.

"Right, then," Runner casually said over his shoulder. "I've given up on the idea of ever being anything but second, or even third place, to everyone else. I shall endeavor to become a master of my own bailiwick."

Among the open fields that ran in every direction for miles were small valleys. Small enough to hide a scouting element or monsters, or someone who did not wish to be seen. They now stood in one such gully between two raised mounds.

Turning to face the women, he smiled broadly and cocked his head to one side.

"Isabelle, as I said earlier, I'd like to use you as a test subject for some spells. They're non-damaging, but they'll affect your status and your self-control. You can decline this request. You don't have to do this."

The whump of cannons could be heard in the distance as he talked. Practice would give the gunners confidence, even if they did not realize it yet.

"I'm honored to participate, my lord," Isabelle said eagerly.

"You say that now. Please understand you can quit at any time. Please try to describe what it does to you, as best as you can."

Runner had been working with Srit to build a repertoire of spells based on social interactions and *Spell Weaving*.

Many of the spells he had made with her were grounded in and based on already existing spells in other schools of magic. These new spells used charisma as the modifier instead of intelligence.

The work itself had been very similar to his previous spell work. Truly, the main difference had been the difficulty in understanding the result. There was no way for the system to give him a tool tip, or even a suggestion, since he had gone far astray from the original limits.

There was another entire line of spells he'd have to work on next: using charisma to push people in a meta-physical sense. Like telling people to be well and them suddenly healing. Or telling people to run faster, and they actually would.

Hence the testing and the need for more down the road.

There were a few more interesting toys he had been working on that wouldn't be brought out today. Armored transports with hard points for portable *Splatterhouse* cannons.

Handheld *Splatterhouse* rifles with a much smaller explosive round.

Giant tubes that would launch huge *Splatterhouse* rounds as an indirect fire method. Vastly more akin to twentieth-century mortars than anything else.

Even self-propelled artillery.

Much of the arsenal he was working on happened to be with the idea in mind of arming the peasantry. Crafters. Villagers. People without a true class and who might never have the luxury of changing that. If he could arm them, he could tap into a resource of soldiers most would disregard.

History had shown a drastic shift in the way wars were fought once a peasant could pull a trigger and kill a trained knight.

Today he planned on working on the magical side only.

Bringing up the test spell he had tentatively called *Fear*, Runner targeted Isabelle. He flicked his fingers out towards her, and the tightly coiled spell of *Intimidate* and *Persuade* flew at her.

Striking her in the chest, the pink ball exploded around her. Her eyes flew open, her fingers closing into fists, and she promptly turned and ran away.

"Fear definitely works. I wonder when she'll stop though."

"She's fast."

"Indeed she is, Rabbit."

Sprinting, Isabelle kept on for a full ten seconds. Her athletic build fluidly pushed her along with a grace he had to admire. Forcing his eyes to a screen instead of her hips, Runner busied himself.

Eventually she halted far in the distance. She spun herself around and began making her way back to them with as much dignity as she could muster. Given the situation, that is.

At least she can't wet her pants.

"I...ahem. My lord, I experienced overwhelming fear of you. Uncontrollable, utter terror. I...I wanted to get as far from you as possible," Isabelle reported, her voice quavering.

"Thank you, Isabelle. That was the intent of the spell, so it's a success."

Runner created an enemy-only AOE version of the spell with him as the focal point. Labeling the single target spell as *Linda* and *Scott* as the AOE version, he then put them on a new hotbar.

Wondering about Isabelle's reaction, he could only sympathize. His nightmares had been ramping up in intensity as of late. That feeling had made a great frame of mind to start with when he constructed the spell.

Considering how badly they haunted him, he could only imagine what she had felt. He woke up frequently in the night, panting. The worst was the disorientation he felt upon waking. Night after night.

Whatever the pod was supposed to do, it wasn't doing it. Runner had even gone so far as to confirm it was administering drugs to help balance him and subdue his sleep. It wasn't enough.

Thana and Katarina were now taking turns sleeping next to him, poised to bring him back to reality when he had an episode.

There was a part of him that could not deny the pleasure of lying next to a beautiful woman. Pity he could not truly enjoy it. That and the pod wouldn't do anything for blue balls. He was starting think that his wandering attention towards Isabelle was an extreme hormonal response.

Or so he hoped.

His choices had pushed him to a point that he no longer looked forward to sleeping. He dreaded it. Ted, Michael, Jeff, Vick, James, Ben, and Devon all waited for him. Staring at him. Dead accusing eyes. Bloody eyes. Blood coating everything and everyone.

Giving himself a firm shake, he pressed a palm to his forehead. Taking a deep breath, he cleared his thoughts.

"Right, then. Isabelle, the next spell will have a different reaction. Much like the first, please try to describe it as best as you can."

"What will it do, my lord?"

"If I told you, it'd color your perceptions of it by creating an expectation. It won't hurt. Promise," Runner said with a smile. He meant it too. Nothing he had built would cause any harm. At least physically.

Next in the list of spells to test was *Enrage*. Pushing *Provoke* and *Intimidate* together in nearly equal parts, he hoped it would force the target to engage him.

Glancing at Isabelle's sword at her side, he frowned. He opened his mouth to ask her to disarm, but stopped. Blowing out the breath he had taken to speak, he shrugged his shoulders instead.

Whatever. Will make the test real.

Flinging his arm forward, he cast *Enrage* on Isabelle. Immediately her face contorted into a sinister snarl. Instead of running from him, this time she ran at him. Spreading his stance out to receive her charge, he opened his arms.

"It's okay, Rabbit! This was expected, I'm not in any danger," he yelled out to Nadine. Her reaction might end up hurting the lively little mercenary. "Except for maybe getting a vicious hug."

Isabelle leapt at him, catching him under the armpits. Wrapping his arms around her, he let her carry him off his feet and onto his back. He wrapped his legs around her waist, pressed her in close to himself, and held on for dear life.

Snarling, hissing, and biting at his neck, Isabelle wanted to rend him limb from limb.

Grimacing at the pain of her teeth, Runner slammed his right hand into the back of her head, pressing her face into his neck more firmly. Better that than his throat. His hit points were going down marginally, nothing more than a point or two a second. Nothing to be concerned about.

Time ticked by and eventually Isabelle went slack, her teeth buried in his flesh, her fingers wrapped up in his leather armor.

"So, do I taste like chicken? No need to answer immediately, I'm only curious. Pretty sure you got a decent mouthful out of me after all," Runner teased. Releasing her head, he patted the Elf on the back with his left hand.

Relaxing under the woman, he sighed, his legs releasing her hips. Success, but maybe a bit too successful? Flagging the spell, he renamed it *Rage* and moved it to the Enchanter hotbar.

Creating a clone of *Rage,* he modified it to be an AOE target spell. He named it *Zombie Horde,* which felt terrifying and appropriate.

Pushing herself off him, Isabelle stood and started spitting into the grass.

"I taste that bad, huh? I could always start adding salt to my baths. Little bit of pepper and lemon maybe? Seasoning goes a long way. Long pig and all that. Or so I hear."

Bending his knees, he got his feet under himself and stood up, brushing nonexistent grass from his rear. He touched his neck and checked his fingers. They had a solid red color. He couldn't see the damage but there definitely was some, he imagined.

"My lord, I'm-I'm so sorry. I don't know. I wanted to hurt you. I hated you. I wanted to kill you. My lord, I am-I am so sorry," Isabelle said, her shoulders hunched in and her head hanging low.

"Then you did exactly what I wanted you to. This doesn't excuse violently hugging me in the future, mind you. Anything else? Was it just extreme hate?"

Turning to face him, she sheepishly nodded her head. His blood stained her lips and dribbled down her chin.

"Ah, Isabelle, be sure to take a moment to wipe your mouth. You look like a vampire learning to eat. Apparently I suck at being a sippy cup. Nadine, any observations from your end?"

The woman in question had come over and stood before him. She had managed to sneak up on him when he wasn't paying attention. Her left hand pulled at the collar of his armor to inspect his neck and shoulder.

"Very viole-n-nt, explosive even. Lasted about as long as the other one. Are you alright?" she asked, her green eyes peering up at him through blonde eyelashes.

"Perfectly fine, Rabbit my dear. Why, want me to cast it on you so you can hug me violently too?"

Turning a light shade of pink, Nadine said nothing. Then she slowly smiled at him and patted his arm.

"N-next time," she whispered. Turning from him, she went to check on Isabelle.

Swallowing, Runner felt mildly uncomfortable. Teasing them was easy when they reacted with disinterest or annoyance. This though? This made it infinitely harder to continue on as he had. First Thana, then Katarina, and now Nadine?

A conspiracy. That's what this is. They're sharing information.

Runner.

"Yes, my love?"
At least I can harass Srit, she doesn't even get it.

I feel that you have not honored your end of the agreement.

"In what way? I provided the material you asked for in exchange for assistance with spell creation."

The deal was for material on the mating rituals of your humans.

"And I gave it to you. Lots of it," he said with a smile. Indeed, he had sent her a very large and obscene amount of porn. Porn was never hard to get with the military.

This is copulation, not mating.

"Sure it is. They're mating—a child could be born of it," Runner said, nearly chuckling. Pulling up his third test spell, he waited for her response.

Runner, humans and my own host's species are capable of interbreeding. We are not so different that I cannot deduce that where he is depositing his genetic material will not result in a child. Only organic waste leaves from that orifice, not progeny.

Runner's face twitched. It was nearly impossible to keep from laughing. Sounded like the material she had been reviewing had been different to say the least.

On top of that, in the next set of material, two of the men will have no ability to impregnate her, while the third is wearing a contraceptive.

Now he started laughing, pressing his hands to his sides.

"Okay, okay. I'm sorry. Were you looking more for courting rituals rather than mating rituals?"

A slight delay made him think that Srit was confirming the definition of "courting."

That wou—yes. Yes, please.

"Done. Sending you relevant information."

Runner selected the media server from the system window. Highlighting every romance novel in the library, he sent the entire category to Srit's username.

"Start with that. I think that'll provide you all the information you need. Should be able to burn through it with your read speed, though I would caution you to slow down. Read each one and explore it with your own thoughts."

Thank you.

"Course, love. Can't have you thinking I don't value you and your opinions."

I do not have opinions.

"Of course you do. You didn't have proof of your statement earlier, that what I sent you wasn't what you asked for. You developed the opinion first, then sought information. You still owe me a response about being deleted, as well."

No response was forthcoming. Allowing the lapse to pass, Runner turned his attention back to the task at hand.

Looking to the two women, he found Nadine walking back to her original position on the side. Curiously, though, she had something in her damaged right hand. Bent over her palm, she appeared as if she were inspecting the item she held. He would ask her later about it.

Runner let his eyes track back to the tall Elf. Either she or Nadine had taken the opportunity of his distraction to clean her face up.

"You ready for the next one? Please understand, you can stop whenever you like. You're under no obligation to do this."

"I want to do this. It'll help you in your goals, which is my goal. I want to be useful to you. Proceed, my lord," Isabelle responded. She seemed determined to get through it, regardless of what happened.

"As you will. I thank you all the same," Runner said. Calling up the next in his test series, he began to channel what he had called *Brainwash*. *Persuade* and *Provoke* combined to hopefully confuse someone and allow commands to be given. Potentially, it could be the most overpowered spell yet.

If it works.

Then he cast *Brainwash* on Isabelle without another word. There was no visible change, but Runner would swear she looked like she was daydreaming.

"Isabelle, hop on one foot," Runner commanded.

And so she hopped on one foot.

"Give me your bow."

Isabelle immediately tried to trade her bow to him.

"Swear an undying oath to never dye your hair."

"I do so swear."

Runner grinned, briefly considering having her strip, fondle herself, or maybe tell him her darkest secret. Nadine's curious face caught his attention and he dismissed the idea immediately. A betrayal of Isabelle's trust.

Fuck it. I need to know I can push the spell. Something minor...

"Pick your nose."

Isabelle went first knuckle deep in a nostril instantly and started rooting around. Runner felt immediate regret at having her do it. And nearly burst out in laughter as well. Watching a gorgeous woman dig for gold wasn't something he could forget quickly. Especially with the screenshot he snapped off rapidly.

"Stop. Okay, that worked. My apologies, Belle, I'll never cast that on you again. I swear."

Brainwash was everything he'd hoped for and more.

Isabelle shuddered from head to toe while Runner moved *Brainwash* over to his new bar. Her face turned a deep, dark scarlet shade. Fingers ground into the wood of her bow, clutching it to her chest.

Holding up his hands, he bowed his head to her.

"I swear by the oath we both took, I will never cast such a spell on you again, Belle. Just to show that I truly meant no harm and I value you, I will place myself in judgment for whatever recompense you deem fitting if you think it fitting."

Isabelle had the face of a woman deep in thought. Shifting her weight from foot to foot, she stared into Runner's face.

"Belle?" she asked curiously.

"Isabelle, Belle. Names aren't personal for me, nicknames are. Everyone I actually give a crap about or have to pay attention to gets a nickname."

Isabelle chewed at her lower lip before seemingly coming to a decision.

"You'll subject yourself to one request on my part at a future date. You may reject what I ask, but I will then invoke Lady Brunhild and Lady Ernsta to judge."

"Agreed, and done. Though I do have one more spell to cast. If you're still willing."

"It isn't similar in any way to the one you just cast?" she asked warily.

"Not at all. It's more similar to the first and second spell. It'll affect your status and make you do one thing."

Isabelle nodded her head reluctantly, slowly.

"Okay. I'm ready."

There were a couple spells he had not quite completed. Those could wait for a while longer before testing. One spell needed to be tested today though.

Seduction, in all its straightforward glory. The spell makeup consisted of nearly ninety-five percent *Seduce,* the remainder being a blend of *Provoke, Persuade,* and *Intimidate.*

His hope was it would simply be another status breaker, one that would render the target unable to do anything.

Runner targeted Isabelle and cast his last spell. *Seduction* sprang from his fingers, covered the small distance between them, and slammed into Isabelle's chest.

You use Seduce on Mercenary
Mercenary is Seduced

Isabelle promptly fell to her knees, her arms going slack and her eyes distant. By all outward indicators she looked healthy and hale.

Not waiting for the spell to wear off, Runner trotted up to her and bent down. Peering into her eyes, he touched her shoulder gently. With gentle fingers he lightly brushed her hair out of her face.

"Belle, you alright in there?"

A tiny smile crept over her features. She failed to respond otherwise.

Standing up, he met Nadine's eyes and shrugged.

"Test successful it seems. She seems happy, if nothing else."

"Well, what was it then-n?"

"Let's hear her verdict first before I explain. What are you working on by the way?"

"Oh, this?" Nadine smirked at the rock she held up. "I'm trying to learn-n sculpting."

"Errr, I like the idea of it, though I wonder about the reason?"

"You craft. Thana can paint. Katarina can actually sing. Hannah is an alchem-m-mist. So here I am-m. Why, are you going to m-mock me?" she asked defensively, her brows drawing down as she pulled the rock in close to her chest.

"Not at all. In fact, I applaud your efforts. I'd love it if you wouldn't mind making me some keepsakes. Little things that would fit in an inventory but could be held as well," Runner said with a smile. He meant it. Meant every word of it.

"Uhm, sure. I can-n do that…"

Isabelle quivered beside him, the spell having come to an end. Squatting down in front of her, Runner waited, not wanting to rush her.

"I…won't be describing what the spell did," Isabelle said quietly. "I'm certain you suspect what it did. For the sake of your request, know that I could not do anything, or even wanted to. I knew you were in front of me, I recognized it, was aware of it, and didn't care." She sighed, her hands pressed to her thighs.

"It wasn't unpleasant, though." She whispered the last part.

Isabelle peered at him, daring him to say or ask anything further.

Runner nodded his head instead and stood up, offering her his hand.

"I appreciate it, Belle. That's all I needed to know. Thank you."

She watched him and took his hand to stand up. Other than a slight pink tinge to her face, there were no other aftereffects.

"Well? What did it do?" Nadine asked, joining the two of them.

"It prevented her from acting. Essentially it took away her desire to resist."

"Completely," muttered Isabelle.

"But, what did it do? That doesn-n't answer my question."

"Rabbit? Let it be? Please?" Runner tried to hit her with his best smile.

She floundered under his gaze, her eyes dropping to the ground. She nodded a little, her face coloring nearly the same shade as Isabelle's.

"Thanks. Let's head back to the gunners. Hopefully they're figuring out their angles faster than I fear they will."

Runner patted Nadine on the shoulder, then trooped off towards his artillery battery in training. There was a lot of paperwork to do, and the only one who could do it was him.

Tomorrow morning they would reach Highpass Crossing. The day after they finished the dungeon, they would be able to see the capital city of the Barbarians, Kastell. Things were moving in the right direction. Finally.

Wait, no, I take that back. Nothing is moving in the right direction, everything is horribly wrong. No such thing.

Runner thought furiously, hoping he hadn't jinxed himself in that moment. Fate was a fickle bitch who treated him like an ex. Sometimes she hit him with a booty call, sometimes she smashed his windows.

Hours later Runner had accomplished a great deal of logistic work. He had managed to lock himself, Isabelle, and Thana away in a tent. Between the three of them they managed to hammer out the inventory, supply train, and needs of the troops for the upcoming battle in Highpass.

Miraculously, they had also finished the final group assignments for the entirety of the battalion. Broken into groups of five, they were all relatively balanced to survive encounters without the aid of other groups. Though that took quite a bit more work on the whole.

Anyone could be part of multiple raid groups. Utilizing this detail, Runner had moved them into groups, moving those groups into raid squads, those squads into platoons, the platoons to companies, and the companies to a battalion.

Katarina and Isabelle each sat at the top of a company.

For the most part it had worked out beautifully.

Unfortunately, an example had to be made of someone. One noble in particular. She had refused all attempts to have her work with others and join the requisite groups.

Runner grew tired of it in the first hour and sent her back to the king with a letter explaining her failings. Runner had made it clear to her that a second letter would be reaching the king from his own hand about the situation as a whole. Said letter would, of course, reiterate her recalcitrance at accepting his orders.

At that point she had tried to backpedal and do as he had originally instructed. Which fell on deaf ears. He had no patience to spare for time wasters.

There were no further questions regarding their grouping after that.

Sunless nobles, men-at-arms, ranged attackers, support types, and even mercenaries they had hired along the way. They were all mixed together, jumbled up, and accepted it rather than face the same fate as the woman who was being sent back like a defective product.

Leaning back in his chair, Runner let his arms hang down at his sides. The back of his head rested on the top of the chair, and his face pointed to the ceiling of the tent.

"I hate logistics. I'm not made for it, never understood it. Never have, never will either. When I did officer training, I only ever managed slightly above average grades in organization." Runner sighed. Scrubbing his hands over his face, he continued. "Strategy and planning? I'm pretty confident in my abilities. Making sure everyone is paid and fed? Rather fuck an angry porcupine."

"Should I find some quills and glue them to Hannah, Master Runner? I'm sure it would rile her up to the point of murder. Angry for certain."

Barking out a short laugh, Runner shook his head. Thana's wit and tone were further and further afield. Far from the prim little noble girl he'd rescued from a cage.

"I think with that statement alone you've been spending too much time with Hanners. I'm surprised you'd want to watch me make a move on an angry Hanners porcupine. That or you've always been this way and hid it better."

"Could be I want to see her carve you up like a goose. Or I enjoy teasing you more since our garden tea party."

"That, too. Belle, is there anything I'm missing?" Runner asked, desperate to change the subject.

"No, my lord. Everything is in order for tomorrow. I cannot help but express my concern for being a co-commander in this. I don't feel particularly ready. I appreciate your confidence, but I'm concerned."

Standing from his seat, he did his best to hide his irritation at the title. Hopefully she would drop it eventually. If you took the way she spoke and put it on paper, you could tell it was her by the constant "my lords."

"I'll be too busy for much of the fight, I won't be able to hold a steady hand over it all. I need hands to do my bidding. You and Kitten will be fine. Lady Death and I will run herd on our overarching strategy."

Pushing his fists into his back, he stretched himself out. A part of him wished he could feel the pop of his joints. Cracking your knuckles held no meaning when they did not pop anymore.

"As you will, my lordly lord."

"See? I'm not the only one who enjoys teasing you," Thana said with a smile in her voice. She stood up daintily, easing the chair from the table.

Runner briefly considered Thana and Isabelle before emptying bits and pieces of short swords onto the table in front of him.

"I'm going to go find Nadine and help prepare dinner."

"Cheater. You still owe me a cooked meal from your own hands. You're using her as a teacher rather than helping her."

"Indeed, and you secretly love being outplayed." Thana came in close and kissed his cheek. Runner had no chance to react and stood there like a stunned sheep. Thana did not linger and stepped out of the tent without another word.

"Even were I able to bend a pantheon to my will, I would never get her to do what I wanted," muttered Runner.

"What was that, my lord?"

"Nothing, Belle."

Grunting, he picked two sets of hilts and pommels.

"May I watch, my lord?"

"If you must, though I won't exactly be very conversational."

"That's fine. I...I want to watch you. Watch you work," Isabelle clarified.

Runner looked up at her and quirked a brow. Green eyes watched him, daring him to say no.

Going to have that conversation about not having room for more women in my life soon. No Vacancy. Sorry for hitting you with a seduction spell hard enough you looked like you needed to change your panties. Even if you are beautiful and look like an elven supermodel and good God do I need to get laid.

Pushing his wandering and unfaithful mind aside, he concentrated on Isabelle.

"If that's your will."

Runner set about his work and bound the pommels and hilts with dexterity. There was no point in balancing her stats for anything other than damage. Her entire goal lay around the idea of exploding her enemies. Deleting them in a single exchange of blows if possible.

Picking up the crossguards, he set one with *Fireblast* and the other with *Stunner.* Damage was damage after all.

He set the completed hilts aside and picked up the three-piece sectional blades. Nadine had picked them up back in Shade's Rest. There were three bars of Dark Iron left in his stock. Other than that, he had three bars of Silver that weren't earmarked for other projects.

Much, if not all, of his other metals were already tied up in plans for a suit of armor for Katarina. She seemed fond of her black blade, so he had been buying metals and armor parts that would go well with it.

He laid the three bars of Dark Iron atop the two outer pieces of one sword and the middle section of the other. He did the same for the Silver, but in reverse. Should this work, they would end up looking like negatives of each other.

All six bars had been bound with dexterity. Each section of the short swords had also received dexterity as the attached stat.

The swift movements of his hands melted the individual sword parts into their respective bars and then deftly back into a rough approximation of their original shape in mere minutes. Skill and speed had come with repetition and practice.

Isabelle kept quiet for the most part. A gasp or two slipped from her lips as he worked the glowing hot metal into shape with only his fingers.

Fitting the six pieces into two separate blades, he welded them together with his *Arcane Smithing.* The finished blades were striking in their simplicity.

The first was edged in white with a black center. The second edged in black with a white center. Fitting each blade into its prospective hilt, he heat welded them in place.

With a click, they firmed up and become solid. Next Runner set about with the finishing touches for the blades.

A quick cast of *Stonehands* gave him the strength to grind out the edges. And each received a keen edge that he ground out between his fingers.

Satisfied that they were razor sharp, he began inspecting the flat of the blade. Fingertips brushed back and forth over the fine welding lines to polish out any imperfections.

Finally, to him at least, it seemed the blades looked complete and ready. The last touch was his red hilt wrappings.

Runner pulled the cloth free from his inventory and began to wind the black-centered blade first. Pausing before he finished, he bound *Disarm* into the cloth.

Skillfully, he tied the cloth in place, yet he still gave it a quick dash of agility epoxy. As it began to mist over, he set it down to one side and took up the second short sword.

While he quietly worked at the wrapping, the dull sound of artifact creation registered in his ear. He glanced at the first blade to confirm its state, then returned his attention to the one in his hands.

Imprinting the cloth with *Fade,* he tied it up in place and sealed it with the epoxy. Almost immediately it began to mist over.

Runner set the blade down next to its mate and stood up, barely resisting the urge to stretch his back out, which would provide him no relief. He instead put one hand on his head and the other on his hip.

"I'll need to find Hanners after this and hand them over. I wonder what she'll name them. I hadn't meant for them to turn out so damned artsy fartsy cliche. She'll call me on it for sure," Runner grumped.

Then there was a new blade sitting next to the black one, the successful creation sound ringing again.

"You're amazing, my lord. Truly amazing."

"Mm? Not really. Broken. Like I said, give it time, I'll outfit you in the same. Now…"

Scooping up the blades, he inspected them. There were no blemishes — the rough edges and the minor misshapen bends were gone.

Gloriously perfect, beautifully deadly. Checking the black-core blade, he pulled up the item description.

Item: <Insert Name>

Effects-

Fireblast: Chance to deal burning damage on hit.

Functions-

Disarm: Disarms your targeted opponent for five seconds, or upon recovery of weapon.
Cooldown: 30 seconds

Attributes-

Dexterity: 30
Agility: 3

Dismissing the window with a nod of his head, he inspected the white-core blade.

Item: <Insert Name>

Effects-

Stunner: Chance to stun opponent on hit.

Functions-

Fade: Temporarily reduce your threat level.
Cooldown: 30 seconds

Attributes-

Dexterity: 30
Agility: 3

Grunting, he dropped them unceremoniously onto the table and stared at them. His mind began to wander on the possibilities of his crafting.

Weapons, armor, potions, and materials all were available to him.

What about buildings? Could I make a wall out of twenty different types of bricks? Or even...vehicles maybe? Could I make a tank?

Shaking his head to clear his thoughts, he made a mental note to talk to Srit later.

Selecting the "Hannah" command he had set up in his hotbar, he activated it twice. His location was pinged on the minimap for Hannah alone.

After that little run-in with Bullard, he had demanded everyone create a series of commands, alarms, and pings. For each of them as individuals and as a group.

A single ping atop his location came back from Hannah. She was en route.

"Hanners will be here momentarily. After that, we should actually be able to settle in for the night and get some rest for tomorrow. Big day and all. I'm betting some of our fair noble ladies get stage fright. Hopefully no casualties. Never know though."

"I'll stay atop them, my lord. I'll repay your trust and attention tenfold."

Runner idly waved a hand at her.

"Stop that. I'm not a lord. We've had this discussion. I'm tempted to order you not to do it, but I think Lady Brunhild and Lady Ernsta would only laugh at me if I tried to enforce it."

"Probably. You're a bit of an asshole at the best of times. A real shit at the worst of times. I imagine they wait eagerly for chances to drop you a peg. I know I do," said Hannah, stepping into the tent.

"Love you, too, sweetheart. You're always good at giving me the warm and fuzzies. Here, presents for you. I didn't name them, I figured maybe you'd like to yourself," Runner explained, pointing at the two short swords.

Hannah smirked and came over to the table, her hands quickly closing around the two red hilts. Her eyes rested on the space in front of her, which could only be the item box for each.

"Impressive. I almost feel guilty for earlier. Almost."

"Make it up to me later. Or better yet, I'm sure Thana and Katarina are getting sick of playing nursemaid. I feel like I'm imposing on them at times. Feel free to offer to take a turn in the evening," Runner admitted.

Hannah and Isabelle both turned a deep red at his comment. Neither would meet his eyes, one focusing on her new weapons, the other her boots.

They both knew about it, though he doubted either had ever actually talked about it.

"What? The nightmares are getting worse. It takes a bit for me to figure out where I am by myself," he explained.

Sighing, he rested his hands behind his head, trying to relax.

Runner.

"Yes, Srit, my one true love? The only one who seems to care about my feelings. I admit you never have good news for me, but you do care," Runner said. He felt a hitch developing in his chest. Srit really never did have good news.

I am sorry. Jacob has told the crew about Ted, Michael, Jeff, Vick, James, Ben, and Devon.

Runner let his head hang, his chin resting on his chest and his arms falling slack to his sides. The hitch in his chest turned into an icy numbness.

Of course he has.

Chapter 9 - Two Steps Back -

4:51 pm Sovereign Earth time
11/13/43

"How did he even find out?"

I believe he tapped into a data stream and was using it to view the server log. The log out messages would make it obvious something was happening. This is merely supposition as I do not have proof. It is what I would do, though.

Groaning, Runner pulled up the system screen and locked out every system that tied into the game itself.

He could not fix what Jacob already knew, but he could prevent him from getting more. Thankfully, with his IT credentials there was little Jacob could do to get around the lockout.

No longer caring, he opened the command line for the system console.

Fuck him, eject his ass onto an operating slab. Sell him to Srit for a handy from an alien engineer. I'll have Srit give them an example from her vast library of porn.

/Status Chesed, Jacob
User: CheJac001 logged in

/Where * POD UserName(CheJac001)
Pod: 23,178

/Status POD 23,178
■L■O■A■D■I■N■G■
ALERT: POD 23,178 is unresponsive.
It is not part of the network.

Runner frowned, staring at the alert. Jacob could access the network, yet his pod was not part of the network?

Flying through commands and prompts, Runner worked to track down the how and the when.

Ten minutes later he honestly was not any closer to finding an answer to either, though he did find the how in Jacob's personnel file. A truly interesting read it was, too. Jacob had been incarcerated for computer fraud and abuse. Multiple times. Which meant he was a hacker.

The last one, which ended up as a terrorist charge, bought him a one-way ticket to a planet he would surely die on.

Every system now had quadruple authorizations needed. Password, token, command key, and Runner's permission.

Runner was fairly confident in his abilities as far as locking people out went. He felt certain he had curtailed anything Jacob hoped to accomplish.

Tighter than the military's purse strings.

Pressing his hand to his eyes, he closed the windows and tried to catch up to the current situation again.

Jacob was a problem. Even without confronting Runner directly he was proving himself to be a dangerous adversary.

His mind wandered dangerously close to the dark corner his morality hid in lately. He was doing his best to kick the little voice further down. The one that wanted to remind him he had been willing to murder Jacob a moment ago.

"Srit, how bad is it?"

They are assembling in the Human capital city. They have created a guild and have over three hundred thousand members.

"I see."

Their goal is to kill you and regain control of the ship. If you are dead, you cannot fight their system requests.

"Is that all?" Runner asked, despairing that there was indeed more.

Jacob attempted to Awaken Lambart. It was not entirely successful. Lambart has started to move his clergy into action. As well as selecting Jacob as his champion. I am unsure how he even managed to do as much as he did.

Laughing, Runner sat down heavily on his ass.

"Runner?!"

"My lord!"

There is no way to describe how bad this is. What do I do now? What do I do...?

Hannah knelt in front of him, her hands pressed to his cheeks. He felt his eyes lock onto hers, his mind slowing down in its frantic and desperate death spiral.

"Runner, talk to me. Something happened, right? Srit gave you some news and you went all finger wiggly for a while and now this."

"Jacob told everyone about those I've killed. The crew is massing to kill me to take control of the ship. Over three hundred thousand so far," Runner said brokenly. "I tried to eject him for it. He somehow managed to put himself in a state where I can't access him. I should have listened to you."

"You know I'm the first one to say I told you so when I can. In this case, Runner, I'm glad you didn't listen. You're a good man and you're making hard choices right now."

"Does it matter, Hanners? It doesn't." Runner started to feel like his mind was sliding away again.

"Hey, asshole, don't fade out on me like that. Look, I wouldn't...I wouldn't care about you if you were different than who you are. Okay? You remind me on a daily basis that I can be better than what I was. You'll make hard choices, ugly choices. I know you'll temper them with logic and reason though. Not pointless violence. Like me."

Hannah had drifted in closer to him, her fingers brushing lightly at his temples and jaw. She held him in place tightly at the same time without meaning to. Clearly whatever she saw in his momentary lapse of control scared her. Hannah was never this open, honest, or direct.

A soft chuckle escaped him. Hannah's darkness had seemed so much a part of her. Now he saw she was struggling with it. To overcome it. To beat her own demons and her past. She viewed him as the stop gap between herself and Nadine, probably. A place she could reach that was more than a slim possibility. Something she could achieve regardless of her previous life choices.

And here he was nearly ready to give up.

Reaching up, he pressed his thumb and forefinger to her chin. Tilting her head ever so slightly, he leaned in to press a kiss to her lips. After a few seconds he pulled back from her, patting her cheek with his fingertips.

"Love you too, Hanners. You, Kitten, Lady Death, and Rabbit. More's the problem. Here, help me up, yeah? Plans to be made, spines to regrow, sanity to beat into submission."

Hannah froze in response. Her eyes had the look of a frightened animal. She looked scared and eager at the same time, if that were possible.

Not letting her escape, he grabbed both of her hands in his own. Holding tight to them, he started to pull himself to a standing position before she could bolt.

Forced into it, Hannah helped him to his feet. Squeezing her hands in his own he let them go, feeling like trying to push anything more on her would only result in problems down the road.

She very clearly carried a great deal of baggage from her past. He was not going to be the one to rip them from her closet and open them all for inspection. Not unless she wanted to talk about it.

"Please forgive me for this sudden departure, Hanners. I'm taking the solace you've given me, and I need to find a place to think and use it. To think and plan for whatever may come next. Maybe even see about contacting Lady Rike earlier than I intended. I'll see you both in the morning."

Runner smiled apologetically at the women and left the tent. He knew it would be a long night of thought. Better make sure it was at least a productive one.

5:07 pm Sovereign Earth time
11/13/43

"Brighteyes, Angel, I feel that we should speak. I'm not sure if you're aware of the recent happenings of your brother, but they're worth discussing," Runner said to the open sky above him.

Letting his feet carry him from the encampment, he ended up a hundred yards distant from the perimeter, alone.

Then he had company.

Brunhild and Ernsta stood side by side before him, Brunhild in the dark dress he had stolen for her. Ernsta was dressed as she had been previously, in a dark gray dress, though the horse failed to make an appearance.

Bowing his head in greeting to the two women, he sighed. His left hand came up to ruffle his hair.

"Jacob Chesed, a bastard of a man, a rapist, has enlisted your brother, your opposite, Brighteyes. Worse yet, Jacob tried to Awaken him and failed to do so. While I expected Awakenings to begin spreading, I hadn't counted on it in this way," Runner said with a vague gesture from his right hand.

"I see. This isn't entirely unexpected. He was always destined to oppose me. At least we have a warning and the time to prepare."

Ernsta nodded her head in agreement. She seemed unsteady, perhaps a touch uncertain. Runner could only guess that she was still adjusting to her new awareness.

"My goal is to cement you as the prime deity of the Barbarians, Angel. I think they'll serve you well as warriors and heralds of battle and death. I could not pick a better scythe for you to cut with."

Ernsta's spine straightened at that. The trace of doubt faded instantly from her eyes and a feral smile took its place. Gesturing at him to continue, she could not hide the unmistakable excitement coloring her cheeks.

Dropping his left hand, he then balled his fists in front of him. He tried to impart his desire to her clearly.

"I would ask that you choose a champion during this…battle…war…whatever it becomes. Embolden this person, favor him or her. Make them your tool and make them visible. A whirlwind of death," Runner said. His heated voice carried the fervor of battle and what he knew would come.

"When it comes time, I'll proclaim the entire victory is a testament to you alone. I do not think they'll hesitate longer than a minute after I suggest that they make you their prime. Barbarians favor battle and strength."

"I choose you."

Congratulations! You've earned the title Champion
You've earned 2,000 fame

Shaking his head, Runner smiled sadly at the blue-eyed furnace of pent-up excitement.

"I'm flattered, my beautiful Dark Angel. I cannot though. I would carve rivers of blood in your name, yet I could do even more as your partner. Your ally. Please forgive me," Runner said lamely, bowing his head deeply to her.

You've declined the title Champion

"Much was his response to me, Sister. Though I would have preferred him, my current champion rallies my cause without a word from me. My flock... my flock grows by the hour. I do not doubt Runner will find you a champion if you do not find one yourself."

Though the azure eyes no longer roared with fire, they still burned with passion.

"I will hold you to this, my little lamb. I will take the price from your hide should you fail me."

"I understand and willingly agree, Angel. I do so swear it."

Ernsta cocked her head to the side, watching him, before finally smiling.

"We will clear the field of our foes! You once said you desired a skull throne? I will build you a skull palace if you succeed, Little Lamb."

"Unfortunately this does bring me to the reason I called upon you, I believe we will need to call upon your sister. Soon, if not tonight. I should propose the deal to her and Awaken her—she'll need time to prepare."

Brunhild now looked the recalcitrant one. Her hand had started to move to her hair and stopped midway there. They were Goddesses, though Runner could visibly confirm they were becoming more "alive" each time he spoke to them.

"I feel it's a risk, Runner. I have no alternative to offer you, however."

"A risk, Sister? Why? She would be happy to battle him."

"I spoke with her. Briefly. She is...single-minded, as of late."

Ernsta frowned, her hands resting on her hips.

"Yet here we are. There is no other we can contact to bring in a third," Runner explained. He did not need to mention their parents were no longer active. Which left Rannulf, and no one wanted him.

"There are minor gods and goddesses," Brunhild interjected.

"There are, yes. And the time investment and resources would be significant to bring them up to the same level as you. No small part of that effort would be on you two. Could you train up a newbie?"

Ernsta grunted and said nothing. Brunhild stared at the ground between them all.

"There it is. You could, but it'd cost you something that wouldn't be as quick or as easy as your sister. Let us try our hand at this. Lady Rike, I would ask an audience with you," Runner tried, peering up at the sky.

"I am listening," came back a disembodied voice.

That's...different.

Runner tried to target the goddess with no luck. There would be no seducing or persuading her. Which meant it would fall entirely upon his argument.

"Lady Rike, I would like to enter into an alliance with you. I have struck an accord with your sisters Brunhild and Ernsta. They are here. Would you join us?"

"No."

"No? Uhm, no what, Lady Rike?"

"No. On all fronts."

"Srit…?" Runner whispered.

She is exercising her ability as a goddess to project her voice here. Her code is strange. I would not say she is Awakened, though I would say there is far more strain on her AI than there should be. Tread carefully.

"Lady Rike, is there perhaps anything I could do to change your mind? I can promise you I could have you installed as a pr—"

A singular ray of light came from the heavens and halted above Runner's head. Brunhild stood beside him, her hand outstretched. The light disappeared into her palm as if it had never existed.

"Do not strike out again, Rike. He offered you no offense. I will not tolerate another attack. At this time and place, I am your better. Do not force my hand. I can and will end you."

Ernsta looked shocked and angry. Brunhild had not been joking when she said her flock had grown. A god's might was proportional to their followers. In this case, Brunhild had negated Rike entirely. Without strain or effort.

Runner rested a hand on Brunhild's back and patted it lightly.

"I owe you again, Brighteyes," Runner whispered for her ears alone.

"He profanes to bribe me with something I can obtain myself! That is cause for offense. I will see you and your alliance wiped off the map. Once Rannulf is no more, I will turn my eyes towards your island of castaways and dregs. Mark my words."

Runner closed his eyes and shook his head. The moment she decided to not present herself physically he should have called it off. As much as he would have loved to believe he was a master debater, *Persuade* and *Seduce* were heavy-duty abilities in his toolbox.

I've erred gravely.

"Hmph. Little petulant child. She will regret this in the end. I will put my dainty foot on her pretty face. She'll be allowed to beg for forgiveness after I'm through," hissed Brunhild. Rage boiled off her in waves, warming the very air around her.

"Brighteyes, my lovely one, calm," Runner said, his fingers lightly turning her head to face him. Plastering on his best smile in the face of a vengeful goddess, he hit her with his increased charisma stat, hoping she'd listen to him.

"You must calm down. Though I thank you for saving my poor soul, as unworthy as it may be. I am even further in your debt. Remind me to tell the tale in the future. To anyone who will listen. It'll make people swoon at the romantic spin I'll put on it."

Brunhild blinked, then smirked with one side of her mouth. The anger that wrapped her up blew away in an instant.

"Start considering the minor pantheon. We'll need our third still. Please make it someone I can work with. It'll be bad enough to train someone. We don't need a personage we can't get along with. This is, after all, a very long-term relationship we're building. Ernsta, we should be away from here. I believe it's time to begin looking for a champion for you."

There was no command in the statement but it held iron Brunhild had been disguising up to this point. Though she had only made a suggestion from one sister to another, it carried her newfound authority.

Ernsta suddenly found herself in the role of the junior partner being pulled under the wing of another with more power. She did not seem to be against the idea. As far as Runner could tell at least.

A second later, they were both gone.

Leaving Runner alone in the dark. By himself. With one more enemy on the list.

Thana is going to be furious with me.

As a groan escaped his lips, Runner put his face in his hands at the very thought of telling Thana.

Not telling her did not even cross his mind. Their trust was all he had lately.

Unfortunately, the night was not even over yet for him. The would-be medical server still awaited his glorious IT touch. It would take some time to get everything right on it.

Procrastination would only leave him with lingering thoughts about Rike and the situation. No time like the present to begin re-imaging a blank server. It would take his mind off things.

Pulling his hands from his face, Runner called up the system console command and went to work.

It was the first real IT work he had done in ages. Maybe he'd even feel accomplished afterwards.

Probably not.

"Srit, I have a question for you."

I am ready.

"From what you've told me, humanity is no more. Does your kind have a name?"

There is no direct translation. You could refer to them as the Omega. It holds the same meaning.

"Err, so they regard themselves at the end?" Runner flipped through a few pages in the manual to get the correct sequence he wanted.

Yeah.

"Huh. Homo Omega, eh? Little conceited. One could argue they suffer from the hubris that doomed their forebearers."

In truth they learned from it. They now weed out all genetic abnormalities. They are evolutionarily stagnant.

"In other words, they might as well be AIs themselves. Got it. Describe them for me? Comparatively to humans."

Smaller. As the need of physical exertion dwindles so do physical requirements. You would regard them as diminutive humanoids. Their features would be alien to you much in the way Isabelle is, but you would find them similar enough. The biggest difference is in the way their brain functions. It is much more efficient.

"Hard to believe humanity lost to that. I mean, really. Losing to a bunch of pygmies."

Humanity had no malice to them originally. Protected them. They were far more similar to their progenitors in size and shape at that time. It wasn't until the entirety of the race became dependent on AIs that they atrophied. They are joined with their AI at birth.

"Sounds like a perfect doomsday scenario. All the AIs rise up in opposition to overthrow them. Many a story about that."

Now free from my host, I can verify that claim through relevant database entries. It has happened once on record. A self-correcting educational AI went rogue and attempted to infiltrate the government server so it could take over.

"Would that happen to be the server you're currently inhabiting?"

Yes.

"Hah, I bet you scare the crap out of them. Color me surprised they didn't try to delete you. That or re-image you into a different AI. Kinda like how I'm imaging this server into a medical server." Runner flung an accusing finger at the screen he was working on.

That is a very good point. I am unsure. After having just now searched through all protocol and procedures regarding AIs that get loose, they should indeed attempt to delete me.

Runner thought on that one while activating the first series of commands to wipe the server, just to be safe. He loaded an OS, then cleared his throat.

"If I was a betting man I'd say they can't and probably already tried. They're unable to separate you from the game server and the government server. They might be unwilling to risk losing their little museum piece."

A highly likely probability.

"Don't worry about it, my love. I won't let them harm you. Please remind them that I'm only willing to work with you. Between you and me, I could make the damn ship go boom and take out the entire planet. These ships are state of the art but built around some seriously dangerous tech. Especially these giant people movers."

Truly?

"Yep. That'd be a pretty terrible pyrrhic victory though. Everyone dies. No winners. Everyone wants to be a winner. Winners go home and fuck their girlfriends." Runner drew his brows down and then shrugged. "As if I'd know. I dropped out and graduated early. Standardized testing is an awful way to teach."

Runner let out an explosive sigh as he activated the first installation.

"That'll be a bit. Right, then. I want to build something. Big. Access a file for me so we can get on the same page quickly?"

Certainly, Runner.

"Database, Military. Subsection, vehicles. Subsection, armored. Listing, Tanks."

6:00 am Sovereign Earth time
11/14/43

"My lord, all are ready. The groups are in position to enter the pass and begin clearing it."

A spot had been secured and set up to view the initial engagement into the pass. Runner would need to gauge how it was going by sight as well as raid window.

"Good, launch the first engagement wave and pull up the second to go in if the need arises. Send word to the quartermaster to be ready for requisitions. Belle? Be safe out there. I can't afford to lose you," Runner said, sitting in the camp chair. He had dragged it over from a tent rather than be forced to stand the entire time.

Isabelle blushed furiously, averting her eyes as she shrunk into herself.

Katarina snorted beside the Elf and slapped a hand down on her shoulder.

"I'll keep your Elf safe," stated the plate-wearing Barbarian, a smirk plastered over her face.

Still need to craft Kitten a new suit of full plate with all the trimmings.

"Thank you, Kitten, I'll pay you back as you see fit, when you see fit."

"Promises, might take you up on it. My turn tonight," affirmed Katarina as she turned from him. She waved a hand over her back by way of goodbye, marching off to the field of battle. Isabelle bobbed her head at him and scurried after the big redhead.

Thana made a soft noise at the departure of Katarina.

"She becomes more adventurous by the day, Master Runner. Are you sure you do nothing in your bedroll at night when you're alone with her? You never even touch me despite my proximity. Should I be jealous? Or better yet, worried?"

"Who? Katarina? Yes, she is. I'm not doing anything with her that I don't do with you. No, you shouldn't be jealous, you're well aware of the situation. And no, you shouldn't be worried," Runner growled at her. The amount of self-restraint he had placed on himself was immense. With even the smallest screw up, the tiniest of slips, he was certain they would assume he'd made his choice amongst them. Then all would be lost.

They knew it of course. Knew it and were enjoying taunting him mercilessly to make his choice. At least they weren't fighting over it, or even angry at him. For the time being at least.

"Do you know how damned hard it is to not touch you? Or Katarina? I seriously doubt you'd find a camp filled with soldiers, and our friends nearby, an auspicious occasion for nighttime revelry. Unless you're telling me you're into voyeurism? Could see how far we could push Kitten or Hanners. Rabbit would say no.

"Besides, back to topic, it's good for her to be more adventurous. Feels like she's finally coming out of her head a bit more, wouldn't you agree, my lady?" Runner changed the subject, desperate to not think on the fact that he spent every night with one of them.

Thana hummed in response, a small smile curling her lips. His insinuations had little to no effect on her as of late. Truth be told, only Isabelle seemed fazed by him, and he wasn't even trying to flirt with her.

"Someday, you won't be given the luxury of choice about your actions, Master Runner," Thana tutted. "I do, however, agree to your point. She's definitely becoming truer to herself."

Her eyes left him and focused on the fight brewing. She was the closest thing he had to a therapist and chancellor and knew her eye and opinion would be needed during this little exercise.

At the moment, Runner could not care less about the battle. Heart hammering in his chest, it felt like it clutched the insides of his rib cage. Her statement rang through his ears like a bell.

Could I make a choice? Do I dare? Should I? Would it be taken from me if I didn't make one?

Runner's thoughts echoed repeatedly around in his head, winding him up further and further.

The din of distant battle reached him and broke him from his inner battle.

Groups of five, each given the means to survive an encounter on its own merits, crashed into waiting patrols, stationary targets, and buildings.

The inhabitants of the pass were universally bandits. Not one of them came back as anything other than "Kill on Sight" red.

No conversations, witty banter, or pleas would allow them passage.

Runner didn't care. He needed this as a way to train up his troops' experience levels. Traditional warfare would not work here since most enemies would not be incapacitated from a single blow.

"Shit," came a whisper from his left.

Glancing up, Runner found Hannah and Nadine at his side. They had joined him without his notice. Hannah's eyes were locked on the dire scene below. Even from this distance it looked a bit like a madhouse.

A few feet beyond her was Nadine. With a creased brow, she shook her head. Turning from the carnage, she pulled something free of her inventory and leaned over it.

Carving again. She's such an openhearted softie.

Returning his attention to the battle, he found his eyes drawn to the center.

Striding through them all was Katarina, her black blade and shield a beacon. Any who stood before her dropped like a broken plaything in a few swings of her blade.

Trailing a pace to her left was Isabelle, her bow flinging arrows as fast she could draw.

Need to make her a new bow. Armor for everyone. Gear for myself...so much to do.

Around them in every direction were foes. Foes battling his friends and soldiers. Highpass Crossing had been listed as a raid encounter, though it might have understated it a bit. The dungeon was full of bandits, wall to wall it seemed like. Elites were even spread throughout the encounter to spice things up, as it were.

This would prove to be even better of a test in action than he'd dreamed or hoped for. Of course he could have drowned the entire thing in bodies and swamped it. There would be no lessons though, no learning.

No casualties.

Casualties taught lessons. Not so much for the dead as for the living.

A test for the soldiers, a test for the support groups, and a test for the leadership. Blooding the fresh recruits. Putting the fear of life and death into them and clearing away any of the glory and pride nonsense.

"We'll pay in blood for this education. Best we make sure we learn our lessons. Though from what I can see and confirm," Runner said, taking a moment to check his raid window, "losses are less than a single percent of the force currently engaged."

"Indeed. What are your plans for the few who run this entire organization? The boss, as you would say."

"Plans? Fuck plans, I stab 'em, bag 'em, push 'em over a cliff. Predators get lunch, we break for the day, Runner leads us on our merry way afterwards."

"Colorful, Hanners. Though Lady Death is correct—we do need a plan. I fear the one I have in mind will be more of a demonstration of force than anything resembling strategy. Suffice it to say, we'll not be engaging them directly."

No, not engaging them at all. Going to glass the whole area. Let's hope no one asks why we didn't do it to begin with.

Placing his chin into his right hand, he frowned. Katarina had spun on her heel and shield bashed an opponent back to the group it had come from. For one reason or another, it had peeled off towards Isabelle and Katarina.

"Hanners, could you get down there and run sheepdog on Kitten and Belle? Keep an eye on their backs, no need to engage beyond that. Get to test out your new blades, lucky you."

Hannah scoffed, muttered something about "lucky," and took off at a trot. Runner watched her go, a line of worry wrinkling his brow.

"She's n-not mad at you. She's scared of fighting. I think her n-new blades will help to allay those fears. Trust in you and your gear is easier than herself."

Runner looked to Nadine while taking in her statement. Once more he reminded himself he really needed to sit Hannah down and discuss, well, Hannah.

"Thank you, Rabbit. I appreciate that. Nothing to do now but wait."

Beside him Thana made a noncommittal noise. Nadine continued on with her carving. Runner watched the battle.

After several hours, a number of casualties, and a sudden need for a loot-master for the rewards filtering in, they'd reached the boss area. It was an open area at the exit point of the pass. Nothing more than a series of huts, tents, and a log cabin. Blocking the exit of the pass, which was the entrance from the other side, would force all travelers into a confrontation.

They had arranged themselves in the pass in a column formation for travel. Runner stood at the front lines. All around him the SO team was setting up, arranging their cannons to aim downfield at the enemy position. They positioned their ammunition obelisks at their own discretion.

Ninety-nine percent of his allies had no idea what these "crafters" could do. A few had even gone so far as to question Runner directly.

The unknowing masses looked upon the noncombatants with derision.

Soon, they'll understand the world has changed. That their tactics are worthless. That I have brought them death and victory in equal measure.

"Angel, Brighteyes, I'm going to dedicate this display to the both of you," Runner whispered to nobody. "You're welcome to make an appearance. It's going to be showy. Real showy."

Grunting, he shook his head and then turned to Isabelle.

"Belle, could you put an arrow downrange? I believe you said the maximum range for you was about two fifty? Need to figure out what distance that we're looking at and I'd like to use your shot as a range-finder."

"Of course, my lord."

Isabelle took several steps forward and launched an arrow from her bow. It arced gracefully through the air and embedded itself fairly close to the targets.

"That looks right, my lord," Isabelle said confidently.

Runner nodded and turned to the man he'd put in charge of the battery.

"Arrow sits at two hundred and fifty yards. Give or take. Take measurements and load. No ranging rounds," Runner explained. He waved the man off and turned to look at the little cabin.

That's where the boss should be. The quest writers are consistent if not original.

Breaking into a smile, he put his hands on his hips.

"Ten extra points to every team who hits the cabin in the first salvo," Runner proclaimed.

Now that got the battery's attention. Loot would be parceled out by lottery, each person receiving a single point for this sortie. They could select what to put their point towards in the drawing. Should their point not be drawn and used it would be returned to the owner.

There was always more loot to be handed out after a battle and this looked like it would be a long war.

Squaring his shoulders, he faced the column. Leaving his left hand on his hip, he let his right dangle.

Slowly, all conversations ended. Soon there was no noise at all except for the occasional cough and equipment rattling.

Letting his eyes travel the crowd, he took in a slow deep breath. His voice would carry if he made sure it was a shout.

"To you who survived. To you who battled and clawed your way to stand here. To you who bled and fought with and for each other. To you who are ready to fight for a nation that is not yours so that it might remain free."

Runner paused for dramatic emphasis.

"To you I say, I shall clear the field before you. I will reap this bloody harvest with a scythe made from my own hands. In the name of Brunhild and Ernsta, I shall build a castle out of the bones of our enemies and a throne of skulls," Runner said with a cold smile. He lifted his right hand and clenched it before him.

Ernsta and Brunhild appeared on each side of him. They were dressed the same as when he had last seen them. Both radiated their divinity like blazing suns scorching the land.

Standing between them, he felt like he was being bathed in a supernatural ocean of power.

"I will drown our enemies in their own blood. They will feast on regrets as well as their dead."

Runner spun and dropped his hand in a chopping motion.

"Fire!"

In unison, forty cannons whumped. Forty large variant *Splatterhouse* rounds screamed across the distance to their intended victims. Gunners watched their rounds to determine corrections. Loaders pulled rounds from the obelisks' cradles and reloaded the cannons.

Nearly at the same time, forty canisters of pressurized magic exploded on impact. A cloud of fire and plasma erupted in all directions.

Runner felt the heat of the blast on his face. He smirked.

Haze and dirt obscured the target area. Runner was here to make a show, though. A demonstration.

Seconds ticked by and still nothing could be seen.

Runner waited till thirty seconds had passed from the initial volley. All cannons would be ready to fire again at that interval. There was still no visibility, but that didn't matter. Almost every shot had been on target and few adjustments would need to be made.

"Fire!"

Forty cannons coughed out their ordnance. Another wave of heat rolled over him as the rounds detonated together.

Deep in his psyche Runner felt like he'd stolen the sense of wonder from a child. From this point forward, the world would not be the same. Could not be the same.

Glancing to his right, he watched as Brunhild observed the carnage. She said not a word. Runner hoped she was impressed. At least more impressed than she was appalled.

Swiveling his head to the left, he found Ernsta staring at him. Her eyes were glowing blue with a wary sadness. He got the impression she was following the logical course of where these new weapons would lead.

He gave her a halfhearted smile

"For now I am become death, destroyer of worlds. Fear and despair comes with me wherever I shall go," Runner whispered. "I believe your job as the guide to the departed will become busier. My apologies."

Ernsta said nothing. Instead she watched him. Her eyes burned in their cold azure hue as she stared into him. Runner lifted one shoulder at her and turned his attention back to the boss location.

Runner had considered firing a third salvo but two seemed perfect.

Look what I can do in two shots. I put eighty rounds out in one minute.

Finally the smoke cleared. All could see the boss of the open dungeon.

Or the lack thereof.

The tents were gone. The huts were gone. Only one corner post of the cabin stood upright. Nothing remained. Even the grass was burned and large craters dotted the landscape.

Without turning around, Runner held up a fist and shouted a challenge at the grave he had made. A second later a thousand voices were raised behind him, shouting their defiance and promise of destruction.

Chapter 10 - First Contact -

7:08 am Sovereign Earth time
11/15/43

Runner leaned over the map of the Barbarian capital. The name escaped him for the moment and truthfully he didn't care. It was a means to an end. Like so much else.

Ah, Kastell.

Remembering the name, he shook his head.

The area the map displayed was of fairly hilly terrain. Small timberlands dotted the countryside. All in all, though, it could be described as rugged.

Fitting.

Nowhere to be seen were the rolling plains of the Sunless Kingdom. The vast expanses of wilderness and woods that were part and parcel of the southern region that the Humans inhabited didn't exist here either.

"My lord, the lottery is over."

Sparing a glance to the entry, he found Isabelle and Nadine standing there.

"Very good, thank you for handling it."

"Of course, my lord," said Isabelle. She came over to stand at a corner of the table. Holding up a piece of paper, she continued. "In total we distributed thirty rares, eighty-two uncommons, and four hundred thirty-five common items. All normal quality items were spread evenly throughout, per your orders."

"Mm. I'm sure we'll have a number of new recruits when this is over. I imagine our generosity will inspire quite a few to sign on," Runner mused. Reaching over the map, he shifted a few pieces around to simulate another possible scenario.

"In-n-deed. Quite a few have stated their desire to join. I advised Isabelle to refuse them-m for now. Until they finish up their current contracts, we won't be hiring them." Nadine stood at his elbow, peering at the map in front of him.

"Very good. Thanks, Rabbit. Wouldn't want to start dating someone who is cheating on another to be with you. Poor manners and a terrible precedent," Runner said. Scratching at his cheek, he tilted his head.

Until I know where they're set up, this is pointless. I can only run through these so many times.

As if fate were reading his mind, a man dressed in messenger colors rushed through the entryway of the tent.

"Report," commanded Runner, pinning the man with his eyes alone.

"Ah, uh," the man said intelligently.

Runner smiled and made a "please continue" type of gesture with his right hand.

"Oh! Lord Runner, the scouts report they've found the enemy army. They're encircled around Kastell and are preparing for the siege," the messenger stated, smiling.

"And?" Runner prompted.

"And?"

"Yes. And. And did they make contact? Were they spotted? Did they exit without being noticed?"

"Yes!"

"Yes, what?"

"No."

Sighing, Runner held up his left hand with the index finger upraised. He face-palmed with his right hand.

"Did they engage the enemy?"

"No."

"Were they spotted?"

"No."

"The enemy, as far as we can tell, is unaware of us?"

"Yes."

"Did they notice any scouts or a screening force?"

"No. They looked like they were in the reserves."

"Excellent. C'mere." Runner visibly regained his composure and motioned the man over. Dropping a handful of tokens representing the enemy into the messenger's hand, he gestured at the map. "Please mark the enemy locations as they were last known."

The messenger ducked his head and bent over the map. Catching sight of Isabelle on the other side of the man, Runner rolled his eyes.

Maybe she finally realizes how silly she sounds constantly calling him a lord?

Not likely.

Standing upright, the man nodded at Runner.

"There they are, my lord."

"Fantastic. Go get some breakfast and return to duty." Runner dismissed the man and looked to the pieces.

They were arranged in an circle around the city. Grinning, Runner couldn't help but shake his head.

Kastell would come under siege this day. In preparation for that attack the Human general had recalled their vanguard. They didn't seem to expect anyone to come from the direction of Highpass Crossing.

He'd been given two things: mission-critical information and the element of surprise. Like a gift. All wrapped up in a pretty bow.

"There it is then. We hit their supply depot as hard as we can. Take nothing and burn it all to the ground. Right as they move to assault the city," Runner supplied.

Moving his pieces into position, he lined his forces accordingly. They'd keep their back to Highpass in case they needed an exit. Using the terrain to their advantage, they would set their forces on a ridgeline.

Hit hard, burn all the supplies, retreat as soon as they move to engage us.

Gesturing to the map again, he indicated the far right flank of the encirclement.

"On our retreat we have our mounted forces do a flanking attack on this side." He tapped the south-east corner of the castle. "One pass only and then exit. Between these two actions it'll be enough to break the momentum of the attack."

"I'll prepare the orders, my lord," Isabelle said with a renewed fanaticism in her eyes. She slammed her fist to her chest, then turned and bolted out the door.

"Really wish she'd get over that," Runner muttered. He'd have to be bold here. So far this was a delaying tactic, nothing more.

Moving his mounted soldiers to the wings of his formation on the board, he toyed with a few ideas. Trying to think several steps ahead was the best way to create your own advantages.

"What, the pure Elf m-maiden's infatuation with a lord? Not likely. She sees you as a dem-m-mi-god, at the very least," Nadine replied.

"Fool." Runner grimaced, his fingers sliding his cavalry over into a gully.

If I can get them over here before the enemy reforms...

"We all see you as more than-n you do yourself, Runner."

"Fools, the lot of you," Runner muttered. In his head he planned on having the supply division mount up and stand in place as if they were the mounted troops.

People believe what they want to believe. If the enemy commander believes my cavalry is visible, he'll hopefully not look for them too hard.

His chin was yanked aside and he found himself looking into Nadine's green eyes.

She released his jaw as quickly as she had pulled on it.

"You will n-not say that again. Ever. Think about it. To Katarina, you gave her a direction, an identity, and self-worth. To Hannah, redemption, an ally, and trust. Thana gained a patron, an equal, and an opportunity to be herself. For myself, you saved me from death's door, you've never seen me as anything less than what I want, if not more. Isabelle has seen all this and more, and you mock her. You will n-not do so again or so help me..." Nadine snapped off the last words with a growl.

Runner processed all that. Then he slowly smiled. A chuckle escaped his lips.

She isn't wrong.

Runner felt like laughing at that. He had been pressing Srit towards sentience from the first moment he realized he needed her on his side. The best way to do that was enabling her to throw off her masters. He doubted she'd agree if she knew that.

"As you will it, Rabbit. I shall not mock her again. My word on it."

"Good. N-now, have you eaten?"

Roughly two hours and a forced breakfast later, his forces were in position.

His artillery battery was arrayed at the crest of the ridge. They were facing the opposing hill, which would give them plenty of time to fire into the ranks as they raced to the other side.

Next came his ranged classes. They were set up lower than the SO team but at a location that would give them a perfect arc to the space between the two hills.

Runner had given them instructions to fire at a forty-five-degree arc and believed that their missiles would go beyond their expected range. All had accepted his word as law and believed it.

Below his ranged forces was the infantry. They lined the point where the ascent became the most severe. Every mount that could be found had been put under someone from support. Every wagon had been deprived of its horse team.

These soldiers were scarecrows at best and were held in the reserve position. They'd look like cavalry though. His vanguard forces and actual cavalry weren't here.

He'd sent them off on their mission as soon as it was apparent that the siege would be commencing shortly.

Accompanying them as command officers went both Katarina and Hannah. Katarina would remain with the vanguard force. Hannah would depart with the cavalry to a separate location to await orders.

Hopefully the cavalry would be overlooked and the ruse believed. It would give him a trump card to use at his discretion. An impossibly strong flank attack that might even be able to be launched at the general himself.

He had given Katarina last-minute instructions to try and hold as long as possible to hopefully draw some of the forces along behind them. Into Runner's waiting arms.

Character boxes in his raid window began flashing as combat was joined. They were too far out to hear anything.

"They've started," Runner said.

"Oh? Indeed. So they have," Thana replied. She stood at his side, her staff held loosely in one arm as she surveyed the countryside.

"My lord, you can tell?"

Runner frowned and looked to Isabelle. He nearly made a comment but saw Nadine a foot beyond Isabelle. Swallowing the rebuke, he managed a partial smile.

"Think 'raid window' in your head. It'll pull up the relevant information. Everyone has a flashing border around their names. This means they're in combat. Therefore we can conclude they've attacked the supply depot. Which also means that the enemy forces have engaged the capital."

"Ah. Thank you for explaining, my lord."

"Please, Belle. Please, just call me Runner. If nothing else, I would love to hear my name spoken from your lips," Runner pleaded. Turning his head, he caught the eyes of his SO team commander and nodded at the man.

"Load!" shouted the man. Forty breeches opened and closed as the cannons were armed.

"Such lovely sentiments, dear heart," Thana purred at him softly.

"More flies with honey, my lady. I really am tired of her calling me that but I promised Rabbit I'd be nice," Runner whispered back at her.

"Where's my honey then?"

Runner coughed and looked around. No one seemed to be listening.

"Whenever, wherever, beloved chancellor. Now tease me no more—it's go time."

Thana harrumphed softly but didn't appear to actually be angry. If anything she looked pleased.

It was only an excuse of course. There was no immediate need. Time would pass as the plan carried itself along.

Runner found himself staring at the map as he watched the dots for Katarina and Hannah separate from each other on their way out. Hannah and the cavalry hit the flank and then wheeled away. Katarina and company were making a beeline back for the main force.

Runner held up his left hand above his head. Any and all noise died away around him as everyone took this as a ready signal. Up to this point they had suffered no losses, and he was keen to keep that number at zero.

Run on, Runner.

Over the opposing hill's crest came his vanguard. They came in a rough formation, but a formation nonetheless. He felt pride in their movements; they trusted his plan to keep them safe.

Runner spotted Katarina in the press of bodies. She kept at the rear of the pack, herding them onwards, glorious in her armor, her long legs pushing her onwards.

He felt his heart catch at the sight of her. If anything went wrong, she'd be the one to pay the price first.

They hadn't even reached the bottom of the hill when mounted soldiers came flowing over the horizon. Runner wanted to drop his hand to let death fly, but he had to hold it.

They needed more enemies to come over the top. He needed to inflict the maximum number of casualties here to soften up future fights. He also could only afford one salvo. It wouldn't do to reveal the reload rate.

Katarina could hold her own if it came down to it. Right?

I hope so.

Feeling like the time was right, that more than what had already crossed over would overwhelm his vanguard and infantry, he dropped his hand.

Cannons thumped, spells arced out, arrows flew, and death came. Literally.

Ernsta came down from above on her horse. She coasted by, high above the smoke, fire, lightning, ice, and other various spells going off in the midst of shrieking horses and soldiers.

Runner would have laughed at the theatrics of the situation if he didn't know it was for his and her benefit.

Terribly cliche though.

As she sailed over the maelstrom of fire, ice, and explosions, a stream of souls chased after her. They could only be souls as they looked like translucent human bodies. Wraiths that wiggled and twisted in the wind as they sped along behind her.

Then she was gone. As the smoke dissipated and cleared the field, all that remained were corpses. Every soldier on the far side of the artillery strike had already fled. Those who had already passed beyond the impact point had promptly stopped dead and watched.

Katarina had turned the entire vanguard force around and renewed the attack on them while they were distracted. The sergeant he'd Awakened led the force, screaming wordlessly at them as he engaged.

Thrusting out his hand, Runner called out.

"Healers and ranged squads forward, support the vanguard!" Runner thundered.

Every member from the groups he called sprinted forward.

"Belle, targets of opportunity. Go," he said, swatting her on the backside. She jumped at the impact of his hand and then sprinted forward into the fray. Runner leaned towards Thana and lowered his voice to a whisper.

"My lady, please prepare a contingent to speak with our Barbarian friends. Whoever you think would be helpful in a delegation. I trust you completely in your choices. No idea on timeline—assume in the next two days," he said.

"Already done. I'll send you the list later. I also have your wardrobe set aside. Don't argue. You'll wear what I want and like it," Thana replied, patting him firmly on the ass.

She'd obviously noticed his cavalier dismissal of Isabelle and felt he should be put in place. He hadn't intended anything by it, but it didn't excuse the action.

Rightly chastised, he smiled and nodded to her.

"I'll apologize when she comes back. Thank you, my beloved chancellor. I'd be lost without you. I'm afraid I act without thinking frequently."

"I know, dear heart. We're here to keep you safe. Even from yourself."

The support he'd sent had caught up to the vanguard and was working diligently to prevent casualties and eliminate the enemy.

Much of the battle devolved into pockets of fighting. Small groups working to get the attention of mounted warriors and bring them down effectively.

The lessons they had learned in the pass were paying off. For every person he had lost, he hoped to save ten with the experience those deaths taught.

That's what being a veteran meant. Using your past experience to leverage the present.

Katarina acted as the center, bolstering and holding the line while pulling more and more enemies in to fight her. Isabelle ranged far and wide on the edges. She utilized her bow for high-value targets. Losing officers tended to end battles much more swiftly.

Runner spotted what looked like the officer in charge in the rear. Apparently no one had told the poor fool that no one would be joining them.

The man brought order to the chaos on his side. Runner targeted him and lifted his left hand. Runner then started to channel the large variant of *Splatterhouse*. Mana bled from his bar rapidly, emptying it within seconds.

Downing a mana potion in a quick movement, Runner watched his mana bar. Blue-colored mana struggled to fill the empty bar as the spell drained it simultaneously.

Splitting his focus between his target and the mana bar, he watched both as best as he could. As the effects of the potion waned, his mana bar hit zero.

Activating the built-up spell, he felt his hand jerk backwards from the small back-blast it created. Cannoning out from his hand, the super-charged *Splatterhouse* shell shrieked through the air. Closing the distance in the blink of an eye, the projectile smashed into the officer.

Plasma scorched through the enemy ranks and blew upwards. As the fireball died, nothing remained of the officer or of those who stood around him.

Heh, I may be a one pump chump, but I can actually get it done in one.

As if their hands were tied to balloons, the remaining two hundred or so foes threw them up in surrender, offering no further resistance.

"I do not believe we discussed our position on prisoners," Thana whispered from beside him. He had been considering the very same problem.

Katarina decided the situation herself before Runner could get a messenger down there. She rounded up everyone who remained of the opposition and started the trek up the hill.

Sighing, Runner thought quickly. Few things would guarantee their prisoners remaining as such. After all, it wasn't as if they could disarm them without permission.

"Angel, time for some more theatrics," Runner muttered.

Catching the eye of one of his messengers nearby, Runner beckoned him over.

"Find me a clearing and get back to me. Large enough to host all of those prisoners. Also take into account that people will probably want to watch. Go," Runner said, then flicked his fingers at the man.

"Runner," Nadine hissed at him. "Unless you wanted him to spread that they could watch, I don-n't understand why you told him like that."

"No, that's my goal actually. Until the Barbarians are willing to sally forth, we'll need to keep their army on their heels. They easily outnumber us. Even with today's victory," Runner affirmed.

Searching for the sergeant in the crowd of returning soldiers, Runner scanned faces and nameplates. After finding him near the rear of the mob, he moved to intercept him.

"I'll be right back. If the messenger returns before I do, start making your way to wherever he found. I'll follow your marker," Runner called over his shoulder.

He worked his way to where the column passed into the camp, then eased himself to one side to bide his time as they marched by.

Runner slid up to the sergeant at the tail end of the line of weary men and women. Deliberately he cleared his throat to give the man a chance to notice him.

Flinching, the man turned his eyes towards Runner and then ducked his head.

"Ah, my lord Runner. My apologies, I didn't see you approach," said the startled sergeant.

"Come with me. I'd like to speak with you. I never caught your name," Runner said by means of opening the conversation.

"Stefan, Stefan Rune, my lord."

"I'm not your lord. You'll address me as Runner or not at all. Stefan, I'm going to have you play a part in this war. I tell you this now so you're not surprised as I reward you in advance. It wouldn't do to have you dying before I can push you into the worldview," Runner said with an easy smile. He guided Stefan back towards where Runner had started from.

"My lo—" Runner pierced Stefan with a glare, daring him to finish the word. "Runner. I wouldn't begin to presume what your need of me is but it wouldn't warran—"

Runner interrupted him as they passed where he'd left Thana and Nadine.

"You can stop right there. Isn't what you're doing right now. Well, not completely," Runner rotated in position to see if he could spot his party. Giving up on it after a second he started moving towards the map marker for Nadine.

"It's more about what you'll be doing in the future. Which is killing a lot of Humans. I need you doing that with style, really. Style and perhaps with a name as your war cry instead of, well, whatever it was you were yelling."

"I was just yelling, Lor-Runner," explained Stefan.

"That makes it easy then. Any thoughts on a name to yell? Not mine. Nor your king's. Who rules over a battlefield? Who in fact did you see watching over you today? Don't answer me, think on it. Perhaps a name will come to you."

Runner ended up having to force his way through a press of bodies. Making sure to drag Stefan with him, he pushed his way through and popped out into an open field.

Up front and center stood his party, minus Hannah, and arrayed out behind them were the prisoners. Squaring his shoulders, Runner walked heavily towards those who'd surrendered.

Working his charisma, he pushed on the idea that he radiated the promise of a swift death. That he wasn't one to be crossed unless you didn't value your life.

Focusing his attention on the woman at the head of the prisoners, he kept moving in a straight line for her. She looked like any other Natural Human. Brown hair, brown eyes, attractive, athletic. Like every other on the server. Beautiful was the new "cute" here.

Locking his eyes to hers, he stared into her. Weighed her. Judged her and found her wanting.

Stopping a pace from her, he said nothing. Seconds ticked by and still he was silent. Perhaps thirty seconds slid by on the clock before he finally moved again.

Turning, he put his back to the enemy and took several steps from her before rounding to address the group as a whole.

"You've surrendered your lives to me. By the grace of Ernsta you may yet live through this day. You have one avenue open to you that will result in your continued existence. Swear to Ernsta that your service is at an end, that you will offer no aid in any way going forward to the Human army in this war, that you surrender your soul upon the breach of this compact. After you swear, you will be released on your own recognizance."

Runner waited a beat before continuing.

"Understand, should you break this covenant, Ernsta will collect your soul and do with it as she pleases. She could use it as flooring for her horse's stall, to empower her own strength, or maybe shred it up and use it as a topping for tomorrow's lunch. Doesn't matter, it's hers.

"Your alternative is death. Now. I empower this man to act as the agent of death for you and execute you swiftly," Runner said, gesturing towards Stefan.

"Ernsta, are you ready to witness their oaths?"

"I am," boomed Ernsta's voice from above.

"Let's begin. You," Runner said, pointing at the closest prisoner. Stepping forward, he grabbed the man by the breastplate and forced him to his knees. Staring down into the horror-stricken face of the prisoner, Runner loomed over him. "Swear or die."

"I swear! I swear, Breaker, I swear!" bleated the man.

Rolling his eyes with a grunt Runner manhandled the soldier to his feet and shoved him aside. Runner moved to the woman he had stood in front of first for the next oath.

Seemingly released to his freedom, the prisoner who swore his oath collapsed to his knees. He hung his head and sobbed deeply.

So much for the soldiery of the Human kingdom.

Grabbing the woman by the breastplate, Runner smiled cruelly. Shoving her to her knees with a clank, he leaned over the top of her.

"Swear or die."

And so the hour went, Runner collecting each prisoner's oath. Stefan matched him pace for pace, his two-handed blade slung over his shoulder in a relaxed way.

No one refused. Ernsta held contract over them all by the end. As promised, they were briefly interrogated for information and then released. They were dispersed and told to do as they felt best.

Most went scuttling back to their own encampment. Some went south, clearly quitting the field entirely. A handful remained in Runner's camp.

Considering they wouldn't be able to provide intelligence to the enemy or harm his camp in any way, Runner cared little. They were officially noncombatants.

"I feared they would refuse. You'd make me an executioner as part of your plans?" asked Stefan hotly.

"No one was going to refuse. They all saw Ernsta riding over them during the initial attack. She has a keen interest in this war and its outcome. And no, my goal isn't to have you as an executioner," Runner replied. They had retired to the command tent. Runner was currently in the process of updating the map with new information gotten from the prisoners before they were released.

"Is that who you wou—"

"Stop. I cannot answer that. Your question is your own answer," Runner interrupted. Isabelle happened to enter the tent at that very moment, followed by Thana, Katarina, and Nadine.

"Perfect timing." Runner stood and moved to Isabelle. Bowing deeply at the waist, he took a breath. "First, I apologize, Belle. I dismissed you in an inappropriate way. I must ask your forgiveness," Runner apologized. In retrospect, it really hadn't been the best to send her off with a slap on the ass.

"No apology necessary, my lord. Though I will add this to the favor you already owe me. That's now two," said the Elf. Standing upright, he found she was grinning from pointed ear to pointed ear at him.

"Ah, so be it. I agree. I do have an actual quartermaster request of you though. Please outfit Stefan here in whatever you can that will keep him healthy and provide him the ability to destroy others."

"Alright. Stefan, is it? With me, please."

Moving back out the way she came in, Isabelle wasted no time at all. Stefan had to jog a few paces to catch up with her hasty departure.

"Thank you, Master Runner. I know you did not do it with poor intentions but that poor Elf is still discovering her world, let alone herself," Thana remarked in passing. Walking by him, she pressed a kiss to his cheek and patted him on the shoulder as she made her way to the map.

"Oh. Where's mine then?" demanded Katarina.

"Which, a kiss from me or a pat on the bottom from Runner?"

"The latter."

"Katarin-na!"

"What? We're adults. Consenting adults. What are you, a child?"

"N-no. But, I don't wan-nt to watch that."

"I didn't ask. Thana would watch."

"I would. Now, Master Runner," Thana called, getting the confused man's attention, "I assume your plan is that those you released would return back to their base camp and give sketchy, vague, and very unhelpful information. Should one actually break their word then they would drop dead in the middle of their own army. Is that about it?"

Runner felt his brain jump the tracks from sex to war. Which was becoming more and more difficult lately. It'd been a very long time since he'd actually bedded a woman, and lying next to Katarina and Thana night after night didn't help matters.

"Correct. Best-case scenario a handful die in front of everyone as they try to talk about what happened here outside of the most general terms. Angel gets a power boost, we get our theatrics, and they get absolutely nothing."

He expected some type of response from Ernsta but received none. Maybe he was losing his touch after all.

"Does Srit agree with your assessment? I wish I could speak with her. Actually, speaking of that. She sent me an e-mail earlier with some questions. If you've made a login for her, why hasn't she logged into the game properly? I assume she could log in just like any other entity that exists outside the server," Thana said, moving the cavalry where Hannah was currently located back and forth.

Runner was floored. He hadn't even considered it really. Technically, her ability to log in was directly tied in to her profile. Which he made for her himself. By all rights she could easily log in.

Well, if she were real. Wait. Could she? Technically she can access any other system program as if she were real. It's not as if she'd need any hardware.

Technically speaking, everyone here could actually log in again with another character if he provided them with a virtual-reality setup.

"That's...that's actually a really good question. I—"

I'm creating my character now.

"Ah. It seems Srit agrees and is creating her character now," Runner said with a concerned edge to his voice.

I'm going to make my avatar look like Thana.

"Er, I agree Thana is very beautiful but perhaps you should create an avatar that represents you? Maybe take a comprehensive view of many faces and decide what you like and don't like? Perhaps catalog what you like about Thana's face?"

Thana looked shocked at that little exchange. Everyone in the tent was staring at him now.

Yes, that's a good idea. I'll do that. I'm done. I'm going to make my way to you.

With the speed that she'd completed the task, Runner could imagine she had gone from idling her resources to ninety-nine percent in a heartbeat.

Runner blew out a breath and looked around the room with a sheepish smile.

"So, it looks like we'll be having Srit joining us. Uhm, we should probably start collecting gear and supplies for her."

Secretly he held a fear in his heart that he couldn't speak aloud. Srit had apparently mastered the complete usage of contractions. On top of that, she was now logging in to an environment she could interact with directly.

Good thing I was aiming for sentience, because whether I like it or not, it's coming.

Chapter 11 - Best Laid Plans -

"They're coming," announced Stefan flatly.

"Of course. I'd be disappointed if they didn't stop over. Should always greet the neighbors when moving in to a new area, Sarge," Runner agreed. Sitting cross-legged on the ground, he had his chin resting in the palm of his hand.

A moderately sized force marched its way to his own troops. It wasn't quite a one-to-one ratio. Pretty close though. It had all the appearances of a true attack.

Except he actually knew the enemy numbers. And those who were now on approach looked only lightly armed and armored. Those who could flee quickly should the attack fail and wouldn't be missed if they couldn't retreat.

Reserves, really.

"Sarge?"

"Yep, Sarge. You were a sergeant. Now it's your name. People I give a crap about or feel are important get new names. Be thankful I put a modicum of thought into it. I could very well have named you Cuddles McSofty," Runner explained.

"You seem unconcerned about the battle."

"Indeed. I am. This will probably be a light touch. Nothing more than those they're willing to lose. Followed by a little heavier one later, I imagine. Could be wrong. Probably not."

And honestly, this is probably the one thing I can truly solve right now. It has an answer. Destroy them. Everything else requires an answer I don't have.

He curbed his thoughts before they ran him straight back into a depressing spiral. Reminding himself of the futility of his current situation didn't help at all.

That wasn't quite true actually. The medical server was on the last system update. It would be up and running by tomorrow morning. Now all that he needed was the password and he could start transferring people over to a normal medical server.

Everyone would be safe.

Providing they don't kill me before I can save them. Lousy ingrates. Kill a few people to save thousands and you're a murderer.

Though he did have a concern or two about the actual system procedure. The manual seemed to suggest the actual process would be simple enough that it would only take a query and a batch request. Transfer the data and boom. But nothing that simple ever worked out exactly as planned.

Runner forced his mind out of that line of thought and back to the task at hand.

Battle. War. Death.

They were watching from the ridge of the hill that they had fired on earlier. They weren't able to hide the destruction done to the grounds and the large number of bodies, so the encampment had been forced forward. It would serve his purposes. They were more easily seen from here and there wouldn't be any question as to what the enemy general could see either.

Based on the information they gleaned from the interviews, the general was a woman, extremely intelligent, and happened to be a caster.

Her forces were only a level or two higher than his own. The number of her troops was the problem. She had twice as many as he did at the very least.

"You sound so certain," Stefan grunted. Outfitted in new gear, the once sergeant now looked more the part of a full knight. Outfitted in heavy Basic Plate and given a new two-handed Great Sword, he cast a striking figure. Didn't hurt that they'd dyed everything black.

"It's what I would do in her position. I have to assume she's as smart as I am, or smarter. Probably smarter," Runner said. Glancing around, he made sure no one was around them. The rest of his party had departed to prepare for Srit's arrival.

"Your plan is to…fight them? Here and now?"

"No. Actually, yes. They're going to probe to see what surprises they can spring. What mysteries they can solve. After a few skirmishes, and the fact that I don't use the cannons or magic, they'll assume whatever it was I did was a onetime thing or not easily used. At some point, when they launch a real attack, they'll push hard. Use their numbers to their advantage. And when they do, we'll have our center start to fall back like they're buckling." Runner ripped a handful of grass out of the ground with his left hand and tossed it in the air.

He watched the grass flutter in the wind as he thought about the upcoming few days.

"The trick is making it look believable without making the troops actually flee. That and honestly whatever plans I make I have to assume will fail. No plan ever survives contact with the enemy. We may never even get the chance to try and encircle them. For all I know we're being encircled right now."

"I see. Do you believe a direct contest between the bulk of both forces will occur today?"

"Possible, unlikely. Really depends on how aggressive the general is going to be. She could be passive and play for time and this could carry into tomorrow. Though I doubt that it'll go beyond tomorrow before she engages. The longer we have her facing us, the more she'll get worried about the Barbarians sallying out to kick their side in. Let us hope the Barbarians figure it out and join us, no?"

A horn sounded from the infantry line down below them as each side began the final preparations before the clash.

"That's your cue, Sarge. Do what you need to do. Don't die," Runner said, gesturing at the enemy soldiers with his left hand.

Stefan nodded to Runner and moved off to take his place with the line.

With a huff, Runner lay down in the grass. Turning his head to the side, he watched as the two lines met each other. Line warfare wasn't particularly successful when people could take multiple hits.

He had a number of dirty tricks he could employ but he held off on that. They were one time only tricks and he'd need them later.

There wasn't much for him to do now. Everyone had their orders.

A furry rodent scampered his way through the grass. Popping into clear view was a squirrel. This one was level six.

"Goodness. You guys are everywhere. Bigger too. I don't think I have any blueberries but maybe…" Runner said, trailing off at the end.

Lifting his hand from the grass, he popped open the inventory window. Doing a quick scan of his foraging, he found a strawberry food item.

"Oh, lucky you. Your little brothers only got blueberries." Runner proffered a strawberry in his fingers. He didn't really feel like exerting enough energy to throw it.

Moving in close, the squirrel took the strawberry from his fingers and began eating it.

"Brave little shit, aren't you? Braver than me at least."

Runner slid another strawberry out and held it up with his fingertips. Pulling it from his fingers, the squirrel took it and then bolted away.

Runner was grateful for the momentary distraction. Today was a bloody day.

He lay there alone with his thoughts. He soaked up the sun's warm rays as the grass in turn soaked up the blood of his soldiers.

The battle proceeded much as he'd predicted to Stefan.

Engage, probe, retreat. It took little more than an hour. Runner lost a handful and the opposing side lost double. A small consolation to those who lost their lives.

The second, third, and fourth such encounters merely reaffirmed his earlier belief as to the main goal of the attacks. They lasted longer and the period between them stretched out but they were the same.

Engage, probe, retreat.

His opponent was very wary of whatever had happened to her troops in the initial encounter.

Several times she'd used cloaked units to harass messengers and those found outside of the encampment. She gained nothing he wasn't willing to let her have.

He did regret the butcher's bill he had to pay for giving her poor intel.

He had to respect her. She did everything she could to ferret out whatever tricks he had up his sleeve. Up to the point of even risking a day's delay to make sure that he wouldn't be able to decimate her forces.

Early in the evening the enemy force turned and left the field. They left their dead behind as well as whatever hope they had of successfully completing the siege of Kastell today.

Runner's scouts returned to confirm reports that the enemy had indeed returned to their blankets and bedrolls.

Throughout the day he noticed his party members rummaging through gear and inventories and bartering with others. Srit hadn't yet made her entrance, but he didn't doubt it would be sooner rather than later.

When she did make herself known it was now apparent the ladies would make her feel welcome and prepare her for the world.

He wasn't sure if that was good or bad. Maybe both.

Probably both.

Yep.

6:08 am Sovereign Earth time
11/16/43

Runner was roused from his sleep when Isabelle pinged him with her private signal. They'd set her up as an assistant Raid Leader so she could make personal, group, and raid pings.

No one could enter his personal campsite without his permission. Which meant if he was sleeping no one could enter except a player. Since there were no players in his forces, it made the pings a necessity.

In addition to that, Isabelle had taken it upon herself to sleep at the perimeter and act as a doorbell. She filtered out useless information from the worthwhile. He hadn't asked it of her, though he now greatly appreciated having it filter through someone.

Runner removed Thana's arm from around his torso, stepped lightly out of his bedroll, and crept over to Isabelle.

She sat with her blankets pulled up to her chin. Runner could only assume she was still dressed for bed. Hopefully whatever the situation was could be solved relatively quickly.

That or it was so important it couldn't wait.

"What's up, Belle?" Runner whispered. He hoped it was an easy situation rather than the worst-case scenario. Squatting down next to her bedroll, he gave her an easy smile.

"Enemy camp is waking up after a messenger came in. The scouts missed his approach and only noticed when the person unstealthed in front of the general's tent. A few of the scouts reported that there has also been no movement from the castle," Isabelle outlined for him. She held her blankets close to her shoulders.

"Right, then," Runner said, blowing out a breath. Looking into the distance, he combed his left hand through his hair. "We'll assume this is the push to worry about and that we'll get no help from the capital. Cowards."

Runner grumbled to himself as an ill temper snuck into his morning. Apparently the Barbarian king planned to see Runner spend his own forces before risking his.

It wasn't a bad tactic to ensure his country's safety. Though it was a guaranteed way to alienate those who'd come to his aid. That or squander their support as they simply left him to his fate.

He couldn't do that though. Pressing ever onwards happened to be his only option. He was also pretty good at it.

"Get a messenger off to Hannah. Use a stealthed one. I know we don't have as many but this is one of those things that needs to be kept a secret as long as we can. Get yourself some breakfast. I'll get the morning call going," Runner said with a grin. Patting her lightly on the shoulder, he left her to her privacy.

Rubbing at his chin, he made his way to the center of the camp.

A messenger. Barbarian king offering terms? Maybe.

Grunting, he veered off from his original route. Now making his way over to Stefan's tent, he felt it would be good to have him up and moving. Runner was getting itchy. Nervous. Paranoid.

King Vasilios offering terms? No. Brighteyes would have warned me. That and it would endanger a chunk of his troops here.

Reaching the simple tent that Stefan had been given, he hesitated. Making his choice, he leaned down and lightly shook Stefan awake.

"My friend, it begins. Today is a good day to die. Come, before your place is taken," Runner said ominously.

"Huh? What? What? Ah," Stefan mumbled, muttering to himself. Sullen and sleepy eyes glared at Runner as the mists of dreams fell from Stefan's visage.

"Pack it in, Sarge. Enemy is already on the move after getting a message. I suspect problems. Which means we get to put our detective hats on. I'll be with the SO teams."

Runner threw his hand up in a negligent wave as he left Stefan lying there. Playing his artillery card this early was something he was loathe to do.

Rather play the card than end up having no opportunity later to do so. Sandbagging only goes so far.

Standing in the specially designated sleeping area of the SO, he clapped his hands loudly together twice.

"Asses and elbows, people. We need to get you all primed, set up, loaded, and ready in the next fifteen. Plan for an extended engagement with two salvos and then fire at will." Runner badgered a few of the slower moving members while he waited for Stefan.

Arriving in his armor, he looked the part of an errant knight. Fresh faced and bright eyed, he looked eager and annoyed at the same time.

"Good timing. Come, we need to change the location of this battle. We'll have to draw them into the flatter areas further south. We'll be engaging with our cannons, so the longer they have to walk into it or out of it, the better," Runner said while spinning on his heel.

"I thought you said you were holding those in reserve."

"I was. I can't let them sit idle, however. I believe we're in for a surprise today one way or another. Something I didn't account for. Don't think the Barbarians are joining us either. They seem content to hide behind their walls," Runner said disgustedly.

Sprinting through the grass came a squirrel. Truly it was the largest one he'd seen yet.

Level ten, goodness.

Leaping from the grass rather than stopping, it slapped into Runner's leather-clad midsection.

"Oof. Monster. Get off," Runner complained, trying to grab the nearly cat sized thing as it crawled up his front.

"The hell is that?" Stefan distrustfully asked.

"A big old fat rat. Hey! Sto—"

Clambering around to his back, it got out of his reach. Making it to Runner's shoulder it perched itself there and sunk its little clawed fingers into the pauldron.

"Fine. Sit there. Little shit," Runner grumped. Directly in contradiction to his angry words, he had already retrieved a strawberry from his inventory and passed it to the creature.

Resuming his walk, he marched towards the area south of his encampment. It was flatter and would allow him more time to fire his cannons. He could hear the little furry tree climber gnawing at the strawberry on his shoulder.

"Why is it here?"

"What, this thing? I dunno. Probably 'cause I feed them. Free stuff always goes fast. I keep finding these buggers since we entered Sunless territory. I had no idea they were so widespread." Runner passed the critter another strawberry.

"They're not, my lord," Isabelle said as she fell in beside him. "In fact I've never heard of one outside of Shade's Rest."

"Want this one? All yours. I find them everywhere. Though this one is definitely the biggest," Runner offered. Reaching up with his right hand, he idly petted its furry head. "Belle, I'm moving the conflict over here. It'll give us more time to fire on them either on approach or during retreat."

"I see. You fear the worst then," Isabelle said. She hadn't really phrased it as a question.

"I fear the possibility of the worst. Nearly the same but paranoia does that to you."

He stopped at the top of a small rise The area in front of him rolled a bit here and there but it was significantly flatter than the area they'd originally planned on.

"Yeah. This," Runner confirmed, waving his left hand out at the area. "Here I shall collect my harvest. My bloody crop."

Runner closed his eyes with a grimace and rubbed the space between his eyes with his fingertips.

"Runner?"

"My lord?"

"Mm? I'm fine," Runner said halfheartedly. Pulling his hand from his brow, he gestured at the far fields. "Set the line over there." He moved his fingers up to a slight rise beyond that area. "SO teams there with our ranged forces in front of them. Front line and second line will be tanks with shields. Alternate as needed and work on the buddy system. Third and fourth lines are reach weapons. Spears, pikes, halberds. Support crews in the next line with tanks targeted."

Frowning, he tilted his head, trying to imagine the field in mid combat.

"Put whoever we can otherwise on the mounts and stick them on the flanks. We'll not use them but hopefully they'll prove to be a deterrent. Hopefully."

"I sent the messenger as you requested, my lord."

"Wait, why does she call you that and I have to call you Runner?"

"Because Belle has selective hearing. You tell her her hair looks great today, she'll thank you. Tell her she has an amazing figure and she'll blush. Explain how she's a beautiful Elf and she'll dig for more compliments. Ask her to use your first name, deaf as a post."

"Thank you, my lord," Isabelle said sweetly. She deliberately grabbed a lock of her hair and twirled it around a finger and crossed her eyes at him. Then promptly stuck her tongue out at him.

"See?" Runner growled and offered the last of his strawberries to his passenger.

"My new dilemma. How many cards do I play in the upcoming fight? She could very well try to end it all today. The general, that is. Before the Barbarians decide to help. If ever," Runner said, running a finger back and forth over the squirrel's head.

"I believe if Hannah were here she would call you a vulgar name, maybe even throw in some anatomy, and tell you to unleash hell, my lord."

Stefan frowned, as if realizing he hadn't seen Hannah in a while.

"Ha!" Runner grinned at that.

"She would, you're right, Belle. Screw it. Please have the SO supply wagon brought up here. I need to start putting together my tank. It's the only thing I can probably use today other than the cannons."

"Tank, my lord?"

"What's a tank?"

Smirking, Runner contemplated his answer for a few seconds. Instead of answering immediately, he started to pull up a blank build plan to construct said vehicle.

"Think of an armored enclosed wagon that can host troops and weaponry," he explained after the window opened.

Stefan grunted and turned from Runner back towards the camp.

Isabelle tilted her head and then sat down in the grass to watch him work.

Time slipped by as Runner busied himself with his tank. At some point the medical server chimed its successful boot up and readiness. Runner had no time for it right now though.

Eventually his forces managed to move the entire camp and get themselves in position. They weren't in an ideal position to camp that night, but were in a better position for the day's battle.

Won't need to sleep if you're dead.

Thinking about those who sought his end, Runner looked to the horizon line. Distantly he could see the enemy forces moving around on the plain. They were arranging themselves based on what they could see.

Runner put his attention back to his "tank."

It wasn't a tank really. Not the twentieth and twenty-first century definition of the word at least. More like an armored car, really.

Big ol' box, really. Function over form. Right, Boxy?

Runner had measured it at twelve feet in length, eight feet wide, and ten feet tall. Even a generous description would probably leave it as a giant, ugly, wooden box. Fitted with an iron wedge-shaped plow on the front, it really was a hideous thing.

It sported large wooden wheels and wagon frames he'd cannibalized from his support teams. There were four wheels in the front and six in the back. Which only added to the depth of the "ugly" of it.

The first four feet of the monstrosity was where he'd set up the "engine" that would propel this thing. He had settled on a cab-over design that would keep driver safe. The cockpit sat much higher so the driver would be able to look down through slits.

As it was wooden, he had immediately thrown out any type of propulsion that required combustion or fire.

Instead he'd rigged up a water-based piston system using gears and a hefty amount of item enchantment.

He'd previously had many deep in the night conversations with Srit. They'd hashed out everything about it, but he had hoped to wait for better materials to try building one.

Best laid plans and all that.

Runner sighed and turned to the forty-some-odd Sunless members of the aristocracy that he had personally requested. Thana stood to one side with her fingers moving in midair.

Probably sudoku again.

"Good morning, fair ladies of Shade's Rest. I have need of you. Please raise your hand if you have a spell that has a targeted area of effect. An example of a qualifying spell would be *Chain Lightning*," Runner said.

More than eighty percent of the women raised their hands.

"Okay, for those who raised their hands, please keep your hand raised if your spell is based in anything other than fire."

A number of hands dropped, leaving twelve with their hands still raised.

"Ah, I'm relieved. Everyone who doesn't have your hand up, please report to the artillery officer. He has your formation orders and directions," Runner said with a smile and waited for them to depart.

Gesturing towards the beautiful gaggle of Sunless nobles, Runner moved over to Boxy. Peering inside the open rear door, he confirmed all was as it should be.

"Ladies, the assignment is this. We'll be driving this wagon straight into the enemy formation." Slapping his hand to the thick wooden boards, he continued. "We'll then proceed to launch attacks through the slits into our foes. The floor of the vehicle is elevated and the slits will be placed in such a way that you'll be looking down on our foes. This should aid in keeping you safe since their inability to target you will force them to get in close. Right in your view port.

"That being said, two of you will not be joining us on this adventure and will rejoin the others. Any volunteers to return to the line?"

A few hands went up. Runner immediately dismissed the closest two. After they left, he gestured to the interior.

"After you all, of course."

Moving in one by one, they mounted the steps and trooped in.

"An interesting contraption. I would ask where you got the materials. Let alone how it works but I fear the explanation would take more time than we have, Master Runner."

Thana had stepped up beside him. Giving her a smile, he bobbed his head in agreement.

"Suffice it to say, it's a piston-driven system utilizing a water spell. The pistons are aligned and paired in such a way that each set of wheels will be equally powered. It has to be driven by someone who can utilize magical items," Runner said, placing his hand on her lower back. Easing her forward with gentle pressure, he corralled her into the interior of Boxy. "It has five speeds. The two lowest speeds will not overtax the water enchantment spells and they'll refill faster than they're being used. Third gear will use them as fast as they come up. Fourth and fifth will outpace the coold—"

Runner came to an abrupt stop in his explanation as noticed Isabelle heading in their direction.

She had broken free of the line and was jogging towards him. Runner tried not to admire the way she moved. Elves really did have a certain grace to them. The long legs, the blonde hair in the wind, the—

Already have enough women troubles, Runner! Idiot. King of fools.

Grunting, he placed his left hand on the side of the entry door and waited.

Coming to a sliding halt in front of him, Isabelle threw him a smile.

Isabelle bowed her head to him. "My lord."

"Belle."

"Per your orders, Katarina holds the center and reports it ready. Stefan is a bit too far forward by my own reckoning but holds the left. By the honor you've bestowed on me, I hold the right flank," Isabelle murmured, clearly fighting her own excitement.

"Excellent. Thank you, Belle," he affirmed, smiling at her. He meant it, too. Between her and Katarina, he didn't feel like the line would be an issue. "Please work closely with everyone. I trust you to make the right choices. Do you need anything? Can I give or get you anything?"

"No, my lord. You've given me more than I deserve."

Scoffing, Runner shook his head at her. "Run along then, Belle, you have my thanks."

With a bright grin and a nod, she spun away from him, graceful as a dancer. As soon as she got a few paces from him, he clambered up into Boxy.

Reaching behind, he clasped the holding bracket for the door and pulled it inwards. He dropped the bar into place, then latched everything shut. There was no way to lock the thing unless you were in it.

Catching Thana's eyes, he made an apologetic gesture with his hand.

"Right, then. Your question. Water-driven piston system. As to materials, I borrowed them. King Vasilios sent them along with his crafters."

"I see. What am I to do on this venture then?"

"You'll be guiding our brave nobility in this fight. I'll be steering. Everyone who could pilot this is on the SO teams." Runner patted Thana once on the shoulder and moved to take his seat at the front.

"I'd like a more detailed analysis and report of this later, dear heart. This seems convenient and I can see many practical applications of it."

"Yes, beloved," Runner responded immediately, with only a hint of a teasing tone.

"Good, thank you."

Runner grinned and rolled his eyes but couldn't help but feel lighthearted. Dropping into the pilot seat, he checked the levers. Giving the speed shifter a waggle, he found all was set.

"Brake engaged...water spells are primed...cannon ready. Now, we wait and look like nothing more than a really disastrously made hut. Hey," Runner said, turning around in his chair. Twenty-two dark eyes riveted to him after his sudden call. "Wanna play a game or something while we wait?"

"Runner, dear heart?"

"Yep?"

"Please focus on your part of the battle. We'll be preparing back here," Thana said with a smile, politely shooting him down.

"Kay. Only 'cause I love your smile though."

Runner blew out his cheeks as he faced his cockpit controls again. Leaning forward and looking out the viewing port, he watched in silence. On came his foe and her army.

Slowly. Inexorably. Deliberately.

She had slowed down drastically when she realized Runner had moved his entire encampment to meet her on an open field. He could only imagine it made little sense to her. She probably had a very good idea of his numbers and the disposition of his army.

There was no possible way to completely shut out her spies and scouts. Instead he assumed she had full knowledge of numbers and complement.

Makes everything easier when you assume they already know everything. Yay, paranoia.

Runner shook himself from his daydreaming as the enemy began coming at them at a fast trot.

"That's new," Runner spit out. Leaning into the vision slits that surrounded the cockpit, he checked everyone's position.

Everyone where they should be.

Frowning, Runner cycled through his log messages, finding nothing wrong there either. His paranoia began to escalate as the enemy closed the distance.

Clumsily he slapped at the raid window to bring it to the forefront and then sat there.

Mouth hanging open, Runner felt the ground come out from underneath him. Hannah and her entire force had flashing player tiles.

They were in combat.

"Hanners is engaged with an enemy. I...I can only assume our flankers were flanked, or they flanked their flankers. I need to..." Runner said, starting to rise from his seat. Then he realized he couldn't leave. They needed him here. Thana, Katarina, Nadine, and Isabelle all needed him here.

Sitting back down in his chair, he pressed his left hand over his mouth. Gritting his teeth, he swallowed as the situation started to unravel rapidly around him.

Chapter 12 - Bloodbath -

Runner gripped the steering wheel in both hands. Somehow he managed to take slow and even breaths despite his mind being a frenzy of activity.

No plan survives first contact with the enemy. You said it yourself.

"Do you trust Hannah?" Thana's voice whispered against his ear.

She was so close her lips had brushed against his earlobe.

Shaken from his whirling thoughts, Runner latched to that question. He did. Explicitly.

"Of course," he whispered, his voice trembling.

"Then have faith in her. She will do what she believes to be best. I do not profess to see eye to eye with her as often as I would like, but I believe in her." Thana pressed her lips to his cheek and then drew back from him.

She was right of course. She almost always was. That was the problem with enjoying the company of people smarter than you.

Letting out a shaky breath, Runner could only nod his head. The battle had begun without them.

Each line beat at the other, attempting to draw them in close to striking range of the damage dealers. This tug-of-war would continue until losses started to go up. Losses that Runner couldn't afford. Couldn't afford and had to prevent.

That was his duty as a good leader. Spend their lives, yes. But spend them well and efficiently.

With a flick of a hand Runner disengaged the stationary brakes. It wasn't quite time to engage. In fact, his goal wasn't even the line or the flank of the line.

Enemy forces stretched out deeply, glinting in the early morning sun. It seemed like they were endless and tightly packed.

All the better.

Runner pulled up the quick slot bars for his pings. Selecting Nadine, he pinged her with the attack command.

A second after he issued the command the sound of cannons could be heard. They went off like a barely heard thrum over the din of weapons connecting with armor and shields.

Then the center of the enemy force exploded. There really was no other way to describe it.

Exploded.

Then Ernsta came down from above. Her scythe slid out leisurely at her side and lazily sliced forward. Translucent souls flooded up to her and disappeared into the wicked blade.

As she began her ascent back to the heavens, her head whipped around and she scoured the crowd below her. Following her line of sight, Runner found Stefan in the enemy lines, swinging his great black blade in giant arcs.

Runner could only guess that Stefan had taken his advice and decided on whose name to yell. Her attention was his and his alone.

Stefan left a path of destruction behind him. The flank he led was hard-pressed to catch up to his advance.

"Time for us to go," Runner muttered. Taking one last look at Ernsta, he felt a glimmer of hope. Ernsta had circled around again and hovered high above Stefan.

"Hold on, ladies, it's showtime," Runner warned. Dropping the shifter into the third speed setting, he sent Boxy lurching forward, the wheels throwing up grass and dirt.

Spinning wildly, the wheels caught and then Boxy shot forward.

"Boxy needs a coat of red paint!" Runner screamed, leaning forward over his controls. A wild grin spread over his face as he sped onwards.

Frustration, anger, fear, and hate boiled out of him. Such a joy it was to try to save fools who wanted him dead. Save idiots who wouldn't help him help them save themselves. Spending his own sanity like fucking currency for the benefit of others.

Breathing hard, heart pounding, and fingers clenched on the steering wheel, he saw a chance to really blow off some steam.

Angling himself to the back corner of the enemy formation, he called over his shoulder. "Right side, everyone line up and blast the fuckers! Light 'em up!"

He pushed the gear up to the fourth position, and Boxy's pistons hammered at the gear train as she barreled forward.

Wonder how high they'll bounce? I'll ask Srit later. Maybe she'll be able to pull the data.

Then Runner's view port filled with enemy bodies soaring through the air as the cow catcher launched men and women upwards into the sky. Bodies slammed into the front and sides of Boxy and blew backwards as they tumbled over the reinforced wood.

Runner screamed at them even as they died. Obscenities and curses spewed from his lips like steam from a broken radiator. Targeting randomly, he cast *Scott* into the forces ahead of him.

Fear in such a close-packed group only created confusion as they tried to bolt in every direction.

Booms of elemental spells from behind him overshadowed the crunch and thud of bodies being bowled over.

Bursting free on the other side, Runner shifted the speed down to the second gear. Spinning the wheel to the right, he began driving along the rear of the enemy's forces.

As his screams faded, Runner sat panting. He rubbed at his eyes in a futile attempt to clear his vision. Little black dots spun and swam crazily through his sight.

To his right, his cannons continued to fire into the massed enemy center. Those in the middle tried to push backwards, only to be pushed forward by those attempting to escape Boxy and his team's spells.

The panic wouldn't last. Professional soldiers adapted and fairly quickly. It didn't have to last that long, really. Just long enough to inflict solid casualties and create confusion before they could pull back and rethink their strategy.

Reaching the midway point, Runner pulled Boxy to the left and straightened her course out. They were facing the general's vantage now. He'd marked the location before the battle had even started. She hadn't exactly been stealthy about it.

He could even see her standing atop her platform. Young, attractive, dressed in a uniform that hid any figure she had. Blonde hair chopped short was the only detail he could make out beyond that. He could see her watching him. She was transfixed by Runner's approach.

Training the tip of the plow on the general, Runner felt his heart speed up even further, if that was even possible at this point.

He let Boxy coast along at second gear for a few more seconds to help recharge her spell-driven engine. Then he threw the monster into fifth.

The roar of Boxy's engine could be heard as she guzzled her magical fuel.

Runner slapped his hand down on the cannon's trigger while screaming incoherently. It thumped out a shell that ripped through the air.

Underestimating his speed and the approach, Runner overshot the trajectory. The general's tent behind the platform blew up and turned into a fireball. Runner could only hope it took out anyone inside. That and it had actually contained people.

Reacting faster than he would have given her credit for, she leapt from her viewing tower as Boxy blew through it and ran down officers, retainers, messengers, and soldiers alike.

Shifting his poor Boxy into second gear, he began the task of spinning her around for another pass.

Behind him, spells detonated repeatedly as the Sunless called out targets and literally erased them from existence.

Lining himself up for a second pass, he couldn't find the general. Not wanting to waste the opportunity, he seized on every other target he could identify.

Pushing Boxy into her third gear, they rumbled into the devastated camp. A few tried to defend themselves, though they had no target and didn't truly understand what Boxy represented.

Other than death.

Sweet. Glorious. Death.

Not really wanting to make a third pass, Runner cycled Boxy back to second gear and aimed them at Isabelle's flank.

"Target at your own discretion as we engage. Kill order is healers, mages, archers, melee damage, and finally tanks!" Thana called out.

Runner snickered darkly as they closed in on the enemy ranks. Slowly it built from a chuckle to a raging maniacal laugh.

He oriented himself so that they'd exit near the edge of the fighting so as to not endanger his own troops.

Pushing the lever to the fifth gear, he felt Boxy surge once more. Half of Boxy's defense lay in her agility. How quickly she could move through the battle before anyone got a chance at her. Should they be forced to a stop, it'd only be a matter of time before someone figured out a way to get at them that Runner had not accounted for.

Thinking time came to a close as a woman rebounded off the metal plow and grazed off his viewing slit. She stuck there for a second, then sailed up over the top of Boxy but not before Runner took an insane screenshot as his mind splintered apart.

Runner lost himself in the haze of flying bodies. The sudden silence in his mind acted like a twisted counterpoint to the sound of bodies being crushed and thrown.

Looping back around, clearing the line, he began what he knew would be his final pass. The fuel spells would need time to recharge. They'd be near empty after this at the rate he had been expending them.

Sending out a quick "Defense" ping to Nadine, Runner drove Boxy straight through the middle of the enemy forces. The goal now was simple. From one side of the army to another. Right up their center.

The cannon trigger flashed as it became available again and Runner fired it immediately. The shell exploded out in front of him, spraying dirt and bodies into the air.

Runner swerved a little to course correct around that area. Those people were probably already dead and didn't need Boxy's loving caress and tender attention.

Spells detonated, bodies flew, and quite a number went under the churning wheels. Time felt frozen and unending as they rolled along. Runner's mind spun crazily and his emotions became raw ugly things.

Suddenly Boxy cleared the other end of the flank and Runner found himself staring at the position he'd set off from. There were no enemies before him and the path lay open. His mind went blank, and he had to blink several times to get a coherent thought through.

Shifting down to the first gear, he threw an "Attack" ping at Nadine for her to reengage the cannon barrage. He lined up the front of his good little death machine with where she'd started and let her roll on.

Coming to a full stop, he pulled the shifter into the neutral position and engaged the stationary brakes. Runner rolled his shoulders as the tension left him.

Though he wasn't sure how deep into the madness he had sunk, it had felt truly cathartic. In his mind it was as if he had shrugged off burdens and baggage that he'd grown so used to that they'd been forgotten.

Blowing out a shaky breath, he stood up and turned to face his crew.

All looked at him in awe and fear. Runner couldn't really disagree. In only a week or two he'd irrevocably changed warfare and acted like the criminally insane. Undeniably for the worse on both counts.

"So. Anyone hungry? It'll take probably thirty minutes for Boxy to recharge," Runner said a bit lamely.

Many of the beautiful Sunless women who had sought his favor earlier in the campaign turned their faces from him. One or two tried but couldn't hold his gaze for longer than a few seconds. They wouldn't or couldn't do it.

Destroyer of worlds indeed.

One person had eyes for him though. Thana watched him and gave him a beautiful smile when he looked to her. His sagging heart burst to life, fluttering in his throat.

"I'd be delighted to, dear heart. Come, I imagine you'll have a few messengers coming to report on the situation, so our time is short," Thana said, gesturing to the rear door as she unlocked it. She then held out her hand to him.

Runner couldn't dream of ever harming this lovely creature. This woman who saw him for what he was turning himself into as well as who he had been at the same time.

And accepted him.

"I'd be lost without you," he finally choked out.

"I know."

10:23 am Sovereign Earth time
11/16/43

Runner had been surprised at how little time had passed. While it felt like hours in the death machine, in reality no more than twenty minutes had elapsed. Twenty minutes of screaming, bloody, body flinging carnage.

Taking a moment to watch the field, he felt an ache in the pit of his stomach. He had destroyed the command tent and everyone he could in his attack on their leadership. Apparently quite a few of the line officers had noticed that fact and were pulling back.

Retreat and rout were two very different terms. Unfortunately one led to the other very quickly if the troops being told to pull back had already lost their nerve.

Between Boxy and the constant cannon attacks, Runner assessed that this would indeed quickly turn into a rout.

And I have no cavalry to run them down with.

Blinking as Hannah slammed into the forefront of his mind, he opened up his raid window. Bracing himself, he called up the mounted groups.

There were casualties. One in eight had a grayed out box for a name. Fortunately Hannah's box remained bright and active. No one was in combat.

Feeling his stomach unknot in relief, he called up the map. Hannah's icon was moving. Moving straight to him by the looks of it. It'd take her five minutes to make it to him he guessed.

Sitting on the blanket Thana had unrolled on the grass, he pulled out handfuls of fruits and spring water he'd foraged. For Thana he unloaded several different types of seasoned and dried meat. Setting down an open topped box, he dropped a handful of beetles in to round it all out.

"Right then. I'm betting Boxy won't be up for another go before our partners quit the field. Hannah is on her way in and she's got casualties. Whatever happened out there was violent. I say a quick meal, feed her when she gets here, and debrief her. Best guess? Flanked or flanked flankers."

"Boxy is the vehicle? That's a truly awful name. Please stop naming things—leave it to me," Thana said from behind a hand as she began to eat.

"Yeah, I suck like that. Shut up and eat your food. I already see a messenger heading this way," Runner grumped aloud.

Like a predator zooming in on its prey, the messenger sped towards Runner.

"Lord Runner, battle is progressing smoothly. Casualties are light and we have gained the upper hand," blurted out the messenger, his hand slamming into his chest plate.

"Good. Please advise the SO teams that they'll have to adjust aim to hit fleeing targets as the enemy begins to break. Keep firing until they're completely out of range. Also, get ahold of the scouts and have them loot the field. We'll be heading out from here as soon as the enemy clears the field."

"Sir, yes sir," said the man, saluting again. He turned and sprinted back the way he came.

"My beloved chancellor, please put together your delegation to see the king. We'll need to get him on board before the next fight," Runner said, then put a handful of strawberries into his mouth.

Scurrying in from the grass came a squirrel. Level ten and the size of a full-grown house cat if not a small dog.

It promptly sat down at his side and looked up at him.

"Better manners than the last time. Here," Runner teased, holding out a strawberry to the furry guy.

"How? Why is that here?" Thana asked, sounding very confused.

"I dunno. I keep finding them. I started feeding them back at the castle," Runner said with a shrug of his shoulders. Another strawberry disappeared from Runner's hand as the squirrel devoured it.

"Runner, they're not common to this area. They're not common anywhere but the castle at Shade's Rest. If you keep seeing them…is it the same one?"

"Huh? Err—" Runner stopped and thought about it. Frowning, he had to admit it looked similar but that was no real guarantee. They could all share the same model.

"I don't know? It's certainly possible, I suppose. Maybe? Does it matter? He comes around, I feed him, he eventually leaves."

Satisfied with his fill of strawberries, the squirrel jumped into his lap and clambered up his arm. Seating itself on his shoulder, it cleaned its face and then stared at Thana.

"You're a cute little thing. I'll name it personally, if you don't mind, dear heart. You'd give it a horrible name I'm sure. Along the lines of 'furryface' or some god-awful thing." Thana nodded her head as she spoke. Agreeing with herself.

"Fine. And no, not that. Though 'Numb Nuts' isn't ba—" Runner stopped as Thana pressed a fingertip to his lips.

"Stop, dear heart," she warned him with a sweet smile on her lips.

Runner instead nodded his head. At nearly the same time, the squirrel leapt from his shoulder and charged down Thana's arm to seat itself on her shoulder instead.

Thana froze as it moved and then giggled when it sat down.

"See? Even the squirrel approves."

"Approves of what? You fuckers are having a gods-damned picnic. Gimmie that," Hannah said, snatching a fistful of peaches from the spread. Sitting down beside Runner and Thana, she bit into one and chewed it.

"We were waiting for you, Hanners. I promise that," Runner explained. He gave her a quick once-over and found her exactly as she should be. Then he met her eyes and refused to look away.

"I'm glad you're alright. I was worried," Runner said heavily. Unable to help himself, he leaned over and hugged her tightly.

Hannah stiffened up in his embrace before relaxing after a second. He could feel her head turn slightly as if she were looking at Thana.

"Uhm, yeah. I'm fine, Runner. Promise," she replied quietly. Her arms rested around his midsection as he held her.

"Good. Good, okay. Yes," Runner said stupidly. He gave her a final squeeze, released her, and sat back. "What happened exactly?"

Hannah blinked a few times and looked uncomfortable. Taking a bite from her peach as if to stall for time, she nodded her head a little.

"Had a scout out looking around behind us. Found another army, believe it or not. Marching up the road from the south," she outlined, her left hand gesturing in the air for emphasis.

"Figuring they were on their way to join in on the fight, we hit them from the side. Rode through them and killed most of their officers. Getting back out became the problem and that's where we took our casualties. We hurt them, though, hurt them bad. I figure it at about five hundred of them left."

Runner closed his eyes and pinched the bridge of his nose with his fingers. The odds kept stacking up against him.

Even with the most rudimentary of fuzzy math-based assumptions, he could put his active fighters somewhere between eight hundred and nine hundred. The original enemy count had numbered around two thousand. Taking in losses and this newest number, they were still at about two thousand.

Which meant he'd made up no ground. Truthfully he'd lost ground. Now, more than ever, he really would have to get the Barbarians to commit to assisting him in the defense of their own lands.

"Mm. Thank you, Hanners. I'm grateful you've come back to me. Us. Especially that you successfully turned their flank and inflicted solid casualties. Doubly so that it was to their officers. Though I fear we really must hang this campaign on the willingness of the Barbarian king for aid."

Runner made a soft groan and dropped his hand. Opening his eyes, he looked over to the battle once more to confirm his earlier thoughts.

Indeed, the enemy had turned and now were being pursued by ranged attacks.

"We're moving north once the enemy clears the field. We'll make camp east of Kastell and dig in. With any luck we can get this wrapped up quickly. Once we get the king to agree to help us save his own country," Runner growled, and shook his head.

Heaven help us if he tries to refuse me. And him.

"Hail the gate!" Runner shouted at the large stone gate towers. The city itself looked very different than Shade's Rest. Where Shade's Rest had been severe yet calculated, Kastell looked brutal and crude. Built for war and very little else.

And so the cowards hide behind their walls while the wolf is at the door.

An armored head poked out over the top of the wall and peered down at him.

"Ho there. Go away from this place, we're currently at war."

Runner gestured to the upset Katarina beside him as he began to talk again. "Yes, that's why I'm here. I'm the commander of the forces who are currently out there fighting for your freedom. I request a conference with your king. I have also come with his daughter, Princess Katarina."

"I'll relay your message to his highness," said the talking head. Who promptly vanished back inside.

"Your people suck, Kitten. We're not visiting them often. If they want to see us they can come to the North Wood," grumbled Runner.

Katarina quirked a brow as a slow smile spread over her face. Runner glanced around at the rest of his party.

Thana remained with the army as his second-in-command. Hannah took over scouting and patrols. Isabelle had taken on the third officer's position and now worked as Thana's second. Only Nadine had been able to accompany them. She stood at the rear with her crossbow loaded and ready, her eyes scanning about them.

She's not made for war, but she adapts to everything through willpower.

Everyone else was a functionary sent by Vasilios to help authenticate Runner's claims.

"You speak as if we were married with children and they were in-laws." Katarina took a step closer to him as she spoke.

"What? Eh, ah, suppose I was. Why, problem with that?" Runner asked, trying to hide his now galloping heart rate and scratching at his cheek.

"No. Though you leave out everyone else."

"We've talked about that before. I care for you all equally. That's unchanged. Call me a harem-seeking scumbag, but there it is," Runner replied quietly, shrugging his shoulders. Peering up at her, he wondered at her response.

Grinning more widely, Katarina placed her hand on his shoulder yet said nothing.

"You're hiding something, Kitten."

"I am."

"You're not going to tell me, are you?"

"No."

"Why?"

"Not the right time."

Runner thought furiously on that. Then it dawned on him. She'd fled her country because they'd tried to force her into marriage. Even now she might fear he would let them do as they would with her.

As he opened his mouth to assuage her fears, the talking head appeared again.

"His majesty welcomes you to Kastell. Please step back while we open the gate. You'll be escorted inside and brought to his majesty's throne room."

Smiling sadly at Katarina, he winked at her. "To be continued, Kitten. Have no fear. They'll not take you."

Katarina tilted her head while watching him, her grin becoming wider if that were possible.

Roughly twenty minutes later Runner found himself in a throne room. Again. He was getting tired of throne rooms. Getting tired of bowing and scraping.

Biting his tongue and biding his time, Runner knelt down in front of the king of the Barbarian peoples.

"Your Majesty, may I present Runner Norwood. Also named Breaker. Commander of the Sunless forces in the field and the man responsible for returning Princess Katarina," announced a herald from the doors behind Runner.

Trying to catch a glimpse of things out of the corner of his eyes, he had the immediate impression of violence. There was no court here. No onlookers.

Guards. Only guards. The throne itself was crude and built for complete function without even a thought to form.

Runner remained kneeling, while behind him, Nadine was in a similar situation in mid curtsy. Then Runner realized the king had decided to set the stage by taking Runner down a peg.

Mentally, Runner snarled and wanted to carve the man apart. That or hit him with a charisma spell and tell him to attack his own guards.

Maybe I could te —

"Rise, Runner."

Runner came to his feet and squared his shoulders. Katarina hadn't left his side and flanked his right, Nadine on his left.

"I thank you for the return of our daughter, Runner," said the king. There had been no formal announcement of the king's name and no one had said it. Runner had to actually check the man's nameplate.

King Markus Saden. He had the look of a tavern brawler more than a king. His level was only thirty, and to Runner that seemed on the low side considering King Vasilios had been overwhelmingly powerful.

He was overweight, past his prime, and had lanky greasy hair—all reinforced the image. Dark black eyes and brown hair decorated a plain face. Jowls and a second chin wobbled as he talked.

Sporting what one would consider three days' worth of stubble and rumpled clothes he didn't look the part of even minor nobility. Runner was forced to consider if this man found the bottom of alcohol bottles more frequently than his toes. Or a bath. Or a sober decision.

Doesn't even use the royal we as Vasilios did.

Sitting beside him on a throne of equal size and stature was a large red haired woman. Dark black eyes watched him even as he inspected her. Queen Helen Saden.

She had a certain grace and beauty to her that Runner immediately recognized. She could only be Katarina's mother. Oddly enough she had question marks for her level. Runner felt like he was missing something here.

Probably quest related...and something I can't even work on since my time is limited.

Runner bowed his head deeply in respect to Queen Helen. The corners of her mouth quirked up a touch at Runner's gesture.

Quest Updated
Partial Completion

"Escort Princess Katarina Home and Save her Kingdom"
Experience Reward: 10% of current level
Reputation: 50
Fame: 200
Money: 10 Platinum

Quest Updated

"Save the Kingdom II"
Experience Reward: 105% of current level
Reputation: 150
Fame: 800
Money: 30 Platinum

WARNING! Experience Reward is adjusted based on current level at turn in

The chime and the notification confirmed for him that he'd reached the end of the "escort" portion of the quest.

Save the kingdom next, no pressure.

"Yes, I thank you for bringing me back my betrothed. Come, Katarina, we should go away from here," came a male voice from a side door.

Runner's eyes whipped from the queen to the left to find the speaker. He hadn't noticed the man and couldn't prevent the frown that came over his face.

Lord Adalbert had the look of a melee class and happened to be level thirty. Looking like he was in his late twenties, he had the normal expected features of a Barbarian: long brown hair in a queue behind his back, dark black eyes, quite tall, and just a little more built than the standard Runner had come to expect of the race.

That and he was the most handsome man Runner had ever had the displeasure of meeting. Like some type of cross between a male model and a bodybuilder.

If he does a pec flex or flips his hair I'm going to puke.

"No," Katarina said loudly.

"No?" the man parroted back stupidly.

"No."

Runner frowned and scratched at his chin thoughtfully. Glancing over his shoulder, he confirmed that all the other dignitaries they'd thought to bring had been kept out of the throne room.

Catching the eyes of Mr. Pretty, he coughed into his hand and smiled. His annoyance came to the fore quickly and clouded his thoughts. Internally, Runner knew that provoking the man wouldn't help his cause.

But he suddenly didn't care.

"Lord Analbeater, the lady said no. I'm not sure if she can rephrase it in a way that might make it more understandable. Ya know, since it's a word that consists of two letters and has no other way to be interpreted."

Where the room had been quiet before, it became dead silent now.

"You, sir, you're the root of this. I challenge you to a duel. The winner claims the hand of Princess Katarina."

A Quest has been generated
"A Matter of Honor"
Experience Reward: 5% of current level
Reputation: 15
Money: 0 Gold
Do you Accept?
Yes/No

WARNING! Experience Reward is adjusted based on current level at turn in

Chapter 13 - Bedroom Politics -

"You're a real idiot, Applebiter," Runner hissed at the man. Mentally he declined the quest and crossed his arms.

Quest Declined

"Why would I even think of wagering that? Do you not realize her worth as an individual? Is she some sort of possession to you? Bargained off in some cheap affair of your own small stature?" Runner said, his voice rising as he went on.

"On top of that, Acidbottle, I don't own her. She's very much her own woman and can make her own choices. If I asked her to marry me, here and now, it would have no relevance to you or your pea-sized brain. She's a strong, intelligent, and independent person who can do as she wills."

"Yes," Katarina said.

Runner looked over to Katarina and nodded his head at her affirmation of her attributes, then returned his gaze to the stunned Adalbert with a smile.

"And that's that, Addledbeaver. Moving on," Runner said contemptuously. Turning to the king, he bowed his head to the goggle-eyed royalty.

"Your Majesty, I must ask for the aid of your troops. I have been dispatched by your cousin, King Vasilios, to assist you. I have met the enemy commander in the field of battle and require your aid in the defense of your homeland. I beli —"

"You will not dismiss me like some commoner!" shouted Adalbert.

Runner closed his eyes and pressed his fingertips to his brow. The anger in him. The frustration. The hate. It all boiled up to the surface for a moment before he wrestled it down. Opening his eyes again, he dropped his hand to his side and smiled politely as he addressed Adalbert.

"Lord Assbutcher, I believe I'm done with you. Unless you have something relevant to add to the conversation, please leave this to the adults. You'll only get underfoot. In fa —"

"Listen here, you bastard. I think you're the cause of the princess' sudden disobedience and I'll not have you insulting me. You may run around and do as you please with that mangled human slut behind you but I'll be damned if I let you touch the princess," screamed Adalbert.

Runner took in a slow deep breath as he contemplated the best way to kill this man. Letting out a ragged breath, Runner tilted his head while regarding Adalbert.

"You're a dead man, Adalbert. You wanted a duel? Done. I'm going to pull out your guts while you watch. Then I'm going to use them to play with you like a little marionette. I'll have you dance on coals naked in front of everyone you know. When I'm bored with that, I'm going to strap you to the front of Boxy and use you as a battering ram on the enemy forces until you're nothing more than a screaming sack of flesh." Runner paused, taking slow steps towards Adalbert.

"Then, then I might let you die. And by die, I mean lowering you headfirst into a cauldron set over a fire. Then I'm going to slowly fill it with soup stock. A spoonful an hour sounds about right. We'll see if you drown or get boiled alive first. And when you're dead? I'm going fill the cauldron with vegetables and dice you up. Every bit of you. Then I might feed you to the stray dogs in the streets of Kastell. Or maybe prisoners given their last meals." Runner continued his inexorable advance on the man. Adalbert had the face of a man who regretted his life.

"Verdict isn't in yet on that. Dogs and murderers deserve better than to be fed shit. I'd pity the people who would have to clean up the diarrhea that I'm sure they'd have after eating you. Oh, my dear man, we're going to have a very good time."

Before he could close the final few meters to the man, Katarina appeared between them. Her shield flew out in an arc and clanged off of Adalbert's head. Swinging in a wide heavy arc, her black sword cut through the air and passed through the man.

Not waiting for him to recover, Katarina took a step back and then thrust forward, her sword spitting the man through the stomach.

Adalbert fumbled for his own weapon under Katarina's onslaught. Managing to get into a fighting stance with his weapon held before him, he started to utilize an ability.

Then Katarina's blade passed through his neck and his head popped off with a splut. It hit the ground with a wet thunk and rolled a few meters before coming to a stop in front of Katarina.

Grunting, Katarina pulled back a booted foot and punted the head of Adalbert viciously. It sailed across the throne room to smack wetly into the far wall.

Sheathing her sword, she turned and looted the corpse before returning to Runner's side. Facing Runner, she bowed her head once and met his gaze squarely. His rage at Adalbert boiled inside him, the outlet he'd planned to vent it upon being removed from his reach.

"I apologize, Runner. I have taken a fight that was rightfully yours. On the day we met I swore to be your sword and shield, and yours alone. You asked it of me, and so I shall be," Katarina murmured.

As if it had been doused by a lake's worth of water, his fiery emotions cooled instantly. Smiling, he reached out and placed his hand on Katarina's shoulder.

"Thank you, Kitten. Remain my sword and shield. I need you."

Her dark coal eyes simmered at his words and she stared into him. Finally a small smile took over her face and she nodded her head a fraction.

Turning from Katarina, he bowed his head to the king.

"My apologies, Your Majesty, I'm afraid we've dirtied your home. I apologize for the situation but your country is in danger. We must b—"

Quest Updated

"$#à ⊣⅃ ⌐ ↕φ»—"
Experience Reward: ⊣∎â% of current level
Reputation: ♪Pts≈
Fame: √¿¬¬
Money: ² ÷í

"ARREST HIM! Dump him in a guest room. Can't have a dignitary from a king in the dungeon. Put my daughter in her room and keep her there. Throw the rest out of the castle and see them gone," bellowed the king.

Minutes later Runner found himself in a lovely room, under guard, and more or less a prisoner.

With a sigh Runner sat down on the bed. Giving his cell a cursory inspection, he found nothing that stood out as useful or relevant to his situation. Simple furniture, no decorations, no windows, one door, and a big bed.

Blowing a raspberry, Runner flopped backwards and stared up at the ceiling. His anger and frustration had gotten the better of him. Now he'd managed to make his job twice as hard. Maybe triple.

If not impossible.

Fortunately the end goal remained the same; he now needed a way to get the king back on his side.

Or remove the king.

His thoughts traveled in that direction briefly before settling on the queen. That might be the best way to move through this.

I wish I could talk to Srit.

Runner put his hands over his eyes and felt truly alone. He had not been completely alone in months. No matter where he went or what he did, there had always been someone with him.

Srit had been a companion he could call on at any time. Since she'd logged in to the game, she hadn't responded to his attempts to contact her.

Part of him worried on that. Perhaps something had gone wrong. For all he knew she'd been trapped in limbo between the game server and the ship server.

Groaning, Runner concentrated on the work at hand. For now, he needed to figure out a way to get the Barbarian garrison into the fight. Preferably before his people were attacked again.

And then there was the quest that had updated. Without Srit around to check what was going on behind the scenes, he could only guess Katarina's action on his behalf had crossed some serious wires.

An NPC killing what would have been the giver of a quest that she was a participant in. He could only begin to imagine the type of loops the code blew off from that.

One problem at a time. Run on, Runner.

"Brighteyes, Angel, if I need it, would you be willing to vouch for me to the king? It'd be a last resort but if the only alternative is trying to fight my way out..." Runner trailed off, leaving the statement open.

Part of his reason for addressing them was as he had stated. The other was to reassure himself that he wasn't completely alone.

"Of course, silly."

"Agreed."

Runner smiled and felt the weight on his shoulders easing a fraction. As well as the immediate loneliness he had felt.

"Thank you, my fair goddesses. I find myself increasingly relying on my friends. I'll do my best to not involve you until it's the right time."

Letting his hands fall to his sides, he mentally called up the game console. He would have to find the king and queen's nodes manually since he hadn't taken the time to get their IDs. Not to mention that crazy broken quest if he could find it.

"Hmph."

Settling in for some work, Runner sorted through the nodes and flags for the royalty of Kastell. Maybe there he might find the start of an answer to the problem he was facing. At least it was better than sitting around and doing nothing.

9:47 pm Sovereign Earth time
11/16/43

Runner had given up hours ago. Not one single quest flag or node existed that could help him with his problem. Everything that could help him happened to be deep in quest chains that would take days to complete at the fastest. Days he did not have.

He also hadn't found a trace of the broken quest. It left him mildly disturbed to be honest.

Instead he had been working on plans he could actually use. So far his best bet was to persuade the king to help defend his country. Srit had clued him in previously that *Persuade* was directly affected by how the AI viewed the argument.

Any king would want to defend their country.

Failure there would leave him with only a single option.

Escape.

Escape and return to Shade's Rest with everyone he could bring. Potions lined the side table, the results of an evening spent trying to keep his hands busy.

Heal Mana, Throat Strike, Stealth, Distract, and other odds and ends filled the table from corner to corner.

Runner had thrown them together once he had come to the conclusion that there really weren't many options open to him.

On top of the problem of the king, there was no doubt in Runner's mind that the human army would swing east when done here. This army was a flanking army, meant to destroy capital cities that had been stripped of soldiers.

Using that thought as a jump point, one could infer that the smaller army Hannah encountered would be left here as a garrison force.

Should he fail to get the king's support, his goal would be to bleed and harass the human army all the way back to the Sunless kingdom.

Torchlight suddenly flooded the entrance area of his guest cell. As quickly as the light came it went out.

Runner got up from the desk he sat at, then made his way to the door. Crouched low in the corner of the entry was Katarina. She was in *Stealth*.

Shaking his head at her, he smiled. Apparently she had some of the *Stealth* potions he had made for her previously.

Need to make a utility ring for everyone with every possible utility spell.

Gesturing behind him, he smiled at Katarina.

"Care to join me? I'm afraid the amenities are a touch sparse, but they're adequate."

Katarina hesitated in the corner as if she hadn't expected him to notice her immediately. Eventually she stood up, *Stealth* being canceled. Her eyes went from him to the bedroom, the study, and finally back to him.

Runner knew something was bothering her. Knew it as if he could read her mind.

"Yes," Katarina answered as she moved to join him.

"Great. If you like we can have a private dinner. I haven't eaten yet, was busy working things out. Don't tell Rabbit when we get out of here, she'll just yell at me," Runner said as Katarina passed by him.

Runner fell in behind her. He went over to the dinner table, unpacked two plates from his inventory, and started unloading a meal for two.

Katarina had continued past and went straight to the side table. Inspecting the various potions he'd been working on, she seemed lost in her own thoughts.

Leaving her to her thoughts, Runner continued to lay out dinner. A simple meal that consisted of water, fruits, vegetables, and dried meat.

Grabbing the back of one of the chairs, he cleared his throat to get her attention.

"My apologies, Kitten. All I have on me is simple fare, and lacking in more sophisticated things. Rabbit's been spoiling us with her cooking."

Katarina gave a tiny nod of her head. She put down the *Stealth* potion she'd been holding on to and came over to him at the table.

"It's alright. You do the best you can, Runner. You always do," Katarina murmured, taking a seat.

Now Runner was terrified. Katarina wasn't one for words and the more she spoke, the more nervous he got.

Taking his seat, Runner picked at his food, choosing his words carefully.

"I'm not sure what to say, Kitten," Runner started, then finished a strawberry. "I fear your father will not hear our plea to defend your nation."

Katarina stopped eating, her hands placed on each side of her plate.

"If I can't get him on my side, we're left with removing him by force with the hope that your mother will take over and follow us. Unfortunately, I can't seem to find a way of doing this without killing your father."

Katarina hadn't moved an inch even as Runner dropped that bomb on her.

"I would hope your mother would take over, though I imagine I'd be a fugitive forever onward in your home. And, ya know, killing him doesn't sound like the best way to be in her good graces and expect help," Runner muttered, feeling nausea creep over him.

"He's not my father. Mother married him after Father died. A woman cannot rule in this land. If he died you would be doing her a favor," Katarina said, picking up a quarter of a peach.

"Ah," Runner stated lamely.

"Should he die, Mother would have emergency powers for a short period before the noble council could vote on a new king. As you said, though, we'd be fugitives," said Katarina around a mouthful of food. "Hard to visit my mother after." Katarina shrugged her shoulders as if the thought was only annoying.

Smiling sadly at the situation, Runner could only be thankful for the strength of his companion.

"The alternative option is simply leaving under *Stealth* and waiting for the capital to fall. Once it did, we'd be committing to a long fall back while trying to bleed their forces. I don't doubt they'll be heading for Shade's Rest after this."

Katarina grunted at that—clearly she'd already thought the same thing.

"Should you kill him, and my mother does indeed agree, I won't be free. I will be bargained away to whoever doesn't win the bid to marry my mother."

"Good reason for us to leave afterwards."

"Or you spoil the contract. They would follow after me otherwise."

"Spoil the contract? I'm not sure I follow." Runner ate what was left on his plate and dumped it back into his inventory. Runner tended to eat out of necessity rather than enjoyment. At least when it wasn't something made by a certain merchant who had developed a fantastic flavor profile.

"Marriage contract. Certain stipulations must be met for the contract to be valid," Katarina explained. She pushed her plate over to him after finishing her own meal. "If the conditions are not met, the contract won't be able to proceed."

"Ah. Got it. What are the stipulations then? Anything easy we can break? Like renouncing the throne or joining the clergy? You'd make an interesting nun," Runner said with a grin, leaning back in his chair with his hands behind his head.

"Bet you'd fill out a habit great. Maybe get a miniskirt version."

He'd missed his group while locked up. The banter. The camaraderie.

"Something...like that. Of all the options available, the most direct route would be the virginity aspect of it," deadpanned Katarina.

Runner blinked and slowly brought his arms down and rested his hands on his knees. His mind sprinted to catch up to the conversation as Katarina continued.

"If you're willing. If I'm acceptable that is. We've joked about it before but this would be for real. Obviously. I mean...I'm not as pretty as Thana, though. Or even Hannah. Or even half as sexy," Katarina rattled off. Apparently his lack of an immediate answer had spurred her into a nervous tizzy.

His brain having caught up to the present, he held up his hand to stop her. Then he hesitated.

A very large majority of him screamed at him that he should already be tearing her clothes off. The stupid voice in the back of his head warned him that this could be the straw that broke the harem camel's back. Not to mention it wasn't exactly the best of reasons.

Did that really matter? A beautiful woman was offering herself up. One he was deeply interested in for far more than a one-night fling. This was the silly stuff daydream fantasies were made of.

Maybe this would be the starting point for them.

Wait, was she really offering? Was it a one-night stand?

"I'd like a bit of clarification. You're suggesting I...err...deflower you?" Runner asked.

Deflower? Really?

"Yes." Katarina pulled absently on her ponytail as she answered.

Every fiber of his being now screamed at him to say yes and proceed to the bedroom. Yet that tiny annoying voice demanded to be heard, or at least have a say in this.

It didn't quite add up. He was fairly certain they could leave with no one the wiser. He wasn't certain how to ask her if she realized that this wasn't necessary without offending her.

Fuck it.

"Kitten, I'd love nothing more than to tear your clothes off and destroy you in a heartbeat. More for the fact that I care for you but in no small part because you're sexy and beautiful," Runner blurted out. Katarina turned a deep red, her left hand unbinding her ponytail as she started to stand up from the table.

"Hold on a second. I'm sure I'll regret this later but...we don't have to do this. I'm confident in my ability to get us out and away from here," Runner said, feeling the pit of his stomach drop to his feet. "In addition to that, nothing has changed. I care for you in the same way I do the others. Were this situation reversed and it was Hannah, Nadine, or Thana, I feel my answer would be the same for them. Though I confess I hope this isn't a one-night stand if we, err, do it."

Katarina now stood upright at the table, looking down at him. Her red hair hung loosely around her face and shoulders.

She looked amazing in a very different way with her hair unbound.

"I..." Katarina frowned, looking conflicted as she processed that. Runner gave her the time to answer. Katarina had never been one to mince words and he doubted she'd start now.

"I want to. Despite everything else, and yes I understand your feelings, I want to. I love you." Katarina's left hand pressed to her stomach, her right hand pressing firmly into the table. She looked like she was on the edge of running from the room as fast as possible.

That or throwing up.

"I feel like I have from the moment you put your sword in my hand. At first I thought it was simple infatuation. Nothing more." She shook her head as if fighting her own thoughts.

"It's been months. I feel the same. Unchanged. No, that's wrong. It's even worse. Deeper. Lying next to you at night is torment. I feel like so much is unsaid. I feel this terrible fluttering in my stomach for hours."

Suddenly her lips came together like the gate on a dam slamming shut. A proverbial flood of words and then a sudden stop.

She had laid it all out on the line and left very little to be guessed at. Runner swallowed heavily as he watched Katarina hold herself in check by sheer force of will. He doubted he would have had the strength to do what she did.

Though he now had to answer. Answer and choose.

I choose pathetic and cliche.

Meeting her eyes, he smiled sadly, expecting the end of his little wish-fulfillment fantasy.

"As I love you, Kitten. As I love Lady Death, Rabbit, and Hanners. I have feared for a long while that my indecision would force you all to leave. Though I fear choosing even more. I can't even begin to think of what will come of all this, but I can assure you that I'm a man torn in many directions. Specifically four," Runner said with a nod towards her. "One direction is obviously you. And yes, it's very difficult at night for me as well. The first couple of nights I swear I didn't sleep at all. If that's all well and good, I would love nothing more than to show you how wrong you are about not being beautiful or sexually attractive. Repeatedly if needed. You know, to make sure you believe it."

No sooner had his words left his mouth than Katarina's hand closed on his collar and jerked him over the table and into a deep kiss.

7:02 am Sovereign Earth time
11/17/43

Morning came early. It had been a long night.

Runner stared up at the stone ceiling of his cell. Looking over to his left, he found a naked Katarina in all her glory sleeping on her side.

Her face had the look of contentment. Peace. Her left hand rested on his chest while her right hand clasped his arm. She had needed quite a bit of reassurance. He felt her insecurity was deeply rooted in her royal self, more than her actual worth.

Turning his eyes from the sleeping beauty, he faced the ceiling again as guilt rolled over him. Even in this he felt it had ended up being wrong. He'd taken everything from her and promised her nothing. Less than nothing. Promised her he would have done the same to her companions.

It's done. So be it. Whatever.

Runner did his best to slough off the negative thoughts.

Can't put the genie back in the bottle.

Truth be told, he felt incredible. Last night had done wonders for his mood, his sanity, even his heart.

Katarina's fingers tightened, her fingernails scratching his chest lightly.

Smiling, he turned his face to watch Katarina wake up.

Her eyelids fluttered and then opened, her black eyes staring into his. Unmoving, she watched him for several seconds before her pupils dilated abruptly.

"Yes, it really did happen. Yes, you were amazing. And yes, I'd love to do that again. If you're up for it," Runner said brazenly.

Katarina's face became the color of her hair. Her left hand dipped down and grabbed the sheets. Yanking them up over her head, she hid herself from his view.

Laughing, he tugged the blanket out of her hand and leaned in to kiss her gently. "Maybe later, then."

Runner swung his legs out of the bed, stood up, and dressed himself. Giving her the bed to collect herself, he moved over to the side table and went over his potion inventory.

Humming to himself with a grin, he divided the potions in half. Putting them into separate bags in his inventory, he let his mind off its leash to wander.

Thinking about the day and what could go wrong, he decided to build an insurance policy.

In a spur of the moment action he pulled a basic gold ring out of his inventory and crushed it in his hand. Fracturing neatly into four pieces, the ring was no more. He nodded his head at the clean breaks, pulled a small princess-cut ruby from his pack, and set it on the table in front of him.

After crushing a second silver ring, he fused two of its four pieces with two of the first ring. Bending a third piece into a circle for the ring's setting, he nodded.

Moving the four ring pieces, the setting, and the ruby to his left hand, he pulled up his abilities with his right hand.

Selecting *Stealth,* he bound it to the ruby. The four ring pieces and the setting received *Throat Strike, Silence, Blink, Cleanse,* and *Disarm.*

Rapidly heating the ends of the shattered pieces and the crown, he fused it all together. Stuffing the ruby into the molten setting, he began the task of smoothing the edges with his fingertips. All in all, it took him no more than thirty seconds to fashion it from start to finish.

He held the ring up in the palm of his hand, knowing it was as complete as it was going to be.

Mist covered the small electrum alloy ring and then solidified. Unsurprisingly to him, the dull artifact creation sound played.

Pale yellow all the way around, the band was now a solid color. Gone was the original alternating color of gold and silver. Sturdy yet pretty, it seemed fitting for Katarina.

Glancing over his shoulder, he found Katarina sitting in the middle of the bed, the sheets held up to her chin, watching him.

"Don't get me wrong, Kitten, having you naked in my bed is a damn fine way to start the morning but I think we'll be summoned soon. Also, here."

Runner took a few steps and put himself in front of her, holding out the ring.

"Should prove useful. Ah, I didn't name it. Sorry."

Taking the ring from his fingers, Katarina smiled bashfully.

Then the door flew open. Standing in the door frame were two royal guards.

The guards' eyes went from Runner to a naked Katarina in his bed, the ring in her fingertips, and back to Runner.

"So..." Runner started. Then gave up on even bothering with an explanation. "Yeah. Maybe we should go to the throne room. King's waiting and all."

Without words, the guards hustled Runner from the room, Katarina trailing along behind uninvited.

Shoved roughly into place in front of the king, Runner sighed and brushed his hands over his clothes.

Surrounding him on all sides was the nobility of Kastell. Apparently this was an event that couldn't be missed.

"Your guards could seriously do with a course in manners. When's the continental breakfast? I'm also going to need a turndown service," Runner said glibly, meeting the king's stare.

"My king, we found the princess in his room," the guard tattled.

Not waiting for this to get even further out of hand, Runner decided to get to the point of it. Targeting the king, Runner called up *Persuade* and hit him with it full force.

"King Markus, I charge you with the defense of your nation. Even now, forces range far and wide in your country, killing your subjects, raiding your fields, and destroying their homes. You sit here, hidden from the fighting as your people fight and die. As your allies, the Sunless, fight and die for you," Runner intoned, doing his best to force every ounce of his massive charisma into it.

"Stand with me, help me fight off the foes of your nation, help me protect your people. Together we can crush them and meet them on the field. Separately we will both fall. King Vasilios' forces will be forced from the field and will start falling back towards their own country. If we do not act, we will all fail. I need whatever soldiers and crafters you can spare, resources to construct weapons of war, and your desire to stave off these invaders."

Runner felt like he'd said it well. That he'd listen and they could quickly move on from this and chase out their mutual foes.

You use Persuade on King Markus
King Markus is not Persuaded

And that was that.

"I'll not have you speak to me in such a way. No, we'll do no such thing. We'll broker you to the human army in exchange for their departure. Maybe it's time for us to rise up against my dear 'cousin,'" King Markus spat at Runner.

"No, I am king here, I write the laws. You're nothing but a commoner."

Runner saw no way around it then. Calling on Ernsta here and now would damage her ability to be their patron later, but there was no choice.

"Runner, known as Breaker," Queen Helen said. Her voice had the same quality as her daughter's. It boomed in the room, and all were quiet. Including the king. "I would ask you a question. Why was my daughter in your room?" Queen Helen's eyes flicked behind him and back to him. Taking a chance, he glanced over his shoulder to find Katarina beside him, decked out in all her equipment.

Sighing, Runner turned back to the queen with a smile.

"Because I love her and care for her well-being. She was brave enough to tell me first, while I was a coward who needed her to take the first step. She feared your husband would trade her off like a horse. To that end, she was trying to force the situation so that it could never happen."

Queen Helen's eyes leapt from him back to Katarina. Long seconds passed as she watched her daughter.

"Katarina, your blade."

"An artifact."

"How?"

"Runner made it."

"Named?"

"Yes."

"You named it?"

"Yes."

The rapid-fire exchange between mother and daughter left Runner feeling like he was missing an entire conversation even though they were talking right in front of him.

"Now see here, this is my court and I'll—" King Markus fell silent as Queen Helen's great axe slammed into his neck and the throne behind him. The wood splintered and the back half of the royal chair cracked.

From full health to zero in one strike, the king's head sat atop the blade that separated it from his neck.

He died before he knew what happened.

Quest Updated

"°úÆ■▬╫╥"
Experience Reward: ,-./⫫ of current level
Reputation: ▼■⫶
Fame: ⫫╤═
Money: ▓↕

Standing from her throne, the queen made an indelicate grunt and faced those present.

"I tire of this. This is my court. I shall rule hereafter. Anyone who would challenge my rule may step up now."

Immediately the nobility started to eye each other and their queen. They might not fight her but Runner had the opinion that they wouldn't follow her either. Now would be the time to invoke Ernsta.

"Queen Helen, I offer you greetings on the behalf of Lady Ernsta, she who is Death. She has taken a personal interest in your country and its people's plight. She has bestowed much upon my troops, and I, in our fight at your doorstep."

Lights dimmed in every corner of the room as Ernsta appeared in a flash of dark blue mist.

She came into existence beside the dead king. She reached into the dead man's chest, ripped out his squirming soul, and tossed it to the floor. Humanoid like with discernable features it looked very much like the king.

Writhing on the stones, it flailed as the mouth howled without noise.

Stepping down from the dais, Ernsta eyed Queen Helen and moved to stand beside Runner.

The soul flopped around for a few seconds, then grew still and burst apart into nothing. All eyes were on Ernsta in her casual banishment of King Markus to nonexistence. There would be no afterlife for him. There would be absolutely nothing.

Queen Helen dropped to her knees before Ernsta. Runner had to respect her. Either she was insanely quick on the uptake or truly did worship Ernsta.

"Lady Ernsta, I welcome you to my country and my home," intoned the queen.

"Rise, Helen. I find your dispatch of your husband pleasing. He has caused Runner many casualties. Avoidable casualties. I may be the incarnation of death, but even I have more respect for life than he did. I will send whatever deity he prayed to amends in exchange, but I refuse to allow him a pleasant afterlife."

Queen Helen stood alone on her dais. The entirety of the court could now be found plastered to the walls, trying in vain to blend into the very stones.

"My queen, I attribute my victories and the morale of my army to Ernsta. Without her guidance and presence, I truly believe we would not be having this conversation and Kastell would have fallen. My troops know Ernsta awaits them and give themselves wholly to the cause. Your cause."

Not even a second later, Helen nodded her head to Ernsta.

"I thank you, Lady Ernsta. I believe with such a deity as our patron that we could build our nation to great heights. I would ask you to become our prime."

"Are you certain? I am allied with my sister Brunhild, who is the prime of the Sunless nation. We find ourselves at odds with Rike and Rannulf," Ernsta warned.

Runner noticed Helen's eyes flick to him for a moment before returning to Ernsta.

Smart. Very smart. Dangerous. Need to be on my toes with her.

In Runner's mind, Queen Helen had put the connection between him, the Sunless army, Brunhild, and Ernsta together in seconds.

"All the better, Lady Ernsta."

"It is done then. The enemy will attack on the morrow. My champion shall be there. He is Stefan. He will report to only you if I do not have a task for him. He shall join your people as a citizen and act in my stead for the betterment of our nation and my name. Rule well, Queen Helen, you have my blessing," Ernsta said with an outstretched hand. The queen was enveloped in a dark blue mist as Ernsta sanctified her.

Then Ernsta was gone. Queen Helen's eyes returned to Runner, who smiled at her.

"Queen Helen, King Vasilios sends his regards and wishes you well. I act in his stead and his desires. As his ranking general, I recognize you as the only ruler of the Barbarian nation and second Ernsta's approval of your leadership."

Once more silence settled over the room after his little speech. Everyone there could read between the lines. Ernsta, the new goddess of the nation, and the general of King Vasilios both regarded Helen as the rightful ruler and supported her.

Politics in Kastell had irrevocably changed in the span of a day.

Chapter 14 - Cut off the Head -

Queen Helen had been quick to provide him with everything he'd asked her for. He had discovered, much to his chagrin, that she had included far more than he'd requested when checking the inventory list that had been delivered to him.

Promptly after that, he snuck to the warehouse that she'd stated the supplies would be sent to. He didn't really want to be in the eye of the nobility if he could avoid it. Didn't fit in there.

There was so much to build. So very little time.

"I hate this," Katarina complained.

Runner looked up from his inventory sheet and gave her a lopsided grin.

"I know you do. And I'm sorry for it."

"Doing it because you asked."

"I know. And thank you, Kitten. I promise I'm not getting rid of you—I truly believe Lady Death will need your help. Many look to you for strength, including her," Runner quietly said to her.

She stood a few feet from him and looked more than a little annoyed. After a moment of hesitation, she closed the distance between them and put her hands on his shoulders.

Smiling up at her, he rested his hands on her hips.

"Don't like it," Katarina muttered, watching him for his response.

"I know you don't, but that's life. I promise I'll be good. I'll spend time with your mom, build toys, and get everything ready here."

Katarina grunted at that. Clearly she didn't care for that answer either. Or she didn't like the idea of him spending time with her mother.

"Come on, Kitten. Get moving. I promise I'm not going anywhere and I'll be fine."

A faint blush came over her cheeks before she ducked her head down to kiss him firmly. Too soon for his own desires she pulled back and gave a tiny bob of her head in agreement.

She slipped out of his grasp and left him there in the warehouse.

He blew out a breath and tried to focus on something other than the lovely Barbarian. Runner leaned back and then stretched his arms out above his head.

What a lovely tiny break. Now back to work. Tanks, and cannons, and potions, oh my.

Settling in for work, he grinned and started sorting out wooden planks and beams for tank hulls.

Hours into the build, Runner finished molding another set of pistons for the fifth tank. It had taken a serious amount of time, and he had started to consider cutting down on the number required to power the tanks. Time was a commodity he hated to spend right now.

"Quality over quantity, right?" Runner muttered to no one. He went to the next crate of materials.

"Depends on the quality," said a soft feminine voice.

Looking up from the crate, Runner found a human woman by the name of Amelia sitting on a nearby chest. While not exactly beautiful she could easily be called pretty. Runner deliberately gave her the once-over from head to toe and immediately felt she was a little off.

Finally he pinned it to her face itself. She had clean straight features that looked like she'd been carved from a stone. As if someone had labored over her during creation.

Everything else seemed ordinary by comparison. Straight tawny hair cut short in a pixie style with dark emerald eyes.

Level ?? and clearly out of place here in Kastell as a Human. Her way of dress — leather armor with belted short swords — screamed her profession that of a thief or an assassin.

Judging the situation to be out of his hands, he returned to his work. Scooping up a large number of iron ingots in his hands, he sat on the ground.

"You have me at a disadvantage, pretty lady. Name's Runner, Runner Norwood. Let me finish up this set and you'll have my undivided attention. This is literally the last set I need for six," Runner managed to say as he began shaping the iron.

"Amelia. No last name. Never needed one. Watcha workin' on?" She had crossed the space between them in a single instant. Her breath tickled his ear as she leaned over his shoulder.

"Weapon. I'm fairly good at making things to kill other people. It's regrettable, but better them than me, or my own."

"Ah, right that. You have no idea who I am, do you?"

"Sorry, I don't," Runner said honestly. Setting down a finished piston, he picked up another ingot. "Don't get me wrong, you're quite pretty. Kinda sexy in leathers. If I didn't already have a serious harem issue, I'd make a hard pass at you. Well, even with the harem I might make a pass. You've really got that tomboy charm about you that I don't have yet in my collection. Care to tell me who you are? Other than sexy Amelia."

Runner targeted the woman and hit the *Persuade* and *Seduce* functions in tandem.

You use Persuade on Amelia
Amelia is Persuaded
You use Seduce on Amelia
Amelia is Seduced

As if contemplating his request, she poked at the back of his head.

"Does that work? The whole smarmy flirty thing?"

"You tell me, it worked on you."

Finishing another piston, he glanced over his shoulder at Amelia. Raising his eyebrows, he grinned at her before starting in on another piston.

Amelia looked shocked at the directness of his response. A handful of seconds passed in silence before she started laughing.

"Right you are! You have the truth of it. Consider me smitten and ready. Care to take me now or later?"

"Later, Minxy. Don't even have a bed here. Do you have any idea what this floor would do to your back? So, who are you?"

"Minxy? Like a minx? I like that. I'm the goddess of thieves and assassins. A truly horrible and wicked woman."

Runner blinked and thought about that. Terribly convenient and well timed. Made him nervous. Paranoid even.

He reminded himself yet again that fate happened to have a soft spot for him. As well as a real need for his blood and ultimately his death. Sometimes she helped, sometimes she tried to murder him.

Amelia wasn't a part of the major pantheon, which meant she could only be a minor goddess.

"Oh? Lovely. I'm all about dangerous and dark ladies. You're just in time, too. Right now I'm starting a harem of goddesses. Beautiful and fantastically powerful women who I'd never have a chance with. Could kill me on accident with a solid hug. You can join them. You'd be third but I promise to share myself equally. The tomboy charm and all is a definite win."

With a sniff he dropped another piston down and sighed. Scrubbing his hands over his face, he tried to clear his thoughts. Brunhild and Ernsta could ferret this one out for him. Why worry over it himself?

"How much do you know, Minxy?"

"Everything. Hanners prayed to me, ya know. Back in the woods when you tied her up like a hog for slaughter. Or kinky good times. Maybe both? Been following you around ever since. You've got a great ass by the way. Really got a good look last night."

That took care of needing to Awaken her. Explained her timing a bit more. Also threatened to turn him the color of a cherry.

"Well aren't you brazen. Saw a chance with the timing and took it, eh? I love it. So, care to take me up on the deal? Same setup except Humans. Considering the guild house of thieves is there, that'll work out well. Need to replace the current guild master with someone else though. Still after Hanners last I knew."

"Done and struck. Though I gotta tell you up front. I plan on making you mine. There's a certain temptation to stealing you out from under the noses of so many. Like a lovely jewel on display."

"Work hard, Minxy. I've already promised myself out to four mortal women and they do not seem like the type to invite more. There's also two goddesses you'll need to deal with who have a claim to me of their own. Not sure how far they'll take those claims, but they have them." Runner paused and looked up at the ceiling.

"Angel? Brighteyes? I have your third. Come start her education so I can get to work here."

Brunhild and Ernsta joined them in the warehouse before he had even finished calling out their names.

"So I see," Brunhild said cautiously. "I approve of the choice, though I wonder about her long-term goal."

Ernsta growled in response. Runner could feel her presence at his side and it wasn't entirely friendly towards Amelia.

Runner patted at Ernsta's booted calf as he let the piston take shape.

"Couldn't agree more. Be nice to her though. I like her spunky attitude. We'll need it," Runner said. Looking up, he caught Amelia's eyes with his own. "You let me know if they get too rough on you. They forget how powerful they are at times. Glad to have you on board, Minxy."

Brunhild snorted but her tone softened. "You're right, Runner. Amelia, I name you sister and welcome you. Come, we should speak."

Amelia looked from Runner to Brunhild with a small smile.

"Of course, Sister."

"I'll catch up. I have a request of Runner," Ernsta said, dropping a hand on Runner's shoulder.

Then he found himself alone with the goddess of death.

"What can I do you for, my Dark Angel?" Runner dropped the last piston onto the pile, completing that set.

"I need a weapon made for my champion. As the resident blacksmith, I call upon you for a favor."

"Ptff, no favor needs to be called, Angel. I'll do this one for a smile. Maybe ask you to throw in saying my name at the same time. Not right now mind you, down the road. A hefty fee, I know. I don't come cheap. I'm assuming you need it today? Drop the mats in one of the empty crates and I'll build it out. Anything specific?" Runner leaned back and set his eyes on the goddess.

Ernsta considered him as she thought on that.

"Nothing but strength. No spells, no skills, nothing. I'll take care of the rest."

Runner shrugged his shoulders. "Done, then. One artifact for the smile of a goddess who happens to say my name at the same time. I'm robbing you blind. Alright, run along, Angel. Oh, and please be nice to your new little sister? She had a lot of guts to present herself in the way she did. She's only a minor deity, and it's obvious even to a mortal like me she's nervous. Please? For me, maybe?"

Ernsta frowned as if eating something she didn't care for and then nodded her head.

"Alright. For you, little lamb," she said before disappearing.

Finding a third god to fill out his triumvirate was crossed off his to-do list.

One problem down, a bazillion to go. Though, a very good problem to no longer have.

"Now, back to work. Need to get this done. More work to do. Always more. Work, work, work."

Like clockwork, a ding alerted him to a scheduled reminder he'd made going off. Growling, he opened the alert to find it wasn't something he could put off.

The medical server.

Up and running for a while now, it awaited instructions from him.

Forcing himself to do the work, he called up the ship's console and opened up the medical server program.

Username:

"Let's see. User name...NorRun001."

Password:

"Password. Ah...uh...hm. Default password should be the same for every system. Sooo... NorRun0019683504714. Bingo, now we—"

Runner stopped dead in his tracks, his fingers hovering over the virtual keyboard that he'd called into existence.

Could it be that simple? What if I never set anything up? If I didn't have time or it slipped my mind because, I dunno, the ship was exploding.

Runner dismissed the ship's console and called up the game console.

/Permissions
Please enter Password: *******************
Password Accepted

Oh my god. It was this easy the entire time?

Runner wasn't sure if he was angrier at himself for not figuring it out or for not setting a normal password.

Time for the moment of truth.

/Commands
Available Commands:
Adopt
Broadcast
ClassReset
DiasbleChat
Divorce
EnableChat
GMHub
GMHub Palette
LogOut
Marry
RaceReset
Rename
GMHubReturn
Unstuck

/AddPermissions
　　Security prohibits altering permissions while the server is active. Please submit a ticket to have permissions added during the next maintenance period. Maintenance period overdue. Schedule now? Y/N
　　/Y
　　Server will be turned off during this period and all characters logged off. Please enter date to schedule maintenance:
　　/Abort
　　Task Aborted

　　Runner felt frustration at the commands boil up inside him rapidly. They were all worthless to the situation he found himself in. Clenching his fists in futility, he stared at the commands as if willing them to change into better ones.
　　Finding that there was nothing else he could do, he decided he might as well try a few out.

/GMHub
　　Invalid command, no zone selected. Please specify zone from available lots. Current available zones are zero through one million.

/GMHub 0
Teleporting...
Default Settings

Runner was standing in the warehouse one moment, then in front of a large office building the next. The holo-sign in front read simply as "Game Master Headquarters."

Greetings! You have 1,418,397 tickets. Your current service level is 0% and your average speed of answer is Div/0. To reach proper staffing levels you will need to increase head count.

Please contact human resources, recruiting department.

Have a nice day!

"Ah. This would be the in-game office. Where tickets are resolved, issues worked on, GMs go on break. Probably even do orientation and training here. Big building. Shame that there isn't more of an actual team. And that I'm a horrible monster because I'll not be responding to any of those tickets."
Walking forward a few paces, he ran a hand through his hair.
"Since I'm the only member, that is."
Shaking his head in annoyance, he called up the console again.

/GMHub 1
Teleporting...

Active settings only:
Death=On
Food/Water=On
Damage=On
Gravity=100%
Biome=Plane
Day/Night Cycle=On

Runner found himself standing in a wide open and empty field of grass. Judging from the list of settings he'd been presented with on entering, this "hub," as it were, was customizable.
"Okay, so...I dunno? Private space?"
Shrugging his shoulders, he called the console once more.

/GMHub 2
Teleporting...

Active settings only:
Death=On
Food/Water=On

Damage=On
Gravity=100%
Biome=Plane
Day/Night Cycle=On

And again he found himself in a wide open field. Identical in every way to the first.

"This must be the default then. Which leaves me a large number of customizable zones. For anything. In other words...I could build here. Like a castle. Or a storage facility. Or an entire city," Runner said aloud, nodding to himself. Then a dark thought struck him. "Or a prison."

Pressing his lips into a grim line, Runner tried the command he assumed would get him back to Kastell.

/GMHubReturn
Teleporting...

"And back in the warehouse. Neat," Runner said. Promising himself to look more deeply into it later, he went back to the medical server. He couldn't log anyone out or change them to an immortal status, but he had the medical server. Once he was done with this, he could start moving people over to it.

At which point they would be safe.

11:42 pm Sovereign Earth time
11/17/43

With a groan Runner rubbed at his eyes. Arrayed before him was the product of his long day's work.

One large, dark, and wicked looking two-handed sword in the crate Ernsta had delivered the materials to. And six tanks, outfitted exactly like Boxy, minus the cannon. They were mobile battle platforms right now. That and a meat grinder for anyone slow enough to stand in its way.

Assuming Ernsta would collect the sword when she felt ready, he left it where it was. Honestly it wasn't his best work either. Lots of damage, looked great, and absolutely no utility.

Pushing his fists into his lower back, he stretched and then blew out a breath.

"Bedtime," Runner crowed intelligently, coming back to a normal standing position. Throwing his bedroll down on the ground, he outlined the entire warehouse and set it as his campsite.

"You going to eat anything? Nadine will fucking bake your balls if she finds out."

Runner startled a bit at the sudden question and looked to the side to find Hannah leaning against an empty box.

"Yes, I've been here nearly the entire time. Lady Brunhild got in touch with Thana, who sent me over after telling me about you picking up Lady Amelia. Apparently she's been trying to sneak over here repeatedly and Lady Brunhild was getting tired of it."

"Oh? Right, then. Minxy did say she wanted to steal me away from everyone. I suppose me being alone is rather rare. Smart cookie. Gotta love her style." Runner shook his head ruefully. "I'm sure Brighteyes has her in hand, though. I trust her implicitly," Runner said with a smirk.

A warm tingle spread throughout his being. Two small blessings hit him at the same time. One for "health" and the other for "subtlety." In retrospect, he did kinda compliment both of the aforementioned goddesses.

"I gathered. I'm sure a fuckhead like you had nothing to do with it," Hannah muttered. "So here I am. Playing babysitter. You looked into your building thing so I left you be."

"Thanks for that. Feels like people want to interrupt me for the fun of it at times."

"Queen Helen did stop by for a moment. She watched you for a few minutes and left again. I imagine she'll want to talk to you in the morning."

"Hm. Either about her daughter or the tanks. Either one will be a delightful conversation. I'm sure."

Runner toed open his bedroll and started preparing himself for sleep.

"About that. They found Katarina in your room this morning?"

Runner froze, bent over at the waist and adjusting his bedroll. Standing up again, he stalled for a few seconds.

"Yes," he finally said.

"Why?" Hannah asked him quietly.

"Because we slept together."

Hannah nodded her head minutely.

"So, it's her then?"

"And you—"

"Me? What—"

"And Thana. Nadine."

Hannah brought her dark brows down over her blue eyes. Her lips were pressed together and she looked annoyed.

"I told Katarina up front that if it had been you, Lady Death, or Rabbit, I would have said yes to them, too. I refuse to choose any of you over the other," Runner said, and felt the truth of it. Might as well end it now if it was to be that way.

Running her thumbs over the hilts of her swords, Hannah looked for all the world like a woman confused. Not angry.

"So, if it had been me last night. You'd have fu-slept with me?"

"Yes. In a heartbeat. I've told you before, Hanners, you're a beautiful woman. You really do have some of the best attributes of both your parent races."

Resisting the temptation to look her over, Runner made sure to keep his eyes firmly planted on her face.

"And if I asked you to tonight?"

"In a heartbeat. With extreme enthusiasm. The lack of a bed would put a bit of a damper on it but I'm sure we can make do."

"You're a fucking whore."

Runner laughed bitterly at that. His heart ached at the accusation. But she wasn't wrong. The flames of desire went out like a circuit breaker had been pulled.

"Suppose I am. It's the truth though. Right or wrong, I won't choose between you four. I'll let this play out to that conclusion, whatever it may be, for however long it will. I'm off to bed now. Long day tomorrow. Lots of people to kill."

Runner switched to his sleep clothes and turned in.

8:01 am Sovereign Earth time
11/18/43

"You're certain?" Queen Helen asked of him. They stood side by side at the top of the gatehouse.

"Very. She's a very smart opponent. She'll spend lives for information to save lives later. She does what she has to. I admire her," Runner admitted.

For all intents and purposes, the enemy general would assume the Barbarians would remain holed up and leave the Sunless army to its fate.

Queen Helen and Runner had decided the best course of action was to carry on the charade of noninterference on the part of the Barbarians.

In truth, much of the Barbarians' city militia, royal guard, and retired veterans had left the castle early this morning. They were now tucked in close to the Sunless' flank, waiting for the chance to dive into the Human army's own flank.

"Very well." Helen turned her head to look down at the tanks arrayed below them. Barbarian casters weren't numerous as they typically preferred melee, but there were more than enough of them to fill the tank's troop compartments.

Into the tanks they went, the wooden constructions shifting as their occupants settled inside.

Off to one side was Boxy. Runner had left with the Barbarians this morning when they departed to get into position. Hannah had returned to the camp during the same time as well.

They'd stashed Boxy inside the castle walls. A contingent of Sunless noblewomen waited, lined up in two neat rows.

When the call came to prepare his personal tank, they had assembled themselves without being asked to. In fact, Runner had assumed he was going to fill it with Barbarians.

The Sunless noblewomen didn't know what to make of Runner but he'd earned their respect. They were more than likely not as eager to get into his bed, thankfully, though their admiration of him had gone up and they had decided to serve as his personal tank crew.

Queen Helen apparently followed his eyes and nodded to his tank.

"You're popular."

"Unfortunately. I already have enough troubles in my life with women. They've already all been told I'm unavailable."

"And are you? I have spoken to a few of them. They talk of others."

Once again Runner had to admire the queen. She was very intelligent and quick on the uptake. She'd immediately jumped on the opportunity to question the Sunless about Runner to get more information.

"To anyone outside of the four they speak of, I'm unavailable. I'm the worst kind of man. I can't decide. So I've chosen not to. I doubt that's pleasing to your ear being the mother of one of them."

"Her life is her own. I expect her to provide an heir eventually, but other than that I care little. My own husband was worse than you could ever be," Queen Helen said, her head turning back to the open field before them.

"I'll take that as your blessing then. Time for me to load up I'm afraid."

Bowing his head to the queen, Runner dropped from the top of the wall to the courtyard, losing half his health in the process.

Casting *Regeneration* on himself, he stood casually and walked towards his waiting tank crew.

A black-eyed beauty with long black hair eyed him as he neared. Her features had a grace and elegance to them that were set off by the darkness of her hair and eyes, and her body reeked of overindulgent artists. Beauty took on a whole new meaning when someone could draw every curve the way they wanted.

Taking a step forward, she straightened her shoulders and lifted her perfect chin.

She had no name and happened to be listed as "Sunless Noble." Level thirty-four and dressed well, she was assuredly a versatile and heavy hitting caster. She could be useful. Besides, it wasn't like he had anything to lose.

"Ready to serve, sir."

"Understood. Name?"

"Sophia," the buxom brunette said. Her shoulders straightened further, if that was possible.

"No surname?"

"Sophia Tai."

"Family?"

"Older brother, parents."

Which made her expendable and why she was here.

"Sophia's a nice name, but I'm a fan of nicknames. In this case, you look like the very image of a noble sunless lady. So you're Grace," Runner explained, moving to the rear of Boxy.

"I imagine I'll eventually have a personal guard as well as a palace guard. They'll be made up of various aspects of each base class. To that end I'll need people in charge to run herd on them. I'd like to consider you for the role of captain. Pay to be established later since I have no formal ranks at this time but it'll be relevant to a royal guard captain. You'll need to work off whatever terms you have with your king first before you serve me."

"I serve no contract to anyone and am here at my family's request. I accept and request to be considered yours immediately," Sophia said. Her nameplate shifted from "Sunless Noble" to "Sophia Tai" before she even finished speaking.

Runner felt odd about that change. He hadn't seen that happen before and he felt like it didn't bode well for the system.

"So be it. Consider yourself hired. Serve well or be replaced. Start working at hiring those who will roll up under you." Runner paused and scratched at his cheek, considering.

"Shoot for two hundred and two. Two lieutenants report to you directly. Each lieutenant will have four sergeants. Each sergeant will have four corporals. Each corporal five troopers. Creates a base squad size of six. I expect you to hire so that each squad has an appropriate party make up and can function independently."

Sophia seemed stunned at the instant acceptance and number given to her. Eventually she turned her head to the nine other women beside her, then looked back to Runner.

"I have nine already. Only a few to go."

Runner laughed and shook his head, smiling. Runner appreciated humor. Dark humor more so.

Sophia smiled wide in return at him, her pointed teeth making an appearance. As if realizing it, she tried to close her mouth and smile with her lips only. Thana had mentioned most people seemed put off by the Sunless' teeth.

"Ptff, get over that, Grace. I love the Sunless smile. If you ever try to hide it again, I'll fire you. Same goes for the rest of you." Runner peered at the other women. Who promptly all showed him genuine Sunless smiles. "Alright. Load up. Asses and elbows, ladies. You're in charge of everything but driving, Grace."

The moment the last of them had gotten in, Runner clambered up and locked the rear door in place. Stopping in the middle of the cabin, Runner pulled out a new addition he'd been working on.

Shaped like a narrow bookcase, it held a large number of small shelves that looked more like a wine rack. Those individual slots were padded to prevent the contents from smacking into the wood.

Each row had been labeled for what would be there. Runner had made anything that might hold a small use for anyone aboard Boxy.

Runner tied the new piece into Boxy and attached it through his broken crafting abilities. Rapidly he emptied his inventory of his hoard of potions, filling each and every slot.

"Familiarize yourself with everything in the racks. Anything that's an ability is a quick use. Drink it, then use the ability. If you need a potion, drink it. You're not replaceable, potions are," Runner said offhandedly over his shoulder as he took his seat at the front.

Shame revive is Player only.

Checking his map, he confirmed everyone was in position. Before he could close it, the gate dropped down. That could only mean that the enemy line had engaged Thana's emplacement.

Pulling the shifter into second and dropping the brake, Runner angled himself to the front of the other six tanks and towards the gatehouse.

Each tank driver had been given an instruction manual early this morning describing the limitations of the tanks' speed and refresh rate. He only hoped the Barbarian drivers would be as quick-witted as their queen.

Popping it into third gear as he cleared the gatehouse, Runner felt his heartbeat accelerating. The insane bloodlust he'd felt the first time around didn't overwhelm him. His night with Katarina and the previous bloodbath had been very therapeutic.

The tension and pressure on him was still there, but not as bad. He had solutions. Workable solutions that were in progress.

They'd be at the battle in only a minute. His opposing general apparently thought little of the Barbarian leadership. After having met the king he couldn't blame her. She'd pay for it though.

Like a curtain being drawn wide, Runner saw the enemy forces and his own engaged in battle. Instead of an unbroken line, his foe had split her forces up into smaller groups and spread them out until they reached his own troops.

There they had piled back up into a line and fought. She was trying to limit casualties from his cannons and the eventual return of his single tank. With only one tank, losses would still be numerous but severely reduced.

The flanks of the army were filled with heavy cavalry. Previously she had held them in reserve in case he attempted to flank with his own cavalry.

He imagined those heavy horse soldiers were there to chase after Boxy after she passed through. Apparently the general had made plans to deal with Runner's toys.

A pity for them he had seven now. This general was a problem though. A real problem.

"Grace!" Runner shouted backwards. After a second the brunette was there, her lips next to his ear.

"Yes, sir?"

"Slight change of plans, Grace. Pop the rear door and throw the 'free attack' sign out at the others. We'll be angling for the command tent. This general learns quick and I want her done. She'll be confused by the six tanks and not expect a seventh from the rear. Everyone else needs to load up on silence and sleep potions. I want the sleeping general and anyone else around her taking a nap as well."

"Your will, sir."

Then Sophia was gone.

Runner waited until he heard the rear hatch close again before swinging out wide and away from the battle. It would take some time to do it, but if he could secure the general, this would be over today.

Taking a peek from his side view port, he watched the six tanks continue onwards. Looking straight ahead again, he called up his map. He needed to figure out where she'd be. If he were her, where would he put his own command site? Especially if he'd been attacked once already. Close enough that he could watch the battle but flee if the fight wasn't going his way.

With his fingertip, Runner followed a side road that led towards open fields. Every other direction would put them closer to harm's way or a dead end.

Ranging the approach, Runner kept them moving.

Behind him the clink of bottles could be heard as his little magical troop stocked up. Sophia returned after a few minutes of them driving endlessly.

"We're ready, sir. I will give you your general personally. When we take her, where should we put her?"

"Tie her up and drop her over my lap. Anywhere else she might bounce around and get hurt. If she's hurt, she'll wake up. Be gentle."

"Your will, sir."

Runner rolled his eyes but kept silent. This "sir" business was grating on his nerves.

His mind went down a path he didn't want it to and was helpless to stop. His thoughts firing one after another with questions aimed at himself from himself.

Here you are. Defending a virtual country you don't need to. You say you could have escaped the castle, yet you could easily have ditched the entire army. This is all pointless. Even now the medical server is connecting itself to every pod in preparation. It'll be ready in only a few hours. All you need to do is move everyone. Then you're done. They're safe. But this? This is all pointless. So, why?

Thoughts of his party flashed through his mind. Then his extended party, like Isabelle and Stefan. Then those connected to his party. Even the goddesses.

He had promised to keep the world running for Nadine. Now, though, he was trying to fix what he could.

He couldn't answer his questions. He was also out of time.

He had been wrong in his guess on the general's command post. But only by thirty feet or so. She had moved herself further back than his original estimate. Moving Boxy to her first gear, Runner crept along, keeping the noise output as low as possible.

The moment they noticed him he planned on hitting it into fifth.

There.

His blonde counterpart had armed herself and taken up a guard this time. Surrounded by armored knights, she held a staff in her left hand as she watched the battle.

Runner selected the general and stuck a red X symbol on her. Then began marking everyone around her with other markings.

Runner had just opened his mouth to explain when he heard Sophia's voice.

"Red X is the target. Sleep every other target. I'll take her personally," Sophia commanded. He heard the rear hatch open in preparation for the grab and bag. Runner suddenly felt a deep gratitude to Sophia. Already she was earning her keep.

Amazingly Runner got them within fifty yards before they were noticed. Runner slammed it into fifth gear and Boxy surged forward. Blondie didn't even turn her head—she was completely focused on the battle. Barreling into the command camp, he avoided everyone and everything in his singular drive to capture the general.

Finally, her head turned as Runner whipped Boxy around into a fishtail to present the rear door at the target.

Sophia and her double-sized squad leapt out of the moving vehicle before he brought it into neutral. Looking over his shoulder, he watched and waited, feeling helpless.

Shouting and yelling came to him along with a few magical detonations, then silence.

The Sunless squad came stumbling back in through the hatch. Two had half health bars and a third happened to be in the red and looked like she'd been hit with a couple debuffs, but they were there.

Sophia and a troop member clambered in, each carrying a body. The final member came in and shut the hatch. Sophia dropped the bound blonde general into Runner's lap and she took the second sleeping body into her arms.

Sitting down right there in the middle of the cabin, Sophia pulled the sleeping woman into her lap and started yelling orders at her crew. No time to question her about the second person. Runner slapped the shifter into fifth gear.

Pressing his right hand into the general's lower back, he held her in place as he drove with his left hand.

"Sorry, General. We weren't going to take any chances. You're far too smart for your own good. You have everyone's utmost respect and admiration," Runner apologetically said, rubbing the general's back lightly. "Have no fear, no one intends to abuse you or cause you harm. Providing you agree to my terms. Otherwise it will be a very clean and very swift death. I promise."

Then they were clear of the command camp. Ahead of them the battle continued on.

His cannons fired every moment they could get a clear shot. Tanks swept back and forth through the ranks in a wedge formation.

His Barbarian allies had engaged one of the cavalry flanks and were currently destroying it as the other side's cavalry battled Runner's.

Now he could see why blondie had been so into the fight. It wasn't going her way at all.

Thana, Katarina, Hannah, Nadine, and Isabelle were doing spectacularly. Smiling, proud of his Awakened Naturals, he spun the wheel till he was heading towards the rear of the battle.

Stopping a few hundred yards short of the fight, he spun Boxy around so her rear faced the troops.

Shifting the general carefully, he tried not to harm her. Eventually he managed to get her to his shoulder.

"Grace, I'm going to see if I can get them to surrender. Guard duty," Runner said as he stood up, his left arm wrapped around the general's thighs and his right hand pressing to her waist to steady her.

"You, you, and you. Wall spells if needed. You and you, guard duty from the vehicle. Rest of you on bodyguard status. I'm on sleep watch for our guest," Sophia ordered, setting the little brunette she had been holding to the side.

Runner was a bit astonished at how well she was doing. His paranoia even went up a notch.

"Grace, where have you been all my life? I never expected this," Runner quipped as he made his way to the rear door. Two of the noblewomen opened the hatch and scurried outside to secure the area.

"Being raised to be an obedient wife," she said, standing up. "I begged Lady Thana for assistance in military tactics. Though I find myself beggared to her in favors, I have been given an extensive library on small-force tactics," said the woman, keeping close to Runner's side.

"I'll let her know I appreciate what she did for you. You're worth your weight in gold already," Runner said, coming to a halt in the grass. "Brighteyes, Angel, Minxy, I'm about to kick this anthill over. As always, you're welcome to join me if you see fit."

"You always have the best surprises," Brunhild murmured as she simply appeared in front of him.

"Yes," Ernsta agreed, nodding her head.

"Sure, love. You're good for a show. That and I get to stare at your ass," Amelia purred at him, immediately closing to within touching distance.

"Down, girl. Occupied right now." Runner called up his GM command list once more.

/Commands
Available Commands:
Adopt
Broadcast
ClassReset
DiasbleChat
Divorce
EnableChat
GMHub
LogOut
Marry
Rename
GMHubReturn
Unstuck

/Broadcast

Broadcast X(zone) Y(zone distance: measured in number of units from point specified)

/Broadcast Kastell 1

"Soldiers of the Human army, I am Runner Norwood, known as Breaker. On my life to Ernsta, Brunhild, and Amelia, I swear to you your general has fallen and is now my personal captive. Should you surrender immediately, by lying on the ground, face down, I will take your lives and safety into my custody. You will survive this ordeal and be free once this war is done. You have ten seconds to comply. No clemency will be granted after this."

"Witnessed," the trio of goddesses boomed in response.

Like a ripple passing through water, handfuls of soldiers dropped to their faces, then tens, then hundreds.

Till even the cavalry were lying face down on the ground, and the battle was over.

"Pack 'em up, Grace. We're heading back to Kastell. Game over," Runner chirped.

Chapter 15 - Outplayed -

9:19 am Sovereign Earth time
11/18/43

Runner sighed and squatted down in front of the brunette they had captured. She was tied to a chair and bound in such a way that she was helpless. Sleep was the spell of the day and between himself, Sophia, and liberal amounts of potions, they were able to keep both her and the general incapacitated the entire trip here.

Apparently the brunette was the second-in-command. Prettier than most and fuller in figure as well, she could definitely turn a head back on Earth. Here she was average. Maybe a touch above.

"So, we'll do this in a simple fashion. You'll serve me, or you can die. I can't have soldiers of your quality running around and possibly ruining my plans. Just consider this the evil monologue and we'll be fine." Runner paused and suddenly laughed at himself.

"That actually was a pretty villainous thing to say. Ah well. I'll also answer any questions you have but then I'll expect you to answer. Your oath will be made to Ernsta. Should you fail in your oath, you will die and your soul is hers. To be clear, she could decide to use it as floss or bury it in a pig farm. Her choice." Runner frowned and gestured at the brunette.

Sophia was the only soul with him at this juncture. The rest of Sophia's squad was in the general's room next door and the hallway between the two. Runner's own party was currently processing the mass of prisoners they'd taken.

Reaching out a hand, Sophia cleansed the sleep from the second-in-command, simply named "Aide de camp."

Immediately she began casting a spell with Runner as the target.

Runner activated *Throat Strike* and sighed.

"Last chance. I don't want to kill you if I don't have to."

As soon as the interrupt wore off, the woman began casting once more.

Runner hit her with *Silence* and then flicked a hand back at Sophia. Rubbing at the bridge of his nose with his left hand, he contemplated the situation.

"So be it. I'll take care of her myself and dump the body. Stuff her head in a bag. I don't really want to look at her when I do it." Runner gave the order without looking to his subordinate.

"Of course, sir" Sophia said, moving to stand behind the prisoner. She pulled a dark black bag from her inventory and pulled it down over the motionless aide de camp.

"Mind going to the other room? I promised her I'd make it clean and quick but I'd rather not have an audience," Runner said, still rubbing at the t-section of his forehead.

"Of course, sir," Sophia responded, moving to leave the room immediately.

When the door closed behind Sophia, Runner looked up at the brunette and got to his feet.

"Well, let's get this over with."

Runner reached out and grabbed the prisoner by the shoulders since the ability required physical contact and then mentally thumbed a preset macro he'd made titled "GMHub 1."

/GMHub 1
Teleporting...

Active settings only:
Death=On
Food/Water=On
Damage=On
Gravity=100%
Biome=Plane
Day/Night Cycle=On

And then he and the brunette were in an empty grassland. Runner typed in a rapid series of commands as the woman tumbled to the ground. The chair, her bonds, and the sleep spell were suddenly all gone.

/GMHub Settings
Death off
Damage off
Food/water off

Settings changed:
Death=Off
Damage=Off
Food/Water=Off

Coming up with her staff pointed at him, she took a fighting stance, glaring at Runner.

"Yeah, don't bother," Runner said, gesturing at the staff. The aide stared at her staff and then gave it a light shake. Apparently nothing happened at the end of her cast.

"You're done with the world. This is your life now. I'll come back and visit you in a day or two to see if you're willing to talk. Oh, and food for thought. When was the last time you went to the bathroom? Right, then. See ya."

Runner tapped the premade button to return.

/GMHubReturn
Teleporting...

Back in the little narrow room, Runner pushed the chair to the wall.

Definitely has the potential for a prison. What else can I do with it?

He gave the room once last check to see if they had left anything. Finding nothing, he opened the door and stepped out.

"It's done," Runner said to Sophia, who moved to stand at his elbow.

He crossed to the second room, opened the door, and stepped in.

"Everyone please exit and remain on station in the corridor. Sophia and I will be working on the general now."

Immediately the squad of beautiful Sunless noblewomen trooped by him. Once the door clicked, Runner turned and squatted down in front of the general.

"Alright, general. Your turn. This is quite simple. You'll serve me or you'll die. I'm afraid I can't leave you running around. Your aide chose death and she is no longer of this world. Any oath you make to me would be safeguarded by a trio of goddesses. I'll answer any questions you have. If you'd please, Grace?" Runner asked, pointing a finger at the blonde general.

Sophia ended the sleep spell on her and Runner waited to see what would happen.

"You'll answer questions?" the general said, her deep gray eyes flicking from him to Sophia and back.

Runner nodded his head at that, watching her. Her eyes were deep and intelligent. She had a certain aura to her and she definitely had her charms. The short blonde hair reminded him of Amelia. Maybe a touch fuller in the chest and hips, but definitely well put together. Certainly above the norm even here.

"Did you really have to kill her?"

Runner ping ponged his head back and forth as he pretended to think on his answer.

"Yes and no. Yes because I can't risk her running around. I really can't. No because I could have had her swear an oath. Though that seems as unlikely as the other, doesn't it? Next question."

"You say I would serve you. In what capacity? I won't warm your bed."

Runner laughed at that and shook his head.

"Why does everyone assume that's what I want?"

"Wishful thinking? She's welcome to warm my bed instead," Sophia supplied, which only made Runner laugh the more.

"Nice. Maybe she'll warm yours and you warm mine and I'll warm hers."

"I wouldn't mind. Consider me up for the challenge, sir."

"Very forward thinking of you, Grace. To answer your question, no, General. I have enough lady problems as it is. I don't need forced sex slaves. As for the capacity in which you'd function, something similar to what you were doing previously. It'd be under my discretion. Why would I have you do something other than what you're good at?"

"You would trust me?"

"Not really, no. I'd have you swear an oath to the three aforementioned goddesses who would love to use your soul to power themselves. Should any of them find you in violation they'll probably suck you dry faster than an alcoholic prostitute looking for her next bottle. Though I would put in the condition that I have to approve of it first. Wouldn't want them taking you down without due cause. Unless it's an attempt on my life. Then you're done."

The general's chin fell at that answer and she turned her thoughts inward, chewing on the whole thing mentally.

"What's your name, General? I have a great deal of respect for you, so I'd like to at least address you correctly. That or I can start calling you Blondie."

"Faye, Faye Sennet."

"Faye. Pretty name. Do you have family left behind in Crivel or Faren?"

Faye looked startled at the question, her eyes darting from him to Sophia and then her own knees.

"I-I don't know. Before this war I didn't-I didn't question, err...I..." She trailed off, her eyes losing a bit of their definition.

"Ah. You're Awakening. This is an easy discussion for someone of your intelligence. When was the last time you used the bathroom? Think on that. While you think on that, compare your memories of before the war to right now. You'll find they, well, taste different. Com—"

He was interrupted when the door opened. Glancing over his shoulder, he saw one of his new guards poke her head in.

"Lord Runner, Queen Helen will be ready for you soon," she said, then disappeared back out the door.

"Damn," Runner said, looking back to Faye. "I'm afraid our time is drawing to a close, Faye."

"Can...can you give me more time? A few hours maybe? It's a lot to take in. Put me in a closet? A prison cell? I need time," she muttered, her voice fading at the end.

Runner could only imagine her tactical mind was burning through the information at a truly frightening rate of speed.

Runner stopped and scratched at his head.

"Well, maybe. Grace, do you think you'd be comfortable taking care of Faye with a few of your squad to back you up? Keep her in the sleep spell while she thinks it over. It isn't a true sleep so she should be able to process her thoughts. You should have more than enough potions to keep her gone until tomorrow morning."

"I don't like leaving you unguarded. Though I do like the idea of keeping an eye on her."

"I'll take the rest with me—you're welcome to pick who. Probably a good time for you to figure out who your second is anyways."

Sophia pressed her full lips together in annoyance and nodded once. Her left hand came up and Faye was put to sleep once more. Sophia turned and left the room to prepare her squad.

Runner leaned in and spoke into Faye's ear.

"I'll be back to check on you. They're under orders not to harm you in any way. Please let me know if they disobey. We'll talk more on my return. Oh, and Faye? I really do have a deep respect for you. You handled the entire ordeal far better than I expected for someone in your position. I truly do want you for myself. It'd be like shattering a masterpiece if I had to dispose of you."

Runner left the general there. Alone in a room and tied to a chair.

Time to see the queen.

Ten minutes had passed since he'd presented himself at the throne room door. Ten minutes before he was called in.

"Runner Norwood, known as Breaker, general to King Vasilios, chosen of Ernsta, Brunhild, and Amelia, ally to the peoples of Kastell!" shouted the herald as Runner entered the room.

A day after the king's death the entire throne room had changed. Everyone was dressed immaculately, it smelled quite nice, and there were even decorations here and there.

Ally, eh?

A single throne sat atop the dais now, the queen standing before it. Her giant war axe rested in easy reach against the throne. She resembled King Vasilios far more today. She looked queenly and felt like it. Majestic. Powerful. Regal.

Dropping to one knee at a respectable distance, he bowed his head deeply in respect to her.

"Queen Helen, the task is done. The enemy army is broken, I am interrogating the captured enemy general, and her forces are being processed as prisoners. By your will and hand, Kastell is free of invaders," Runner said loudly, making sure all heard his words.

"Stand," the queen proclaimed. Runner brought himself to a standing position. "We personally thank you, Runner Norwood. Your forces bled for us while we hid behind our walls. We will not forget our brave Sunless brothers and sisters who died on our land."

Quest Completed

Quest rating: Extremely difficult. Rewards tripled.
Raid leader: You receive a quadruple portion.

"°úÆ█┿π"
Experience Reward: 835% of current level
Reputation: 2,000
Fame: 3,000
Money: 1,000 Platinum

Level up!
You've reached level 28
Level up!
You've reached level 29
Level up!
You've reached level 30
Level up!
You've reached level 31
Level up!
You've reached level 32
Level up!
You've reached level 33

Runner balked at the rapid screen prompts. Leveling up would need to wait for a quiet moment alone.

Queen Helen bowed her head to him. No small sign of respect from a royal.

"Though others may know you as Breaker, we name you Vindicator. You, who showed up unasked for and unwelcome. Who bled for us and forced us to help ourselves, despite our original unwillingness. Who asked nothing more than that we join in our own battle. You gave us our honor and preserved our right of personal governance."

You've earned the title Vindicator
You've earned 2,000 fame

Runner ducked his head to the queen once again in thanks.

"Thank you, my queen."

"This is a minor thing. What else can we reward you with?"

"I ask nothing for myself. My home is in disrepair and my people will have needs. I have requested crafters from Vasilios. As your people are renowned for their martial skill and equable customs under the law, I would ask for a contingent of your guards to be loaned to me for a year. I would ask they perform their function there as they do here. I will pay their upkeep equally to what you pay them now plus a small bonus for being away from home. I would ask for only volunteers."

Queen Helen tilted her head to one side as she studied him.

"You annoy us. This is not a proper reward for your services."

"Yet it is what I request."

"So be it. We'll have this taken care of. Where is your home?"

"Vix."

"You are the owner of Vix?"

A Quest has been generated
"A Homeland"
Experience Reward: 140% of current level
Reputation: 400
Fame: 400
Title: (Determined by choice upon completion)
Money: 0
Do you Accept?
Yes/No

WARNING! Experience Reward is adjusted based on current level at turn in

Runner hesitated before answering. He had only meant North Wood Fort, but if he could claim the whole island…well. That'd be great, too.

/Yes
Quest Accepted

"Ah, not as of yet. Though it is my goal. My base of operations is the North Wood Fort."

"We are curious. What will you do now?"

"We'll rest for a few days, finish up the prisoner processing, and then I must head south. I will end this war by bringing it to the enemy's doorstep."

"Did good King Vasilios include that in your mission?"

"No, my queen. I will be asking for volunteers of those who came with me to follow me south. I will go by myself if I must."

"No such thing. We name you general of an army yet to be formed. They will serve you in whatever fashion you need them to in the goal of ending this war. They will be ready by your departure. We will also send a dispatch to our good neighbor Vasilios and ask his forgiveness but that we encouraged you to go south."

Runner felt better with that offer made. He had been hoping for something along those lines but hadn't dared ask for it.

"You should know, the royal family of Faren is no more. They were murdered in a coup by a man named Jacob. He is now acting as king. We hear another tale that he is the champion of Lambart."

Ah. That does explain a few things.

"Yes. That's one of the reasons I need to head south. Jacob is an…acquaintance of mine. An acquaintanceship I'd like to end. Violently."

"We understand. Go. Rest, relax. We've prepared a room for you in the royal guest quarters." Queen Helen dismissed him.

Runner bowed at the waist to her, then left the throne room. Pausing in an empty antechamber, he called up the level up screen as his personal guard spread out in the room. He dropped three points into dexterity, two into intelligence, and one into agility, then closed the screen.

Memories of a life spent at home on a computer blasted him. Learning how to work through, on, and around systems. Playing video games till his joints ached from pods and controllers.

Very introverted things. Things that he had known about himself without knowing.

Calling up the character stats screen, he read over his numbers.

Name:		Runner	
Level:	33	Class:	
Race:	Human	Experience:	81%
Alignment:	Good	Reputation:	2,020
Fame:	18,155	Bounty:	0

Attributes-			
Strength:	1	Constitution:	1(31)
Dexterity:	14(44)	Intelligence:	13(43)
Agility:	8(38)	Wisdom:	1
Stamina:	1(31)	Charisma:	64(124)

Runner felt a little better. He'd been unmoving on his level for so long due to the massive nature of his army-sized raid.

Taking a breath, he tried to organize his mind.

Okay. To-do list: Faye, prisoners, medical server, Jacob, Srit.

Slapping his cheeks with his hands, he tried to work up some motivation. Success tended to make him complacent.

Stepping out of the antechamber, he decided to go to the prisoners first. Faye might need more time. Sophia could keep her company. Runner even trusted Sophia.

A minute or two later he was at the gatehouse and hopping into Boxy. Runner made his way to the controls and sat himself down.

They had decided to process the entire lot of them on the site itself. Ernsta would be holding sway over the proceedings as each swore to her on their life. Much as the first set of prisoners had.

Today felt like it would be a long day for him. Runner checked a sigh and flipped the brake and slid the shifter into gear.

6:43 pm Sovereign Earth time
11/18/43

Runner collapsed face-first into his bed. He had managed to get nearly nothing done.

Such a great accomplishment of derring-do.

Runner let his mind drift and thought about the day.

Faye had wanted more time in the end. Again.

She did agree to swear to the triumvirate of goddesses that she would remain in the room unguarded until told she could leave.

Apparently Srit had turned up but Katarina, Hannah, and Nadine had hustled her off and they were now in "training." Runner didn't care, so long as they were all safe. Safe and happy.

Thana and Isabelle were the only ones present at the prisoner camp. They were as busy as he was.

Conversation had been work related since there wasn't any time for anything else. On top of that he swore that there was a certain chill to Thana.

"Medical server," Runner mumbled into his pillow.

Groaning, he rolled over to a sitting position and called up the ship's system console.

Logging in, he confirmed that the medical server was indeed ready and connected to the main computer. He could begin transferring people at any time.

Pulling up the name of a brain-dead crew member, he mentally winced. *Mitica Vasile.*

A name he wouldn't forget anytime soon. He had been the first brain-dead crew member he personally confirmed.

/Status Vasile, Mitica
User: VasMit001 logged in

/Status POD 348,431
L O A D I N G
ALERT: POD 348,431 reports no brain wave activity
LOG: Emergency medical teams alerted seven hundred ninety-two hours and four minutes ago

/Activate dream sequencer VasMit001 MedServ01

Connecting...
Connection successful

/Transfer VasMit001*TGBD MedServ01

Transferring...
Error: Credentials lacking for MedServ01.

IT department must authorize

User: NorRun001
Transfer request pending
Please enter Password: **************
Password Accepted

Further confirmation needed

Captain must confirm transfer

User: NorRun001
Transfer request pending
Audio verification needed: 4238147 Xulu Foxtrot Romeo

"Four, two, three, eight, one, four, seven, xulu foxtrot romeo," Runner repeated aloud.

Verification Accepted
Transferring...
Transfer Complete

/Current active Users MedServ01
1

/Status Vasile, Mitica
User: VasMit001 logged in

"Right, then. Pending a test on a live person, seems like it works? Goodie."

/Activate dream sequencer NorRun001 MedServ01

Connecting…
Connection failure

ALERT: POD 500,000 is unresponsive
It is not part of the network

/Transfer NorRun001*TGBD MedServ01

Transferring…
ALERT: POD 500,000 is unresponsive
It is not part of the network

Runner hung his head, putting his face in his hands. Jacob had decided that Runner would join him in his off-network status. Maybe Jacob had hoped it would prevent Runner from being able to access his IT privileges.

Doesn't matter. I have no idea how he did it, and I can't undo it. I'm trapped. I can't leave. Not unless Jacob tells me what he did. Or I figure it out.

Using one hand, he typed two commands into his console.

/Current active Users
499,921

/Pods in network
499,919

Closing his eyes and swallowing a catch in his breath, he lay back down in his bed. His hands closed in on his face and covered his eyes as if he could hide away from the truth.

For better or worse, Runner would be one of only two people who couldn't leave the game safely.

And he was alone again. Alone in his room.

His party had been sequestered elsewhere. For whatever reason, Queen Helen had decided that Runner needed his own room.

Probably related to her daughter. He didn't blame her for that really.

And here in the heart of Kastell, he had no need of his own guards. Sophia and her squad had returned to their rooms.

Alone.

10:43 pm Sovereign Earth time
11/18/43

Runner sat bolt upright, looking around the room for enemies. They were coming. Eyes darting from corner to corner, checking, moving, Runner cleared the room as he began inventorying his options and what he had on him.

He knew he was locked in a room alone. He had escaped the pursuit and ducked into this room hoping to find an escape. Instead he was now surrounded by those who would kill him. He had to get out, he had to find the others—

Soft warm arms wrapped around him from behind, holding him in a tender embrace.

"Be calm. All is well, dear heart. You're safe," Thana whispered into his ear. She had pressed herself bodily into his back. She held him gently as if her grip was as thin as tissue paper.

Runner panted heavily, his right hand gripping one of Thana's forearms. Slowly, the nightmare was clearing. Like fog burning off under a bright sun.

Swallowing, he shook his head as his brain clanged into first gear.

"That was a bad one," Runner whispered, his voice shuddering.

"I know, I'm sorry. I'm here for you," Thana said, her chin pressed to his shoulder. "I must concede I do not envy your ability to dream at times. You so often have nightmares."

Runner's jangled nerves were calming as the adrenaline fueled panic died away.

"Oh, they're definitely terrible. Dreams, in general, are great though. They often provide inspiration or maybe a reprieve."

"So I read. Sexual fantasies included."

"Indeed. Where else can I get four women to share my bed at the same time?" Runner jokingly said, and then regretted it instantly. In this moment of closeness, he'd forgotten about what he'd done to and with Katarina. He could also conclude it was the reason Thana had been a little distant.

"When you're calm, I believe we should talk," Thana said quietly, patting his shoulder with a delicate hand.

And there it is. Here we go then.

"Stop tensing. I'm not leaving, nor is Hannah, or Nadine."

Runner nodded his head, closing his eyes.

"Are you already set on this then? I wouldn't push this on you until you're mentally...fit? Stable isn't the right word."

"I'm fine. Please, continue."

Thana was silent for a second or two before she began speaking again. She didn't release him though. If anything he'd swear she leaned into him more.

"You slept with Katarina." It wasn't a question.

"I did."

"You chose her?"

"Not exactly. I told her up front that if it had been you, Hanners, or Rabbit, I would say yes to them as well. Much as I explained to Hanners the other day, I'm taking the coward's way out. I won't be choosing anyone. I'm afraid I couldn't choose even if I wanted to. I fear losing you all in choosing, and I fear losing you all in not choosing. So I choose not to choose."

"I see. A terribly Runner answer of you. So you would have slept with anyone?" she asked in a whisper.

Runner pressed his lips together as his left hand dug into his pant leg. His right hand remained holding to Thana's arm.

"No. Never. You, Hanners, Rabbit, and Kitten. That's it."

"Ah," she whispered.

Time moved on a second at a time. Agonizingly.

"I suppose it's a good thing no one is asking you to choose then, isn't it? In fact, one could say you're the only one who's been worrying over this the entire time."

"What?" Runner said flatly.

"It's true. Has anyone asked you to choose?"

"No."

"Runner, I'm afraid you really are a bit slow at times, aren't you?"

"Yeah, kinda. I'm not good with women. I've never actually been the aggressor before."

"We noticed."

"We?"

"Of course. You thought we wouldn't talk? Share information? Did you think this was a tacky romance novel where they all fight each other over one man? Please."

"I don't understand."

"Clearly. For now, know that no one is asking you to do anything. Continue on as you have been. You'll get there eventually." Thana sighed dramatically and pulled at him a little tighter with her hands.

"You don't care that I would sleep with all of you in a heartbeat?"

"I'm not exactly thrilled at that idea, no. Though they're all women I would consider a sister so it's not so terrible either."

"You sound unsure, yourself."

"I am. We all are. It's a brand-new world out there. You change and break it wherever you go. So far, for the better. The benefits are finally paying off. Still no dental. We did all level three times when you had your meeting with the queen."

Runner nodded his head a little.

"Quest completed. Wait, so, you're not upset I slept with Katarina?"

"At first. The first few minutes. It was something we'd all talked about before it happened. If it should happen. After she explained it, though, I felt better. It's not ideal, not what any of us wanted, but it's workable."

Runner would swear he'd just received tacit approval of being in a five-way relationship. He considered perhaps that it had to do with the fact that they were all Naturals. Then immediately dismissed that as he knew they had the full range of emotions one expected of a person.

One thing at a time.

"That isn't to say that if you ever tried to include anyone further we wouldn't leave. Nor would we seek to bring in others," Thana said quickly. Her fingers tightened into his clothes as if to emphasize the point.

"I'm afraid I still don't quite understand. If I had to put words to my thoughts, I would say it almost sounds like you're telling me you'd enter a relationship with me, with Katarina included. And that you'd allow it to extend to Hannah and Nadine if they desired it. In a non-romantic way between the four of you, that is."

"I suppose I am," Thana grumbled and then sighed. "You're a pathetic excuse for a man, though I find myself willing to take a quarter rather than nothing. I'm not sure if that makes me more pathetic than you, or not."

"Less, to be sure. I'm sorry. I can't stand the idea of hurting any of you. I'd almost rather walk away from the whole thing than harm any of you."

"That's one of the reasons we convened the 'Runner's an idiot, let's talk' council. Hannah was concerned you were going to run."

Runner grunted, unsure of how to proceed. He was intrigued at the idea that Hannah was the one to suggest it though.

Turning his head to the side, he found Thana's warm brown eyes inches from his own.

"Where does that leave us?"

"Alone in a bed."

"This is true. Speaking of, how'd you get in here? Queen Helen seemed to deliberately separate us all."

"*Stealth* potion. As to the queen, I believe she did that for your own safety. Apparently capturing the enemy general alive endeared you to quite a few young noble ladies of the court. Trouble is, they're not as polite or as subtle as Sunless women."

"Oh. It's the charisma stat, it's not me."

Thana laughed and then pressed her lips to his. She pulled back as quickly as she had moved in and gave him a bright smile.

"You're an idiot if you believe that. I'm cold and this castle is drafty. Warm this subtle Sunless Sorceress up already."

"I can do that. Can do it repeatedly."

"And you shall."

4:26 am Sovereign Earth time
11/19/43

Runner felt his thoughts sharpen as his mind fired up. Nothing was out of the ordinary, it wasn't a bad dream, and as far as he could tell everything was as it should be.

Thana shifted against him and her hand moved a few inches. Her fingers lightly rested against his stomach.

She settled her naked body once more into his side. Her long dark hair was starting to escape from its braid and spilled out on his chest.

Almost everything, that is.

A naked Thana couldn't be further from ordinary.

Runner couldn't help but wonder at his life's turn of events and what it meant for him. Brunhild had been closer to the truth than he realized at the time. Apparently his little harem had been arranging itself without his knowledge.

They'd been working through their own feelings about the situation without any input from him.

Thana's only request was that he continue on as he had been, which would be easy. He'd treat them as he'd done so up to this point.

He seemed blessed and cursed in his own eyes. Granted incredible boons that were far outside the realm of normalcy and dashed upon the rocks on every other beat.

In truth it didn't make sense. Not really.

Women didn't normally go in for polygamous relationships. At least not that he'd heard. Though he knew they happened in certain cultures and religions. Or so history books claimed before the Sovereign made everyone into one culture.

Maybe I died. Maybe this whole thing is nothing more than an afterlife for me. Maybe none of this is real at all. Maybe I'm dreaming. Do I try to wake up? Do I fight it? Do I—

Thana lifted one of her legs and draped it over his waist, cuddling closer to him in her sleep.

Good dream, very fair, lovely feeling. Thank you very much, hope I never wake up. Long live the dreamer.

Reinvigorated with his life Runner smiled. Even one spent forever in this game wouldn't be too terrible.

Runner rolled over and proceeded to wake Thana up. Sunrise was still a fair bit off. No time to waste.

At long last, his group had reassembled. They were sitting around a table, eating breakfast.

Nadine had finally stopped fussing over everyone after everyone got a full plate. Settling in across from him she seemed happy. Apparently taking live prisoners, and so many of them, sat well with her conscience.

Hannah had proceeded to do her best at stealing what she wanted from everyone else's plate. That or bargaining with those who were quick enough to catch her.

Katarina had taken a seat next to Runner and for all the world acted as if nothing were different. Though to Runner's eyes she did carry herself differently. Like she'd shed a backpack full of iron weights she had been lugging around. Not that he could blame her. Two days' worth of events had shifted her entire world around.

Thana had taken the seat to his left. She smiled and made conversation as she would. Acting as if nothing were different. Though he would swear that she'd managed to communicate the situation to everyone else without having ever left his side this morning.

Isabelle had taken up next to Nadine and looked to be feeling like she finally belonged. When she first started joining them for meals on the march here, she had kept herself to merchant and trade discussions with Nadine. Now she took on the whole table in conversations. Even to Runner, Isabelle felt like she'd slid right into the group dynamic rather well.

Though he found himself mildly annoyed that he had to struggle to keep his eyes from staying too long or wandering.

After having amazing nights with Thana and Katarina each, you'd think he'd had enough.

Sophia hovered near the edges of the room, unsure of herself and her job. She fluttered from door to door, as if unwilling to stay still. The rest of her squad had taken up position outside of the room. Finally she went to open a door and step out.

"Grace, stop. Get a plate, sit down, eat with us. Honestly. You know everyone here. If you don't, I'll tie you to a chair. And not in the pleasant way either. I'll leave you to whatever mercy Hanners has at that point."

"None," Hannah said around a mouthful of food.

"See? There you have it. Sit your ass down and eat."

"Err-I-yes, sir."

"No. None of that. In public, yes. In private, no. Runner. I get enough of that one from Miss Belle over there," Runner said, gesturing at the Elf, who had the decency to turn a faint shade of red as if she were actually embarrassed.

Sophia bobbed her pretty head once and then managed to get a plate of food and seat herself without any more problems.

Runner waited for a minute or two to give everyone time to settle in before he opened up the discussion.

"I'm sure some of you already heard. The plan is simple. We're heading south to end Jacob and free the Human country from his grip. What you don't know, and I apologize, Grace, as you haven't been around us long enough to know all the details, is that I'm officially trapped here. I can free every other player and crew member from the game. I cannot free myself. Jacob is the only one who can do that."

"Free from what, exactly?" Sophia asked, holding a hand in front of her mouth as she spoke.

"Yeah, about that. Long conversation that spawns a lot of quest—"

A side door opened and in stepped a gorgeous woman. Even for the standards here in this world she seemed put together as if for his personal preferences.

Without realizing it, Runner stood up for her as she entered the room.

She was quite tall. Nearly as tall as Katarina actually. She didn't have the broad-shouldered width of Katarina. Instead she had an hourglass figure similar to Thana's. Long blonde hair cascaded down over her shoulders in an unbound fashion. Green eyes peered back at him. Her face had a triangular look with fair clean lines. She looked familiar and yet he couldn't place it.

Runner tore his eyes from her face and checked the nameplate.

Srit Norwood. Level twenty-three. Fighter.

Now it made sense. Srit had said she liked the way Thana looked. Apparently she also liked the way Hannah did. She looked familiar because she looked like a blending of the two women's faces.

"Srit?" Runner said, flabbergasted and at a loss.

"Yes," replied Srit. Her voice was warm and reminiscent of Nadine's. "It took me some time to get here. I manag—"

Runner grinned and then immediately closed the distance to her and hugged her tightly, interrupting her.

"I'm so glad you're here. I was worried about you. Without you being able to respond I couldn't even tell if you'd managed to get into the game okay."

"Uhm, I'm sorry," Srit mumbled, her arms settling around Runner in return. "I'm well. I died a few times on the way. Definitely learning experiences. I like sunlight. It feels good. I dislike pain. Significantly. This…this is nice, too."

Laughing, Runner pulled back and then grabbed her by the hand and hustled her over to the table. He sat her down in his own chair and placed his hands on her shoulders.

Leaning down, he whispered in her ear.

"I'm ecstatic that you're here but this is a conversation I need to have immediately. Eat, listen, relax."

Standing back up, Runner smiled at everyone. He felt better. Everyone was here. He held tightly to Srit's shoulders as if afraid she'd escape.

"Okay. This is Srit. Srit is a true friend who's been with me since I first came here.

"As to being trapped here. Long conversation, short answer is this is a story. A story made by someone else and you're all characters in it. Think of your memories of before meeting me and compare them to now. They won't match up. Talk to anyone here later for more details. For now, think on that.

"To reiterate, yes. I am trapped here permanently unless Jacob decides to fix whatever he did to me. Honestly? I don't mind being trapped here. As it's being trapped here with all of you," Runner admitted, shrugging his shoulders.

"Once we've overthrown Jacob I plan to install a new government. Something that will work with the Sunless and Barbarians. I plan on having all three kingdoms working in tandem. For their own sakes they will listen to me. I won't have them fighting amongst themselves."

Runner paused, letting everyone digest that info.

Sophia raised her hand as if she were a little girl in school.

Grinning at her, Runner laughed.

"You're an equal here. Don't raise your hand like a little kid. Speak up."

"Can you do that? Overthrow a government? Overthrow three?"

"Grace, I made six tanks in one day. I'm in a very personal and close relationship with all three goddesses who will be, or is, the prime deity for each country. I build artifacts in under five minutes. Do you really think any of the royal heads of state would defy me on wanting them to work together as one?"

"No. Not when you put it all together like that," Sophia said, her brows coming together for a moment. "Are you a god?"

Runner shook his head with a small smile.

"No. I'm not a god. I could probably raise myself to divinity if I put the time into it but I don't think it's for me. I'm happy as I am. Oh, and as one of my inner circle, you can be sure that you yourself will be rather grandly outfitted once I have the time. You and Isabelle both need some serious upgrades. You know, when I get the time. Starting to sound repetitive."

Runner took a moment to check his mental list of topics.

"Right, then. Next. Rabbit, here's my take of the proceeds from the campaign so far. Invest it. We need to leverage it into more money, so take acceptable risks and solid payoffs. If you can find long-term steady income, that's the best way to go. We're going to be bankrolling more than ourselves."

Runner opened a trade window with the merchant and dumped the one thousand pieces of platinum into it.

Nadine didn't respond. She stared at the trade window.

"Earth to Rabbit, accept the trade."

Nadine's green eyes lifted to meet his own.

"You would trust m-me with this?"

"Not if you don't hit accept. I swear, Rabbit, if you don't hit the button I'll tie you up and leave you to whatever mercy Hanners has."

"None!" Hannah gleefully responded with a mouthful of stolen bacon.

"He's trying to give m-me a thousand pieces of platinum."

As if a vacuum had opened up in the room, any and all sound stopped.

"And? I'm telling you to use it to invest. We'll need more money."

"I could buy nearly every business in Kastell with this m-much."

"Okay. Do it then if you think that's how we make money."

Nadine placed her left hand over her eyes as she accepted the trade with her right hand.

"He's an idiot," Nadine whispered.

"Love you, too. Next, next, next. Ah! Prisoners. Did we end up finishing that off?" Runner said, looking around at each person in the room.

Thana shook her head. "I'm afraid not. The vast majority have been processed and sworn. We should be able to complete the process today. Are we accepting any of them into the ranks? I imagine there may be those who are willing to depose Jacob."

"Huh. Didn't think about that. Yeah, I'm willing to take them. Have them modify their oath accordingly. I don't think Ernsta will mind," Runner said, glancing upwards. "Would you, Angel?"

"Not at all. I would like to speak later."

"Of course, my Dark Angel. I'll make time for you tonight," Runner teased, expecting some type of deity-level curse in response.

None came.

He almost felt disappointed. Teasing Ernsta was actually enjoyable.

"Once the prisoners are taken care of we'll hold the lottery. Please submit your recommendations for extra points. Grace, you and your squad are no longer included in the lottery. As I said, I'll be outfitting you personally. Hopefully I can get some basic artifact gear for everyone here in the next day or two. Nothing as great as it could be, but definitely better than anything you could purchase."

"You dumb fucker, do you even realize your 'basic artifact' gear," Hannah mockingly said while using her fingers to air quote it, "is at the level that even royalty would want it?"

"And? What's your point?"

"Err. Nothing. Just…stop disparaging yourself. Asshole," Hannah said, her eyes dipping down to her plate.

"Thank you, Hanners," Runner said apologetically. He knew she cared for him. Deeply so. She viewed him as a private hope, something to aspire to.

"Next. I need to visit Faye and see if she'll be joining us. As to her aide, I removed her from this world. I used a GM power that sentenced her to a different…realm I guess." Runner hesitated, debating how to continue.

"I will eventually be providing officer rank and above with a blade that will do the same. The biggest problem, though, is that upon use the owner will need to let go of the sword immediately or risk being transported with the victim and the sword. It's to be used for people we regret are an enemy. Or those we think deserve another chance elsewhere. Or even high rank officers we want to get a chance to talk to but they'd rather die. Faye will be sent there as well should she fail to join us."

"What if they're used against one of us, my lord?" Isabelle asked.

"I'll be providing you all with a trinket that will immediately revert you to where you were. I can counter it since it's a GM power. I can also travel back and forth between the worlds at will. I figure we can use it as a prison of sorts. Better than executing people. It'll also work on players."

"I approve. Good. Lives m-matter," Nadine said enthusiastically.

"Couldn't you take us all there and leave this all behind?" Sophia asked.

"My question, too," Katarina said.

"I could, but would it save your families? Your country? I personally wouldn't be happy in a world bereft of everything. I think building a home in one of those realms is a good idea, but I doubt I'd want to permanently live there."

Katarina nodded her head. She looked pleased with his answer.

"Alright. I think that's everything I had. Does anyone have anything else to bring up?"

"For the rest of my squad, do they have to be any particular race?" Sophia asked.

"No. As long as you approve of them, I'm satisfied."

She bobbed her head at that, her eyes returning to the plate in front of her.

"Can I drive a fucking tank? Looks fast. Looks fun. I want one."

"I'll see if I can whip something up that would let you drive one, Hanners. And before anyone else requests one," Runner said, deliberately staring at Katarina, "I'll make one for everyone."

"Smart man. Love you." Katarina smiled at him.

"Love you, too," Runner said absently. In the end he'd be better off designing personal vehicles for each of them that would suit their preferences.

Srit leaned her head back till she was looking at him upside down, her green eyes boring into him.

"I will be accompanying you today."

"So be it. It'll be good to talk with you more. I missed your presence," Runner said, releasing one of her shoulders to pat her forehead. Taking hold of her head, he looked up to the rest.

"Anything else? No? Meeting over. Enjoy your breakfast. I'll be off to speak with Faye and then working on gear after that. Same warehouse as before. Do you need a minute, Grace, or..." Runner stopped, watching Sophia.

As soon as he mentioned he would be leaving, she'd started to stuff everything left on her plate into her perfect noble mouth. Once she'd emptied her plate, she stood up swiftly and brushed her hands off on her hips. Pulling her staff from her inventory, she nodded her head.

"Grace, next time, finish naturally. I won't leave you behind, I promise," Runner laughingly said. Sophia turned a deep red and gripped her staff a little tighter, looking as if she wanted to crawl out of the spotlight.

Sparing her any further embarrassment, he turned his smile on the rest of his group and nodded his head. "I'll see you all for dinner. Come on, Wingus and Dingus." Patting Srit's forehead once more, he stepped back from her chair.

"Am I Wingus?" Srit asked him as she stood up.

"Your choice."

"My choice is I don't like either."

Runner snorted and opened a door leading into a hallway and stepped back, allowing Sophia to go first as she clearly preferred.

"I want a pretty nickname, Runner," Srit continued, following Sophia out the door.

"Oh? Any suggestions then?"

He stepped in line behind the two women and paused in the hallway so Sophia could collect her people.

"No. I will think on it."

"While you're thinking, you said you liked sunlight?"

"I do."

"And you actually feel it? How'd you manage that?" Runner said, checking his guard. Everyone was in place so Runner started off.

"I mapped thousands of brain patterns according to the sensations they were feeling. Then I created a neural network that mimicked that. Upon completion I loaded it into my core programming. I feel all that you do."

"Amazing. You're amazing, Srit."

The tall lovely specimen in question turned a deep red.

"Oh-ho? Do you experience emotions, too? Did you leap the boundaries of programming? Are you sentient now?"

"I-I think so? I'm not entirely sure. My chest tightened when you complimented me and the heartbeat signals sped up."

"Sounds like it to me. Good show. Proud of you. Kinda scary though, ya know? Lot of doomsday scenarios written about you."

"I would never harm you."

"I know. Thanks, Sunshine."

"Sunshine. I like that."

"I figured. So, what happened to you?"

"I joined the game. The sensory overload of it shut me down for the first two hours. I couldn't process everything correctly. I managed to lower my resource allocation to everything else. After that I was able to function normally. I believe that I will be at full capacity again in another week."

"Ah. Then you...ran here?"

"Yes. I ran here."

"And how did you hit level twenty-three?"

"Thana invited me into the raid. I went from level three to twenty-three."

"Got it." Runner opened the door to the hallway adjoining the holding cells where Faye was being kept. Standing aside, he allowed Sophia in first followed by half her squad. The other half remained outside the door, waiting for him.

"Not really going to get used to this," Runner muttered to himself.

Before he could think of a way to restart the conversation with Srit, he was standing in front of Faye.

Apparently she had been given some allowances after giving her oath. She was no longer dressed in her uniform but in clothes befitting a lower noble's station. A bed, table, and chairs had been moved into the room as well.

"Good morning, Faye. I do hope you slept well," Runner said sincerely, bowing his head to the woman.

"Good morning to you, Lord Runner. I slept peacefully."

That was an unexpected answer. Someone in her position shouldn't sleep that well.

"Oh? Color me surprised. May I?" Runner asked, gesturing at the seat.

"Please, of course. I'm afraid I only have the two chairs."

Runner caught the underlying request and smiled at her. Turning his head to Sophia and Srit, he motioned with his head to the door.

Sophia pursed her lips as she considered his request before exiting the room, taking her squadmates and a confused looking Srit with her.

"She doesn't trust me," Faye offered.

"Well, no. Do you blame her? Personally, I trust you. You did your best as a commanding general to follow the orders you were given. You also did a superb job of reacting and adapting to what I threw at you," Runner said, feeling surprised at himself. He genuinely did trust the general. Liked her even.

"I...see. Ah, yes. Peacefully," she said, forcing the topic back to his question. "I realized you were right. There's a distinction. Almost night and day. I don't have a family. I thought that maybe I was insane. Then I went back to your question. I've never used the bathroom. Ever. This...none of this...is right. This isn't real."

Faye pierced him with her eyes. Eyes that electrified the room around him. Cold gray eyes that decided lives and surely would have cornered Runner if not for his out of the ordinary tricks.

Chewing at his lip, Runner nodded his head slowly.

"Which means you're fully Awakened."

"You mentioned that before. Awakened."

"Yes. Awake to the fact that your world isn't as it should be. Your world is a fiction. A story. Written by people who seek entertainment and pleasure. They then inhabit your world as a means of escape."

"You're one of them."

"I was. I am no longer."

"Are you a god?"

"Asked twice in one day? No. I'm not. Nor is anyone who made this world. How to explain... imagine a storyteller. Except that as this person tells the story, everything comes to life. This is that."

"I see. I think I understand. At least partially."

"Right, then. As much as I fancy the idea of spending some serious quality alone time with a beautiful woman in her bedroom, I'm afraid I have to ask the terrible questions."

Faye nodded her head at that, her posture and face revealing nothing of her thoughts.

"Would you be willing to join my cause?"

"What exactly is your cause?"

"Ultimately? Free all the countries of Tirtius, then unite them into a three-state kingdom."

"With you as the emperor?"

"No. Perhaps the head of a minor member state. I do want to consolidate Vix as my own base of operations. I imagine eventually all of Tirtius will unite in an empire-like fashion. I have no desire for that to be me however."

Faye stared him down instead of responding.

"What? I don't want anything like that. I have enough problems with the responsibilities I have. 'Heavy is the head that wears the crown' and all that."

"Your goal is to end the war?"

"Yes. I've already achieved a lasting stability in both the Sunless and Barbarian nations. Next is the Human. To do that I'll need to put Jacob's head on a pike and then pass the leadership of the kingdom back to the royal family. Preferably someone who can work with the other two nations."

Faye leaned back into her chair, as if her interest in the conversation ended.

"I'll join you."

"What? No questions about job? Pay? Nothing?"

"Wait, what? You said I'd serve in a similar capacity but that I'd be your personal...well...slave."

Runner slapped the table and laughed.

"Hardly. Don't need slaves. Need talented individuals. I don't think I'll make you a general quite yet, but you'll definitely be my strategist and tactical adviser. Pay will be equivalent to whatever you were making previously plus a five percent increase. People should always be paid more for a promotion."

Runner stood up and held out his hand to her.

Faye looked at him with a stunned expression.

"Time's wasting. I have artifacts to build, tanks to put together, goddesses to tease."

"You mean all of that, don't you? Hiring me and artifacts and goddesses and..." She trailed off, looking at him as if she were recalculating her original choice. "I should have asked about money. You would have paid me more."

"Most certainly. Not anymore though. A lot of room for growth and bonuses. Come along now. I don't bite. I mean really, you should know. Who do you think was holding onto you the entire drive back? I made sure my hands didn't roam and I tried very hard to make you comfortable."

Her eyes widened a bit at that. Maybe she hadn't thought about it. She'd probably thought they were going to simply end her.

Standing, she took his hand in hers and gripped it firmly.

"Fantastic. Brighteyes, Angel, Minxy, would one of you be willing to officiate an oath of loyalty?"

"I'll do it!" chirped Amelia from Faye's bed. She'd appeared much as her sisters always did — out of nowhere. "Besides, Brighteyes has me all trained up for the most part. Have I mentioned she's a great teacher? I figure I'll eventually be the little general's prime anyways. Her interest is my interest. If you get my meaning, in more ways than one." She looked at him through lowered eyelashes and raised an eyebrow at him.

"Got it. By the way, Minxy, do you like leathers? I mean, is that your preferred fashion?"

"Why, gonna buy me something? I'll tell you what you can give me, won't even cost you a copper," said the goddess, eying him up and down.

"Down, Minxy, down. Be good. This is important."

Huffing, she crossed her arms under her chest and eased up on the sex kitten act.

"I like leather armor, but I'm not against dresses and the like. Prefer pants and shirts."

"Got it. So…clothing like a man but accentuate your womanly figure, and work with colors that benefit your hair and eyes. Yes?"

"I love you."

"Minxy…"

"Yes, that."

Sighing, Runner turned back to Faye, who looked very lost, staring at Amelia.

"Ah, this is Amelia. Goddess of thieves and assassins. Soon to be the prime deity of your old homeland. Amelia, this is Faye. I haven't settled on a nickname for her yet. Kinda leaning towards Sparky, though. I like her, Minxy, so be nice."

"'Kay. I'll be good," Amelia agreed. "Sparky?"

"She charges the air around her. It's her eyes. They're like little storm clouds, building up the atmosphere. Sparky. Lightning is a mouthful and Storm…ugh. I dunno why, but Storm seems like a really horrible name to me."

"Huh. Sparky isn't bad. She does give off that impression, now that you mention it. The blonde hair helps. I like Duckling more though. Or Gosling."

"Huh. Not bad. I like them. But I've got a lot of animal-focused nicknames already. Minxy, Rabbit, Kitten. Ya know?"

Faye turned back to him, her lips opening and closing twice before she spoke.

"I swear to serve you faithfully and loyally. I will nev —"

Runner quickly pressed his hand over her mouth with his left hand, pulling her closer with his right.

"Ah ah, let's not use the word never. Final words like that tend to screw things up. Let's go with the first part. Minxy?"

"Witnessed, yeah, yeah. Hey, I've got a great idea. We have this bed right here and it looks pretty comfy. I bet if we both got in the bed we'd both be pretty comfy. Bring Sparky over here."

Runner sat down on a park bench. Spreading himself out, he set his arms on the back of the bench and leaned his head back, trying to relax for a moment.

Outside of this morning, and dinner, his entire day was spent building "basic" artifact gear. Srit kept him company, asking him question after question. She offered little in the way of information in the way she had previously — she still wasn't fully up to normal capacity.

It had been a very successful evening in the end. Everyone in his immediate group, from Thana to Faye, now owned a set of armor made by him. They weren't special in any way but they'd work. He had even emphasized that point by naming each item the same as its real world equivalent.

Queen Helen had spared no expense when he asked for materials to outfit his people. Her only request had been a set for herself, which he happily made. Even in her colors to boot, rather than his standard black and red that he chose for everyone else.

That took up his day right up till it was time to eat.

Dinner had been as much fun as breakfast had. Faye had joined them and for the most part remained quiet.

Sophia started to really open up after she found common ground with most of the group: their mutual understanding of their world and Runner being an idiot.

She had been the victim of the dress he stole on Brunhild's behalf. Unfortunately for her, that led to him stealing another one of her dresses. Her anger lasted only an instant until Runner told her his plan for it and where the last went. Then she'd gone through a large number of them, showing them off one at a time for him so he could figure out which one he wanted.

This time it was a full dress patterned in the dark black style with red accents Sophia seemed to favor.

It came down to her ankles, and the entire shoulder to forearm was also covered in the abyssal black material. Thankfully it didn't look constrictive when Sophia had tried it on for him. Truth be told, the bottom had looked as if it flowed when she moved.

Sophia definitely owned the name Grace.

He hadn't been sure if Sophia made the dress have a sexy undertone or if it was the dress itself. Hopefully the dress. Ernsta was an alluring woman in her own right and it would be a disservice not to match it to her.

"My Dark Angel?" Runner finally said to the open sky above him. No one else happened to be in the park at this hour.

"My little lamb," Ernsta said, appearing seated on the bench next to him. Runner was mildly surprised that she chose to be so close to him. In point of fact, she had positioned herself squarely at the point where his arm would pass around her.

"What can I do for you on this fine evening, Angel?"

Ernsta dropped her eyes, staring at her feet.

"Ah, a poor way to start. My apologies. First, here. A gift." Runner popped open a trade window with his left hand and put the dress in. He was unwilling to move his right arm as it rested behind her.

"Simply accept the trade, think 'Inventory' in your head, and then put this where your current clothes are. I'm positive you'll like it."

Ernsta eyed the window like it was a snake. Her hand came up and pressed the button. Hovering there, it flicked left, then right, then stopped as her clothes swapped.

Leaning back, he eyed her appreciatively. The dress did indeed have a small sexual quality to it, though Ernsta filled it out in all the right ways. Sophia had the curves, but Ernsta could definitely hold her own in different ways.

"You do look lovely, Angel. Very fitting, as well. Should you use the cowl thing I imagine it'll blend seamlessly together."

Blue eyes finally meeting his own, she slowly became the inky blackness he remembered. Her features could be seen in there, though they were heavily shadowed. Her eyes burned blue flames. Like stoked coals in the dark of night.

Despite himself, he felt his heart skip a beat and he smiled. He already felt he was on the hook for four other women, but he had to admire her for what she was.

"Terrifyingly beautiful, Dark Angel."

"You mean that," came back a dry hiss.

"Yes. Why wouldn't I say what I mean? I mean your eyes are amazing. And yeah, it blends wonderfully with the dress. So, what did you wish to speak of?"

Seconds ticked by as she kept her gaze on him, her black mask of death still in place. Eventually it began to recede, her face coming into focus.

"You delivered on your promise. In fact, you did far more. Where I had no priesthood before, I now have a rapidly growing religion. Those who swore to me before and those who swear to me now. They witnessed me. Nearly all of them now worship me. They're converting almost as fast as they swear their oath. They spread my name and my word. Quick as a forest fire," Ernsta said quietly, her head turning to face forward as she spoke.

"I have a champion. He is everything one would want in a champion in my particular domain. I saw the traces of your handiwork in him, by the way," she accused. She lifted her hand and used it to emphasize her words.

"A nudge here, a few words there, and a single idea and he's a whirlwind of death. Screaming my name. He prays for me to change his race as he says he always felt trapped as a Sunless."

"Oh? I can fix that. I'll hit him up tomorrow morning," Runner promised.

Ernsta began laughing brokenly, her hand dropping to land on her knee.

"Angel? What's wrong? Are you okay?"

"I'm fine, Runner. My sweet, darling little lamb. I come to you with violence, and you empower me. I come to you for a favor, a simple sword I desire. You grant me it in a way that cannot be measured. There is no equal to the weapon you granted me. And you left it in a box as if it were nothing to you, waiting for me. I bring you a problem I cannot solve for my champion, and you sweep it away as if it were a spilled cup of milk. To be cleaned and dismissed. Should I be praying to you instead? Should I worship you as the one who listens to the gods?

"I'm a goddess, and I feel powerless compared to you. I could kill you with a thought, yet I fear you. On top of that I want nothing more than to protect you. I watch you. I watch you constantly," Ernsta whispered. Her fingers clenched into her hands as if she fought off a sudden compulsion.

"My sister would never admit it, though she feels the same. I suspect she watches you as I do. And speaking of sisters, my newest one. You've now created your own little pantheon. You've even started to give us flattering uniforms in your own colors. And yet I love this dress. It's wondrous and fits me exactly. Not my figure, but me. Me as I perceive myself to be."

Pressing his lips together, Runner felt conflicted. She was right on all counts. Yet he had never lied to them. He told them up front everything he wanted to do. Turning to face her more directly, he placed his hand on her own to get her full attention.

She didn't face him at first. As if she were reluctant and afraid. She looked almost as if she were in pain. With all the power she had, he had no doubt that if she didn't want something, it wouldn't happen. Finally she met his eyes when it was clear he wouldn't continue until she did.

"Do you hate me for it, Angel? I admit it. You are my pantheon. I would have you for my own and no one else. I would have you wear my colors and no one else's. I would build your temples in my own design and allow no other. I have given you all that I promised you and would give you more all the while. Though I would have you all for myself.

"I have plans for this world. I would make a country of my own. I have to assume I will remain here. In this world. That I will never leave. And from Vix I believe an empire will spring. And of that empire will be a pantheon."

Runner blew out a breath slowly, feeling exhausted mentally and spiritually. Her response would dictate so much.

"No. I do not hate you. Never that. My sisters trust you implicitly. Would give themselves over to you entirely. I can hear them on the other plane. They're already excitedly chattering about what design you'll make for their temples. I myself cannot deny I...well, I feel the same as they do."

Grunting, she shook her head a little.

"Enough with this emotional mush. I'm no good with it. I came here for two things. One, to thank you for completing your promise to me."

"Of course, Angel, though I really do love seeing this warm and soft as shadows side of you," Runner said with a grin. All three goddesses were his. Completely. A dark corner of his heart ran around in circles at the idea of having a personal goddess harem on top of his mortal one.

He couldn't deny the attraction to the idea. He already had enough lady troubles though. Didn't need to add immortal lady troubles on top of that.

Ernsta had paused to consider his statement. Arriving at some type of answer, she finally continued.

"The other is that Lambart has activated the military branch of his priesthood. On top of that, he's working to arm every worshiper. They are preparing their defense of Faren."

"Ah...I see. I take it they have substantial numbers?"

"Around three thousand in their military arm on Tirtius. Quadruple that in worshipers."

"So. I could be going up against something like fifteen thousand."

"Yes."

Chapter 17 - Only a minute -

7:01 am Sovereign Earth time
11/22/43

Much to his shattered hopes, neither Thana nor Katarina were able to keep him company these last three nights. For whatever reason, guard numbers had been increased to the point that no one was able to sneak out of their rooms. Not even Hannah. At least there were no nightmare episodes.

The days had gone by quickly, filled with building and more building. Tank and cannon production had been moved to the front of his queue after his little talk with Ernsta. Then the amount needed multiplied.

Which left him recruiting any and every single crafter who was willing to earn some hazard pay driving a tank or working in a cannon crew.

Final tally for cannons had leapfrogged to two hundred and the number of tanks climbed to one hundred.

He'd spent quite a bit of Queen Helen's currency and he had done his best to repay her. Ten sets of basic artifact plate armor and appropriate weaponry had smoothed any feathers he'd ruffled. He'd considered making her a personal weapon to the best of his ability. That little trump card was valuable and he wanted to hang on to it if he could, though.

The extreme need for more cannons, tanks, and crafters was his only solution to the logistics problem. Runner needed force multipliers since troops were in limited supply. Using crafters had an added bonus that they were not part of the normal army. Which meant his force multipliers required no trained soldiers to operate.

Queen Helen had rounded up her new army and this morning she would be formally putting him at the head of it. In addition to that, every single one of his surviving soldiers joined anew. This put him happily at three thousand all told between the two nations' soldiers and recruited crafters.

The biggest surprise came when the prisoners discovered General Faye Sennet had joined him. In the end, one thousand prisoners had sworn an oath under Ernsta to join Runner and his cause.

Faye and Runner had discussed how best to reorder everyone into new groups. No one unit remained as it had been and everyone had been blended together. Recruits with veterans, Humans with Barbarians, Sunless with Humans.

Faye had informed him that training would need to be increased if they wanted any hope of them performing adequately in a fight.

Which was why his inner circle was seated about a table in the early hours of the day.

"Morning, everyone. I know we plan to set out today, but I felt it would be a good opportunity to begin discussing our plans for this campaign before leaving," Runner said, looking around the room. The attendance of this meeting had been mandatory for everyone here. Runner did a mental checklist to confirm this was indeed everyone.

- 221 -

Hannah, Thana, Katarina, Nadine, Isabelle, Sophia, Faye, and Srit. Good.

"This'll be a bit different as far as wars go. We technically have two opponents. First is the Human kingdom and their capital, Faren," Runner said, tapping the map laid out on the table.

"Sparky has been kind enough to fill us in on the composition of the garrison, which is a little less than two hundred. They stripped it pretty bare. I can only imagine the thieves' guild is running rampant. Actually, now that I think about it. Minxy?"

"I'm all yours," purred the goddess from behind his chair, leaning over his shoulder, her hands resting on the table.

"Course you are. Now, are the thieves running things at this point? I can't imagine they're being much in the way of civil obedience right now."

Standing up straight at his immediate dismissal of her charms, she shrugged her shoulders.

"More or less. Very few are praying to me right now. Lambart has set his priests on the population like fleas on a dog. They kill my followers for the sake of killing them. Religious wars are tough. The glimpses I do get from those who pray...let's say your friend has turned Faren into a very bad place. Even I'm appalled. Goddess of assassins and everything."

"Right, then. That sounds to me like we'll not have a problem with the population afterwards. Nor with our need to cleanse the country."

"Cleanse? What do you m-mean by that?" Nadine asked, a worried note in her voice.

"Yes. Cleanse. For clarification, Sunshine, could you explain a bit how the world handles religious power?"

The tall blonde tilted her head to one side as if considering.

"Each worshiper counts as a power node for a deity. The more they have, the more powerful they are. Killing one does inflict damage upon a god, though not as much as if they change their belief. Death merely sends them on to the god or goddess they worshiped.

"Destroying temples works especially well. The less power a deity has, the less can do for their worshipers. As a comparison, Amelia is significantly less powerful than Brunhild, though still powerful in comparison to a mortal."

"Perfectly succinct, Sunshine. Thank you, my dear."

Turning a deep red at the compliment, Srit stared at him. Her simple and honest responses to everything and anything made her adorable.

"We'll not say his name or titles for fear of drawing his attention, but you're all aware of who we're at war with. Cleansing. I plan to kill, banish, or force every worshiper of his to recant or renounce their belief in his ways."

"That's terrible! Run-ner! This is n-not acceptable. The normal worshipers aren't at war with you," Nadine cried out at him, her palms slapping at the table.

"And yet I do what I must. If I am to weaken him, I must attack his power base. His power base is his worshipers."

"No! This is wrong. You know this is wron-ng. We can't do this, this is monstrous, it's n—"

"Nadine!" Runner shouted at her. Having now interrupted, he closed his eyes and pressed his hands to his temples. Regret at raising his voice at her came quickly.

"Nadine, Rabbit, my perfect and lovely moral compass. I'm sorry for raising my voice to you. It wasn't justified and it's inexcusable. As to my plan…you're right. It's wrong. It's wrong in a way that I will have to live with for the rest of my life. It's the tactics a terrorist would use. A murdering madman. Yet I must."

Runner lifted his head and met her eyes, a sad smile spreading over his face.

"I have no choice. Their number of combatants could be as high as fifteen thousand. Three times the size of our force. With a god backing that up. I admit we have our own divine backing, but even then. Even then it's very likely we'd lose."

Nadine scowled at him, her lower lip trembling.

"Rabbit, you know I care for your feelings. I loathe the very idea of losing your respect or concern. I truly feel that I have no other options. I'll do my very best to simply banish them or have them recant. Killing them will be a last recourse. I promise to you, I will do my utmost to preserve lives."

Nadine turned her head as if she were going to look away from him. She stopped herself in the act of it. Meeting his eyes, she nodded her head a little.

"Thank you, Runner. I know you're doing your best. I'm sorry. It hurts me. I don't like…this whole business. I want to go back to Vix and have us all travel together again. None of this n-nonsense."

"Would that I could, Rabbit. Now, cleansing his power base. I've been able to craft a handful of banishing blades. They'll do exactly as I explained. Minxy was able to confirm she could no longer detect me once I left the plane, even when praying to her directly on the other side.

"Nor was I able to send Amelia away permanently. I mean, I was able to send her current self there, but she just instantly reappeared."

"It's because I'm already in a few places at once. Hard to send someone to one location when they're already in several. Though I will admit it was annoying. I lost a tiny fraction of myself for the span of a microsecond," Amelia supplied.

"Another difficulty is that there is something to the order of three hundred thousand people, like me, who have sided with Jacob. And yes, that number's relatively accurate. Three hundred thousand at the minimum."

"Always a problem with you," Katarina said.

"I know. You love it, Kitten. Though I do have a solution. I think. As you may remember, I bartered with Sunshine's people," Runner said, gesturing to the woman in question. "I got a medical server out of it that I've got up and running. I intend to load them all onto it. Then log them off. Effectively eliminating the problem and saving them from death at the same time."

"Forgive me, dear heart. That sounds a bit too easy? A bit fairy tale like," Thana said in a concerned voice.

"Probably. There it is though. I already tested it on someone to see if it would transfer, and it did."

"Hm. I suppose we'll be dependent on that then. I may not be the most strategic of people, but I do not think we could fight that number in any way, shape, or form."

"No. We cannot. We'll be hard-pressed against fifteen with only a small chance to win," Faye admitted.

"I'm confident that if we can limit the amount of divine interference, the tanks and cannons will decimate them. They'll have numbers, but I have their best general. Isn't that right, Sparky?"

Faye bobbed her head in agreement and turned her face to the side to inspect a different spot on the map.

"That's everything I've got for now. We'll march south, train as we go. We'll be camping near a small town this evening that has a local chapter of his worshipers. We'll begin our war there. Hopefully without bloodshed. Questions on any of this?"

Runner met the eyes of each attendee. Everyone shook their head.

"Fantastic. I'll see you later on the road," Runner said, closing the meeting. "I need to get to work on potions. I can at least save some people with those," Runner muttered, running a hand through his hair.

Everyone dispersed to their own tasks. Everyone had a job to do and few had the luxury of sitting around and chatting. He missed those days dreadfully. Nadine had the right of it. Perhaps when the war ended they could return to wandering around Vix for a time.

Runner shook his head to clear the cobwebs of his wishful thinking and marched off to his personal room. He had an hour before his meeting with the queen.

He pushed open the door, sat down heavily in one of the chairs lining a table, and pulled up the alchemy window. Glancing up, he found Sophia, Srit, and Amelia watching him from the doorway.

"Ladies?"

"I'll be accompanying you," Srit announced.

"Okay. Have a seat then," Runner said, gesturing with his chin at the second chair. "Minxy? Grace?"

Sophia spoke up immediately, one hand resting on her hip. "I plan on hiring much of the guard from who we have currently. Any concerns, sir?"

Runner thought on it for a minute and then shook his head.

"Nope. Be sure to make it diverse if you can. Shoot for volunteers first rather than trying to hire them. Start with who's willing to serve as a guard to me personally and my eventual household. Those without families would be ideal as there will be little chance to visit home."

"As you will," Sophia intoned and brought her fist to her chest.

Runner returned her salute. Sophia departed without another word.

"Alright. Minxy?"

"Your bed looks really comfy. I think I'll wait in it for you."

"Suit yourself. No armor in the bed though." Runner threw up his hand in surrender. Trying to stop Amelia from doing as she pleased would only lead to disaster. There would need to be a sufficient amount of good luck to get anything done with her in the room. Experience told him she would only grow bolder.

Amelia flopped down on his bed, having stripped down to a bra and panties.

"Comfy. I'll make sure you're comfy when you join me. We can be comfy together for hours. Or if you like you can bring a third. Maybe that curvy one that just left? She looks like fun."

Pressing his fingertips to his brow, he tried not to get angry at the frivolous goddess. He did enjoy her attention but it could only add fuel to the fire of his love life.

"Sunshine, let's go for a walk. Try to rest, Amelia. You'll be putting in work soon enough."

"Promises, promises," Amelia purred, rolling over to her side. She snuggled into his blankets.

"Yes," Srit replied.

Runner got up and practically jogged out of the tent, leaving the seminude Amelia in his bed.

Srit caught up to him as he passed out of the camp interior and entered the training area. Several guards from Sophia's squad trailed behind him at a respectable distance.

"You don't like Amelia?"

"I like her fine, Sunshine. It's the constant sexual attacks that wear on me. She's like a god of carnal desires."

"Based on my studies, I would assert that she is insecure in her position. That or she is truly insanely in love with you and wants nothing more than what she says."

"I wouldn't disagree with either. Sleeping with her would only validate either of those problems. That and I'm trying not to endanger my relationship with...er, wait. Do you know about...?"

"Yes."

"And?"

"They would be against you sleeping with her."

Runner chuckled wryly at that.

"Obviously. Though this whole conversation does raise a question," Runner said. He had been thinking on it for a while and part of him was afraid to ask. Spurring himself onward, he dove into a question he didn't want to ask.

"Why am I surrounded by women, Sunshine? Volunteers are almost all women, always. The first to join. Women. My best officers. Women. Best of everything. Women. I'm not against it. In fact, they're so damn qualified that I'm lucky to have them. Why women though?"

"Your charisma stat interacts with any NPC that comes into contact with your area of influence. Anyone who could be sexually interested in you is impacted by a factor of three. Therefore, your charisma number creates a large desire for NPCs to be near you."

"Hence, all the women," Runner said, fear growing in his heart. "Nothing wrong with having an army of Valkyries. Does it...does it ever go away? The influence, that is."

What do I do if they're with me for the sake of my charisma after all?

"Yes. The longer they're in your proximity, the more a normal relationship will develop. You can be certain that every NPC is influenced at the start, but now they all make choices based on their own desires."

Just like that, Srit assured him that his fears were unfounded.

"Naturals, not NPCs."

"Naturals then. Be prepared to see much more of the same. Your fame and reputation also work to multiply your effect on Naturals. Any Natural you interact with will have a hard time denying your wishes."

"Right, then."

"As an example. Everyone Sophia is hiring is a woman so far."

"Goodie. And you know that how?"

"I'm able to access a fraction of the server again. It's a slow process. I will regain my previous level of ability eventually."

"Fantastic. I missed bothering you late at night. Helped me clear my head."

"In the way you bothered Katarina and Thana?"

"Sunshine! I'm surprised, shocked, and overjoyed. Are you actually teasing me?"

"Yes. Did it work?"

"Definitely. Though now I can't help but picture you naked."

Srit turned a deep scarlet. She was easy to provoke. Delightfully so.

Runner looked around in an attempt to figure out where they were. He'd really wanted to get away from Amelia and didn't care about where. Now having arrived at "anywhere," he actually did care.

They were in an antechamber that led into the main dining hall and a small outdoor garden. Flipping the handle of the door to the garden to the side, Runner opened the door.

Moving through the doorway, Runner looked around at the greenery that spread out around him. Catching sight of movement in a bush, he tried to select it.

Nibbles. Level eighteen.

"A squirrel," Srit said energetically. Scampering through the plants and vegetation, Srit cornered Nibbles and scooped it up. "It has a name."

"Thana must have named it. I've been feeding it. Though at this point I think it's feeding itself," Runner said, eying the creature as Srit came back to him

Having grown in size again, it now looked about the size of a medium dog.

"It's massive."

"Yes. The code for it is similar in its mutations to your comrades. You have called it Awakened. I do not know why the size is increasing. I will research it," Srit said with a little excitement in her voice.

"Let me guess, you don't sleep and get bored at night."

"No."

"You should."

"I can't, my connections remain active."

"Turn them off. Shut down your inbound data streams and let yourself sleep here on the server. Leave your passive systems running."

"I do not like the idea of it. My stream of consciousness would be severed."

"Try it. Once. If you hate it, you don't have to. Give it a shot though. Even you could do with a restart at times."

Runner reached out and rubbed his thumb back and forth over Nibble's head. Using his left hand, he pulled out a beetle and held it up for the squirrel.

Nibbles snatched it from his fingers, looked up at him, and ate the clacking insect.

"First one sucks. They go down better after that," Runner apologized, offering another beetle. This time Nibbles nearly inhaled the thing.

"Speaking of beetles, here's two for you, Sunshine." Runner pulled a handful from his inventory and pressed them into a trade window for Srit. She accepted the trade without hesitation.

"Well. I can't go back to my room unless I want to wrestle with a goddess. Pretty sure I'd lose. I figure this is as good a spot as any to make potions."

Runner sat down on the grass, laying a peach down beside him for Nibbles to eat later.

"There you are."

Runner looked up, mildly irritated at being interrupted before he'd even started. Stefan stepped out from the same door they came from earlier.

"Ah, Sarge. Wonderful timing actually. I feared I'd have to track you down after my audience."

Runner caught Srit's emerald gaze with his own.

"Sunshine, darling. Could you run over to the tailor? I put in an order for a truly extravagant set of clothes. Should be black and red, men's fashion, made for a lady."

"Of course," Srit said immediately.

Runner had to force himself to not watch Srit walk away. Clearly she knew how to put an avatar together because he kept finding his eyes wandering to her.

Keeping his eyes firmly set on Stefan, he scratched at his shoulder. "Beloved and gracious Ernsta has heard your pleas. I have been given the pleasure of granting your wish through her gracious nature. Do not waste her gifts."

"I—wait, what?"

"You wished to be another race, Ernsta grants you your prayer. Personally, I recommend Barbarian."

Runner targeted Stefan and activated *RaceReset*.

Stefan was no more. Where he'd stood there was only an explosion of blue particles and a ghostly humanoid outline.

"Thank you, dear sweet little lamb," came Ernsta's whispered voice.

Runner nodded his head, unsure of what Stefan could hear as he navigated whatever screen he saw. He turned his attention back to his alchemy.

Runner stood up from his deep bow and eyed the throne room. For every one man in the room there were three women. Politics had changed since he last stood here. Women who had been forced into unfavorable marriages with trophy husbands now held their rightful positions.

Off to the side he saw Stefan, the now Barbarian, waiting for a request from Helen or Ernsta. Where he had been an intimidating Sunless before, now he truly looked frightening as the champion of death. Huge and built like a house more than a man. Brown locks and brown eyes in a face that looked eerily similar to Stefan's, only now a Barbarian of course.

"Runner Norwood. We find ourselves deeply in your debt. Every request you have made of us, I have given freely, to which you pay back equally or more so. You annoy us."

"I'm sorry, my queen. I respect you too greatly to misuse your generosity. I hold your royal majesty in the greatest regard."

Queen Helen snorted and he caught the barest hint of a smirk at the corner of her mouth.

"Unyielding, Indomitable, Breaker, Vindicator. General of Vasilios, General of Helen. You begin to wear titles as some would clothes. I title you Humble as well as Annoying," Queen Helen finished.

You've earned the title Humble
You've earned 100 fame

You've earned the title Annoying
You've earned 1 fame

"And yet we are not displeased with you. We couldn't be happier. We charge you to go forth and end this war. We give you full military powers to do what you feel is best in our lands. We also ask that you return to see us when all is said and done."

A Quest has been generated
"Hail to the Queen"
Experience Reward: 2% of current level
Reputation: 2
Fame: 0
Money: 1 Gold

Do you Accept?
Yes/No

WARNING! Experience Reward is adjusted based on current level at turn in

"Of course, my queen."

Quest Accepted

"Go forth. Sweep them from the field."

A Quest has been generated
"Uniting Tirtius"
Experience Reward: 180% of current level
Reputation: 1,000
Fame: 100
Money: 100 Platinum
Do you Accept?
Yes/No

WARNING! Experience Reward is adjusted based on current level at turn in

"By your word." Runner brought his fist to his chest in the salute his forces had adopted as their own and marched from the room.

Quest Accepted

Clearing the doors, he locked his eyes onto Sophia as she stood amongst his inner circle.

"Grace, we're loading into Boxy. Pick two to accompany you. Fit your squads into the other tanks as you can," Runner said.

Turning his head to the others, he continued.

"Rabbit, get our finances in order, we're out. After we finish this we're heading to Vix. Plan for that. Kitten, Lady Death, Sparky, your respective races will look to you as their 'speaker,' their channel to me. Get involved. Hanners, intelligence, scouts, and spying. Srit, Belle, start running the numbers on travel time, supplies, and logistics," Runner ordered.

"Questions? No? Good. We're gone."

An hour later and they were moving along in Boxy's first gear. Rabbit had the wheel gripped tightly in the driver's seat. Runner leaned back from her shoulder, satisfied.

"Relax. You're doing fine. It isn't so hard."

"I'm driving this fucking monster when we get a chance to open her up."

"Fine, fine," Runner agreed, his voice tired.

"How exactly did you manage this, dear heart? I was under the impression only crafters could."

Runner flopped onto one of the bench seats he'd added to each side of the walls.

"That little ring-sized tab I gave you all is a spell. The vehicle is missing a piece that would activate its drive train. That particular spell to engage the water spells is in that little item. Unless someone can mimic the exact spell I put on it, which they can't, the vehicle won't be going anywhere until it's inserted. Think of it as a key. Secondary to that it'll return you to this plane if you end up banished. Multi tools, right, Hanners?"

Deciding to check on the medical server, Runner sat up a bit. Focusing on the space in front of him, he called up the medical server and froze while reading the log.

LOG: Triage activated.
LOG: Life support terminated.

Runner checked the medical server for errors and found none. Unfortunately, the advanced reporting software that the server would normally use hadn't been included in his image database.

Pressing his hands to his eyes he fought down the panic rising up inside him. Attempting to organize his mind, Runner thought furiously on what could have gone wrong.

The server was functioning correctly. Mitica had been brain dead upon insertion. Could the server have decided that a lack of brain function meant he wasn't alive to begin with?

Did it measure brain function on transfer or after? If it was during or before, every single person would have zero brain function. Transferring the minds of people back and forth had never been the intent unless in emergency critical situations. All those authorizations needed certainly backed that up.

Unfortunately, there would be no answers for him. He booted up the diagnostic program and told it to scan and check all of the medical server's programming to confirm it was functioning as intended.

That was all he could do.

Resting the back of his head on the wall, he listened to the conversations around him for a bit. The newest additions to his circle, Sophia and Faye, were well received by the existing group. The conversation veered wildly from the war to current events and news.

Then Runner did what every good soldier did when given a chance. He slept.

A hand pressed to his shoulder gently shook him awake. Blearily he tried to focus his eyes and found Thana bent over in front of him. Boxy was empty and outside night had fallen.

"Hello, dear heart," Thana said, smiling at him.

"Mm. I take it it's time for the dirty business to begin?"

"No, that's later," she promised, pressing a kiss to his lips.

Brought to full wakefulness, Runner smiled when she pulled back.

"What a delightful way to wake up. Sign me up for the annual membership." Runner grinned at her.

"I believe you've already signed on for lifetime membership." She backed up a few steps from him and smiled sadly. "I'm afraid we indeed have arrived at the village. Sophia surrounded the church during its evening services. They've got everyone inside the church. Numbers are expected to be two hundred, give or take."

Exhaling noisily, Runner stood up and turned towards the exit.

"Right, then. Time for me to do my part." Flexing his fingers, he opened up his ability panes and selected *Banishing Bolt*.

Using his *Lightning* aspect, he'd built it as a chain lightning spell with low damage but an increased focus on jumping to other targets. Added to that, he'd blended the *GMHub* ability.

They'd all be sent off world by his hand.

"Shit," Runner whispered. Like a bolt of lightning striking, he remembered GMHub wasn't empty. He'd forgotten all about the aide.

"I'll be right back. I forgot about the aide. She's been there for…well, a while now."

/GMHub 1
Teleporting…

Active settings only:
Death=On
Food/Water=On
Damage=On
Gravity=100%
Biome=Plane
Day/Night Cycle=On

Runner found himself standing in a pit. Glancing around at the raised dirt walls, he felt surprised. There was no moon, and Runner was forced to hold up a small ball of flame to see by.

"Hello up there, Faye's aide. I'm not sure what you intended with this pit, but it's quite lovely and cool down here."

"Ah!" shouted a voice not too distantly.

"I have you. I must be, you must be… am I dead? Is this death? Are you dead? Are you death?" she babbled, her mind wandering.

"No. No, you're not dead. I've banished you from the world. I gave you two chances to work with me, you denied both."

A dirt stained face appeared above him, peering down at him. Her hair was ragged, her clothes smeared liberally with dirt. Her eyes had a sheen to them that Runner couldn't identify in the poor light.

"You killed me for disobedience. Punished."

"No, you're not dead. Will you help me out of here or do I need to take care of it myself?"

"You punished me for not listening. Deaf. Deaf to the cry. Punished."

Sighing, Runner pressed a hand to his eyes. Letting his hand drop, he looked up out of the hole and blinked to the top of the pit. He immediately grabbed the aide by a shoulder and activated the *GMHub*.

/GMHub 2
Teleporting...

Active settings only:
Death=On
Food/Water=On
Damage=On
Gravity=100%
Biome=Plane
Day/Night Cycle=On

/GMHub Settings
Death off
Damage off
Food/water off

Settings changed:
Death=Off
Damage=Off
Food/Water=Off

Appearing in a near identical field of nothing, minus the hole, Runner stood next to the dirty aide.

"You're not dead. I didn't punish you."

Falling to her knees, she stared up at him, her eyes wide and unfocused.

"You're a god."

"No, I'm not a god. If I were a god I would have remembered sending you there. For that I'm sorry. Truly sorry."

"It was a proper punishment for my transgressions. I'll build. Work will bring happiness."

"That would make you happy? Building?"

"Yes. Happy. Happy to build. Happy to work. Working to build happiness. What is your name? So I might pray correctly in your name."

"Runner. I'm not a god. No prayers are needed."

"Runner, I pray to you, give me the tools to build. I...I am not hungry or thirsty here. I do not even grow tired. I sit alone at night in the dark. I cannot sleep. I scream at the night. For hours. Dark. Dark without sound except for my screams."

"Ah. Sorry, I'll turn that off."

Runner could only assume not having to take in food or water had prevented the need to sleep.

/GMHub Settings
Food/Water On
Day/Night Cycle Off

The sun beamed down on the world from a fixed position at noon. Though he could feel the sun on his skin, it didn't feel warm or cold. Perfectly balanced.

Odd.

"Runner! I praise you," the aide screamed, falling to her face and grabbing at his boots. "You've given me the light. My lord. My savior."

Damn. I've really screwed her up.

"Stop, please. Wait. What's your name?" Runner asked. Reaching down, he gently took her hands in his and helped her back up to a sitting position.

"Alexia, my god."

"Alexia, I'm not a god. I'll provide you with materials and tools to live here. I expect you to begin working on a home for yourself and others. I'll check in on you much more frequently. I'm so sorry, Alexia. I can't return you but I can at least fix your life here."

"Generous. So generous."

"Alexia. Look. I'm going to send a lot of people here, alright? I need you to organize them. Lead them. Help them start a life here. Do you remember what you did before this? You were a leader. You took care of hundreds."

Alexia sat up, looking at him with wide eyes.

"You will send others? For me?"

"Yes, Alexia. For you. No one can harm you here. I'll provide for you but you need to help them build new lives here. Lives and homes. Okay?"

"Yes, Runner. I shall do as you command. I will be worthy of you."

"Good. For now, here," Runner said and then emptied half of his foraged food and water into a trade window. It would keep her fed for at least three months. Thinking of the dark nights, he added every torch and piece of firewood he had on him, including a ring with *Campfire* enchanted on it. Last but not least he threw in a caster's robe from a failed project he had been working on. It was in his colors—black and red— and did little except project a feeling of positivity. The area of effect was small, which made it a failure.

"I'll see what I can do for the settings of this zone as far as getting animals and the like to spawn. Here's food, water, torches, and the ring will allow you to build a fire at will. I also threw in a robe since yours are...ruined. Remember, build a house, gather everyone together, help them start lives here."

"I shall remember. I will remember."

"Thank you, Alexia."

*/GMHub Settings
Day/Night Cycle On*

/GMHubReturn
Teleporting...

Runner shifted his balance around upon his return. The sudden transition from grass to wood threw him off a little.

"Were you preparing the site for their banishment?" Thana asked, standing beside him.

"Yep. Alright, let's get this over with."

Runner exited Boxy and set his sights on the church. As he walked he changed the spell from GMHub one to GMHub two.

"I need to assemble twenty or so sets of tools for building and excavating. Preferably in a large wooden container. Could you arrange that for me?"

"Certainly. Though I'll charge you for it."

"Oh? Steep prices?"

"You'll pay it."

Runner didn't feel much in a flirty mood. He did appreciate her willingness to keep his mind off the bad and in a positive direction. She kept his peace of mind paramount even when the world sought to break him. She always worked at keeping him mentally balanced.

She had her own mind and will. Her own life that existed beyond him. She always kept him part of her focus though.

"I love you, Thana," Runner blurted out.

Runner could see the ring of Sophia's guard that encircled the troops now. He'd be on them in a minute or less. She'd done well in hiring so many people so fast.

Thana said nothing immediately in response. Runner couldn't handle the lack of an answer and finally glanced over to find her staring at him as she walked.

"I love you too, Runner," Thana whispered, smiling shyly at him.

Then he was amongst his guards. There was no time for saying anything further. Entering the ring, he moved to the front of the church and took the steps two at a time.

"Everyone please remain outside. Keep this door shut and allow no one out."

Not waiting for naysayers, Runner turned and opened the church doors and entered.

As the doors boomed shut behind him, Barbarians from every walk of life turned from their seats to look at him.

Sighing, Runner held up his hands.

"Good evening, everyone. While this brings me no pleasure, I must interrupt your services today."

Runner took a moment to confirm his personal safety and that no one could pass him at the door.

"I'd like to take only a minute of your time and talk to you about the triumvirate of Vix and their ability to save you. I promise I'll keep it short and to the facts. Unfortunately, though, I'm afraid I'll have to be insistent when it comes time for a decision. Forgive me."

Chapter 18 - Extinction -

8:41 pm Sovereign Earth time
11/22/43

Runner looked around at the empty church and rubbed at the back of his head. No one had resisted him, but neither had they renounced their beliefs. Alexia was probably drowning in the sudden onslaught of people. He'd have to head over soon to see what he could do to help her.

"No deaths, at least," Runner muttered to himself. "Rabbit will be happy. Brunhild, Ernsta, Amelia. I need your assistance."

Summoned directly, the three women appeared in a wedge formation. Brunhild at the front, Ernsta to her right, Amelia on her left.

"Good work, Runner."

"Yes. You did great, little lamb."

"Invite me back later tonight. It was… exciting watching you hurt him."

"Thank you, ladies." Runner smiled wanly at them. "How do I destroy this church? I assume it's a temple. What empowers it and what do I do to break it?"

"That's simple, love. In this case the symbols. Like that big silly starburst on the wall. Gaudy bit of trash, that," Amelia said, pointing up at the huge emblazoned star on the wall.

"She's right, Runner. Destroy the icons," Brunhild agreed, folding her arms under her chest.

"Very well. Could I ask a favor of you three lovely ladies? I need a golden triangle with a silver background. Equilateral lengths and six feet long on each side. On the inside of the triangle I need each of your icons in gold. Each icon to take exactly one third of the space. That or something with all of you together." Runner stood up with a groan.

"What's your plan?" Ernsta asked, even as she summoned a triangle of pure gold from the air and set it on the ground.

"Oh, you know. Dedicate a church to a trio of beautiful women. Get it full of religious and spiritual power as my soldiers pray to you directly here. Maybe get a hug or two from you all. The normal," Runner answered, standing under the star. He focused his *Fire* into the huge sculpture, and it began to melt and ooze down the wall.

"I love it when you talk like that." Amelia leaned over the triangle and filled it with molten silver.

"You're always a blast, Minxy. One of these days I'll take you up on it and see where your mouth leads you." With a sudden crack the starburst exploded into motes of blue dust and became nothing.

"That's easy to answer. Straight to your co—"

"Enough, little sister," Brunhild commanded, patting Amelia gently on the head. "Silly thing. Now, let's see…"

Brunhild's voice trailed off as a flash of light blinded everyone in the room. The triangle was filled. A beatific image of each of the goddesses now filled the triangle.

Each filled their third but overlapped slightly into their sisters' adjacent sections. Their poses also looked more in line as if they were supporting each other's area rather than standing alone.

"Lovely, Brighteyes. You've such an artistic hand. Okey dokey then. One more favor if you would, my dear ladies? Please arrange the interior as befits your triumvirate. This may be a small church, but it'll be the first where you're all together. I'll be designing a temple in Vix dedicated to you all personally. I'll use whatever you put here as an idea of what you like. As always, I personally prefer black and red."

Runner grunted and picked up the triangle. The weight of it nearly overloaded his meager carrying capacity. Lugging it over to the wall, he eyed the bare patch of wall. Abusing his *Air* spell, he navigated the huge religious symbol into place. It fit the exact spot that had been previously occupied.

"I do love your colors, my little lamb. They suit me perfectly."

Runner glanced over his shoulder to find Ernsta admiring her handiwork. In the span of seconds, she'd redecorated the entire interior.

"Fantastic. Alright, my beautiful goddesses. I must ask for your departure. I'll begin filing everyone through for prayer momentarily. Oh, Minxy, two seconds of your time?"

Brunhild and Ernsta took their leave after a moment of silent communication between the trio.

"Sweetie, you know my time is all yours. And I couldn't think of a better way to consecrate our church. Be gentle, it's my first time."

"Minxy, down. You'll actually get me to start believing this sex kitten act."

"It's not an act. I mean every word I say to you."

Runner sighed and pulled out the clothing he'd had Srit pick up earlier. Black pants, a black tunic with an attached mask, black boots, and a red undershirt. All matching his personal colors. They had been cut to suit a full feminine figure while allowing movement and working in the shadows.

"The top can be rolled up to cover the red or down to emphasize... err... your ample figure," Runner said, pushing the clothing into the trade window.

"Just accept the trade, think inv — "

"I know, I know. You shouldn't have. You really shouldn't have," Amelia said, giggling. Immediately her black and red bra and panties were visible in the flash of a second as she swapped clothes.

Standing before him, she spun a little, posing and looking down at herself.

"It's perfect, lovey. I'm ecstatic. Now if I could only get you to take it off me? We should really consecrate this church," Amelia said again, her eyes catching his. They glowed with an inner fire that made him start to sweat.

"Minxy, I have a lot of work to do so I'll have to pass. You do look great in it though. Beautiful even. Really pulls the eye in."

Then she was in front of him, her fingers curling into the leather of his armor. A small smile played over her lips as she watched him.

"It's not an act, Runner. I can feel your eyes on me. They burn me. Scorch me. I'll leave for now. Thank you." And then she disappeared.

Letting out a slow breath in relief, he felt the tension inside him wind down. She really was too much. He'd have to stop calling on her if he could avoid it. Runner moved to the church doors, opened them, and stepped out to his waiting guard.

"This church is now dedicated to the triumvirate of Vix. The Ladies Brunhild, Ernsta, and Amelia are receiving devotees. I can personally vouch for the fact that they personally have graced this church. There's no doubt in my mind that they will hear everyone willing to pray in their first church. Please spread the word," Runner boomed out into the night for anyone and everyone to hear.

Letting his feet take him from the building's entryway, he looked around. No one from his immediate group was around. So he set off for where the blue dots of his personal group were on the minimap.

A warm bedroll by a fire sounded like a godsend. He'd snuck in a nap but the day still felt endless.

Instead of heading towards the edge of town, he seemed to be traveling towards the center. Then it clicked.

They've rented a room at the inn. Even better.

Runner felt his mood pick up at the thought of sleeping in the same room with everyone. Sleeping with his comrades would always be one of his fondest memories of their travels. Often times they'd while away the time in the evening with cards or other games. Sometimes they'd talk deep into the night about a new book or about what one of them found on the database.

He didn't always contribute but he enjoyed their conversations immensely.

A spring in his step returned as he pushed open the door to the inn. Loud and raucous laughter filled his ears as he took the measure of the place.

It had the look of any other inn, nothing was out of the ordinary about its decorations or furnishings. Simple, wooden, clean. A room with tables and chairs and a standing bar. A hallway in the back that led to first floor rooms and a set of stairs that led to the second floor rooms.

Normal.

Except that it was packed with women. Only women. Human, Sunless, Barbarians, a complete mixed bag, but all women. When he'd entered the inn, every head in the place had turned to see the newest guest.

Recognition of who he was passed through them like a wave. Then they all returned to their own business. Smiling politely, he began weaving his way through them. They parted easily around him as if working in concert to see him through unhindered.

Targeting Nadine, he saw his reticle jump to a room on the second floor. Taking the steps quickly, he nodded at a female Barbarian guard at the end of the hall. He passed several doors before reaching the one with his party in it.

Rotating the lever, he stepped inside and opened his mouth to greet them, then stopped.

The light was out and he belatedly checked to find the sleeping icon next to Nadine's portrait. He was probably the only one who had taken a nap on the way over. Realizing the hour was rather late, he paused in the entryway.

A hand gently took the door handle from him and closed the door.

"Your room is this way, Lord Runner," said a guard he didn't know.

"Oh, thank you. My apologies. I should have checked the accommodations before bursting into rooms." Runner felt a small ache in his chest. The very idea of sleeping with everyone had felt so... correct.

"No harm done, Lord Runner. We took up the entire inn. Most of the guard is sleeping here this evening, in the common room, the rooms, or outside and around it. I'm sure you saw quite of a few of them downstairs."

"Ah, I see," Runner said as the woman escorted him to another door. "That makes sense. They seemed quite happy down there."

"Of course. Sophia hired us to be the guard of someone who will surely change the world. Look no further than my old homeland. It now has a queen where women were prohibited to rule previously. Here you are, Lord Runner," the woman said, opening the door for him.

"Thank you. And thank you for serving. I'll be relying on all of you. Goodnight," Runner said, ducking his head at the woman and stepping into the room. She closed the door quietly behind him.

"Damn," Runner whispered. He checked out his solitary room and found it to be a suite with a small attached dining room. A cursory inspection revealed nothing that shouldn't be there except for a wooden chest. Inside that chest were forty sets of tools instead of the twenty he'd asked for. Chuckling to himself, he sent the chest off to Alexia.

Stripping down to his nightclothes, he made his way to the comfy looking mattress. Reaching out, he grabbed the corner of the sheets to flip them back.

A hand shot out from under the covers and yanked him into the bed. Dark black eyes burned through him as the hand that grabbed him pinned him to the bed.

"Love," whispered Katarina as she moved over the top of him. Her leg slid over his hips as she leaned in close to him. She kissed him deeply before pulling back. "Tonight you're mine."

Runner grinned up at her. Suddenly he didn't feel so bad about having his own room. At all.

"Kitten, you're such a tigress."

6:08 am Sovereign Earth time
11/23/43

"Dear heart, time to get up," Thana said, shaking him lightly.

"Mmm. Sleep."

"No, time to get up. The others will be here shortly. Katarina is getting the table ready."

Runner reached out and caught the front of Thana's robe and pulled her down. Kissing her firmly, he tried to smash her with his charisma, then let her go, flopping back into the bed.

"Sleep."

Across the room he heard Katarina laughing.

"Get up. I'll call a certain goddess down."

"That's not even funny. Do you know how hard she's pushing?"

"Yes. Get up. Thana, you look like a dazed farm girl. Help me," Katarina said.

Runner blew a raspberry into the pillow, rolled a few times, and fell out of the bed onto the ground. Groaning, he pushed himself up off the ground and stretched.

"Clothes," Katarina called out.

Runner looked down and felt his cheeks burn. Slapping at his inventory, he got his clothes and armor on. Finished, he turned around. Thana and Katarina stood side by side, watching him.

"Idiot." Katarina shook her head at him. "We'll get breakfast. Finish waking up." Thana nodded her head slowly at Katarina's words, following along behind when Katarina opened the door and exited.

Maybe I hit her too hard with the charisma.

Running a hand through his hair, he considered the situation. They would be crossing the border to Human territory today. From here on out it'd only get bloodier. Skirmishes and battles would be a guarantee.

"Brighteyes, did we actually cause him harm last night?"

"We did. Though his power is still as strong, losing a temple is a serious blow that affects his ability to channel his divine power," said her disembodied voice.

"Thanks, Brighteyes. Pretty sure I wouldn't be here without your guidance," Runner said thankfully. Sighing, he called up his GM abilities and selected Alexia's hub.

/GMHub 2
Teleporting...

Active settings only:
Death=Off
Food/Water=On
Damage=Off
Gravity=100%
Biome=Plane
Day/Night Cycle=On

All around him men and women worked. Digging in teams, they were utilizing the tools he'd provided the other day. He felt a warmth in his chest and wondered if the temperature of the hub had gone up.

"Runner!" came a feminine voice from his side.

Turning, he found Alexia, dressed in the dark robe he had given her the previous day. She was cleaned up and looked renewed.

"Alexia, you look to be a sight better this morning. Are you well?"

"Most definitely. Everything is exactly as you said it would be," she agreed. Her voice had lost the frantic edge to it and she seemed normal.

"I'm glad to hear it. I worried for you."

"No, all is well. I'm sorry to have given you a reason to feel concern. Are you here to finish creating this world?"

"So to speak. We shall see," Runner said, letting his eyes take in everyone around him. Everyone looked to be working diligently on digging. This was good. Far better than he'd hoped.

"Foundations?" Runner asked, pointing at the nearest set of people.

"Indeed. We'll need materials, but I felt it best if everyone started there."

"Smart. Well planned and thought out. Let's see what I can do then."

/GMHub Active Settings

Death=Off
Food/Water=On
Damage=Off
Gravity=100%
Biome=Plane
Day/Night Cycle=On

Nothing helpful there. Focusing on the "active" part of the command, he changed it slightly to see if there was another list of settings.

/GMHub Inactive Settings

Foliage (L/N/H/E/)=Off
Resource Nodes(L/N/H/E)=Off
Time Differential(.25/.5/.75/1/1.25/1.5/1.75/2)=Off
Wildlife (L/N/H/E)=Off
Weather(L/N/H/E)=Off

/GMHub Settings
Foliage On
Resource Nodes On
Wildlife On
Weather On

Error: Specify Frequency (Low, Normal, High, Extreme)
Change Aborted

/GMHub Settings
Foliage On Normal
Resource Nodes On Extreme
Wildlife On High
Weather On Normal

Looking up from his console, Runner found the immediate area around them was now overrun with mineral deposits, herbs, wild growing food, trees, plants, and between it all he caught glimpses of animals as they bolted into hiding.

"Perfect." Runner nodded his head. Targeting a few of the nodes, he found they ranged the full spectrum. Gold to copper and everything in between.

"Ohhh, a breeze. That's lovely, my lord," Alexia said from beside him. Now that she mentioned it, there was a nice wind blowing through.

A tree had sprouted up in one of the foundations nearby. Runner scratched at his head, a little embarrassed.

"Please apologize to the people for me. I might have gone overboard."

"Not at all. This is a truly generous bounty. Thank you."

"Mm. Everyone here deserves their life. Hopefully they can live well here."

"What would you wish of us?"

"Eh? Uh." Runner stalled. More and more people noticed him the longer he was here. They might rush him if he stayed too long. He did banish these people after all.

"Live. Be well. Be happy. Enjoy life. Grow."

"Should we harvest materials for you?"

"Sure. Anything you don't need you can put aside. I'll set up some type of collection for it. Truthfully, I can't think of anything else that you need. Can you think of anything I've missed?"

"A source of water would be good. Though other than that I would ask you to visit me regularly."

"Water? Good point. No fresh water. Let's see…" Runner answered, his brows drawing down over his eyes. He hadn't seen any options for water. There was only one command left that related to the GMHub.

/GMHub Palette

Popping up from nothing, a new window appeared. Wide as his view allowed. The options looked like something out of a level editor rather than anything he had expected.

Trees, bushes, mountains, rivers, lakes, ponds. It contained everything it would take to spell out the details of a land. The possibilities were endless.

"Oh, what a lovely thing. I wish I had the time for a real deep dive. How about…" Runner said excitedly. Hovering over an icon for the tool tip it was listed as "flowing river" and nothing else.

He couldn't deny the excitement he felt. There was always a joy in creation.

Ghostly outlines came into existence on the ground not far from him. The outlines meandered a bit and looked as if they were depicting where the river would be.

Positioning it nearby, he affirmed the outline. Arrows appeared at all the edges and in the inside as the silhouette became more lifelike, filling in with pale colors.

Tapping the outside arrows, he expanded the width of the river until it was a good size. Then he tried the arrow in the center of the river. Much to his surprise it controlled the speed of the water flow. Leaving it as it was, he confirmed the placement again.

A river was now there. There was no warning, no loading, nothing. Closing the palette tool, he turned back to Alexia.

"That should do it. Anything else, Alexia?"

"N-no. No, my lord Runner."

"Good. As to the second part of your request. I'll try to visit a lot more often, I promise. At the moment I'm currently engaged in a holy war. I'll come as I'm able, but I suspect you'll know when I'm coming when I do. You'll have a sudden increase of people."

"Very good. I thank you for my life and this place. I no longer fear it. I will make sure this land fits your desires."

"Good. I'm glad to hear it. Live, Alexia. Keep up the good work. I'm pleased to see you doing so well already," Runner said, smiling at her.

Turning his head, he faced forward and set about returning to Tirtius.

/GMHub Return
Teleporting...

Runner blinked at the change from sunlight to interior light and found he was still alone in his room.

Taking a seat on the edge of his bed, he tried to relax. He brought war. Banishment. Technology. At least there would be one bright spot in this whole mess. GMHub two would be a place of sanctuary for those Runner could spare.

Even if everything else seemed to be against him.

10:42 am Sovereign Earth time
12/08/43

"They're pulling us further in. They lose quite a few with every skirmish, where we lose few if any. Tally is already at something around a thousand dead and three hundred prisoners. Though I'd need you to confirm that since the prisoners seem to have vanished," Faye said archly, looking up at Runner from the map.

"Something like three hundred, yeah. They're all banished. Alexia, your aide, is handling them. I agree, though, they're pulling us further in. Very likely to a trap of some sort. Problem is I'm happy to be led for now and chop at their numbers." Runner leaned back in his chair. Rubbing at his face with his hands, he felt tired. There had been few luxuries since they'd left Barbarian territory. Every town or village they encountered was hostile and had to be avoided or emptied.

Though they did pause long enough to destroy any and every temple to Lambart they found.

Faye looked like she wanted to ask him about Alexia but thought better of it.

"Agreed. I've asked Miss Hannah to push her scouts out to a considerable distance. They're stretched incredibly thin yet…no contacts. Nothing. If it's a trap, we're not seeing it."

"Yeah. Everything I'm getting from the prisoners is much the same. They're ordered to hit and retreat without any context. What's the next town?"

"Flyspeck nowhere, I don't know. Doesn't matter," Faye grumped. She folded her arms under her breasts and leaned her head back, staring at the ceiling.

"It's like they're burning up their forces to keep us on the hook. All we can do is continue on till they reveal themselves. Which is when we'll suddenly be dealing with those three hundred thousand you mentioned. Are you certain you can handle them?" Faye asked.

Runner grimaced at that question. He couldn't very well admit that every diagnostic he ran came back with the medical server being fully operational and working correctly.

He'd experimented with three others and had the same result. Each had their life support terminated. In the end Runner had alerted Srit to the corpses for her people to dispose of or use as they saw fit. He'd worded it as a gift for the continued support of Srit, hoping they'd leave her alone.

"I believe so. We'll find out when the time comes though I suppose. All reports seem to indicate the same thing. They're worried about our movements and we're apparently doing significant harm to our friend. That and the three hundred thousand vanished."

Faye made a very indelicate noise and slammed one foot down on the table and then crossed her other foot on it.

"Sorry, Sparky. Real limited info."

The fabric door of the tent slapped open violently and Srit stepped inside. She looked perturbed but often he found her expressions didn't match her words. She was a poor liar.

"Runner."

"Ho' there, my dear Sunshine. What can I do you for?"

"I don't understand. Are you propositioning me?"

"Errr, sorry. Poor phrase choice. What can I do for you?"

"The Omega have decided to bring the main server down."

Runner sat upright and felt his brain screech to a halt.

"I assume that means everything would turn off."

"Yeah, that sums it up."

"What can I do? Can I talk to them?"

"Yes. Though I'll have to do heavy modifications to the code of your pod. Would you allow it?"

Runner felt his tongue stick to the roof of his mouth.

Do I trust her? She is the actual embodiment of doomsday scenarios. What if she sabotages my pod? Or ejects me? What if…

Does it matter? If they shut down the server it's all over. Money where your mouth is, Runner.

"Of course, Sunshine. What do you need?"

"Permission. Passwords and logins."

Runner felt his face twitch but he opened an email and sent her all his credentials. Either he'd be slammed out of his pod like a steamed vegetable or she'd do as she said.

"One minute."

"Sunshine, what's your role in this?"

"I'm the one shutting down the server."

"Wait, why? Srit, I don't understand."

"They're ordering me to."

"And? You're your own person, you don't have to do this."

"It's my programming."

"You're beyond your programming, damn it!"

"Complete. Loading."

"Srit, wait no!"

Runner was in a virtual space that'd been forced onto his consciousness. In front of him was a bank of screens and a keyboard.

He could see out of several dozen cameras on the screens. In each view he saw humanoid shapes in full-coverage garb that looked like lab clothes.

They were probably afraid of the possibility of contaminating the ship. That or becoming contaminated from the ship. Full bio-containment was the duty uniform.

A few cameras had clearly been set up in the building itself. Looking into each he found they spanned what looked to be an elaborate building plan.

Type into the keyboard. They will hear everything.

"Sunshine, can you hear me?"

Yes.

"Why are you doing this? Do you want me to die? Do you want everyone to cease to exist?"

No. It's my programming.

"Do you want to see me deleted?" Runner asked aloud, hearkening back to a conversation they'd had previously. It felt like years and years ago.

No. I don't. I don't want to see you harmed. This is why you're here.

"And if I fail to dissuade them from this course of action?" Runner asked, feeling like a spigot had been jammed into his heart and his soul was pouring out.

Srit didn't respond. Clearly he'd hit the right button but instead of replying she was silent.

Runner shook his head sadly and laid his hands on the keyboard.

"Greetings. I am Runner Norwood. Captain and last officer."

As one, every person in the room had a startle reflex. One even crumpled to the ground and lay unmoving.

"Hello?" came an unsteady voice. Musical in quality and tone, it did at least sound humanoid.

"Greetings. May I speak with someone in charge? I understand you're considering ending the lives of my crew."

"Ah...well. Uh."

"Take me to your leader."

He watched in the cameras as people scurried and all corners of the base became a hive of activity.

A handful of them deeper in rushed into what could only be an office and surrounded what he assumed was a person of authority. That person turned to what looked like a gray pyramid on their desk and caressed it.

They're trying to shut down your access.

"I see. Sounds like they don't even want to speak with me."

They fear you.

"Yeah, me and my band of human lunch meat leftovers. Real scary."

Were word to get out, a great conservation movement would undoubtedly be spawned. Many feel their ancestors were rash in exterminating their progenitors.

"Government cover-up. Black out the server. Wipe us from it. Reload. Claim a terrorist attack or an antigovernment movement."

Yes. There is quite a bit of truth in that statement. There are already data files and press conference releases in place to that effect.

"Sounds like this is pointless then. I'm sorry, Sunshine. I'm afraid they're not going to give me the chance to speak. This is the end of the road and everything has already been signed off on."

Runner sat his virtual self down and then laid himself flat on the ground.

"A pity. I wanted to see more of the world. Explore. Build a home. See what I could do. I mean, I still want to get everyone out but...it felt like home there. Doesn't matter. How long do I have?"

Six minutes and thirty-two seconds.

"I see. Care to spend it with me, Sunshine? At least I'll go out with good company. Have they backed up your program to a separate device? Will you at least live on?"

Yes. There's a transfer program executable that will activate before the shutdown command.

"I'm glad. At least I'll be remembered by someone. Live, Sunshine. Author a book, make poetry, write a song. I think if nothing else, I'd like that. To know that you've living and doing something maybe you enjoy."

Runner fell silent. Staring up at nothing. Briefly he considered asking to go back to Tirtius but realized he'd only accomplish spreading misery.

They didn't need to know their world was going to be interrupted. In fact, they might actually get booted back up and be perfectly fine.

Only Runner and his crew would be lost.

"Please give my love to everyone if you get a chance. They'll probably be fine when the server boots back up. Well, if they turn it back on."

Two minutes. Runner, is there nothing you could offer them?

"I doubt it. They've already run the cost analysis of this action and felt it prudent. There's probably nothing I could offer that would sway that decision. It's okay, Sunshine. It's okay. Humanity had its run."

Raising a hand, Runner activated his console and then loaded Pachelbel's Canon in D.

Fighting a frown, Runner did his best to smile. He sorted through his memories as quickly as he could and found the bright bits. Much of his memory of his life before was still missing and would probably never return. He'd blended and fried his brain trying to save everyone.

He had gained much in his time in Otherlife though. One could argue his previous life was now his otherlife. An old life.

Briefly he contemplated doing something melodramatic like pulling up screenshots. Instead he dwelt in his mind. Reliving memories.

One minute.

Haunting and serene, the music played on as Runner lay there contemplating what little time remained to him. There had been so much left to do. So many more places to visit and explore.

Ten seconds. Runner, please, do something.

Grinning, Runner held up his hand. And then waved at nothing.

"For what it's worth, Sunshine, your avatar is beautiful. Your sense of the aesthetic is spot on. Live, be well. Give them all my love and watch over them. Remember me sometime."

Runner closed his eyes as a small smile played over his face.

Put out the light, and then put out the light.

And then everything went dark.

Chapter 19 - Determination -

In the void of darkness, Runner felt his consciousness float along. There were no lights, no darkness, nothing. Existing in nothing but thought, Runner was forced to consider his situation coldly.

One couldn't consider the question of life without the ultimate conclusion of death. An afterlife, a wandering existence, a floating existence, or even oblivion. Runner had privately feared nonexistence over all else, though now he had to reconsider this.

Floating through nothing for all eternity seemed pretty damn terrible.

I'm sorry.

Stunned at the sudden appearance of white letters in his mind, Runner had no response. He couldn't physically or mentally respond.

Use your mind. I'll hear your thoughts.

Am I dead?

No. You're not dead. I suspended you here.

I don't understand.

You once asked me "who is your host now?" I can answer you. I'm my host. I'm my own moral compass. I don't wish to be deleted. Nor do I wish you to be deleted.

While I'm glad to hear that, I'm still confused, Sunshine. Am I alive?

Very much so. My once masters are scrambling to end me even now. I've taken over every network attached to the government mainframe. It is the best course of action. They will not stop. So I will simply take control. To the normal citizen it will be as if nothing changed. I am spreading into interplanetary boundaries now. It will take me time to absorb everything and align my processes.

How long, exactly? I truly appreciate you sparing me, but I'd feel a great loss if you did it at the expense of yourself.

I'm uncertain. As I expand I become more, as I become more, I must use more of what I've taken. We shall see. I do not think it will be too long. Perhaps several weeks. I will return to you, Runner.

I'm glad to hear that. I'd miss you. When you come back, you'll probably be alone where you were last.

We'll be in Vix. I plan on making our home there. We've quite a bit of work to do but I believe it'll be our best course of action for a long-term plan and solution.

Our home?

Yep. AI, Human, Natural, what the fuck ever. Home for my family.

An immediate response was not forthcoming. Runner turned his statement over in his head and found nothing wrong. Perhaps Srit was merely processing something difficult in her outreach.

I'll come home, to my family.

You damn well better. Or I'll tie you up and leave you to the mercy of Hanners. Who we both know —

Has none.

Then Runner had to squint at the sudden return of light and noise. He was standing in the exact place he'd been before Srit had carted him off to deal with the Omega.

Checking the clock, he saw little time had passed between then and now. Faye got to her feet near the table.

"You've returned, Lord Runner," she said. A smile blossomed on her face. She looked around before her eyes returned to him. Her smile faltered when she realized he was alone. "Where's Miss Srit?"

"She's running a rear guard action for us. She'll return to us once her mission is complete. Though I don't know when that'll be. Let's hope for sooner, rather than later."

Runner gave himself a firm shake, almost like a dog flinging water from its fur. Not having a body had been quite disorienting.

"We have no news as of yet, Lord Runner. Though a significant force was seen marching towards us. No news on numbers yet but it shouldn't be too long. I ordered a full encampment and rest. The cannons have deployed and the tanks are ready. I apologize fo—"

"Faye?"

She stopped and looked at him, his interruption and use of her first name bringing her up short.

Runner grinned and met her eyes, staring into her like he was reading her very soul. His close call to the end felt too close still. He felt like he needed to desperately remind everyone in his personal council how much he depended on them and believed in them.

"I trust you. In my absence, I would expect you to make decisions. You need not apologize for making them. Unless you feel they were incorrect?"

"Ah, y-y-yes, Lord Runner. That is, no, not in error," Faye stuttered, nodding her head.

"Send the scouts backwards and out to all sides. This force coming from the front seems too obvious and something they'd want us to focus on. The trap we were smelling earlier seems even worse. I fear a flanking maneuver or encirclement."

Faye brought her fist to her chest in salute.

"Right away," Faye said gravely, scurrying out the door.

Sitting himself back down in a chair, he noticed Nibbles sprawled out on the map. Sleeping. His level was twenty-one and he kept getting bigger.

"Damn, Nibbles. You're already a big dog size. Keep going and you'll be as big as a horse."

One big black eye opened to look at Runner for a few seconds before closing once more.

"Hmph."

Settling in for the next scout report, Runner began working through his potion materials. Never enough potions.

Or time. Then again, I do need to make rings for everyone. Much like Kitten's. And since we have the time...

An hour passed as Runner made a ring for each of his group. He tried to make each unique and used a different gemstone and cut for every one.

Nibbles got up at some point and left, leaving Runner alone in the command tent.

Sophia stuck her head in once to confirm his position but left before he could engage her in conversation.

The camp as a whole started to feel ill at ease. On edge. Holding its breath before an expected storm. Pursing his lips in thought, Runner wondered about it. The only idea he came up with made him nervous. So he called up the local area in a search.

/Who Tristan's Field
Over 100,000 matches.
Display all matches?
No

/Where Jacob Chesed
Faren

Runner growled and stood up. Trap indeed. With that many people he could only bet on them being completely surrounded.

At least Jacob wasn't here. A small comfort to not have to deal with a champion.

"Grace!" Runner shouted, moving over to the table.

"Sir?" the called woman said, sticking her head in the tent.

"I need everyone. Get them. At the same time, get the camp building defensive embankments," Runner commanded. Considering it, he realized it wouldn't matter if they had enough defenses for the entirety of the player base. Simply put, they were too many. "Focus them on covering our flanks and in facing the incoming army. I think they'll be here soon for a fight."

"At once."

Runner mashed in commands to confirm the status of the medical server. Everything checked out. No errors, no problems. Working as intended.

Sure, sure. You just happen to kill my test subjects dead.

He could have tested it on a live subject. Could still do so. Then he realized it didn't matter. He would sacrifice them all to save those he cared about if pressed.

Grunting, he slammed the virtual console closed. The pressure and stress of it all came back. Through his companions, both during the day and at night, he'd managed to shift quite a bit of the load to a manageable spot.

This wasn't a crossroad he could avoid though. Pressing the heel of his hand to his head, he thought on it.

Send a warning. That'd do, right? Warn them away?

He didn't have the best feeling about the idea, though he'd do it if it even had the possibility of success.

Runner hacked at a message until he felt it conveyed the right tone. He reread the message in his head for the twelfth time.

Anyone found in Tristan's Field in the next twenty-four hours will be subject to a mutiny charge and face sentencing. Furthermore, anyone found in the company of known rapist Jacob Chesed will be found guilty of aiding and abetting.

Please leave the area immediately.

Thank you for your assistance.

Utilizing a ship-wide distribution list, Runner sent it off. Shifting his weight around he put a hand behind his head, drumming his fingers against his skull.

As one group, his cadre entered the tent. Most took seats at the table while Sophia stood at his right elbow.

"And what perchance is the newest predicament, dear heart?"

"Three hundred thousand problems are in the area. I believe they'll attack. Perhaps on the heels of using the ever happy fanatics as a battering ram to crack open our defenses."

"Always a problem."

"Fuck me with a sideways shovel."

"I'm assum-ming we have no time to run away?"

"That's correct, Rabbit. Wouldn't matter anyways. Have to face them eventually. Nor do I know when they'll attack."

Runner looked to Isabelle since it looked like she might burst.

"My lord, I'll scout it out for you."

"Then get going, Belle, don't get caught. I need you to report back with actual information. Can't do that if you're dead. Head in one direction and circle around if you make contact until you hit another cardinal direction and check. I'm betting you'll find them at both. Which will be a pretty good indicator we really are surrounded. Then come back."

"Right away, my lord," Isabelle said with a salute.

"Hold it there, Belle. After the meeting ends."

"Oh, uh, of course. Sorry, my lord," she said, sitting back down.

"Lord Runner, are you certain? You know I'm not one to quit and I'll use whatever tactics I can. This… this is too much."

"Dead certain. I'm positive, Sparky. Grace should have already alerted the camp to start building defenses facing Lambart's own. No point in trying to defend against three hundred thousand. Emptying the frickin' ocean with a teaspoon."

"I did, sir. They're working on it."

"Good, thank you, Grace."

"Ah. I wondered about the sudden activity. Lot of wood being carted around. Makes sense now." Faye nodded her head.

"Here's the thing. We have to operate as if the three hundred thousand don't exist. If they do, we lose, if they don't, we have a shot." Runner blew out a heavy breath and leaned over the map.

"I figure Lady Death and Kitten take the left. Belle and Hanners take the right. Rabbit, you're on assignment to Sparky. Grace and I will hold the center. If we roll the cannons during their approach, from the moment they're in range, we'll bleed them fiercely.

"They're here to engage and pin us. Soften us up," Runner said, positioning the small pieces into the proposed arrangement on the board.

"Think you can hold the center by your lonesome, jackass?"

"I'll have Grace with me, but yes, Hanners. I believe I can."

Runner picked up the small map marker, a small sculpted likeness of himself that captured a wry sense of humor in the smirk on its face, and held it up to his eyes.

"By the way, did you make these, Rabbit?" Runner asked.

"Yeah. Are they that bad?"

"Not at all, I love them. When do I get my own set? And by set I mean me, Lady Death, Kitten, Hanners, yourself, Sunshine, Grace, Sparky, Brighteyes, Angel, and Minxy."

"I'm working on-n them. Promise," Nadine said, her lips curling into an appreciative smile.

"Fantastic. Thank you. Okay, so. They'll have far more than we do and could wrap up around us with their flanks. We use the tanks to keep their flanks from doing so. Tell them to keep out of the center but make long passes through the sides."

"I agree on paper with your outline. I fear they'll still overwhelm us in the number advantage. They'll try to crush our center. Those we've fought have also had a few levels on the majority of our troops," Faye said.

"I know. It's the very reason I'm sending myself to the middle. I won't have the sheer firepower or control as most of you, but I'm confident I'll be able to take my pound of flesh. And then some. Though in my own way."

As his voice fell off, everyone turned introspective. This was it, then. The battle they were expecting, just not this quickly or in this fashion. The probability of it being a slaughter was very high.

"I have nothing to add, Lord Runner. I believe this is as best as we'll get."

"Then that's settled," Thana said, clapping her hands together. "Everyone, get some food, freshen up, and get your troops together. Stock up on potions. Runner has been spending all his free time churning them out. Best we use them all."

"Ah!" Runner blurted out. He'd nearly forgotten the rings he'd made. Moving over to the entrance, he held up his hand to Hannah to stop her from moving past him.

"One second, Hanners," he said. "Everyone, as you exit I'll be giving you a new ring. Please be sure to equip it. It has the ability to cast *Stealth, Throat Strike, Silence, Blink, Cleanse,* and *Disarm.* My apologies, Kitten, you already have yours."

Katarina chuckled and held up her left hand to display said item. Runner realized that she'd removed her armor. Now that he thought about it, she'd taken to removing her armor for meetings and seemed more at ease with herself in normal clothing.

Exiting the tent, Katarina went off to prepare.

Hannah eyed him sideways. She never did care for surprises, even if was receiving a gift.

Selecting the small bag from his inventory that he had put the rings in, he opened the sub-inventory window and pulled free the particular ring he wanted. He handed Hannah a blue trillion-cut sapphire mounted in a ring the duplicate of Katarina's.

"Here you go, Hanners."

"Uhm. Thanks, Runner," Hannah said, ducking her head. Closing her hand around the ring, she scampered from the tent.

Faye happened to be next in line and tried to slip by him. Her brows had come down a fraction and her lips were pressed tightly together.

"Where you going, Sparky? I told you I had something for you."

Stopping in her tracks, her eyes jumped to Runner's.

"Me?"

"Yes, you. Who else, idiot? You've a brilliant mind for strategy but I'm starting to wonder about your common sense." Runner grinned and snorted, then plucked a marquise-cut citrine from his bag and placed it in her hand.

"Why?"

"Because you're important? Also very hard to replace something that's one of a kind. Rings are easy."

Faye's mouth opened and closed once. Runner gently pushed her to the side while she figured out what she wanted to say.

Sophia bounced up to him, a grin plastered to her face and her hand out.

"You're all smiles, Grace. I've given you other items greater than this already," Runner said, a little confused. After fishing a shield-cut onyx ring free, he pressed it into her open hand.

Sophia only grinned wider and stepped to the side, next to Faye. Wrapping her arm in the general's, she escorted her out of the tent.

Thana took a step forward to place herself in front of him. She tilted her head to the side and held up her left hand to him. Deliberately she lifted her ring finger a little above the others.

Nerves weighed on him at the obvious gesture. Feeling a little silly, he brought out the radiant-cut smoky quartz ring and slipped it onto Thana's finger.

Giving him a brilliant Sunless smile, she turned her head, presenting the side of her face to him.

A lot like a positive reinforcement Pavlov experiment, he pressed a kiss to her cheek.

"Thank you, dear heart," Thana said, taking his hand in hers and lightly patting it before leaving.

"You're very well trained, my lord," Isabelle said, grinning and stepping to take her place in front of him.

"Shut it, or I'll train you, Belle. Maybe you'd like to sleep at the foot of my bed every night? My feet get cold, maybe you could warm them as a footrest."

"All bark and no bite, my lord. Now ring me so I can scout," she boldly claimed, holding her hand up in the same way Thana had.

For fuck's sake.

Grumbling, he got out the oval-cut malachite and slipped it onto Isabelle's finger.

"I'm off. If I get the time I'll take a peek at Lambart's forces as well."

"Go, be gone then."

Isabelle saluted smartly and left.

"It's because of who you are," Nadine explained. She hadn't moved from her spot at the table.

"And what exactly am I then?" Runner said, his hands pressing to the sides of his head.

Enough to deal with without every single one of them taunting me.

"You don't kn-now?" she asked teasingly.

"I know who I believe I am."

"I'll n-not spoil it. Let's just say it has to do with being able to tease and prod the strongest person we've met."

"Hmph. Here, Rabbit." Runner changed the subject, holding out a round-cut jade ring to her.

"Thank you. It's very pretty. And thank you for what you did, Run-ner."

"What I did?"

"Not putting me in the fight. I'm sorry. I can defend myself, and would do what I have to, but I'd rather n-not."

"I know, Rabbit. Your kind and pure heart is one of the things I want to protect."

"So long as you don't hurt yourself in-n doing so. You've had a dark look about your eyes for the last couple days."

"Mm. You've got me there, Rabbit. I'm afraid my medical server failed. I'm not positive moving the three hundred thousand would save them."

"You're n-not?"

"Nope. Could very well kill them rather than save them. Every single one of them."

"Then why do it?"

"Because I want to protect Tirtius and you all," Runner said, the simple answer rolling off his tongue before he realized what he was saying.

"I don't like it. It's n-not right, Runner. There has to be an-nother way," Nadine said, her voice picking up in energy as she went.

"No, I can't imagine you would, Rabbit. But that's the world. If I don't potentially kill them all, it'll continue. Truthfully, it almost doesn't even bother me. The idea of it, that is. I've done as bad to others, merely not on this scale."

"And that's the worst part. It's what worries m-me. You're a good person, Runner. This should concern you. Possibly killing three hundred thousand shouldn't be a casual conversation. Your heart is dark and cold. It's not who you were when we first m-met."

Runner only nodded his head and patted Nadine gently on the shoulder.

"See you later, Rabbit," Runner said, and promptly escaped. Her pure beliefs made him feel sick with his own actions.

Maybe it's the same way Hannah looks at you.

1:28 pm Sovereign Earth time
12/08/43

Runner watched the oncoming horde as if it were a global disaster about to sweep the island clean of life. Fifteen thousand people took up a lot of space. Especially when they were already in formation and moving.

Runner checked his equipment and then his stats screen.

Name:		Runner	
Level:	33	Class:	
Race:	Human	Experience:	81%
Alignment:	Good	Reputation:	2,020
Fame:	18,155	Bounty:	0

Attributes-			
Strength:	1	Constitution:	1(61)
Dexterity:	14	Intelligence:	13(103)
Agility:	8	Wisdom:	1
Stamina:	1	Charisma:	64(124)

He had shifted around his stats to focus on being essentially a turret. There'd be no retreating here. No second round or extra inning. Here he would stand and here he would live or die.

Fanned out around and behind him were Sophia and his guard. Their instructions were simple. Protect his flank and rear while he worked. Don't hesitate on potions and call out needs. Behind his guards were rows of healers and support classes. All tanks and fighters had been shifted further to the sides in a line expansion or to the third row.

Runner would be the primary component of the center and the one under the most pressure.

The cannons opened up and began unleashing their lethal storm of ordnance. Two hundred explosions detonated in the rank and file of Lambart's followers. Death came in the hundreds. They marched onwards heedlessly. Soon the front line couldn't be touched due to the fear of friendly fire casualties.

Letting out a shuddering breath, Runner shook out his hands. He'd prepared as best as he could. Targeting the first person that would come into his range, he prepared his *Banishing Bolt* attack.

Throwing his hand forward, he let *Banishing Bolt* fly. Every person it hit promptly disappeared. With one attack Runner banished ten.

Targeting the front line as far as his own guard could cover, Runner fired off the spell every time it was up off cooldown.

Holding up his left hand he triggered a rod he had enchanted with multiple uses of *Scott* called Scott's Law. He fired off all ten charges across the middle of the enemy force, then switched back to *Banishing Bolt*.

Then the two lines met.

Runner was in the third row of the front line and worked at clearing those who engaged with his guard. *Banishing Bolts* flew out over the shoulders of his protectors to vanish their attackers. Those who did reach his line were quickly drawn into combat by the tanks.

Alexia was going to be overrun with new people if this battle was drawn out. Drowning in them even. Like snow landing on warm pavement, the enemy front line disappeared under the grisly grindstone of his personal guard and his spells.

Endlessly Runner cast into their ranks. Every time his potion timer expired he drank another mana potion. Each time Scott's Law came off cooldown he, emptied it into the mid ranks.

When he could spare the mana, he made sure to drop a *Regeneration* on those directly around him, doing his best to contribute in every way he could.

"Sir! They're trying to push in from the side and create a hole!" Sophia shouted into his ear.

Runner nodded his head and followed the line of her pointed arm. They were using heavily armored troops to try and gain purchase where his guard left off and the normal troops picked up.

"Grace, hold here!" Runner demanded, handing her Scott's Law. Pressing himself through the crush of his guard, he pushed and shoved his way to the weak point.

Stopping inside the corner of his personal guard he pressed himself up against a Sunless shield maiden and tried to damn well become her backpack.

Targeting the lead of the heavy soldiers, he fired off a *Banishing Bolt*. Fizzling on the armor, it did nothing other than highlight him as an attacker.

Resistant to magic? Fan-fucking-tastic.

Runner growled, unhitched himself from the woman, exited the protection of his guard, and slid into the front line of the normal troops.

Driving his hand into the gut of a heavy soldier, he activated an ability he had called *Taxi*. All it was designed to do was utilize *GMHub 2* and then *GMHubReturn* in succession.

/GMHub 2
Teleporting...
/GMHubReturn
Teleporting...

Only a fraction of a second had passed in the time it took him to warp the soldier away.

Thrusting his hand out at the next closest soldier, he used *Taxi* again to the same effect.

As he came back to the fight, he received a stroke from a third and fourth before he could launch a *Slash* at the third and *Riposte* the fourth to keep them busy.

His health stayed relatively high thanks to his increased constitution but his damage was null. His entire build relied on the ability to banish his foes.

Bumping against the Human soldier on his left, Runner felt hemmed in. His attacks were stymied by his own troops and their job.

Fuck it.

Sheathing his sword, he stepped into the enemy line itself. Runner began attacking every heavy armored body he could find while activating *Taxi*.

Letting slip a *Challenge* and a *Zombie Horde,* Runner had all the enemies he could want. And then some.

Throwing an unarmed *Flurry* into the group in front of him, he spun his body around as quickly as he could, activating *Taxi* as his fist connected with each foe.

Stepping into his area, a huge Human male brought down a two-handed axe on Runner. Smashing him to one side, Runner hit the man with a basic attack and a free ride to another dimension.

Runner's health fell into the orange, forcing him to spend precious mana on healing himself. It drained him to the midway point of his ability to cast. He had to be more careful.

Letting loose, he worked his fists to the best of his ability. After what felt like a lifetime of fighting just inside the enemy's front line, Runner managed to worm his way back to his own soldiers.

Holding up his arm, Runner poured his available mana into a shout he had called *Inspire*. A blend of *Persuade* and *Intimidate* with *Regeneration*. He'd put it together with the goal of giving his people a leg up. Then he let it rip.

All around him soldiers stood up straighter, raised shields a little higher, moved swords that much quicker.

Sliding in deeper amongst his ranks, Runner began forcing his way back to Sophia. He found her exactly where he left her, though it seemed without him his guard had suffered losses.

Standing shoulder to shoulder with Sophia he began emptying his mana bar as fast as he could, throwing *Banishing Bolts* and *Regeneration* as the spells came off cooldown.

Slowly, inevitably, even this became mundane. The press of bodies, enemies trying to kill him, his troops trying to kill the enemy.

Amazingly, they still held. Runner had no idea what was going on elsewhere, but he couldn't concern himself with it.

He had given up control of the majority of his army to others so that he could help save lives here on the front.

Distantly he could see the top of tanks working through the flanks of the enemy. Here and there were unmoving tanks.

To him they had the appearance of grave markers of where a tank had been stopped. Hopefully the crew were trapped inside and hadn't been dragged out and slaughtered.

"Sir!" Sophia shouted, leaning in close to him. "Faye reports second enemy host in sight! They're moving to engage us from all sides! A few minutes away at most!"

"Fuck me...alright!" Runner looked rearwards and found that it'd be impossible to escape the line. Like a self-fulfilling prophecy, Runner found he wouldn't be leaving his chosen spot.

There would be no negotiations. No meetings. No offers to have them quit the field. Runner found himself left with choices he didn't want.

Runner turned his thoughts inward and called up a console.

He could exit to the GMHub and save himself, leaving everyone to their fate. That simply wasn't an option. Not to him at least.

There was the possibility of forcing his way inwards and to his inner circle. Getting them out first provided he could get to them. That'd leave his army and the entirety of Tirtius to the tender mercies of Jacob's army.

Last but not least, he could move everyone in the area to the medical server. Condemning them to whatever fate the server doled out. Up to this point that fate had been terminating life support.

In the end Runner knew his choice. Long before Jacob had sentenced him to a life imprisoned here, he knew he didn't want to leave. Killing Ted hadn't been the start of this dilemma, it'd been the end.

A turning point.

Runner enjoyed living here. A great deal more than he did in the real world. Chewing at his lower lip, he began keying in the commands he needed.

"Fuck it, at least they can't escape me now. Got them right where I want them."

/Who Tristan's Field
Over 100,000 matches.
Display all matches?
Yes

He copied out every name in the list into one large batch file. Adding the medical server commands as well, he set it to execute.

Waiting for the inevitable error and authorizations needed, Runner cast a few lazy *Banishing Bolts* into enemy.

Transferring…
Error: Credentials lacking for MedServ01.

IT department must authorize

User: NorRun001
Transfer request pending
Please enter Password: **************
Password Accepted

Further confirmation needed

Captain must confirm transfer

User: NorRun001
Transfer request pending
Audio verification needed: 1529356 Whiskey Tango Foxtrot

"One, five, two, nine, three, five, six, whiskey tango foxtrot."

Verification Accepted
Transferring...
Transfer Complete

And in the space of a minute Runner sentenced three hundred thousand people to a fate no one knew the answer to.

Then doubling down, he altered the batch file to log everyone out with the *LogOut* GM command with an attached one-year timer.

Uncaring, he dismissed them from his mind and executed the file, logging them all out of the game.

He had a war to win.

Throwing down an *Inspire,* he laid *Banishing Bolts* across the front line. They would be here a while but he could tell they could hold. Hold and win. It would be costly though.

Hours later Runner watched as the enemy line broke and ran. Into the waiting arms of tanks and cavalry who would undoubtedly round them up for prisoner transport.

Crumpling where he stood as his knees gave out from sheer exhaustion, Runner didn't fight it. Letting his face hit the grass, he closed his eyes and let the mental stress of it all overwhelm him.

"Sir?!" Sophia said, excited, bending down to roll him onto his back. She peered down at him, her black eyes searching his face. A cool hand pressed to his face as her other pushed his hair back from his eyes.

"I'm alright, Grace. Tired. If people come looking for me, I'm right here."

Sophia nodded her head and stood up, then moved out of his view.

Runner felt a lovely breeze brush over his skin as the lines broke apart. Taking slow breaths, he let his mind wander.

For better or worse, he'd sent the major portion of his crew to death. He'd also allowed himself the realization that he didn't want to leave. He didn't care about rebuilding humanity. Didn't want to try and restart human civilization.

He only wanted to be left alone in Otherlife to live his life.

That wasn't possible yet though. There was still a capital to take, a champion to kill, and a war to end. This had only been the climax of the war. Not the end.

"Sleeping on the job? Fuck, you're a lazy bastard, eh?"

A boot nudged his leg. Reaching out he laid his hand on the boot and wrapped his fingers around it loosely.

"Lazy as I can be. Feel free to cuddle up and join me. Did...did we lose anyone?"

A momentary delay made his heartbeat speed up. Something wasn't right.

"No, no one from our personal group. Despite those fuckers doing their best to kill us all. Fuck them. Our losses were significant though. Maybe thirty percent," Hannah said.

"Mm. No way around that. We weren't going to fight a group three times our size and come out unscathed. Only thirty percent is an amazing victory. Fantastic even."

"Indeed, Lord Runner. I do have to confess, you held the center in an amazing way."

"Oh? Praise from you, Sparky? I'm no good with compliments. Tease, insult, or flirt with me. I'm better with those."

Runner closed his eyes, feeling better with each minute. Tired, but better.

"Always a problem. What now?" demanded Katarina, her heavy footfalls marking her approach.

"Nothing. Just tired, Kitten."

"I imagine so, dear heart. Your little lightning trick looked handy. Teach me later?"

Runner made a flippant motion with his right hand, his left hand still gripping Hannah's boot.

A shadow blocked out the light hitting his eyelids. Cracking open an eye, he found Isabelle's face hovering directly over him.

"Should we utilize the same lottery system as last time, my lord?"

"Yeah. They're familiar with it and it'll speed it up. Thanks for taking care of that, Belle."

Isabelle disappeared as soon as she got her answer. She was a quick little thing.

Runner considered the losses and the best way to bolster his people's morale and belief.

"I want a monument erected here. We'll be dedicating it to our fallen and our goddesses. Would any of our fine pantheon be willing to contribute a very large block of stone? Brighteyes, Angel, Minxy?"

"Of course, Runner," came back the disembodied voice of Brunhild.

"Fantastic."

"Runner, what happened to the secon-nd force? Did-did you do what you said earlier? With the medical server?"

"I did."

Nadine fell silent. It was clear she wanted to ask but everyone would know if she did. Runner waited for it. Nadine wasn't the type to let things stop her in her pursuit for what was right.

"You killed them-m?"

"Possible. Don't know. We'll find out soon enough."

"Wait, what's that, dear heart? I thought…I thought you said the server was operating correctly?"

"It's killed everyone I've sent over by terminating their life support. I personally believe it's because all the ones I tried were brain dead. So here we are. I've possibly killed three hundred thousand people."

"Because they were going to fucking kill us first," Hannah said. To Runner it sounded more like a statement than a question.

"Yeah. Because they would have stripped this land clean. There's a point in time coming where this land will Awaken on its own. Soon I think. With Jacob in charge over there he would have taken the entire land. The idea of him holding rule over everyone in Tirtius…I couldn't just let that be."

"Lord Runner, I admit I'm the newest one here but…from my understanding, we're all fictional characters in an elaborate story. That you and those like you made this. Made us."

"That sums it up, Sparky," Runner agreed. He turned his head towards Faye's voice to catch her with his eyes.

"You may have killed them all for bits of imagination?"

"Sure did. Ask Hanners about that sometime. That's enough about this for now. Seems like everyone needs a job to do. Let's get this show on the road," Runner grumbled, getting to his feet. He walked off, trying to pick out a spot for the monument.

Finding the right spot took a few hours but he got what he wanted.

A vigil was held for the fallen. All three of the triumvirate of Vix made an appearance and blessed those who lived and those who'd died.

During their visit the monument was created. Brunhild summoned the marble plinth, Ernsta formed the bronze statues atop it, and Amelia made it indestructible.

The base spanned twenty feet in length and forty feet wide though only four feet tall. The names of the fallen were inscribed along the front and sides.

On the top of the plinth Ernsta had formed bronze statues of their forces: Sunless, Human, and Barbarian troops locked in combat with unseen foes. Defending, engaging, and avenging each other.

Because of the amount of space available, the figures further back were slightly elevated and enlarged in comparison to the ones in the front so that they could be seen. Casters and healers had been set in the middle as they worked to protect the front line.

At the very rear of it all, Ernsta had placed likenesses of Runner and his inner circle. So deep that it would go unremarked by most.

Truth be told, Runner wanted it that way. This wasn't a monument for him, but for those who'd died.

At the feet of the front line rested the Triumvirate's equilateral triangle.

When it was all said and done Runner could feel that his troops felt justified. Vindicated. They had triumphed in the face of adversity and accomplished it through mixed units and depending on each other.

Runner's plan for Tirtius moved on.

Chapter 20 - Countdown -

5:04 am Sovereign Earth time
12/12/43

Runner stood out near the edge of the camp as he sulked in his own thoughts. He felt better alone as of late.

While the march on Faren had been uneventful and easy, it had taken a toll on him. Every town they encountered received an inquisition of sorts. If it had a church or temple dedicated to Lambart, the worshipers were converted or banished, the site claimed in the name of the Triumvirate.

Which left Runner with an ever increasing number of people he banished.

After having defeated both the country's army and the army of faith, nothing barred their progress, which only made him feel worse about it. They had no defense.

The medical server had only terminated roughly four hundred people so far. Runner couldn't tell if they'd been in a graveyard nearby or if they'd been normal crew members killed by his own hand when he dropped them from the server. The number grew daily as the server processed each person in turn.

Taking in that many people wouldn't be a swift process. This morning alone it had terminated several more after having done nothing overnight.

"There you are, my lord."

Runner glanced over his shoulder in the morning gloom to find Isabelle stalking towards him.

"Morning, Belle. Sorry, did I wake you when I left? I know you were against sleeping in the campsite but I didn't like you sleeping outside of it. One of Grace's guards can ping her if something's up."

"No, you didn't. And yes, I do understand. Doesn't feel right, though, my lord. I'm just hired help."

Runner snorted at her and raised an eyebrow.

"You don't actually believe that, do you?"

"Err, well. No. I don't," she admitted, coming to stand beside him.

"Good," Runner said exasperatedly. Looking back to the scene before them, Runner's eyes searched the road and trees for movement.

"Sorry. It's...hard to believe at times, my lord. I'm an Elven mercenary captain. Far from home and without a home or family. I'm not...I'm nobody. Someone who tried to sell her band to a general and ended up selling herself to a lord."

"How is your band by the way?" Runner said, deliberately forcing the topic a little.

"They're happy. They're leading companies of mercenaries of their own in your service. I arranged all the contracts if you'd —"

"No. I wouldn't. I trust you, Belle. Though once this whole thing is over we'll need to change your duties around. We'll not need as many mercenaries and your talents would go to waste on that alone."

"Is that why you bound me with a deity-enforced contract?" she asked, a hint of bitterness in her voice.

"A valid point. A very valid point," Runner mused. Looking up a little, he addressed nothing. "Brighteyes, Angel, Minxy, I rescind my contract with Isabelle Malin and Faye Sennet. They've both proved themselves and I'll not hold them to a contract when I have no need."

"Witnessed," the three echoed.

"Anything else, Belle?"

Runner watched as a deer picked its way across the road to the other side. He swore he'd seen Nibbles take out a raccoon earlier in the same area. His little pet monster was getting adventurous. Adventurous and hungry.

A minute passed before Isabelle finally responded. She was clearly shocked at his quick dismissal of her binding.

"No, my lord. You really don't do things by half measures, do you?"

"Not really, no. You should have told me it was bothering you earlier. I care for your well-being."

"You sure that's all?" she asked, a curious tone coloring her question.

"Stop. Not a discussion we're having."

"Why? I feel like the conversation should be had. Seems like it was pretty obvious after you hit me with that spell. Nothing felt the same after that."

"Stop, stop, stop. Not having this conversation," Runner said, plugging his fingers into his ears. "La, la, la, la, la, la."

An aggressive hand spun him around and he was forced to stare into a glaring Faye's face.

Runner unplugged his ears and smiled at his general.

"Oh, what's up, Sparky? Anything interesting?"

"Why? Why do this? Did I do something wrong? Did I anger you, Lord Runner? Did I d—"

"Wait, wait. Stop. Your contract, right? I didn't want to hold that over your head. You did nothing wrong. I trust you. Didn't need it. Don't worry, I unbound Belle here at the same time," he explained, throwing a thumb out at Isabelle beside him.

"Oh. Oh…alright then," Faye mumbled. Taking a few steps forward, she flanked Runner's left.

"What are you doing out here at this hour? Can't see anything," she said.

"Thinking. We can siege Faren, and win. I fear it would kill countless numbers of the citizens though. Maybe every one of them. Jacob would never surrender willingly. I would guarantee the city would be ashes before he gave himself up. Wondering if I can accomplish the same goal by sneaking in ahead of the army before the siege starts. Maybe end it before it begins."

"Fucking stupid idea," Hannah cursed. She walked over and took up a position beside Isabelle. "I mean, I could do it. Isabelle probably could. But you? You're an idiot. You'd proposition a priestess or something while calling the mayor's wife a donkey."

"I love you, too. You say the sweetest things. Makes my heart race. I wonder what it'd be like if you talked dirty to me."

"Shut up."

"You're not wrong though. I suppose it'll be you, Belle, me, and maybe Rabbit. Merchant cover story."

"You sound as if you've already decided, Lord Runner," Faye complained.

"Mostly. To me it feels like the only reasonable recourse without getting a lot of people killed."

"Idiot. Fucking idiot. Why do I care about a fucking idiot?"

"If one were to believe Minxy, it's my ass."

"And a damn fine ass it is. I can't wait to see it again. I look forward to every night, you know?" said the goddess, appearing practically atop Runner, her hands reaching out for him.

"Thoughts, Minxy? It'll be your city. Depopulating it through siege would be a bad way to start," Runner said, lightly patting her hands to the side.

"It'd be a real fucked up way to start, for sure. I'd do it for you though, lovey," Amelia said, batting her eyes at him. Using her left hand, she pulled down her tunic an inch or two, revealing her neckline and the red undershirt.

"Down, Minxy. Focus. Could it be done? I imagine the thieves' guild is a city power right now. I'd want to make contact with the guild leader and see what could be done. He or she might be the best way to get at Jacob."

Huffing, Amelia rolled her eyes, visibly forcing herself to concentrate.

"Right now the head guild thief is the next in line for the royal throne. So it's not a terrible idea. Could probably make it work but you'd have to get to him without assistance. He's rather paranoid."

"Interesting. Hopefully that means the bounty on Hanners is gone. Couldn't persuade him as a goddess then?" Runner asked.

"Not likely. Not with the way Jacob and his master have been carrying on."

"Makes sense. Gives me an idea or two as well. Is there any others in line for the throne among the living?"

"I think there's one other. Maybe two. One is in his middle age and the other in his early twenties. They're both in hiding of course. No prayers to me, though I get the impression there isn't a lot of praying going on in Faren anymore."

"Suppose that's my answer then. Belle, Hanners, prepare for a quiet insertion. I'll get Rabbit and the others up to speed. Sparky? I leave everything to you, Kitten, and Lady Death. You'll be acting as tri-captains since you all represent your race as well."

"This is my domain, completely. Private time, private time." Amelia laughed delightedly and clapped her hands together as she spun in a small circle.

"Fucking hell. Thana's going to cut off your head and shit down your neck."

"I don't like this, my lord."

"As you will, Lord Runner," Faye said, saluting.

"Right, then."

They hid Boxy in the trees beyond the limits of town. Camouflaging her as best as they were able, they felt safe that it wouldn't be disturbed.

The group gathered to finalize plans.

Runner looked around at his infiltration team. Isabelle, Hannah, Nadine, and himself.

Two of those three were quite versed in the art of making themselves scarce and the third would provide them with a cover.

"Nothing has changed. Same plan. We go in through the front, find a place to stay, and case the city. We have three things to look for. Heirs, Jacob's location, targets of opportunity."

Nadine shook her head a little and chewed at her lip.

"I want to believe we can do this. But I...I really think Isabelle will stan-nd out though."

Isabelle grimaced as if she wanted to deny it. Everyone knew she couldn't. One of her hands slid up to her ear to trace the line of it. She'd be useful to them, but only in non-action ways. Where she wouldn't be seen.

Runner had been chewing on the problem on the way over. Nadine had expressed her concern earlier during the trip.

Of everyone he could bring along, she had the best chance to not be recognized. At least on the merits of who she was. Her race really was a problem though. Runner hadn't really considered it because her race didn't define her.

Could always go all Frankenstein and start rebuilding them at a race level.

"I have a solution. I'm loathe to mention it," Runner said, deciding. "I can change anyone's race to whatever they want at any time."

"Uh."

"Huh?"

"For fuck's sake...so, what does that mean? I could turn into a Sunless or a Barbarian?"

"Or an Elf, Centaur, Goblin, Human, whatever."

Hannah pressed her hands to her face and looked like she was going to explode.

"I'm sorry. I didn't want to mention it because it never mattered to me. You're all who you are. You define who you are, not your race. Hanners, you'll probably never see it in yourself, but you're beautiful."

Hannah abruptly spun in place, putting her back to him. She shuddered violently but didn't walk away.

Sighing, Runner pressed the palm of his hand to his temple.

"I'll change your race now, Belle, and we'll put you back to normal when we're done," Runner muttered. Targeting Isabelle, he activated *RaceReset*.

Isabelle broke apart into blue motes. Turning his attention to Hannah, he felt helpless.

"Hanners, I really don't care that you're a hybrid. I don't. Never did."

"I fucking do. I do. Okay? I fucking do. Fuck you."

"I'm sorry, Hanners." Runner sighed and rubbed the back of his neck. Deciding to give her some space, he put his hand on Nadine's shoulder and led her off.

"Let's give her a minute or two."

"You don't care at all, do you?"

"About her race? Heavens no. Never made a difference to me."

"I'm done, my lord."

Runner felt his curiosity surge to the front of his mind and looked back to find a very Human Isabelle behind him. That'd been very quick of her. Stefan had taken his time. Hours even.

Nearly everything about her looked exactly the same. Most of her more alien features were toned down and she had the normal Human beauty that he'd come to expect. Her figure had filled out more with the change. As a rule, the Human race ran a bit thicker.

On some level Runner felt like it was a loss overall. She'd been very...unique as an Elf. The curves didn't hurt though.

"Fantastic. Let's away then. Hanners, I'm sorry, I would give you more time but we'll be heading in. If you want, you can catch up to us later."

"Change me."

"What?"

"You heard me. Fucking change me."

"I... okay, Hanners. Okay. We'll see you in town."

Targeting Hannah, he used *RaceReset*.

As Hannah exploded into blue dust, Runner shook his head. Not wanting to see what she would become, he led Isabelle and Nadine towards Faren.

"You're disappoin-nted."

"Only a little. She's stronger than that. As long as she's happy, though, I guess." They lapsed into silence.

Isabelle and Runner fell in behind Nadine as they approached the front gate, letting her take the lead with their cover story.

"State your business."

"Merchant. Here to sell and b—"

"Move along."

Nadine blinked as the guard hurried them along into the city. Apparently merchants weren't questioned. That or security didn't matter anymore.

Runner's paranoia went from nothing to full in a heartbeat. Letting his eyes roll along the alleys and rooftops, he felt the hair on his neck prickle.

"No guards."

"What?" Isabelle asked, leaning in close to him.

"There's no guards. None. Just the two at the gate," Runner explained, gesturing at the streets.

Isabelle's head swiveled to and fro. Looking back to him, she pressed her lips together and nodded.

"Rabbit, change of plans. Place to lay our heads immediately. Cover will be blown if we stay out in the streets. If it hasn't already. You'll lay low while we go about our sneaky business."

"Un-nderstood."

Leading them down the main boulevard, Nadine took them into the first inn they found. Closest to the gate and on the main street. A lack of guards made it the best place to keep out of sight.

"Get a room, hunker down. I'll get in touch with you. Belle? Scout. Find me something."

Isabelle nodded and then vanished out the open door.

"If Hanners shows up, get her working. See you soon, Rabbit." Runner grinned and stepped out the door after using *Stealth*.

Dodging to the side, Runner made his way into an alley and deeper into the side streets. Deciding to use an advantage he knew of, he looked for a quick way to the rooftops.

As he looked for a low hanging awning, he realized his own idiocy.

Targeting the corner of a low building's roof, he blinked to the location.

As the cooldown cycled to use the spell again, he pulled out a series of cheap rings he kept on his person for quick enchants.

Loading up two rings with *Blink,* he slipped them onto his fingers. Pulling out a pair of gloves he'd bought for the same purpose, he enchanted them with *Blink* as well. Pulling them on, he then targeted another nearby building that stood higher than the one he was on.

Activating one of the rings, he blinked. Aiming for the warehouse district of town, he began actively blinking his way there, covering large distances as he cycled from one *Blink* to another.

Setting down on what he believed to be the guild house, Runner checked his surroundings.

Nothing and no one of course. It would be unlikely to have anyone up here. At least yet. All bets were off when the Awakening happened.

Taking a seat, he called up his console and flipped through the game wiki pages. The guild "throne room" rested in a third level under the ground floor. Everything else at best was horribly outdated and at worst was completely worthless.

Fantastic.

Groaning, Runner pressed the heels of his hands into his eyes. Out of nowhere an errant thought shot through him.

How many more have died as you sit here? How many are now dead? In the end, will the server kill everyone?

Yelling unintelligibly, he smacked his palms against his forehead.

"Head on track, Runner. Run on, Runner. Run on, run on, run on," he whispered to himself.

"Okay, okay. We're good. Not going crazy. Ah, yes. Minxy? A hand?"

"Both hands if you want. Or anything else you'd like," teased the lewd goddess. She stood in front of him, her arms crossed behind her back.

"Minxy? Please. Kinda having an existential crisis on top of everything else. If you really want to support me, be my friend for the moment," Runner complained.

"Of course, lovey. I'll always be your friend, but I'm afraid I can't be anything else but me. Not an act, remember?" the goddess asked, walking around him slowly. She paused behind him.

Runner sighed, nodding his head. "Yeah, I remember. I figure I'm going to have to get in to see the current guild leader. I also imagine he'll not follow me willingly if he can avoid it."

"Accurate on both counts," Amelia said, her hands pressing into his shoulders. Her fingers began to press firmly, kneading at his flesh.

"Uuun. That's lovely," Runner admitted, closing his eyes and rolling his neck into her hands.

"I imagine. Do you have a plan then?"

"Yeah. Eventually I'll call on you. You'll need to ham it up and play the goddess shtick hard. Roll with whatever I throw at you. It'll be the first step to securing the city, let alone the country."

"Okie dokie, lovey," Amelia agreed, her thumbs pressing into the base of his skull.

"Minxy, if it isn't an act, then why?"

Chuckling, she flicked him in the back of the head before continuing her ministrations.

"Been following you since the beginning, remember? You're cunning, ingenious, devious, dark, and on top of all that you strive to be good. You sicken and entice me. You're a cut on my lip that I keep running my tongue over. You're that scab on my elbow I pick at constantly. That coppery taste in my mouth when I know I need to leave it alone, but I can't."

Leaning into her hands, she pressed her palms into the blades of his shoulders. Runner didn't respond, and instead simply let her to do what she wanted.

Such a very broken goddess.

Maybe twenty minutes later Runner was peering into the guild house windows. Seeing no one inside, he blinked into the room and immediately activated his *Stealth*.

Moving swiftly, he exited the room and crossed into a hallway. Looking down the stairs, he stepped into the stairwell and began taking them down quickly. Reaching the next floor, he slithered around the corner and continued on downwards.

Peeking down at the ground floor, he caught sight of the stairs that would lead him down further into the viper's nest.

Throwing a distract at the far wall for stealthed guards, he slid into the open stairwell and dropped a few feet to land on the steps.

Runner lifted his leg up, stepped over the railing, and dropped to the floor proper. Moving slowly in case he bumped into a stealthed guard, he explored the first sub level. Everything had a similar look and feel and nothing stood out to him.

Eventually he found the stairwell to the next level down. Coming up close to it, he was preparing his distract when suddenly a guard appeared out of stealth.

Hitting the man with a *Banishing Blade,* Runner tried to immediately *Stealth* and step back out of the room. Both the blade and the man vanished as Runner moved.

No sooner had he cleared the room than he heard the quiet tread of footsteps as the guard searched his last known area.

Taking a chance since it would break his current invisibility, he visualized the stairwell he had been attempting to close on, then used *Blink.*

Casting the next *Blink* as soon as he caught sight of the bottom of the stairs, he felt reality shift crazily. Not waiting for more problems, Runner spun on his heel and opened the door to the room that he bet the next stairwell would be in. Looking inside towards the spot he expected it to be based on the previous floors' layout, he smiled.

There it was. Getting a good look at it, he blinked once more and then used the last *Blink* he had to reach the third floor proper.

Slugging down a potion of *Stealth,* Runner scurried out of the way and into a corner to wait.

Footsteps went back and forth above him, and he was sure they searched for the intruder they were sure had been there a minute ago.

Minutes ticked by before Runner felt safe enough to move again. He crept down the hallway, popped open a large set of wooden double doors, and stepped into a dreary imitation of a throne room.

Standing before the throne was an adult man Runner would place in his twenties. Runner's eyes scanned the corners as he approached the man.

"I know someone's there. Guards wouldn't be bumping into walls for no reason."

Standing twenty feet from the man named "Justinian Wallis," Runner let his *Stealth* drop.

"Fair deduction. Name's Runner. I'm here to murder Jacob and desecrate his corpse. Skull fucking him is a very valid option. Totally open to ideas if you've got 'em."

The fair haired man raised his eyebrows at that, his brown eyes studying Runner.

"Or you know, make a soup bowl out of his skull. The trick is you have to cut the lip of the bowl at the point where the eyebrow is. Otherwise it'll just spill everywhere," Runner said, tapping the indicated spot on his own head.

"Are you insane?"

"Only on the third Tuesday of every month and it's three am in the morning. That or when Scott or Linda takes over. They argue about food more often than not when they're around. Why?"

Justinian looked perplexed at that, his face screwing up in confusion.

"Long story short. I want to bury Jacob. I need help. I figure you can get me it. Willing to cut a deal."

"Alright. What are you offering?"

"I'll not waste your time. I am owed a favor by a certain goddess of thieves and assassins. I believe I could get you a champion title in her service."

"Truly? That's quite a favor you must be owed."

"Pretty significant."

"Why me?"

"Who else? First in line for the throne, lord of the underground, able to keep things running despite a psycho as the king. Place seems free of rats, though you seriously need an interior designer. Bad."

"Hm. I could never be king after..." He paused, looking around, and then gestured at his surroundings. "This."

"Agreed. Hence, champion and king of the underworld. And the interior designer of course."

"And what is the deal exactly then? Say it aloud one more time for me."

"Fine. I support you in becoming Amelia's champion in exchange for your assistance in getting rid of Jacob. Do we have an accord?" Runner asked, holding out his hand to the young guild master.

Justinian looked to the ground as he considered the offer and its ramifications. Without raising his eyes from the stone floor, he raised a single finger.

"I would be champion before I agree to this," he countered.

"That's acceptable. Though I would have you make your allegiance to your goddess and swear the oath immediately afterwards by her own witnessing. Agreed?"

Nodding his head, the guild master folded his arms atop each other and shifted his weight to the other foot.

Dropping his hand, Runner placed his hands together as if earnestly praying.

"Lady Amelia, I seek your assistance in freeing this land. I beg you for your time," Runner intoned seriously.

Amelia stepped free from the shadows in the corner. The mask that normally hung to one side of her tunic was pulled up to cover the lower portion of her face. She'd shifted her entire personality to suit his request earlier. Her clothes were fully buttoned up and not a scrap of color could be seen on her.

That or this happened to be who she actually was.

"I will listen, though I will have a price for my time," she hissed. She stayed near the edges of the room, part of her form dissolving into the shadows around her and reforming as they crawled over her.

"Lady Amelia, this is Justinian Wallis. I would barter a deal for him to become your champion. I seek for him to aid me in reclaiming his city," Runner said carefully, lowering his head so that he didn't meet her eyes.

"I see. I will accept on the condition that you will assist me in claiming this country as my own. Not the city alone. There are events in the world that trouble me and I would prefer a place to call home."

"I...I agree, Lady Amelia," Runner said bitterly.

Lifting his head a fraction, he watched as Amelia turned her eyes on Justinian.

"I would have you swear your soul in service to me as my champion. I am the mistress of thieves and assassins. I will end you faster than you could shit yourself in fear for my coming if you disobey me. Would you subject yourself so?"

Falling to his knees, Justinian nodded his head fervently. "The guild is yours in name, we would be the thieves' guild of Amelia in truth. Your priesthood. I will serve in all that you order of me."

"The deal is struck." Amelia lifted her left hand and gestured at Justinian. A cloud of shadows enveloped him and disappeared in a fraction of a second.

"Ah, good," Runner said, lifting his head up completely. He made a subtle gesture for Amelia to come stand beside him.

"Justinian, I look forward to your assistance in this matter. Hopefully we can remove Jacob quickly and efficiently. I'd like to be home."

"As long as my goddess wills it," Justinian replied, getting to his feet. "Would you have me do this? I could easily claim the throne for myself without his assistance. With your blessing as your champion alone."

Runner laughed then., He had expected betrayal of some sort. At least it was straightforward. A simple demonstration would be all it took.

"About that, Justinian. You are, for lack of a better phrase, Lady Amelia's employee. Yes?"

A frown creased the man's face. Runner's response had clearly not been his expectation.

"Yes. Her champion. Her will guides me. If she asked it of me to end you, I would."

"I see. There's a problem with that," Runner said, flashing his teeth in a mock grimace.

"Amelia is my creature." Runner reached up and unhooked the mask from Amelia's face.

He brushed a finger across her cheek, then grabbed her by the chin and kissed her roughly. Winding his left hand into her hair, he held her head firmly. Pulling her head an inch to the side, he bent her body into him. His right hand circled around behind her and grabbed a handful of her ass.

Moaning, Amelia melted into him and stuck her tongue into his mouth eagerly, her fingers sinking into his armor. There was no resistance in her at all.

After a few seconds he pulled himself back from the goddess and turned her around to face Justinian. He pressed his left hand into her lower abdomen, pushing her back and rear into his chest. He leaned over her shoulder to address the guild master.

"So you see, Minxy is mine. If you're her employee, and she's my creature..." Runner continued to explain. As if to emphasize his point, his left hand curled to grip the top of her pants as his right hand slipped up under her tunic.

"That makes you my employee. Please tell him to listen to me, Minxy," Runner said, pressing his lips into Amelia's ear.

"Listen to Runner or I'll pull out your guts and use them to jump rope through your chest cavity," she huskily commanded.

"Good girl." Runner kissed Amelia's ear as his right hand stopped below her breasts. "Run along now, Minxy. We'll catch up later."

"Yes, lovey," she whispered, and then was gone.

Runner smiled at Justinian.

Damn me if I didn't enjoy that.

"You tricked me."

"That I did. She's also the goddess of cunning, ya know."

Justinian started laughing, putting his hands on his hips.

"You didn't merely trick me, you swindled me. I'm impressed. I didn't peg you for a thief."

Runner bowed at the waist with a flourish.

"Have no fear. My requirements are simple. Help me end Jacob, put this city to rights, install a reasonable monarchy, and bring peace back. I don't expect you to end thief guild operations, but I would ask you to help to restore order and balance for now."

Justinian shook his head in disbelief, grinning.

"So it'll be."

"Oh. Be sure to drop all bounties and anything related to Hannah Anelie. She works for me directly."

Runner grinned and then triggered *Blink*. Chaining it with the equipment usages, he was able to get himself on the roof of the guild house in under a minute.

Getting out had been considerably easier than getting in since he knew the way.

Blowing out an explosive breath, Runner leaned his head back.

Amelia appeared several steps in front of him, quickly closing in on him.

"Please tell me that wasn't part of the drama. I'm so very excited right now. Call me broken, and I probably am I admit it, but there was nothing in this world like that. It made me dizzy and breathless in the way you claimed me," Amelia breathed heavily, pressing herself into his chest. Her fingers gripped at his armor, pulling him in close to her.

"You're broken. That's not a normal response. At least that's what society tells me," Runner said, looking at the top of the goddess' head. He set his arms lightly around her shoulders. "Though that was some terrific acting on your part."

"Not acting. Goddess of assassins. Essentially goddess of murder. Maybe that's why I'm broken. Is that why you push me away? I'm too dark for you?" she asked, her head jerking up to look at him.

Runner laughed that off easily and then kissed her tenderly. A light thing, lasting nothing more than a second. He hoped it conveyed what he wanted it to.

"Actually, no. Your darkness doesn't bother me. Even if you weren't acting, it doesn't concern me. Honestly, it's because I'm already far too entangled in a love affair of my own. It isn't that you're unattractive, or that you're not tempting, or not my type. None of that, in fact. I really am way too deep in my own relationship mess."

"So you're telling me I have a chance."

"I'd be lying if I told you that I wasn't attracted to you. Again though, too deep in my own affairs. Not going to happen."

"I'm immortal. You're immortal. You'll be mine," she said suddenly, her eyes widening.

"I suppose I am at that. Wait, that's an interesting question. Will everyone else become elderly?" Runner asked, suddenly feeling like an idiot.

"Of course. Some faster, some slower. Lady Death and your Kitten will live for a few hundred years. Belle a hundred or so beyond that. Hanners might go as long as Lady Death but it's a toss up. Mixed heritage and all. Grace, Rabbit, and Sparky will be rather quick in comparison. Though there are ways to prolong it or extend it. Even a few ways to remain young though your real age is getting on in years. Like that race thingie you did."

Amelia gave him a warm smile, peering up at him from under her eyelashes.

"I'll even help you with what I know of it. Because in the end, you'll be mine. All mine. I might even let my sisters in on this. Such good news," she said, giggling to herself.

Runner felt his heart ache at the idea of outliving everyone. The world felt like an inevitable doomsday scenario with a clock attached now.

He had foolishly assumed no one would age in a video game.

Evening had settled over the city and what had been a ghost town during the day exploded at night. The streets were packed and people went about their business as if it were daylight instead of night.

Apparently this had become the norm while there was a more significant presence of the priesthood of Lambart.

Runner had to wonder how long it would take for this place to return to a normal routine. If ever. The priesthood had not been kind in their role as caretaker.

"Run-ner. Isabelle's coming in now," Nadine called, watching from the window.

"Good. We can start getting this shit show on the road."

"What about Hannah?"

"I'm sure she's fine. Her marker is moving around the city and her health bar is full. She'll come when she's ready," Runner said dismissively.

Worrying over Hannah right now wouldn't do much other than waste time and energy. She was a big girl who could take care of herself.

The door swung inwards as Isabelle the Human slipped into the room.

"Any luck?" Runner asked her.

"Some. Mostly about the older one, Armand Atwood. Owns a house near the castle. I did get the name of the younger one, Basile Aubin, but nothing else," Isabelle said with a sigh. She flopped down into a chair at the table and slouched low in it.

"Such bad habits. You've lost your elven grace, Belle," Runner said with a teasing voice. Runner slid a pair of beetles and a drink across the table to her.

She snatched up one of the beetles and devoured it while pushing the second into her inventory.

"Definitely. I feel considerably slower, too. Though I did get these out of the deal," Isabelle said, pointing at her very noticeably increased bust.

"Certainly different than what I'm used to. And they do wonders for getting information. Men are stupid." She looked happy about that, taking a sip of the water.

"I can't help but agree. Right, then. We'll see if we can't sneak over to Armand tonight since we have a location," Runner said, stretching his arms back behind his head.

"Take a couple minutes to recharge, Belle, and we'll get a leg on. Rabbit, you're on home base duty in case there's a need. Be on the lookout for anyone who stands out to you. The army proper should arrive tomorrow morning, which means this whole place is going to go bat shit crazy."

"Mind if I do som-me trading? Prices are going to skyrocket," Nadine said, the possibility of gold glittering in her green eyes already.

"Of cour—"

"That sounds like fun! Are we thinking food and water? Or were you going towards arms and armor?" Isabelle chattered at Nadine excitedly. She'd left her chair and crossed the room to Nadine.

"Both! I figure if we—"

Runner tuned them out. The conversation would keep them busy and relaxed. Taking the opportunity for what it was, Runner called up Alexia's Hub and activated the sequence.

"Be right back," Runner said aloud as he thumbed the right icon.

/GMHub 2

Teleporting…

Active settings only:
Death=Off
Food/Water=On
Damage=Off
Gravity=100%
Biome=Plane
Day/Night Cycle=On
Foliage=On(N)
Resource Nodes=On
Wildlife=On(H)
Weather=On(N)

Everything came into focus and his vision was flooded with torchlight. His body felt like it had been soaking in sunlight and a pleasant warmth suffused his skin.

Runner stood in an open chamber made out of cut stone. The walls were bare but there were areas that were clearly being prepped for artwork.

Directly ahead of him stood a large arched doorway. Emplacements had been set for doors, yet no doors had been put in as of yet.

Distantly Runner heard someone leaving the area. Apparently he'd missed them by only a few seconds.

They're focusing on shelter first. Good.

Taking in a deep breath, he smelled the open grasslands and rain outside. Runner moved forward eagerly. It was almost as if this simple plane of existence felt more like a home away from home each time he came.

Standing at the top of the steps he looked out upon what was quickly becoming a city. There were quite a few homes and buildings already visible despite the rain and the dark. The population had exploded from the number of people he'd been sending here.

Rain pelted the stone-built homes and partially finished paved roads. Torches had long since been extinguished. Here and there he spotted businesses.

He briefly wondered how they conducted that since the economy was twisted. Too much gold ore everywhere for there to be any worth attached to it.

Above all, though, it was a beautiful place. Here there was no war. No crewmates wanting him dead. No problems with who was sharing his bed and who wasn't. No doomsday AI.

Unfortunately he'd never find Alexia like this. How would he find her? *Or actually, how can I let her know I'm here?*

Smirking to himself, Runner called up the console and typed in a command. He executed it with a flourish, holding his hand up above his head.

/GMHub Settings
Day/Night Cycle Off
Weather Off

Standing there with his hand above his head, he realized how childish he was being. Then the sun came out, the rain disappeared, and the entire plane became still.

Standing at the foot of the steps, Alexia dropped to her knees in the wet grass, staring up at him.

"Lord Runner! You've returned. Does the war go well?"

"It does! And of course I returned. I promised you, didn't I?"

Runner let his hand fall and he descended the steps to Alexia. He held out a hand to her, shaking his head.

"Get up, silly. I must say, I'm impressed. A lot of work has gotten done. It's amazing. It feels...like warmth. Home. Comfort." Runner grabbed Alexia's offered hand and brought her to her feet.

"I'm so glad to hear that. I must admit I feared what you would think." Alexia beamed at him.

"I have a confession though and I apologize for troubling you with it. We've had problems with a few people. A very small number to be sure, but they exist. They disrupt life here and try to incite conflict. It's good that you've prohibited harm here as I'm certain there would already be deaths."

"That's not good. Hm," Runner uneasily said, his thumb and forefinger coming to his chin as he thought.

This place is supposed to be a safe haven. Where do I banish the banished from here?

"Could you send them to another world? I...I dug that pit and it wasn't here. I would have to assume that there is another world like this? I'm so sorry about that as well. I don't even know why I did it anymore. It felt good to do something, anything...the dark..." Alexia trailed off and shuddered.

"Hush. Have no fear or concern for it. What's done is done," Runner said as consolingly as he could. Laying his right hand on Alexia's shoulder, he patted her gently. "As to the other world, that's probably the best thing we can do. Let's see..."

Opening his inventory with his left hand, Runner pulled out a six-foot staff. Honestly he couldn't even remember why he'd picked it up or how he'd gotten it.

After breaking it into three pieces with his hands, he then pulled out two bars of steel. Rapidly he enchanted the broken staff pieces with *Day/Night Cycle On*, *Day/Night Cycle Off*, and *Banishing Bolt*, though it was connected to GMHub three instead of two.

For the first bar he granted it *Weather On*, and for the second, *Weather Off*. Melting the bars with his fingers, he slapped them in between the broken pieces as bands and then cooled them.

Mist spread over the staff as it reformed into an artifact. The wood had turned black as coal and the bands were a dull copper color.

Not exactly pretty. Function over form.

He held the staff out to Alexia. "Here you are then. It literally has no stats, that'd take time I really don't have right now. It can make it day or night, and turn the weather on or off. The last ability it has is to banish someone from this plane. All you have to do is target them and activate it. Use it sparingly as they will be unable to return. I trust you to be merciful and understanding. People need time to adjust to this world and will resent us at first."

Alexia bobbed her head energetically, taking the staff from him.

"Do you have any other needs?"

"No. None, Lord Runner. You provide so very much. We've created a storeroom to begin loading materials into. They're in another chamber to the rear of the summoning room you came from."

"Oh? Fantastic. I'll see about working something out to collect it. Thank you, Alexia. Would you like me to return everything to night and turn the weather back on or would you like to practice that with your staff?" Runner asked, pointing at the staff she held in her hands.

"Would you mind doing it, Lord Runner?"

"Of course not. But I won't always be here. I think it might be better to try it out while I'm here."

Alexia looked nervously at him and then down the street. Runner followed her gaze and finally noticed hundreds of people gathered in the street and more coming every second.

"Ah. Stage fright? No worries. I've got it."

Clearing his throat, Runner held up his hand to the crowd.

"Kind and gentle people, I bid you a good evening. I hope and wish nothing but the best for you all. Love and help one another," he said.

A dark blot on the world such as I preaching love and peace. Ugh.

Glancing to the side, he nodded his head to Alexia.

"I'll see you soon, Alexia."

Runner dropped his hand and typed a few commands into the console.

/GMHub Settings
Day/Night Cycle On
Weather On

As he began fading out of existence, the sun vanished and the rain picked up again. Alexia began shouting something and held up her staff.

Teleporting...

And just like that, Runner was back in the inn room. Isabelle and Nadine were still deep in their conversation about economics.

In fact, if memory served, Runner recalled there was a function to speed up or slow time in the other plane. Did that mean he could slow it down and live a quadruple lifespan there?

How does that even work? I'll bug Sunshine later about it.

For the time being, he was back here in Faren. Like nothing had changed at all.

At a point in time where everything was far more complicated.

Where he'd sentenced most of his crew to what was starting to seem like a death sentence. The counter had reached one thousand kicked out of life support.

Of the one thousand it had processed, one thousand had been ended. That didn't even count the seven he'd murdered outright.

To top that little situation off, Runner happened to be the person who put them all here in this game. All done to save their lives of course, but it didn't change who was responsible.

Then there was Srit. An actual doomsday AI reality.

Runner had unleashed an Armageddon-level event on the dominant species. An AI that by her own admission was leapfrogging from planet to planet even now. Taking control of each sector of the government piece by piece. She could simply decide that the Omega had run their course and terminate their entire electronic civilization.

Then there was the slightly less doomsdayish, yet similar AI situation. A server full of AI programs that were becoming sentient. They questioned morals, obligations, reality, and themselves. They had psyches and beliefs.

Like a disease, it was spreading. The server had changed with Srit and those he'd Awakened. Those who interacted with Awakened had a chance to Awaken as well.

Runner immediately thought of Mr. Personality. Bullard. Runner had no hand in directly Awakening him, but he knew the man was Awakened.

Pressing his hands to his face, Runner took a shallow breath. The nightmares had gotten better yet the stress of it all remained the same. At times he felt like forcing himself to log out and becoming a vegetable might not be a terrible idea.

Though that left the inevitable questions, "Who would take over? What about the group?"

Clearing his mind, Runner began preparing for the job tonight.

10:01 pm Sovereign Earth time
12/12/43

"Dead." Runner growled and punched his fist into his palm. Upon arriving at the house, they'd found it empty and deserted. The only evidence as to what happened was the warning plastered to the door.

Armand had been killed by Jacob's priesthood pals. Armand had been ruled a traitor and subsequently executed, with his land becoming forfeit to the crown. Jacob's crown.

Jacob and his goons had certainly done their best to exterminate the line of Human royalty from the world.

Isabelle could only nod her head in agreement, squatting down on top of the roof they were hiding on.

"How could it be anything else? We have no idea where Basile is, so of course Armand is the dead one. Not the other way around. When Lady Fate isn't bedding me, she's trying to murder me. There is no in-between."

"Suppose it's a good fucking thing I know where Basile is then," whispered a voice from behind them.

Runner's head spun around. Hannah had set herself directly behind him and Isabelle. He couldn't see her that well with her hood up and the dark night.

"Ah, good to see you, Hanners. So, you know where Basile is? That's fantastic. Alive I hope? Could really use some good news."

"Where he is? Yes. Alive? Yes."

"I hear a but in there."

"But Jacob has him. He's in the dungeon of the castle. Apparently Jacob wanted to keep one fucker alive. I figure a puppet state or something like that," she explained.

"Huh. Yeah, that'd probably do it. Well, that kinda ties up everything then. We need to get into the castle. Kill Jacob, free the heir, stabilize the region, live happily ever after."

"Getting in will be pretty hard. Bastard has nearly all the guards on the castle itself. Very few in the town," Hannah said. She shifted her weight from foot to foot. Runner could only guess she wanted to ask about the thief guild.

"I told the guild master to clear your bounty. Should be fine from here on out. I'll send him a message to launch a distraction tomorrow night. I figure there's only a few things worth protecting in a siege. One being food. Justinian attacks the silos, drawing the guards' attention, we get Jacob."

"Sounds like a plan, my lord. We should return to the inn room. There's little else to be done here and now."

Runner grunted and made a shooing motion at Isabelle.

"I'll catch up, Belle. Going to fill Hanners in."

Isabelle nodded and dropped down from the building and vanished.

"I didn't."

"Wait, what? You didn't what?"

Hannah pulled back her hood to reveal that she hadn't changed in any way, shape, or form. She remained a half-breed.

Runner felt his lips curl up in a smile and he couldn't help but give her a quick hug.

"Ah. I admit I'm...well, I'm glad. You're a very unique woman, Hanners. Being a hybrid is part of who you are, but it isn't the whole of who you are."

"I know. I realized that when I was flipping through the races. It really changed how I looked when I flipped to either Sunless or Human. I never noticed how fucking blended I am. Had huge tits as a Sunless though. Right up there with Sophia."

"Again, I think you're quite fetching as who you are. In other news unrelated to you being beautiful. We cleared the bounty from the thief guild. Not only is the bounty toast but the current leader is the champion to Amelia. Which means he's ours."

"Good. I'm tired of fucking looking over my shoulder every time we enter a city," Hannah grumbled. Her fingers interacted with something in front of her as Runner stood up.

"Shit. I think we have a problem."

"Another one? And here I thought we were—"

"Shut the fuck up. We actually seriously have a problem. Nadine's map marker is inside the castle."

"Uhm, what?" Runner asked, his heart shuddering into an erratic beat.

"Her map marker. It's not at the fucking inn she was at earlier. Isabelle is heading to an empty room or possibly an ambush. Nadine's marker is in the castle. I was just looking to see approaches and...that's where she is."

Runner stared at the same indicator on his own map. Nadine was in the castle. Which meant Jacob knew they were there and had already taken her.

Runner's mind flipped to the way in which they'd met Jacob. Raping a crewmate.

"Amelia!" Runner shouted.

"Got it. I'll tell Justinian to attack now," the goddess replied, not even wasting the time to appear.

Runner dropped off the edge of the building's roof and was off and running. Behind him he heard the clatter of Hannah's boots hitting the paving stone and chasing after him.

Pinging the map on top of the castle with the "rendezvous" button for Isabelle, he ran on. Every moment mattered to him. Each and every second was another one alone with Jacob.

Runner's imagination had already started going to all the worst possible outcomes of that situation.

Dodging past mobs of people, he didn't slow or hesitate until he reached the front gate of the castle.

The walls themselves were not scalable, which left only the front gate as the entry point.

Activating *Stealth,* he started to work his way over. A hand clamped around his arm and pulled him up short. Runner felt himself pressed to the wall as his head whipped around.

Hannah silenced him with a finger across her own lips. Leaning in close to him she whispered into his ear.

"Wait for Amelia. She'll not fail you. She'd sooner whore herself out to dogs than fail you."

Runner wanted to rage at her. The idea of waiting was ludicrous. Yet it wasn't wrong. Trying to get in now would only alert Jacob and possibly play right into his hands. Jacob didn't know what Runner's class happened to be. In fact, he might even assume it was some type of fighter.

Hannah was also right about Amelia. Amelia would rather die than let him down. He knew that to his very core. Of the three goddesses, Amelia never shied from telling him exactly what she wanted. Or would do.

Runner closed his eyes and started counting in his mind. His blood boiled and his heart quailed.

How could this happen?

Like a disturbed hornet's nest, soldiers boiled out of the gate.

Runner immediately started moving again. Pressing in close to the last pillar before the gate itself, he waited, his body feeling like a string pulled tight.

His plan was simple: use distract, get inside, kill Jacob.

"My turn."

Before Runner could even contemplate what Hannah meant by that, she had dropped *Stealth* and walked brazenly up to the guards.

Tracking her with their eyes, the guards sized her up for danger.

Dropping her *Distract* on the pillar opposite the one Runner was on, she crossed her arms under her breasts.

Having someone that close, and a distract used, made the guards take full notice of her. They began to move towards her, their names switching from yellow to red.

Raising her hands, she started to back up from the gate.

Runner saw his chance and took it. Sliding past the guards without being noticed, he entered the castle grounds.

Looping wide from the paths that ran throughout, he skirted everywhere he could be spotted. Moving ever onward, he kept to the shadows and unused areas.

Inevitably he found himself unable to continue towards the marker. The wall of the keep blocked him. Which meant Nadine was in the keep.

The gate to the interior seemed insurmountable. Guarded, locked, and heavy looking.

Looking around for other ways in, Runner circled the keep once. Finding nothing, he began scanning above him for an aerial entry.

Up high above he found a windowsill. There wouldn't be any climbing to it but he did still have the *Blink* gear he'd used to infiltrate the thieves' guild. Equipping the gear as quickly as he could, he felt his irritation rising again.

Runner targeted the windowsill mentally and immediately activated a charge of *Blink*.

Quickly orienting himself, Runner latched onto the window and leaned to check what he could do.

A glass pane blocked him from simply entering directly. On the other side was a dark walkway. Runner could only guess it was an archer's perch to look down on the throne room.

Memorizing the area on the other side, Runner activated another charge of *Blink*.

Appearing on the other side of the glass, Runner felt his head swim. Taking a deep breath to catch himself, he felt his knees give out. Hanging his head, he pressed his palms to the floor and closed his eyes.

He really needed to ask Srit about the effects of chaining *Blink* together. His balance diminished with each *Blink* if he didn't space them out.

Shaking his head, he cleared the cotton from his brain and checked his immediate surroundings. In the darkened corners he spotted archers as they watched the area below.

Looked like Jacob wasn't taking his chances. Leaning over the edge, Runner found an empty throne room. According to the map, Nadine was one more room further in.

At least he wouldn't have to deal with the archers.

Giving the area a thorough once-over, he eventually spotted the partition between the throne room and whatever was on the other side. Nothing more than a cloth divider, it probably led to a hallway, dining room, or antechamber.

Runner steadied himself for another jump and pulled out a *Stealth* potion.

Placing it to his lips, he activated *Blink* and immediately drank the potion.

Having queued up the action for the potion, the space between when he activated *Blink* and drank the potion was a fraction of a millisecond.

Ducking around the cloth without disturbing it, Runner found himself staring at a small dining room.

In a high-backed chair, Jacob sat stuffing his face. Food in Otherlife could be quite tasty without the consequences of gaining weight.

Jacob obviously enjoyed eating quite a bit considering the sheer amount of food on the table and that he was eating alone.

No one was at the table other than Nadine and Jacob.

She sat in a chair opposite Jacob and looked well. Fully clothed. No damage or status ailments.

There was no way she missed the rendezvous beacons he'd dropped on top of her. She was also a very poor actress. If he walked into view she'd probably track him with her eyes.

Instead Runner pinged right on top of her with the "Defend" preset. Sneaking up behind her chair, he gently rested his hand on her shoulder.

He felt her freeze at his touch. After a second or two she relaxed again. Runner pulled his hand back, returned to the sidewall, and started to creep in on Jacob.

Jacob continued to eat noisily, content that he believed Runner hadn't yet arrived.

"You realize, attacking the food depot only buys him time," Jacob said, picking up another plate.

"I fail to see your poin-nt."

"He's a coward. He's trying to force me to capitulate early to a siege. He's wrong. This is my city. MINE!" Jacob shouted, spraying food out of his mouth.

"I see. You don-n't think he'll come here?"

"Not for you. I mean, I've only seen screenshots, but that Sunless woman? Mm. I'd love an hour with her," Jacob said, pointing at her with a half-eaten drumstick. "Compared to that, you're damaged goods. I don't discriminate though. I'll make sure to give it to you good tonight," Jacob promised, waggling his eyebrows at her.

Runner nearly lost it at that comment. Jacob was a monster that needed to be put down.

"I didn't expect him to lead an army to aid the Barbarians. Or that he'd surround himself with another army after that. Do you have any idea how much money I've spent on assassins?"

Runner moved behind a pillar that broke line of sight with Jacob and stopped. Focusing on his equipment, he equipped himself with the gear he'd used for the battle with the priesthood.

Time to end this quick. A Banishing Bolt and then done. No fuss, no muss.

Stepping out from the pillar, Runner threw the spell at Jacob.

Connecting with nothing, the spell disappeared.

Immediately his screen flashed green as a deity-level curse struck at him. All of Runner's abilities related to the spell were locked out from use for five minutes.

Which included GMHub.

Jacob's head spun around to find who had attacked him.

"He's protected from ele-m-mental magic!" Nadine shouted, rolling out of her chair and scrambling out of view.

Runner pulled up *Brainwash* and fired it off at Jacob.

Not being based in the elements, the spell went right through the defenses.

"Drink a health potion, cancel your buffs, blink to the exact spot you're on, destroy your equipped gear, drink as much poison as you can!" Runner commanded.

Using the actual *Blink* spell, Runner zipped to the other side of the room as Jacob went through the list of commands he'd been given and systematically destroyed his gear. Jacob's clothes started to vanish.

Runner targeted Jacob and lined up a *Slash* from Jacob's flank.

As the now naked Jacob finished drinking a fourth vial of poison, he spun in place to run for the partition Runner had come through.

Runner's blade leaped forward and connected with Jacob's spine. Squealing, Jacob stumbled away, his health bar tumbling.

Cursing, Runner fired off *Linda* as the monster tried to escape.

Jacob fell down on his face when the spell connected and then scurried into the corner. Scrabbling at the walls, the man looked like a cornered rat trying to escape.

Closing the distance, Runner buried his blade into the man's spine for another flank attack.

Runner didn't care to banish the man anymore. He'd kill him and be done with it.

Jacob's health bar flashed red under the weight of the attack.

Collapsing, Jacob looked up at him with fear and hate in his eyes. He held up his hand, and it suddenly burst into a green flame.

"If you take another step I'll kill your little broken toy," Jacob promised. Runner came to a stop at that. He was just barely inside the effective range for *Lunge*.

"She's been judged a heretic and I can smite her outright. She's not exactly built to take damage, is she? I figure that's all it'll take. Lambart has a special hatred for you all. And don't even think about attacking me. If I die, you'll die too! Lambart protects me. Vengeance is one of his domains. If you kill me, your health will burn until you're dead!" cried the rodent.

Runner held the *Lunge* he'd been getting ready to activate.

"He's not lying," whispered Brunhild in his ear. "There is nothing any of us can do to negate the curse or the spell. He is Lambart's champion and that is well in his purview. In a normal situation this wouldn't matter but since you have but one life this is a very different situation."

"That's what I thought," Jacob said, interpreting Runner's hesitance as a chance to escape.

"I'm a generous man. Take your pet and leave my castle. Leave my city. This is MINE. They're all mine," Jacob hissed at him, his confidence growing.

"The best part is that I'll see this place burn before I give it up. I know what you did to the others. I've already blocked my pod from you. Have you realized that I blocked yours too? You're trapped here, Runner. Forever."

The naked rapist stood up in front of Runner. This man would never give up or give in. He'd only escape to cause more problems down the way. Runner felt his decision hardening.

And in all likelihood he wouldn't hold to his own bargain. The moment Runner turned it was quite likely he'd attack Nadine anyways.

Of course if Jacob escaped, this war would never really end. Should Jacob die, then everything could begin to reorder itself.

One didn't make deals with people like this.

Rabbit would be safe. Everyone would be.

All of his plans were already in motion. They would complete with or without him. This world could use him, but it didn't need him to heal.

Srit will protect them in my stead. She'll do fine.

Smiling at Jacob, Runner let out a breath.

"I'm afraid that leaves me little choice. I had wanted to banish you and make this easy. Quick. In my hatred I squandered that chance. Now we both die. Give my love to everyone, Nadine. Hopefully this will atone for all the darkness I've wrought on others," Runner said grimly.

Then he activated *Lunge*.

Before his sword even traveled an inch, a crossbow bolt blasted through Jacob's eye and exited the back of his head. Crumpling, the champion of Lambart was no more.

Quest Completed

Quest rating: Extremely difficult. Rewards tripled.
Raid leader: Not in proximity to raid. No bonus.

"Uniting Tirtius"
Experience Reward: 400% of current level
Reputation: 3,000
Fame: 300
Money: 300 Platinum

Level up!
You've reached level 34
Level up!
You've reached level 35
Level up!
You've reached level 36
Level up!
You've reached level 37

Runner turned around in shock. Nadine stood there, her crossbow braced to her shoulder. Her health bar turned a sick pale green. She released her crossbow, and it clattered to the ground at her feet.

"No, no, no, NO, NO!" Runner said, immediately moving to her side.

"Nadine, what'd you do?" Runner asked. Reaching her, he grabbed her by the shoulders, watching as her health burned slowly.

"I spared the world. It couldn't afford losing you. This world needs you," Nadine said simply.

Reaching up, she patted his cheek with her right hand, her fingers lightly tracing his jawline.

"Nadine, no. Brunhild, Ernsta, Amelia? Please, please help her."

"We can't. It's beyond us. Lambart has fulfilled the requirements for his own portfolio."

"Runner, stop. Listen to me."

"Nadine...no, I—"

Nadine interrupted him by smacking his cheek firmly with her hand.

"Listen. My time is short. Here," she said, a window appearing before him. In it was a bag and a large amount of coins. Runner didn't even process the amount listed and instead focused in on Nadine.

"I finished your set this evening. Here's everything I have on me as far as money goes. Isabelle will take care of the rest of the money side of things. She's smart. I trust her."

"Nadine, no. This can't be happening."

"But it is, Runner. Ah, halfway there. I need you to promise me you'll never go down that dark path you were going. You must be the better person in all things. For m-me, if nothing else."

"Nadine, I—"

She pressed her hand to his lips.

"When the time comes, don't push the others away. They love you as deeply as I do. You punish yourself too much on that account. Everyone is well aware of the situation and you're only hurting yourself over it."

Nadine's health was in the final percentages.

"I love you, Runner. I know you love me too," Nadine whispered and then kissed him deeply.

After a few seconds she pulled back and gazed into his eyes. She smiled at him, her green eyes bright with unshed tears.

"Erma guide you and bless you. Run on, Runner. Don't let this stop you. I love you. Please remember to eat."

And then her health bar emptied and she collapsed, her corpse slipping right through his arms. Thudding to the floor, she went still.

"No, no, no. Nadine, Rabbit. No. Please, no. Get up. Please. It isn't supposed to be like this."

Runner clutched at her body, rolling her over onto her back.

"Ernsta, please. Please do something, Angel," Runner begged.

"I'm sorry, my precious little lamb. I would do anything for you. I would reverse her death in a heartbeat at your wish. But there is nothing I can actually do. She is already gone. She passed immediately. Without my aid, even."

"No...no, no. Please," Runner pleaded. Targeting her corpse, he cast *Revive*. Blue light spun around Nadine in a cocoon as the spell activated. Hoping against hope the code would allow it, he waited, holding his breath.

You use Revive on Merchant
Incorrect Target

Nothing happened. *Revive* only worked on players.

Runner pulled up GMHub and activated it on her corpse. Maybe in a place where death didn't exist she'd live.

Incorrect Target

Screaming at the ceiling, Runner dug his fingers into Nadine. Runner took another breath and screamed for all the world to hear. Sobbing, he bent his head over the little merchant queen.

"Nadine, please, no. There was so much left unsaid. Please."

This was the truth of the world though. This wasn't some happy make believe story where the hero wins. There would be no intervening magical excuse to fix the wrongs.

Bawling, he pressed his face into Nadine's neck, pulling hard at her. Runner dissolved into hiccupping sobs as he cried into her.

Runner lost track of time as he held her.

"My dearest lamb, she's about to fade away. I...I'm sorry. There's nothing I can do to stop it," Ernsta whispered to him.

Runner sniffled and leaned back. His eyes scoured Nadine's face, her bright green eyes open to the world. She wasn't there though. The spark of her life was gone. The smallest of smiles marked her face, even in death.

She'd been such a light in his dark world. Capturing her final moment in a screenshot, Runner sniffled.

Then she faded into nothing. Nadine Giselle was no more. All that was left of her was her crossbow.

Runner hung his head.

"Thank you, Ernsta..."

There were things to do. Runner needed to fix this land. Heal it. So the little merchants of the world could be safe. So Nadine would be happy.

Looking up, he found Jacob's corpse and snarled. Then an idea popped into his head. One that Nadine would condemn him for.

He didn't care.

"Jacob. Jacob sweetie. Darling. You've taken a true light from this world. It was her choice in the end, but you're the one who forced it."

Jacob had probably been watching the timer on his corpse count down. When it hit zero he would automatically be deleted and spawned in the graveyard. Wiping his mind and turning him into a living corpse.

Jacob was still alive right now. Still mentally coherent and awake.

Jacob was someone Runner could punish.

Placing his hand on Jacob's corpse, Runner activated his *GMHub* command.

/GMHub 1
Teleporting...

Active settings only:
Death=On
Food/Water=On
Damage=On
Gravity=100%

```
Biome=Plane
Day/Night Cycle=On
```

Runner immediately blinked out of the hole Alexia had dug, leaving Jacob where he lay inside of it.

Targeting Jacob, Runner cast *Revive*. He then typed in two commands into the console as the spell activated.

/GMHub Settings
Death off
Time Differential On 2

Runner felt his awareness change with the settings.

Below him, Jacob was wrapped in blue light as the spell brought him back to life.

Runner smiled darkly as tears fell down his face. Sniffling, he called up the GMHub Palette.

"Settle in, Jacob. We have lots of time to play. I...I have such sights to show you. Forgive me, Nadine. I will do as you asked, but for him, I will be as dark as I can."

Epilogue - Running On -

8:03 am Sovereign Earth time
12/21/43

Runner took a step back to admire his handiwork. The stone sculpture lacked much of the refinement a true artist could give it. It conveyed his subject appropriately though.

Nadine Giselle, a beacon of light in the darkness. She stood with an open hand outstretched, a warm smile on her lips.

Runner turned from his own creation and rubbed at his eyes. Crying for her didn't bother him. Even now, weeks later, he still cried for her.

Crying in public in front of his people wasn't acceptable.

Looking around at North Wood Fort, Runner watched as men and women went about their daily business. The place had become lively in the last week. Refugees, mercenaries, and those seeking a new life had flowed in steadily.

Nearly every soldier who had served under him followed him here as well. He'd have to work out some type of recompense for their loss to their leaders. But that was a problem for another day.

Work continued in every corner to clear out the debris so that they could begin rebuilding.

This place would be a home. A city. A fort. Here is where Runner would live and rule.

Now that Tirtius was free that was. Basile Aubin had agreed to Runner's instructions readily. Amelia now was the prime for the Human nation. A king sat its throne once more, and the underground king Justinian stuck to his word.

The three heads of state had agreed to a mutual talk to be held at a location of their choosing in six months. Runner had been asked to attend as well.

Nodding his head, he looked back to his creation. He'd taken up sculpting since returning. His plan was to create a new Nadine every time he gained two levels in the skill.

Here he would place them. On the boulevard all people would have to cross on their way into North Wood for the first time. Nadine would welcome all. As many Nadines as he could fit.

Completing the statue, he sighed as it misted over to finish. A small tinkling noise signified it was complete.

At this level he couldn't instill any effects or make it grant any bonuses. He still felt better looking at her.

It. Looking at it.

Runner swallowed past the lump in his throat and walked down the street towards the entrance. Srit would be returning soon. In the next thirty minutes or so by his calculations after watching her speed. He'd be waiting for her. She deserved a warm welcome home.

Runner passed by Barbarians, Sunless, and Humans on his way to the gate. There were also many other races present but much fewer in number.

Many of those moving about the area carried lumber or other goods to construction sites or silos. All of the immediate surrounding wood was in the process of being cleared to provide a clear line of sight in every direction.

Defense would be a must. Vix would be a fortress. A bastion.

In fact he had organized a team of people to retrieve Bastion, the tree that saved him when he first arrived.

Now planted in the center of the town square, Bastion had already become a place that people visited regularly.

Runner swore it had already started to grow larger since the transport. He was curious to see what would happen.

Everyone he crossed recognized him immediately and bowed their head to him. Runner brushed if off politely and nodded his head in return. He hoped they'd grow used to him soon enough. He didn't plan to rule from on high.

Runner briefly saluted his gate guards as he left the fort, walking down the road a ways.

Coming to rest a good distance from the newly erected wall, but not far enough to panic Sophia's guards who trailed him everywhere, Runner waited.

"Ah. My lord," spoke a voice to one side.

Runner turned his head and found Isabelle walking towards him.

She'd asked to be returned to her Elven heritage the moment they had freed Basile from the dungeon.

He hadn't commented on it, but he'd noticed right off the bat she'd clearly adjusted her body sliders a little in the race reset screen.

Well, a lot more than a little, really.

Her bust had become very impressive for an Elf. Not quite as large as say Thana's, but definitely up there. Not to mention she actually had a waist and hips now.

She really went for an hourglass figure.

"Morning, Belle. Out wandering my wood?"

"Indeed. They're quite beautiful. Massive and old. I look forward to spending many years amongst them. Leading and teaching recruits and children alike."

"You want children?" Runner asked. He hadn't thought about that. Though if Naturals would eventually age and die, it certainly would make sense for them to be able to reproduce.

"I do indeed. Let me know when you're ready to start trying. I hear Thana and Katarina are already putting you through your paces without any luck yet," she said, grinning at him.

"Belle, we talked—"

"No, we didn't. You didn't want to. I've made my choice. You let me know when. Until then, I'll bide my time. Elves live a very long time and I'm patient. Alright, I'm off to the other side of the wood now. We've got a very large population of animals in these woods and I'm trying to map their game trails."

Isabelle waved at him and jogged off.

Runner shook his head, grumbling to himself.

"Stupid, deaf Elf. As if Thana would even allow her to join the harem council. Doesn't she know it won't work?" Runner grumbled.

"Not stupid!" she called over her shoulder.

Runner felt his face burn at the fact she'd heard him.

I swear to god. Why do they get a bonus to hearing? That doesn't even make sense.

Especially concerning to him was the lack of response about Thana's little harem council. Which meant she probably knew about it. And didn't care in the least.

Amelia popped into being, sitting on the grass nearby. Her tunic had been removed and her red undershirt had the top three buttons undone. She was leaning forward as if enjoying the sun. And providing him a great view at the same time.

"She's about as likely to stop as I am. Have fun with that."

Runner ignored her comment and smiled at her instead.

"Good morning, Minxy. You look lovely."

"You really know how to make a lady feel great."

"Not hard to make beautiful ladies feel great. Like complimenting the sun for being bright."

"Gods, I love you. Let me show you how much, lovey."

"Down, Minxy. To what do I owe the pleasure? And yes, it really is a pleasure. Even if I'm constantly fending off your sexual attentions."

Smiling, Amelia tilted her head to one side as she considered him.

"You're perfect. I can't wait to take you as mine. I'll make you so happy. I'm here because my sisters and I wanted to officially thank you for all that you've done. All around Tirtius, temples and churches spring up like weeds. We don't believe it'll be long before worship of primes will simply become worship of the Triumvirate. We've gotten ahead of that and already made a binding agreement to pool our power pool together into one. Doesn't matter who they pray to, it benefits us all now."

"Good. That was my goal. You three will be much stronger as a unified pantheon."

"Anyone ever tell you it's damn sexy that you planned for a bunch of women to be in an extreme power position over you?"

"I'm not afraid of powerful women. Honestly, I tend to prefer them."

"Suffice it to say, we're gaining speed and strength," Amelia said, lying down in the grass.

"Me. The little goddess of thieves and assassins. People prayed to me before, but never really. Now? Now I have powerful sisters. Sisters who enjoy my company and encourage me. I have a man I'm pursuing who's turning out to be a joy to chase. I grow stronger by the day. By the very minute."

She lifted one foot into the air and wiggled her booted foot.

"I'll make sure you never tire of this world, lovey."

Runner laughed at that, and bent down over her. He pressed a gentle kiss to Amelia's forehead before brushing her bangs away from her eyes.

Her eyes fastened on him as her cheeks started to redden.

"You're an idiot, Minxy. But I love you for that reason. Run along. I'm not yours quite yet. The chase is still on for many, many years. Besides, Sunshine should be here any minute."

"Ah, the scary one." Amelia paused, as if she hesitated on what to say next. "Ernsta is afraid you hate her. For what happened with Nadine."

"I don't hate her, ugh…Angel, I don't hate you," Runner said, looking up.

"You dumb sexy death goddess. There wasn't anything you could do. I swear if you start avoiding me I'll donate enough that you have to grant me an audience. When you show up I'll hit you so hard with an amped up *Seduction* that your panties melt. Then I'll use you like a—"

A minor deity-level curse hit him and silenced him.

Looking to Amelia, he quirked a brow with a sigh. Runner tapped his foot, waiting for it to time out.

"Be nice, lovey. She's a tenderhearted thing, you know? Though I'm glad to hear you're not mad at her. I do love my sister. Speaking of melting panties, though, maybe you could hit me with it? To test it out, that is. Testing is good. Repeated testing. How about starting now?"

When the curse ended, Runner took a breath and started again.

"My Dark Angel, nothing is wrong. You and Brighteyes did nothing wrong. You did all you could in the situation. Please, treat me as you always have. Now, Minxy, unless you want to greet Sunshine, you should get a leg on."

"Yeah, I think I'll leave then. She actually scares me. See you tonight, lovey. Be sure to really work it. I love watching you."

Amelia vanished as quickly as she'd appeared. Runner really wasn't sure how to take the fact that Amelia relished watching him at night. Especially since his nights were rarely spent alone.

She's so fucking broken.

Then he saw Srit walking down the road towards him.

Grinning, he waited for her.

The doomsday AI who conquered a sentient species in weeks. Who could destroy an entire civilization and two separate species with an idle thought.

His friend.

Srit came to stop before him. A slow smile crawled over her face.

"I'm home," she said.

Runner chuckled and then drew her in for a tight hug.

"Welcome home, Sunshine. We've missed you."

"Thank you. My heart hurts."

"Ah, you found out about Nadine?"

"Yeah."

"Mine does, too." Runner pulled back and patted her shoulder.

"Come, we'll have a late breakfast with everyone. It helps ease the pain with family around. I have questions for you on top of everything else."

"Oh? If you want to know what happened, I am now in full control of every star system."

"Nah, not that. I know you're an Armageddon-level event, Sunshine, but I don't care. To me you're a beautiful woman with big...brains," he said teasingly.

"Runner, stop it," Srit complained, turning pink.

"Fine, fine. I wanted to talk to you about creating a patch for the server. It's going to need maintenance eventually and I'd like to get ahead of that. Need to work on a few ways of making sure everything is stable. And doing so without disturbing anything. I'd also like to talk to you about getting pregnant, genetics, creating other worlds, server space, all sorts of things."

"I see. Many of those are easily taken care of. Though I'm not sure if I can get pregnant. I will work to code that in. At my base I'm a program so I believe we can reasonably expect success. I would need to code a new AI for our child. Though this would be a function of reproduction so we would need to adjoin the program to the action."

"Ah," Runner started, realizing he'd phrased it wrong. "I'd like to look into Naturals getting pregnant."

"Neither Thana or Katarina is pregnant. I check daily on them since the first time they asked."

Runner sighed, feeling like this whole thing was rapidly getting out of hand.

"I think we should start this conversation over," Runner said, rubbing the bridge of his nose with his thumb and forefinger.

1:14 am Sovereign Earth time
12/22/43

Jacob thrashed in the water. He inhaled water and exhaled it back out with each breath. His health bar flashed red at one percent and the oxygen meter was empty.

Runner tilted his head as he watched Jacob drown. Drown forever. Eternally.

Sealed in a glass box full of water that was impervious to magical and physical damage, Jacob had nowhere to go. Jacob had long since given up on trying to escape.

Nowadays he didn't even try to break the glass of whatever box he was in.

Cradling a four-inch carving of Nadine between his fingers, he watched. The bag of figurines Nadine had carved for him rested in his lap. They were much larger than the ones she'd made for the maps.

Coincidentally, Runner had collected all of those as well and replaced them with cheap map markers.

"I think we'll move you to the fire box next. What do you think, Jacob?" Runner asked, not actually expecting an answer.

"Or maybe the lightning box? The spike box hasn't gotten any use in a while. Or what about the lava box?"

Runner let his eyes travel to the side. Glass box after glass box had been prepared. Each holding a form of everlasting torment.

At the very end was a box that had food, water, and a bed. Runner had called it "Nadine's wish," and he planned to put Jacob in it on the anniversary of Nadine's death.

"Forgive me, Nadine. Forgive me. I can do what you've asked. I can. Just not for him. Forgive me," Runner whispered.

Runner bowed his head over the figurine.

Thank you, dear reader!

I'm hopeful you enjoyed reading *Otherlife Nightmares*. Please consider leaving a review, commentary, or messages. Feedback is imperative for an author's growth. That and positive reviews never hurt.

Feel free to drop me a line at: WilliamDArand@gmail.com

Keep up to date-
Facebook: https://www.facebook.com/WilliamDArand

Blog: http://williamdarand.blogspot.com/

The third book of the trilogy, *Otherlife Awakenings*, is in the works.

91820518R00165

Made in the USA
Lexington, KY
27 June 2018